PRAISE FOR STEVE BERRY AND HIS COTTON MALONE NOVELS

THE BISHOP'S PAWN

"Berry's most personal novel to date."   —Associated Press

"As fast-paced and exciting as all his previous books, this is another winner in the author's bestselling series. Berry's fans will not be disappointed. He has a knack for presenting alternative history that seems as though it might be true."   —*Library Journal* (starred review)

"It took him a while—a dozen books—to get around to it, but Berry has finally written Cotton Malone's origin story . . . [an] exciting tale of historical intrigue."   —*Booklist*

"Berry has always 'hit it out of the park' with his books; with this, he's basically hit it to the moon and back. It is *that* good. Berry is outstanding, taking people on a hunt through the past that brings even more suspense to a crime that has never been forgotten."

—*Suspense Magazine*

"This Cotton Malone case is a fast-paced, heart-pounding thriller with dark corners and passageways. The action hits the ground running and does not let up until the end. Steve Berry is a talented author who shakes things up by presenting alternate versions to historical events."

—*RT Book Reviews*

"Berry mixes historical facts with his own fictions in a manner that readers of this terrific series have come to love. *The Bishop's Pawn* . . . keeps the suspense building until the final pages. It's one of the best books in a wonderful series."   —*Connecticut Post*

"Berry doesn't so much as up the ante here as change the game. And the result is a tour de force that's everything a great thriller is supposed to be."   —*The Providence Journal*

"Bery deftly weaves historical facts and made-up fiction."
—*The Florida Times-Union*

"A riveting adventure told in Berry's trademark style of pairing meticulously researched history with unexpected twists."
—*Southern Seasons*

THE LOST ORDER

"Combines the history of a secret society with a look inside the Smithsonian Institution—and it's terrific." —Associated Press

"A page-turning read that is hard to put down."
—*Library Journal* (starred review)

THE 14TH COLONY

"Berry's modus operandi is always all-action . . . Berry gunfights his way entertainingly enough to the save-the-world conclusion."
—*Kirkus Reviews*

"Berry makes history exciting, and he has written another winner."
—Associated Press

THE PATRIOT THREAT

"Blistering reading entertainment at its level best." —*The Providence Journal*

"A fast-paced and entertaining traditional thriller along the lines of *The Da Vinci Code*." —*Pittsburgh Post-Gazette*

THE LINCOLN MYTH

"All action all the time as Malone once again yanks civilization back from the precipice." —*Kirkus Reviews*

ALSO BY STEVE BERRY

COTTON MALONE NOVELS

The Lost Order

The 14th Colony

The Patriot Threat

The Lincoln Myth

The King's Deception

The Jefferson Key

The Emperor's Tomb

The Paris Vendetta

The Charlemagne Pursuit

The Venetian Betrayal

The Alexandria Link

The Templar Legacy

STAND-ALONE NOVELS

The Columbus Affair

The Third Secret

The Romanov Prophecy

The Amber Room

THE
BISHOP'S
PAWN

STEVE
BERRY

MINOTAUR BOOKS
NEW YORK

For Patricia June Goulding
And a long life

Published in the United States by Minotaur Books, an imprint of St. Martin's Publishing Group

www.minotaurbooks.com

Designed by Steven Seighman

The Library of Congress has cataloged the hardcover edition as follows:

Names: Berry, Steve, 1955– author.
Title: The bishop's pawn / Steve Berry.
Description: First edition. | New York : Minotaur Books, 2018.
Identifiers: LCCN 2017044458 | ISBN 9781250140227 (hardcover) |
    ISBN 9781250194053 (signed edition) | ISBN 9781250194060 (international, sold outside the U.S., subject to rights availability) | ISBN 9781250140234 (ebook)
Subjects: LCSH: Malone, Cotton (Fictitious character)—Fiction. | Political fiction. |
    GSAFD: Suspense fiction.
Classification: LCC PS3602.E764 B57 2018 | DDC 813/.6—dc23
LC record available at https://lccn.loc.gov/2017044458

ISBN 978-1-250-14025-8 (trade paperback)

Our books may be purchased in bulk for promotional, educational, or business use. Please contact your local bookseller or the Macmillan Corporate and Premium Sales Department at 800-221-7945, extension 5442, or by email at MacmillanSpecialMarkets@macmillan.com.

First Minotaur Books Paperback Edition: August 2019

10 9 8 7 6 5 4 3 2 1

ACKNOWLEDGMENTS

Again, my sincere thanks to John Sargent, head of Macmillan; Sally Richardson, who captains St. Martin's; and my publisher at Minotaur, Andrew Martin. Also, a huge debt of gratitude continues for Hector DeJean in Publicity; Jeff Dodes and everyone in Marketing and Sales, especially Paul Hochman; Jen Enderlin, the sage of all things paperback; David Rotstein, who produced the cover; Steven Seighman for the interior design work; and Mary Beth Roche and her innovative folks in Audio.

As always, a bow to Simon Lipskar, my agent and friend. And to my editor, Kelley Ragland, and her assistant, Maggie Callan, both of whom are wonderful.

A few extra mentions: Meryl Moss and her extraordinary publicity team (especially Deb Zipf and JeriAnn Geller); Jessica Johns and Esther Garver, who continue to keep Steve Berry Enterprises running smoothly; Glenn Simpson, superintendent of the Dry Tortugas National Park, for showing me an extraordinary national treasure; Dan Veddern and Glenn Cox, who, over dinner in a French château, helped me work through the plot (it's not exactly what we discussed, but it's close); Melisse Shapiro and Doug Scofield for introducing me to Palm Beach; Wanda Smith, who made a great case for the inclusion of Starke and Micanopy, Florida; and Grant Blackwood, novelist extraordinaire, for helping unstick me.

My wife, Elizabeth, once again was there every step of the way, pushing me along with this first incursion into the world of first person.

This book deals with courage and fortitude, so it's only fitting that it be dedicated to a friend of ours who is currently going through a tough struggle with cancer. It was something that sprang up out of nowhere, with no warning whatsoever. But instead of feeling sorry for herself or wallowing in pity, our friend has accepted the struggle and bravely faced the challenge head-on. Thankfully, she has a loving husband and four wonderful sons, all of whom are with her every step of the way.

Elizabeth and I have no doubt she will win the war.

In the meantime, this one's for you, PJ.

They said one to another, behold here cometh the dreamer, let us slay him and we shall see what will become of his dreams.

—GENESIS 37:19–20

PROLOGUE

HOW IRONIC, I THINK, THAT THIS ALL STARTED WITH A MURDER, and now it appears it might end with another.

I've been summoned to a famous address, 501 Auburn Avenue, Atlanta, Georgia. The house is a two-story Queen Anne with a porch, scroll-cut trim, porthole windows, and a gabled roof. Part of a neighborhood with a famous name. Sweet Auburn. Once the home of hardworking, middle-class, urban families, sixty years ago the neighborhood became the epicenter for a movement that ultimately changed the country. The African American couple who'd lived in this house had not wanted any of their children born in a segregated hospital, so all three arrived into the world right here. The first, a girl, Christine, came early, before a crib had even been found. So she spent the first few nights of her life in a chifforobe drawer. The youngest, Alfred Daniel, found the world on a hot July day. The middle child, a boy, born ironically in the middle room upstairs, appeared on January 15, 1929. They called him Michael, for his father. But five years later, after a trip to Berlin, the father changed both his and the son's name to Martin Luther King, one senior, the other junior.

I'm standing in a quiet downstairs foyer. The invitation had arrived a week ago at my Copenhagen bookshop by regular mail, inside an envelope hand-addressed to me—Cotton Malone—and contained a note that simply read:

Fifty years have passed.
Bring them.

And then:

April 3. King house at MLK Center. 11:00 P.M.

With no signature.

But I knew who had sent it.

A few night-lights burn here and there in the darkened ground-floor rooms. Years ago, when I'd lived in Atlanta working for the Magellan Billet, I'd visited here one Sunday afternoon with Pam and Gary, a rare family outing of mother, father, and son. We'd taken a tour of the house, then walked the entire King Center, trying to impress upon Gary the importance of racial equality. Both Pam and I prided ourselves on not having a prejudiced bone in our bodies, and we wanted our son to grow up the same way.

I glance into the front parlor with its famous piano and Victrola. The guide that day had told us how King himself had taken music lessons on that keyboard. Not one of the middle child's fondest childhood memories, if I remember correctly.

We'd also learned a few other things about Martin Luther King Jr.

He'd attended elementary and high school nearby, and college across town at Morehouse. In 1954 the Dexter Avenue Baptist Church in Montgomery, Alabama, called him to be its pastor. But in 1955 when Rosa Parks was denied a seat in the front of the bus, for 381 days he led the Montgomery transit boycott. In 1957 he became president of the fledgling Southern Christian Leadership Conference. Three years later he moved back to Atlanta and shared the pastor's pulpit with his father at the Ebenezer Baptist Church, which still stands just down the street.

From there he evolved into the heart and soul of a great movement.

So many memorable speeches. Two massive legislative successes with the Civil Rights and Voting Rights Acts. A Nobel Peace Prize. Thirty arrests for the cause. All leading to Memphis and April 4, 1968, when an assassin's bullet ended his life.

He'd been but thirty-nine years old.

I stare at the man standing in the shadows at the end of the ground-floor hall. He's definitely aged, but his face seems to have only become stronger with the years. His hair is grayer, the frame thinner, but the same air of gentle intellectualism remains, as does the stooped gait and short shuffle to each step as he approaches.

"Tomorrow will be a big day here," he says in the low voice I recall. "Fifty years since King died." He pauses. "Nearly twenty years since you and I last talked. I still feel the pain every day."

A cryptic comment, but I expect no less. "Out of curiosity, how did we get in here tonight? This is a national historic site."

"I have connections."

Of that I have no doubt. It was the same years ago when all of this started.

"Did you bring them?" he asks.

I reach into my back pocket and display what he'd asked for. "Right here."

"You've kept them all these years, along with the secret. Quite an accomplishment."

"My career was the protecting of secrets."

"I kept up with you. You worked for the Justice Department what, ten years?"

"Twelve."

"An agent with the Magellan Billet. Now you live in Denmark and own an old bookshop. Quite a change."

There's a gun tucked at his waist. I point. "Is that necessary?"

"We both knew, at some point, it would come to this."

Probably so.

"You managed to move on," he says. "Everything that happened only pushed you forward to greater things. That's been impossible for me. I'm amazed I've lasted this long."

It's true. My life has been altered in ways I could have never then imagined. But what happened also taught me a valuable lesson.

"I came, tonight, *for you*," I tell him.

"Lay everything on that side table, please."

No point arguing, so I do as asked.

"The King family lived in this house a long time," he says. "They raised three children under this roof, one of whom grew up and changed the world."

"We both know it took more than just him to make that happen. You were a big part."

"That's kind of you to say. But it's no consolation."

Only a handful ever knew what really happened, most of whom are now dead.

"Do you ever think about those few days?" he asks.

My time with the Magellan Billet exposed me to some amazing things. Templars, a ruthless Central Asian dictator, Charlemagne's secrets, the lost library at Alexandria, modern-day pirates. But nothing compares to what I was involved with during my first mission.

Before there even was a Magellan Billet.

"All the time," I say.

"Should the truth be told?"

A fair question. Fifty years have passed and the world has changed. But I point again and have to ask, "Is the gun for me, or you?"

He does not immediately answer.

I learned a long time ago that people's actions are nearly always less tidy than their minds. So I decide to be cautious.

"I want to talk about it," he finally mutters.

"And your choices of listeners are limited?"

He nods. "It's eating me up. I need you to tell me everything that happened. We never had this conversation back then."

I hear what he has not said. "Before what?"

"Before I decide which one of us this gun is for."

JUNE
18 YEARS
AGO

CHAPTER ONE

TWO FAVORS CHANGED MY LIFE.

The first happened on a warm Tuesday morning. I was cruising on Southside Boulevard, in Jacksonville, Florida, listening to the radio. A quick stab at the SEEK button and through the car speakers came, "Why does New York have lots of garbage and Los Angeles lots of lawyers?"

"New York got first choice?"

Laughter clamored, followed by, "How do you get a lawyer out of a tree?"

No one seemed to know the answer.

"Cut the rope."

"The other day terrorists hijacked an airliner full of lawyers."

"That's awful. What happened?"

"They threatened that unless their demands were met they would begin releasing one lawyer every hour."

More laughter.

"What do lawyers and—"

I turned the radio off. The disc jockeys seemed to be having fun, lawyers apparently a safe object of ridicule. Hell, who was going to complain? It wasn't like gay jokes, Polish jokes, or anything even remotely sexist. Everybody hated lawyers. Everybody told a lawyer joke. And if the lawyers didn't like it, who gave a damn?

Actually, I did.

Since I was a lawyer.

A good one in my opinion.

My name, Harold Earl "Cotton" Malone, appeared as one of thousands at the time who held a license within the State of Georgia, where I'd taken the bar exam six years earlier. But I'd never worked at any law firm. Instead I was a lieutenant in the U.S. Navy, assigned to the Judge Advocate General's corps, currently on duty at the naval station in Mayport, Florida. Today, though, I wasn't acting as a lawyer. Instead, I was doing a favor for a friend, a distraught husband going through a divorce.

A favor I was beginning to regret.

The wife, Sue Weiler, possessed the cunning of a dictator and the boldness of a stripper. She'd spent yesterday parading across Jacksonville from apartment to apartment. Four in all. Men she'd met here and there. Fast sex with no strings. While sitting outside Apartment Number 3 I'd seriously wondered if she might be a nymphomaniac, as she certainly possessed the appetite.

Just past 5:00, after a surprisingly brief visit at Apartment Number 4, she folded her long slender legs into a sparkling new Cadillac and headed onto a busy boulevard. The car was a rosy shade of white, so pale that it looked pink. I knew the story. She'd specially ordered the car to enrage her estranged husband, the stunt entirely consistent with her taunting personality.

Last night she'd headed straight to an apartment complex on the south side and Boyfriend Number 5. A month ago she'd done the same thing and, being the pal that I was, I'd followed her then, too. Now the soon-to-be-ex-husband's lawyer wanted pictures and, if possible, video to use in divorce court. My buddy had already been socked with temporary alimony, part of which was going to pay for the Cadillac. Proof of adultery would certainly stop all alimony. Especially since Sue had already twice testified that she possessed no lovers or hardly any male friends at all. She was an accomplished liar, and if I hadn't seen the truth myself I would have believed her.

A light rain had fallen all yesterday afternoon, and the evening had been typically hot and humid for Florida in June. I'd spent the night rooted outside the apartment of Boyfriend Number 5 making sure Sue didn't slip away. Fifteen minutes ago she'd emerged and sped off in the Pink Mobile. I speculated where she might be headed. An apartment complex out at the beach and Boyfriend Number 6, a title insurance agent with the advantage of forty pounds more muscle and twenty fewer years than her husband.

The morning was bright and sunny, the roads filled with commuters, Jacksonville traffic always challenging. My metallic blue Regal easily melded into the morning confusion, and following a nearly pink Cadillac presented little difficulty. Predictably, she took the same series of twists and turns across town until her left signal blinked and the Cadillac veered into another apartment complex.

I noted the time.

7:58 A.M.

Boyfriend Number 6 lived in Building C, Unit 5, with two assigned parking spaces, one for his late-model Mazda, the other for a guest. I'd discovered those details a few weeks ago. Half an hour from now, allowing plenty of opportunity for them to climb into the sack, I'd find a good spot to grab a little video and a few snapshots of the Cadillac beside the Mazda. In the meantime I'd wait across the street in a shopping center parking lot. To pass the time I had a couple of paperback novels.

I flipped on my right blinker and was just about to turn into the shopping center when a Ford pickup shot by in the left lane. I noticed the cobalt color, then the bumper sticker.

MY EX-WIFE'S NEW CAR IS A BROOM.

And knew the occupant.

My pal, the soon-to-be-ex-husband.

I'd last talked to Bob Weiler at midnight, calling in the bad news, none of which he'd liked. Him being here now meant only one thing—trouble. I'd sensed a growing resentment for some time. The seemingly blasé attitude the wife took to her husband's jealousy. A delight in emotionally building him up, then enjoying while he crashed before her eyes. An obvious game of control. His for her affection, hers for the pleasure of being able to dictate his response. But such games carried risks and most times the participants could not care less about the consequences.

Bob's pickup, in defiance of some substantial oncoming traffic, flew across the opposite lanes, tires squealing, and shot into the narrow drive, barely missing the carved cedar sign proclaiming the entrance to The Legends. I aborted my right turn, changed lanes, and, taking advantage of some rubberneckers, followed. Traffic momentarily blocked my approach, and by the time I finally made the turn into the complex Bob was a good ninety seconds ahead of me.

I headed straight for Building C.

The truck was stopped, its driver's-side door open. The pink Cadillac sat parked beside the Mazda. Bob Weiler stood with a gun leveled at his wife, who'd emerged from her car but had yet to go inside. I whipped the steering wheel to the right and slammed the Regal into park. Groping through the glove compartment I found my Smith & Wesson .38 and hoped to God I didn't have to use it.

I popped open the door and slid out. "Put it down, Bob."

"No way, Cotton. I'm tired of this bitch playing me for a fool." Bob kept his gun trained on Sue. "Stay out of this. This is between me and her."

I stayed huddled behind my open car door and glanced left. Several residents watched the unfolding scene from railed balconies. I stole a quick look at the wife, fifty feet away. Not a hint of fear laced her gorgeous face. She actually looked more annoyed than anything else, watching her husband intently, the look reminiscent of a lioness surveying her prey. A stylish Chanel purse draped one shoulder.

I turned my attention back to Bob Weiler. "Put the gun down."

"This bitch is milking me while she screws whoever she wants."

"Let the divorce court handle her. We've got enough now."

He turned toward me. "The hell with courts. I can deal with this right now."

"For what? Prison? She's not worth it."

Two shots cracked in the morning air and Bob Weiler let out a groan, then his body crumpled to the ground. Blood poured from a pair of holes in his chest. My gaze darted toward Sue. Her gun was still raised, only now it was pointed at me.

Another shot exploded.

I dove into the Regal.

The driver's-side window, where I'd just been crouched, exploded, spraying glass on me.

She fired again.

The front windshield spiderwebbed from the impact but did not splinter. I snapped open the passenger-side door and slid out onto the pavement. Now at least a whole car was between us. I sprang up, gun aimed, and screamed, "Drop the gun."

She ignored me and fired one more time.

I ducked and heard the bullet ricochet off the hood. I came up and sent a round her way, which pierced Sue's right shoulder. She recoiled, trying to keep her balance, then she dropped to the pavement, losing a grip on her weapon. I rushed over and kicked the pistol aside.

"You no-good piece of crap," she yelled. "You shot me."

"You're lucky I didn't kill you."

"You're going to wish you did."

I shook my head in disbelief.

Wounded and bleeding, but still venomous.

Three Duval County Sheriff's cars with flashing lights and screaming sirens entered the complex and closed in fast. Uniformed officers poured out, ordering me to drop my gun. All of their weapons were pointed my way, so I decided not to tempt fate and did as they asked.

"This bastard shot me," Sue screamed.

"On the ground," one of the cops said to me. "Now."

Slowly I dropped to my knees, then lay belly-first on the damp parking lot. Immediately my arms were twisted behind my back, a knee pressed firm to my spine, and cuffs snapped onto my wrists.

So much for favor number one.

CHAPTER TWO

I SAT IN A WHITE, WINDOWLESS SPACE MADE OF CONCRETE BLOCK. Interestingly, no one had read me a single constitutional right, nor taken a fingerprint, snapped a mug shot, or made me change into an orange jumpsuit. Instead, I'd been led into the Duval County jail and locked in a holding cell all by myself. I stared up at the walls and ceiling, wondering where the microphones and cameras might be hidden. The trip into town from the apartment complex had taken half an hour in the patrol car, my hands cuffed behind my back. Taking advice that every arrestee should heed, I kept my mouth shut, only providing a name and phone number for my commanding officer.

Sue Weiler had been taken away in an ambulance and, if the level of her shouts was any indication, her wounds were not life threatening. Bob Weiler died before his body hit the ground. There'd been a slew of witnesses, so trying to find out what happened would be a mess. What was the old Russian saying? *He lies like an eyewitness?* The deputies had not appreciated my staunch support of the constitutional right to remain silent. But too bad. I was still processing. Never once had I even struck someone in anger. Instead, I'd bypassed all of the various and sundry misdemeanors and gone straight to felony aggravated assault, shooting another person.

And I felt no remorse.

I'd also witnessed someone die.

Another first, which tore at my gut.

Bob Weiler was a friend.

The silence around me was broken by an occasional disembodied voice, the hollow echo of footsteps, and the soft whine of machinery. The jail was not unlike the many I'd visited before, each in their own way forlorn and depressing. My cell was about six by eight with a metal bench and a toilet with no seat. A single opaque window, recessed into the block wall at shoulder height, was protected by a steel grating. I'd never been a guest in a jail before, always a visitor. Being locked behind bars was definitely different. No freedom. No choices. Your autonomy surrendered to strangers. Certainly all of the powerlessness and petty humiliations designed into the building were intentional, there to sap away courage and strength, the idea being to replace any positives with a docile helplessness.

I knew I should call Pam, but I wasn't in the mood to hear her moralizing. She'd told me more than once to stay out of the Weilers' business, but you didn't turn your back on a buddy in trouble.

At least I didn't.

My own marriage hung in jeopardy, the warning signs all there. Short tempers, quick judgments, zero patience, lack of interest. Something Clark Gable once said had come to mind of late. *Love is heading toward your house, knowing that on the other side of the front door is a woman listening for your footsteps.* Pam quit listening two years back when I did something stupid and forgot that marriage was suppose to be monogamous. I'd violated her trust and hurt her deeply. I'd apologized profusely, and she'd supposedly forgiven me. But that was not the case. And we both knew it.

I'd screwed up.

Big time.

And changed a wife into a roommate.

A clang disturbed my thoughts, then one of the corrections officers appeared and opened the cell door. I took the cue and rose, following the woman down a sterile tile corridor. Her rhythmic stride, slow and steady, would have pleased any drill sergeant. Cameras bristled like gun emplacements over every door. A strong chlorine odor tickled my nose.

I was led to another brightly lit, windowless space, this one not a cell but an interrogation room, equipped with a long metal table and six chairs.

Most likely for lawyers and clients. A woman waited. Middle-aged, thin, attractive, with short, light-colored hair and a confident face. She wore a smart-looking wool-skirted suit. She would eventually become one of my closest friends, but on this day we were perfect strangers.

My first impression of her was never in doubt.

Law enforcement.

And not local.

"My name is Stephanie Nelle," she said.

The corrections officer left, closing the door behind her.

"What are you? FBI?"

She smiled and shook her head. "I was told you were intuitive. Give it another shot."

I tried to think of a clever retort, but couldn't, so I simply said, "Justice Department."

She nodded. "I came down from DC to meet with you. But an hour ago, when I showed up at the naval station, your commanding officer told me you were here."

I was in my second year of a three-year tour at Mayport. The base sat a few miles east of Jacksonville beside a protected harbor that accommodated aircraft-carrier-sized vessels. Thousands of sailors and even more support personnel worked within its fences.

"I'm sure he had nothing good to say about me."

"He told me you could rot here. It seems he considers you nothing but a problem."

Which, believe me, I'd tried hard not to be. I'd served at bases in Scotland, Connecticut, and Virginia. I knew the word was out I was a maverick, tagged with stubbornness, arrogance, even a little recklessness, with an occasional confrontation with authority. But by and large I toed the Navy line, and my service record was exemplary. Next up for me was sea duty, which I wasn't looking forward to. At least three years' worth, if I ever wanted to advance to commander. Pam, God bless her, followed me to each duty station, finding a job, making a home. Which made my past idiocy even worse. We'd talked about her going to law school. She had an interest and I liked the idea. Or having a baby? Maybe one of those, or both, might save us. Bob Weiler's death had brought into sharp focus the horror of divorce.

I slid one of the chairs away from the table and sat. The sleepless night was catching up to me. My visitor remained standing.

"Nice aiming out there," she said. "You could have killed her, but you didn't."

I shrugged. "She didn't appreciate the favor."

"Your first time shooting someone?"

"Does it show?"

"You look a little rattled."

"I watched a friend die."

"That would do it to anyone. Sue Weiler wants to press charges against you."

"Yeah. Good luck with that one."

She chuckled. "My thought, too. I was told you can handle yourself under pressure. It's good to see the intel was correct. You flew fighters, right?"

That I had. For a while, at least. Until I was talked into a career shift by friends of my late father. Two admirals and a captain who seemed to have made it their life's mission to look after me. My father would have been flag-rank-eligible by now, too, if not for his submarine sinking with all hands lost. No bodies had ever been recovered, little known about the mission. In fact, the whole thing was stamped classified. I knew that because I'd tried, without success, to access the court of inquiry's investigative report. I'd been ten when the men in uniforms came to the house and told my mother the bad news. Nothing about it made sense then, and it would be many more years before I learned the truth.

"I read your personnel file," she said. "You specifically requested flight training, and your skills were top-notch. Mind telling me why the shift to law?"

I trained my eyes on her like gun barrels. "You already know the answer to that question."

She smiled. "I apologize. I won't insult you like that again."

"How about you get to the point."

"I have a job for you."

"The Navy has first dibs on my time."

"That's the great thing about working for the attorney general of the United States, who works for the president of the United States, the commander in chief. Jobs like yours can be changed."

Okay. I got the message. This was important.

"The job I have in mind for you requires skill and discretion. I'm told you possess both qualities."

I decided to do a little testing on my own. "Was it the two admirals or the captain who told you about me?"

"All three, actually. One led me to another to another. They sang your praises. But the question is, do you live up to that advance billing? Your CO doesn't think so."

Screw that idiot. He was an ass-kissing paper pusher and always would be. A career officer focused on doing his twenty years, then retiring out with a pension while he was young enough to double-dip in private practice.

That path had never interested me.

But over the past few years I'd started to wonder if that might be my fate, too. Those friends of my father always liked to tell me they had a plan. Just go to law school, get the degree, then opt for JAG. Which I'd done. But I'd been beginning to wonder if they'd forgotten about me.

Now here was an opportunity.

Sent by them.

What did I have to lose?

Most likely my CO was going to strap me to a desk for at least the next month as punishment for drawing attention to his command. Forget about the fact that a friend died and the other person fired first.

"Am I off the hook for Sue Weiler?"

She nodded. "I had a talk with the sheriff. No charges will be filed."

I was impressed. "The sheriff himself?"

"I saw no reason to start any lower."

That was my first of many later moments appreciating Stephanie Nelle. She was a person who could make things happen. On that day, though, I only saw her as a way to make an end run around the asshole waiting for me back at Mayport.

"Okay," I said. "You did me a favor. I'll do you one."

My second in twenty-four hours.

And nothing was ever the same.

CHAPTER THREE

I SLID INTO A BOOTH ACROSS FROM STEPHANIE NELLE. WE'D LEFT the jail and driven east in a rental car out Atlantic Boulevard toward the naval station, bypassing the road for the base and ending up in Neptune Beach. Pam and I lived nearby, and being the curious sort that I am, I'd learned that the name dated back to 1922 when an enterprising resident built a train stop next to his home and christened it Neptune. He'd been told that if he built a station the train would be required to stop, which would eliminate his walking two miles to Mayport every day in order to catch a ride to work into Jacksonville.

Smart guy.

It worked.

Now Neptune Beach was a lovely seaside community lined with brick-paved streets and lots of artsy shops and crowded bars and restaurants. A happening place year-round, but especially from Memorial to Labor Day.

The Sun Dog Diner was one of my favorites. It had the metallic, tinny look of an old-time roadside café decorated with the obligatory slick vinyl and shiny linoleum. Friendly, too. The people treated you like a neighbor, the kind of place where if they hadn't seen you lately they'd pour you a free drink, offer a seat, and chat awhile. It sat on the main drag, across from another of my favorite places, The Bookmark, a local independent haunt. Its owners, Rona and Buford Brinlee, had become friends. I loved books, and always had. Eventually they would become a livelihood, but back then my collection was only beginning.

"Have you ever heard of a 1933 Double Eagle?" Stephanie asked.

I shook my head.

"It's the rarest coin in the world. Ninety percent gold, ten percent copper. Millions of Double Eagles were struck from 1850 to 1932. They were America's gold pieces, and they're still prevalent in the coin market. But in 1933 something different happened. 445,500 Double Eagles were struck that year, but none of those were ever issued to the public. FDR banned the private holding of gold in April 1933. Since the coins had already been produced when that happened, they were simply held at the Philadelphia mint and eventually melted down."

A waitress sauntered over.

"What's good to eat?" Stephanie asked me.

"The meat loaf is top-notch."

"Then we'll have two," she told the server. "I'll drink water."

"Iced tea for me."

I could tell Stephanie Nelle was comfortable being in charge, so I let her be in charge.

The young girl left.

Out through the front window I watched as people walked in and out of The Bookmark. I could already see her problem, so I asked, "How many of the 1933 coins managed to escape the smelter?"

"That's been a mystery for a long time."

I listened as she explained how the 1933 Double Eagles had evolved into the Holy Grail of numismatists. Only two of the coins were intentionally kept back at the mint, both given to the Smithsonian. They should have been the only two in existence anywhere.

"But more surfaced," she said. "Twenty that we know of. Best guess is they were stolen by an employee at the Philadelphia mint who sold them to a local jeweler, who sold them to collectors, until the Secret Service got wind of it in 1944. Eventually nineteen of the coins were reclaimed."

"And the last one?"

"That's where you come in."

I liked the sound of that.

"The Secret Service has been tracking that coin for decades. It's at the top of their most-wanted list. I know. I know. It seems silly. A sixty-plus-year-old gold piece. But they take their job as protector of the nation's currency seriously. They hunted the others for decades."

"What's it worth?"

"That's hard to say. Best guess is around $10 million. But remember, it would still be illegal to own it, as it's stolen government property. So any buyers would be limited to rich collectors content never to show it to anyone. Right now, that last 1933 Double Eagle, that we know of, is in south Florida."

She explained that it had been brought north by boat from the Caribbean two days ago. But the boat broke anchor and foundered on a reef, settling in about forty feet of water. The coin's owner had learned of the sinking and was en route to try to retrieve his property.

"I want you to get it first," she said.

I wasn't quite sure if she thought me stupid, gullible, or just ambitious. I discounted the first one, since no one wanted to be considered an idiot. Gullible? I'd never been accused of that. My inclinations actually tended more toward highly suspicious to paranoid. Ambitious? That's possible. I was young and hungry and eager for a change. I'd pondered for a long time what life had in store, hoping to God it wasn't handling court-martials and kissing the asses of higher-ranking officers. Truth be told, I'd already had my fill of the Navy, and the prospect of working for some civilian law firm was simply not appealing. This woman, who'd come from DC just to see me, had obviously pegged me right. I wanted out. That meant, for the moment, I'd allow her the luxury of thinking that I didn't realize she was playing me. What had Kenny Rogers said? *There'll be time enough for counting, when the dealin's done.*

So I kept listening as she dealt away.

"Your personnel file says you're a certified diver. This one's simple. Forty feet of clear, warm water down to that wreck."

"And what am I after?"

"A black waterproof case, about eighteen inches square. I want it brought up intact."

The waitress arrived with the food, which looked delicious. I hadn't eaten since yesterday afternoon.

I dug in.

"We're confident the Double Eagle is inside, but that will be for me to determine. The case should not be opened. Those friends of your father's told me that I could count on you to follow instructions."

I enjoyed the meat loaf and noticed that she was ignoring hers. "Why me? You must have plenty of other agents at your disposal."

"This job requires an element of independence, outside normal channels. It's a sensitive, internal matter within the Justice Department. One I'm handling. So I need a fresh face. One nobody knows."

Which tickled my lawyer bell big time. Three years of law school and six years at JAG hadn't taught me much, but they both ingrained a healthy curiosity. A host of questions popped into my brain, none of which, I realized, this woman was going to answer. Not now, anyway. So I kept my inquiries to myself. Besides, I wanted the job. So why antagonize the new boss?

Still, I couldn't resist. "What if I say no?"

"Now who's underestimating who?"

I grinned. "Is it that obvious?"

"You've been waiting for an opportunity like this a long time."

She knew me. Which was scary.

"You just didn't know when it was coming. Guess what. Moving day is here. Lieutenant Commander Harold Earl 'Cotton' Malone, your time has finally arrived."

"What about my command at Mayport?"

"Your CO told me I could have you. Apparently, you don't play well with others and you like to improvise far too much for his taste. For him, that's an impediment. Lucky for you, both of those qualities appeal to me."

CHAPTER FOUR

I PARKED NEAR THE DOCKS, THE TIME JUST BEFORE 7:00 A.M. THE drive south down I-95, from Jacksonville to Key West, had been a long one, which I'd endured yesterday after leaving Stephanie Nelle. I'd been able to get my car back from the Duval County impound lot without even having to pay a fee. Good to have friends in high places. My first stop after we parted had been home, where I packed a bag, telling Pam that I'd been dispatched on a special assignment. I was unsure how long I'd be gone, but would call when I knew more. She wasn't happy, to say the least, which I added to the growing list of our woes. I told her about Bob Wieler, shooting Sue, and going to jail, which elicited only the obligatory *I told you so.* I accepted her rebuke, not wanting to argue, and conceded that she'd been right all along.

I hated what was happening between us.

A Navy career was not conducive to good marital relations. Its hit-and-run existence added nothing but strain. The divorce rate was sky-high, and not just with enlisted. Misery stretched all the way up the ranks. The closer you got to retirement, the greater the chance of a split. But my self-inflicted screwup had only poured salt onto that potential wound. A friend of mine liked to say that *once you leave the marital bed, you never return.* He might be right, because returning came with a host of heavy baggage. Truth was not a one-way street, and it really did take two to tango. For Pam and me the truth would be a long time coming between us. Many years would pass before we both learned the whole story, eventually ending our marriage first as bitter enemies, then as friends. But back then I genuinely hoped Pam and I weren't finished.

Stephanie told me to get a good night's sleep and be at the Key West Bight at seven. Last evening I found a nearby motel and took her advice, the same one Pam and I visited last year on a long weekend. A truly enjoyable three days for us. We'd played, talked, and there'd even been sex.

Good times.

Laid back, free-spirited, artsy, quirky, scenic, you name it, Key West definitely shifted left of center. Pirates once made it the wealthiest place in Florida, at a time when Miami remained an uninhabited swamp. The town sat at the end of a rocky chain of low-slung islands. Its tropical climate lingered year-round, along with a seemingly continuous happy hour. People came to fish, escape, carouse, and rejuvenate. Nonconformity seemed a religion. Hell, it even seceded from the Union back in the 1980s, declaring itself the Conch Republic, then promptly surrendered to the United States and requested a million dollars in foreign aid.

You had to like that spunk.

I was told to find one boat among the charters that called the historic harbor home. Today not that many people buzzed about, probably thanks to a clinging canopy of gray sky, which looked ugly and threatening. A steady breeze swept in from the sea carrying a tide of warm moisture, the air thick like being submerged. A storm was definitely coming. Not a day for deep-sea fishing and not good for my car, which was minus one window.

I found the boat, the *Isla Marie,* at the end of a dock, a forty-footer with a wide stern, twin inboards, and an enclosed upper bridge. A sheltered rear deck offered sun protection for any fishermen, and a spacious forward cabin accommodated overnight stays.

A man emerged onto its rear deck.

Short, stout, square-shouldered, thick-necked. His tanned skin contrasted with thin, silvery hair. He was potbellied, dressed in khaki shorts, a dark Key West T-shirt, and a battered ball cap. Around his neck hung a gold doubloon on a chain. Just as with Stephanie Nelle, I knew the look.

More law enforcement.

"Trying to fit in?" I asked the guy from the dock.

"I'm retired. What do I care?"

Good point. "You Captain Nemo?"

The guy smiled. "I don't miss all the stupid intrigue."

Stephanie had told me to use the code name.

"And you are?" he asked.

"Cotton Malone."

Which sounded like a code name in and of itself.

"Where'd you get a name like Cotton?"

"It's a long story."

He flashed me an amiable, toothy smile. "That's good. 'Cause we have a long trip. Hop aboard."

"Where we going?"

He pointed a finger out toward open ocean.

"Seventy miles that way."

We stood in the enclosed bridge, the *Isla Marie* fighting hard against a stiff headwind, the beat of the engines steady under my feet. The farther west we cruised, the worse the rain became. Windblown spray and gusts of bright foam flew up from the bow as we knifed a choppy path through the churning water.

"Nobody will be fishing today," my host said.

"Haven't you forgotten something?"

No name had yet been offered. At the docks I'd understood. *Loose lips sink ships.* But we were long gone from Key West.

"Jim Jansen, once with the FBI."

"Now with the Justice Department?"

"Hell, no. I was asked to help Stephanie out. A favor. Like you, I'm told."

The entire boat shifted like a seesaw. Thank God I wasn't prone to seasickness, otherwise I'd be tasting my breakfast twice. Jansen seemed to have a good pair of sea legs, too.

"Are you local?" I asked.

"Born and raised in the Keys, then spent thirty years with the bureau. I retired two years ago and came back home."

I knew the score. Generally, FBI special agents had to go when they turned fifty-seven or completed twenty years, whichever came later. Extensions could be granted, but they were rare.

"You a conch, through and through?" I asked, making sure I pronounced the *ch* with a heavy *k*.

"Absolutely. We have a lot of freshwater varieties, transplants from every place you can name. But the hardcore saltwater species, the true locals, we're getting rarer and rarer. Take the wheel."

I grabbed hold as Jansen found a map, unfolded it, and laid it across the instrument panel. The rain kept slapping like pellets, splattering the windshield in drenching waves.

"Time for you to know some things," he said. "We're headed for the Dry Tortugas. Ever heard of them?"

"A little bit. Didn't Billy Bones mention them in *Treasure Island*?"

He pointed a stubby finger at the chart. "It's a cluster of seven tiny islands, not much more than sandbars with some trees and bushes, set among a slew of coral reefs. It's the end of the line for the Florida Keys and the last speck of the United States. Less than a hundred acres of dry, uninviting, featureless land at the edge of the main shipping channel from the Gulf to the Atlantic. Ponce de León himself discovered them. He called them the Tortugas for all the turtles."

"And the 'dry' part?"

"That came later to let sailors know there's not a drop of fresh water anywhere. But the islands offered great anchorage from the weather and a perfect resupply and refit stop."

"Why are we out here in the middle of a storm, headed for them?"

"Stephanie a little tight-lipped?"

"More like lockjaw."

He chuckled. "Don't take it personal."

"How long have you known her?"

"Just met the other day."

Which told me nothing, so I asked, "Tell me about the boat that sank."

"It was a dump. Looked like the *Orca* from *Jaws,* after the shark got hold of it. I don't know how the thing even made it here from Cuba."

I heard the magic word and tossed Jansen a hard look. "You're kidding?"

"Makes it all the more interesting, doesn't it?"

That it did. Cuba lay only ninety miles away, and as far as I knew it was illegal for any boat from there to be in American waters. No exceptions. Ever. Stephanie had not mentioned a word of this detail, saying only the craft had come north *from the Caribbean.*

"Two days ago the boat was docked off Garden Cay in the Dry Tortugas. I was there, watching. The wind was howling like today and it was raining hard. The tidal currents are real bad there, they flow against the prevailing winds. The harbor has long been a sanctuary, a safe haven from enemies and weather, but you have to know what you're doing. This captain didn't. The boat broke anchor, drifted west, and hit a reef. Gone." Jansen snapped his fingers. "Like that."

I kept a stranglehold on the bucking wheel. "I'm not an expert on driving a boat. You want to take this back?"

"Nah. You're doing fine. The boat went down here." Another stab at the chart, just west of a small, slender island. "Just off Loggerhead Cay. The guy who brought it north was held up at the campsites on Garden Cay, at Fort Jefferson. Here. Which is a few miles to the east."

The fort I knew about.

Built in the mid-1800s to defend what was at the time the world's busiest shipping lanes, it eventually evolved into a jail for Union deserters during the Civil War. After, it continued to serve as a prison. Dr. Samuel Mudd, convicted in Lincoln's assassination, was its most famous inmate. Disease and hurricanes forced its abandonment, and it eventually morphed into a late-19th-century coaling station for Navy steamers. The *Maine* left from there for Havana and history. Now it was a national park, showcasing the largest masonry structure in the Western Hemisphere. I'd seen pictures. A massive brick hexagon, hundreds of feet long, walls fifty feet tall and eight feet thick that consumed nearly the entire high ground of a featureless cay, making it appear to float atop the surrounding turquoise water. Its massive gun batteries, mounted in multiple-tiered brick casements, had been meant to hold their own against an entire enemy fleet. A perfect example of the old adage that forts were built not where convenient, but where needed.

"It's got to be remote as hell out there," I said to Jansen.

"It ain't the Four Seasons. But there'll be few people to get in our way."

"You said the guy who brought the boat *was* on Garden Cay. Where is he now?"

"In custody. Good for us it's illegal for someone from Cuba to be here."

Yeah, good for us. "Am I going down to the wreck in this storm?"

"We have no choice. The boat's owner is on the way, and we have to get that waterproof case before he does."

"Where's he coming from?"

"Cuba. Where else?"

Of course. How silly of me to ask.

A wave pounded the port side and the boat reeled. I compensated and brought the bow back on its previous heading. I then caught Jansen's eyes with my own. His were deep-socketed, with a nervous blink, and I wondered what this man knew that I didn't.

A blast of air slapped more rain against the windscreen.

"This is nuts," I said.

"It's the smart play. Nobody will be out in this mess. Especially the park rangers. We should have an open-field run."

A mass of black clouds, loaded with thunder and lightning, swirled overhead. The entire ocean seemed to be boiling.

"If you were there when it sank, why didn't you make the dive?"

"Do I look like Lloyd Bridges? It's not in my skill set. So Stephanie went out and got herself a young buck."

"You don't approve?"

"Not my call. I'm just a volunteer."

"How much do you know about her?" I tried again.

"I guess you deserve a little info."

That was the way I viewed it, too.

"She was State Department, then moved over to Justice. I remember that she worked close with the FBI when I was with the bureau. Still does, I'm told. A lawyer, but government through and through."

I heard his unspoken praise.

A prosecutor. Good people. On the right team.

As long as the man was talking, I tried, "She told me about the 1933 Double Eagle. Seems like one special coin."

"It could be the last of a species."

Valuable enough that we were out in the middle of a storm trying to retrieve it. But nothing about any of this rang right. A coin that shouldn't exist. A boat from Cuba suddenly sinking. The owner, from Cuba, too, on his way. The Justice Department allowing all of that to happen. And all for a waterproof case that had to be retrieved intact.

Unopened.

I'd tried enough court-martials at JAG to be able to read juries and witnesses, and though I might be the designated young buck I was no fool.

Something stunk.

Bad.

CHAPTER FIVE

I spotted Fort Jefferson through the rain.

The trip from Key West had taken nearly three hours, the going slow thanks to the storm. Jansen was back at the helm, navigating us beyond Garden Cay and the fort, heading toward Loggerhead, the largest of the seven islands, which accommodated a lighthouse whose piercing beam could be seen through the storm.

"The boat broke anchor just over there, then drifted off the south point of Loggerhead," Jansen said. "That's where the reefs on the other side got it."

The squall had eased, but the rain continued. A couple of catamarans, sailboats, and a few power cruisers sat at anchor five hundred yards to our left. We passed the south tip of Loggerhead and I spotted something bobbing in the water. A plastic milk jug with a piece of yellow rope attached to its neck.

"I tied it off to a coral head below," Jansen said. "The reef is shallow here so I could snorkel. The wreck is fifty yards west of the marker, in a little deeper water."

"Isn't this a national park? How'd you manage to tag the wreck?"

"With all the bad weather, that jug hasn't been noticed. But another day and it would have been."

He eased back the throttle and held the boat steady. "I'll keep above you with the engines. Careful with the props. Go ahead and gear up. Everything you need is down on the deck."

It had been a while since I last dove. The Navy taught me. Pam learned in Cozumel a few years ago. But she'd only made two dives. On the second, an encounter with a nurse shark proved that being underwater was not her thing. So she'd spent the next three days on the boat, waiting for me, which seemed the story of our life.

I climbed from the bridge and found the gear. Standard issue. Nothing fancy. I screwed the regulator onto the tank and tested the pressure with a hiss. Then I adjusted the shoulder and waist straps and buckled on a weight belt. Overhead, lightning flickered and I flinched against another jagged stab that seemed like it was meant for me. The tumult of thunder and the beat of the rain remained steady. How many safety rules was I about to violate? Like never, ever go into the water with lightning. Or alone. In restricted waters. The deck tossed in violent, unpredictable lists and I decided this was no place to don heavy equipment. So I slipped on my mask and fins, tossed the tank over the side, and rolled off the gunnels into the water.

I dropped beneath the turbulence and found the sinking tank. Leaning forward, I inserted both arms through the shoulder straps inside out, then hoisted the weightless mass, bringing it up, over my head, and down on my back, keeping my arms out straight until the straps rested comfortably on my shoulders.

I found the regulator and purged it of water.

Ready to go.

I kicked toward the bottom where things were much calmer. Jansen had been right. The reef was shallow here. Maybe ten feet at most, then a sharp drop down to white sand and thirty-plus depths. A little farther out the real drop happened to deep blue water. The dingy day offered challenging illumination, but visibility was excellent.

The water teemed with life.

A barracuda appeared, hanging around with its mouth open, exposing some impressive fanglike teeth. With an incredible burst of speed, it disappeared into the blueness. A forest of living coral, in shades of tan, yellow, and brown, sheltered countless inhabitants. I recognized lavender triggerfish, banded butterflies, black and yellow angels, and red squirrelfish. I also kept watch for sharks at the outer limits of visibility.

And then I saw it.

The wreck, angled to its starboard side, the white wedge of a hull settled into the sandy bottom, its bow pointing skyward. What paint there was remained, as the hulk had not been down long enough for algae to take hold. It was every bit thirty feet long, and not all that dissimilar in configuration to the *Isla Marie* waiting above. A gash large enough to swim through ran down the length of the port side, confirming what Jansen said.

Reef hit.

I swam around to the stern, poking my head into the main cabin. Furniture and equipment lay helter-skelter. Not much there. The rear deck was likewise sparse, except for some diving equipment strapped to the bulkheads. No black waterproof case in sight. I took a moment to survey the sandy bottom surrounding the wreck and saw nothing there, either.

I stopped and gathered myself.

The warm water felt good, and my breathing had slowed to steady and calm. This definitely beat the hell out of a courtroom. I kicked toward the upper bridge and stopped at the door, which remained open on its hinges.

And there it was.

A black waterproof case, about eighteen inches square, just as Stephanie Nelle had said. I grabbed its handle and was surprised. Heavy. A bit too much to haul to the surface, especially since I wore no buoyancy vest.

Which raised a question.

What else besides a coin was inside?

I took a second and assessed things. The smart play was to move the case out to the seafloor, then head up for some rope. No sense trying to haul it up, then fight the storm to get it on the boat. So I worked the container free of the bridge, kicking hard, breathing harder, and finally gliding out beyond the wreck, settling the container on the sandy bottom. A quick glance up and I saw the *Isla Marie*'s keel bobbing on the surface, the engines grinding back and forth, maintaining its position.

I headed up for it.

Breaking the surface I spit out the regulator and caught Jansen's attention with waving arms. "I need rope. Fifty feet or more."

"We've got company," he hollered back through an open window, motioning toward the stern.

I popped up as best I could to see over the rolling crests. A small boat was coming our way, closing fast. Could be the park rangers from Fort Jefferson.

"Get the rope," I yelled again.

"We need to go."

"There's time. We can do this. Get the rope."

I wanted these people to know I had nerve. If I was ever going to get out of JAG and into the action, I had to prove myself. I had a talent for sharp thinking in a crisis. Time to put it to good use. The other boat was coming, but I should be able to get down and back—if Jansen would just toss me the damn rope.

Which he did.

A coil of yellow nylon landed atop the water.

"The case is heavy," I yelled. "I'll tie it off and yank a signal, then you haul it up. I'll be right behind."

I grabbed the end of the coil, stuffed the regulator in my mouth, and plunged back beneath the waves.

CHAPTER SIX

I CLAWED MY WAY THROUGH THE WATER, HEADING FOR THE BLACK case that lay beyond the wreck. On the way down, using some of my clear-thinking-in-a-crisis, I decided to wrap the rope around the exterior and not trust the handle. Its unexpected weight remained a puzzle. I was no stranger to working in the dark, as few people facing a court-martial ever leveled with their lawyer, especially someone who was an officer in the same Navy prosecuting them. So I was accustomed to half the story or, worse yet, total lies. Eventually, though, the truth always prevailed and I assumed that would shortly be the case here, too.

What an idiot I was.

I reached the bottom and saw I had plenty of slack in the rope, so I worked the yellow nylon beneath the case and wrapped it around a couple of times, forming a makeshift sling that should remain firmly attached. Overhead, I heard a new rumble of engines and saw the black outline of a second keel powering to a stop. Small, oval-shaped, like an inflatable or a dinghy. Out in this chop that had to be a rough ride.

Two divers entered the water.

Both carried spearguns, their fins kicking furiously as they headed toward me.

A little extreme for park rangers.

If I yanked the line, the divers would make it to the case long before Jansen could haul it to the surface. Knives were affixed to each of their legs—it would be an easy matter for them to cut the rope. So I abandoned the case and headed for the wreck. My pursuers were nearly to the bottom. I glided across the rear deck and into the main cabin just as a spear thudded into the wood behind me.

I hadn't heard it coming.

Unlike in the movies, there were no whining sound effects signaling its path through the water. The thing just appeared.

Definitely not park rangers.

I rolled onto my back and watched through the cabin's rear windows as one of the divers swam my way and the other headed for the black case. I'd never been trained to handle this kind of situation, but that didn't mean I was in over my head.

I spotted a short set of steps that led down into a bow berth. The gash I'd seen outside should be there. A diver with a still-loaded speargun arrived at the stern. I needed to slow him down, so I pushed the cabin's rear door shut and latched the bolt. Not perfect, but it should buy a few moments. My eyes locked with the diver outside, who didn't hesitate aiming his weapon. The wooden door was half glass, protected by a broken metal grille. I couldn't assume that the spear would be stopped by any of that, so I kicked twice and dropped down into the forward berth. Behind me the spear burst through the glass in the door, thudding into wood across the cabin.

I immediately saw that I was right and a bow gash opened outward. It would be tight, but possible. So I wedged myself through and came up behind the second diver, who was approaching the black case. He laid his reloaded speargun down on the sand and reached for his knife, surely about to cut the rope. I had maybe ten seconds to do something. So I kicked hard and reached around, yanking the regulator from his mouth and popping off his face mask. The assault caught the guy off guard and I used his confusion to wrench the knife away. Drifting back, I drove the heel of my right fin into his forehead, further dazing him.

The other diver from the wreck had found his way to the hull gash. I knew there'd be a moment of awkwardness before he could maneuver himself through. I was running out of options, the first diver working to find his regulator and face mask. The man inside the wreck disappeared. Then I realized. He was reloading, readying himself for a shot out the gash.

I heard an engine roar louder.

The *Isla Marie*.

Jansen was leaving?

I yanked hard on the rope.

Several times.

The engines above revved and the slack in the rope began to recede. I snatched the other gun from the sand and sent its spear through the gash. Whether it hit anything didn't matter. It would buy me time and give the guy in there pause. I grabbed hold as the rope went tight and both the case and I were dragged away from the wreck. I didn't want the heavy case to strike anything, which might compromise its watertight seal, so I slipped down to the container, secure in its sling, and wrapped my arms around it. Jansen had throttled up the boat and I was now being propelled through the water, speed adding buoyancy.

Some kicks of my fins and the case and I rose.

A quick glance back.

The other diver in the wreck was free, aiming his speargun.

But I was now out of range.

The boat stopped.

We were beyond the reef in deep blue water, the bottom beneath me not visible. I was still bear-hugging the case, breathing harder than I should. So I told myself to calm down.

I felt pressure on the rope.

Jansen was pulling it in.

I released my grip and kicked for the surface, breaking through into the rain. I stayed with the case as Jansen brought it closer to the boat.

"Climb aboard," he called out.

I didn't want to risk the case slipping free, so I stayed with it in the water until the container nestled the stern, then I slipped off my fins, tossed them onto the deck, and climbed the metal ladder. Jansen had a death grip on the rope, and I helped him bring the case up and over the gunnel.

"Amazing how one gold coin can be so heavy," I said.

I saw that Jansen did not appreciate my sarcasm. Too bad. He hadn't just been shot at with spearguns. I released my waist belt and slid the tank off. That dive had taken a lot out of me. I scanned the seam of sky and sea and noticed that we'd gone far enough out that the other boat could not be seen through the murky storm.

"The third guy up here in that inflatable started to get frisky," Jansen said. "I had to use this." He reached behind and withdrew a semiautomatic from his waist. "I figured you were in trouble."

But I wondered.

Jansen had powered up and moved *before* I yanked on the rope. Then there was that moment of surprise I'd caught on his face when he saw me on the surface.

"The water was churned up," Jansen said. "But clear enough for me to see those two guys after you. I decided it was time to go and was hoping you were hanging on."

"Who are they?"

"I imagine they work for the coin's owner. One of those boats we passed at anchor might have been his. He apparently arrived sooner than we thought. You did good getting this up here."

I'd had enough, so I grabbed Jansen by the arm. "It's time to end this bullshit. You understand what I'm saying."

He glared at me. "Don't get your panties in a wad. This is all par for the course. It goes with the job. You did good. You've got balls."

I released my grip.

I neither believed nor appreciated any of what he was saying, but I was in no position to either argue or barter. I was the new kid on the block, and to make friends I had to play nice.

"What now?" I asked.

"I told you we have a guy in custody. But there's another person, on Loggerhead Cay, who's camped out waiting for him. She came yesterday afternoon to make a deal with the guy who brought the boat from Cuba. There is a 1933 Double Eagle involved, but it's not in that case.

It's on Loggerhead. The woman who came yesterday was going to use it to buy what's in this case."

"And what is that?"

He shook his head. "That's above my pay grade. Not for either of us to worry about. Since we have the case, why don't you take the place of the guy we have in custody and make a deal for the coin."

"You're going to give her what's inside?"

"Hell no. I'm going to help the FBI arrest her. But first we need to know some things. Get her talking. Find out what you can. Can you handle that?"

Sure.

Sounded like a plan.

CHAPTER SEVEN

I HOPPED ASHORE ON LOGGERHEAD CAY.

The rain had eased, the clouds separated, and a harsh sun was now streaming down soothing the sea and warming my body. Jansen had eased to a dock that extended out past a narrow beach to drop me off, then motored on toward the north point of the island where he'd be waiting. We hadn't seen the inflatable with the divers on our return.

Loggerhead sat three miles west from Fort Jefferson. The black-and-white conical tower of its signature brick lighthouse continued to flash, as did the one across the water, atop the fort, each winking to the other in the ever-brightening midday. The island's landscape was flat and uninteresting, barely a few feet above sea level, covered in low scrub and thick stands of a short, squatty pine. A beautiful thin ring of white sand wrapped its edges, dissolving into the transparent water. The reef where I'd dived lay off the far side, toward the southwest. Here, on the east, a cluster of low-slung buildings guarded the lighthouse. Jansen had told me that only a few caretakers lived here. Birds seemed the main residents along with, I assumed, its namesake turtles, which surely used the beaches for nests.

Jansen also told me that a handful of campgrounds were scattered across the forty or so acres, concentrated at the south and north extremes. No food, fresh water, electricity, or medical assistance existed.

Each person had to bring everything they needed and take everything away. The remote sites were first come, first served. The contact I sought waited at the north point.

I wore a Jacksonville Jaguars T-shirt, a pair of Nike shorts, and tennis shoes, projecting an image of island simplicity. But a clean-shaven face and a regulation haircut might give away my military status. I was in good shape, the dive had just proven that. My waist remained thin, my hair a sandy blond. Middle age was years off, and thankfully my metabolism burned more calories than I took in.

Weather here seemed to change in a blink of an eye. The storms from earlier were vanishing, replaced by clear skies and sunshine. But it was also hurricane season, and I imagined that this was the last place you'd want to be if one of those paid a visit.

A concrete walk led from the dock to the lighthouse, which sat roughly at the island's center. I avoided that path and headed north, up the beach, following the wet sand. Thunder continued to rumble in the distance as the storm moved eastward. The only other sounds were the wind, a gentle lap of tiny waves, and the shrill cries from birds overhead.

I felt like a castaway.

The whole cay was only about two hundred yards wide. If not for the thick stands of pine, you would have been able to see from side to side and end to end. At the north point I spotted a green Sundome tent, its rain fly unzipped, set among what looked like foundation ruins. A weathered placard identified the site as the former Tortugas Marine Biological Laboratory, established by the Carnegie Institution in 1904. I had no idea what I was walking into, but since there was no choice I left the beach and followed a narrow trail through prickly pear cactus.

"Are you the person who made the dive on the wreck?"

The words were delivered in Spanish, and hearing a disembodied female voice where there'd just been nothing startled me. Thankfully, languages were familiar to me. It was a side effect of an eidetic memory that came courtesy of my mother's side of the family. Not photographic. Just a mind that retained facts like a magnet, which had made it easy for me to learn Spanish, French, and some passable Italian. My hope had been that the skills might come in handy one day.

A woman emerged from the tent.

She was a little over five feet tall with shoulder-length dark hair and smooth brown skin. No makeup marred her attractive face. Her almond-shaped eyes sized me up with a tight, almost uncomfortable gaze. She was trim and fit with healthy curves concealed by jeans at the limit of their embrace and a loose-fitting blouse. Being a lawyer and asking a million questions had taught me that conversations hated a vacuum. If the questioner didn't rush in to fill the silence, the subject usually would do it for you, often to their regret.

So I stayed quiet.

"Can you understand me?" she asked in Spanish.

The accent was American, with a touch of the South. Like my own. I said, "No Spanish."

Better to keep my linguistic abilities to myself.

"Is this better?" she said in English.

"Works for me."

"You can't be Valdez. He sounded older on the phone."

"I'm not."

"Are you the fellow who dove the reef?"

I nodded. "You watched?"

"From the beach. I was wondering if anyone would come. I heard about the wreck yesterday when I arrived. But since I'm stuck here till later today, I had no choice but to wait and watch."

"Do you have a name?"

"Coleen Perry."

"I'm Cotton Malone. I came for the coin."

"You work for Valdez?"

There was that name again. New in the mix. But I knew the correct answer. "I do." I had to tread carefully since I had no idea where this was headed. So I stuck with the facts. "I have what you want." I pointed off toward the water. "It's on that boat, anchored out there."

Jansen had assumed a position about a hundred yards off the north point, near where the water transitioned from turquoise to blue. Once I'd learned what I could, a signal from me would bring him back around to the dock where we would take this woman into custody. Since there was literally nowhere for her to run, that task should be easy. Interestingly,

Coleen Perry did not appear anxious in any way and I surmised that this might not be her first rodeo.

"Who were the other guys that went down with you?" she asked.

"Some additional help that I didn't need."

"I noticed your boat left in a hurry."

"You want to deal or talk?"

She reached into her pocket and found something, which she tossed across to me. I caught the offering and saw that it was a plastic sleeve protecting a shiny gold coin a little over an inch in diameter. One side showed Lady Liberty holding a torch and an olive branch backed by lines of glory. The other depicted a bald eagle in flight, with more glory lines and the familiar motto IN GOD WE TRUST. Above the eagle the face value read $20.

"It's still illegal to own it," she said.

"Yet you have it."

"Not anymore. Where is Valdez?"

"He doesn't get out much."

"We were supposed to talk."

I glanced back at the coin in my hand and something occurred to me. If this Valdez was in fact from Cuba, getting paid in cash would not be the smartest move. True, U.S. dollars were used there, but not in the quantities this coin commanded. So what was in the case that was worth millions of dollars?

Time to see what I could learn.

"I'm not in the loop here," I said. "Just hired help. But I am curious."

"That's what got the cat killed."

"But satisfaction brought it back."

She smiled. "Okay, what do you want to know?"

I motioned with the coin. "How did *you* get this?"

"I didn't. My father did."

"And it's too nosy of me to ask where he got it?"

She shook her head. "If Valdez isn't here, I just want my documents."

Another new piece to the puzzle. *Documents.* Now I knew what had made the waterproof case so heavy.

"Like I said, they're on the boat. I'll signal and it will meet us at the dock."

"Do it."

The sound of propellers biting air disturbed our tranquility. I glanced up and saw a single-engine Cessna seaplane dropping from the eastern sky, descending rapidly, skimming the choppy surface, and making a landing not far from Jansen's boat.

"Are you expecting somebody?" she asked.

I watched as the blue-and-white plane taxied toward the *Isla Marie*, killed its engine, then nestled close. I caught the tail ID numbers: 1180206. Was Jansen in trouble? Movement on the rear deck drew my attention. The plane blocked a clear view, but I could see someone hoisting something from the boat. Then people hopped into the plane, which drifted away, its engine restarted. There was nothing I could do but watch as the plane gathered speed, then lifted off into the midday sky.

I turned back to face Coleen.

Who held a gun in her hand.

CHAPTER EIGHT

I DEBATED WHETHER TO KEEP TO LIES.

Frankly, I wasn't sure what was what at this point.

"I want my coin back," she said. "It seems you don't have the documents anymore."

Fair enough. I tossed the packet over. "You may not believe this, but that plane was as much a surprise to me as it was to you."

"I don't believe anything, except that Valdez is apparently a double-crossing crook. What was the plan? You get the coin. He gets back his documents? I get screwed."

I needed to see about Jansen. Hard to tell exactly what had just happened on the boat. He might be hurt.

"I have a friend out there who could need help."

She lowered the gun and shrugged. "I don't care. I have my coin. Get the hell out of here."

I ran toward the water and plunged in, shoes and all. The sea remained churned, surging around the flat spit of island. Jansen had been right about the local currents. They were formidable. But thankfully they were headed out to open ocean, which allowed me to negotiate the hundred yards quickly.

"Jansen. Jansen."

No reply.

The *Isla Marie* twisted around its anchor line. I heard a plane in the distance and saw another making a water landing near Fort Jefferson. A bad morning was turning into an okay afternoon and tour operators out of Key West had to make a living. I grabbed hold of the stern ladder and climbed up onto the deck beneath the sheltered roof. The dive equipment still lay where I'd left it. Water dripped from my wet clothes.

"Jansen," I tried again.

I checked the forward cabin. Empty. I climbed to the upper bridge. Empty, too. Jansen was not on board. Had he been taken by the people in the plane? Or had he gone voluntarily?

I climbed back down to the main deck and considered my options. The waterproof case was gone. It had been here when I'd left earlier. Clearly, it had found its way onto the plane.

Then something caught my eye.

A red-and-white Igloo cooler, which hadn't been there before.

Maybe Jansen had brought it up from below? I glanced out across the water and saw another seaplane. But instead of vectoring for Fort Jefferson it turned west and headed my way.

Then I noticed something else.

A wire leading from the Igloo, draping the port rail.

Alarm bells rang in my brain.

I rushed to the cooler and removed the top. The inside was packed with plastic-wrapped clay bricks. Metal posts were buried into the top layer. Wires led to an electronic device.

A detonator.

No timer was visible, which meant it was probably remote-controlled. The exposed wire leading out had to be an antenna.

I darted to the rail, glancing up to see the seaplane bank north and start a low sweep that would take it about a quarter mile off the stern. I caught the coloration. Blue and white. Then the ID numbers.

1180206.

The same one from before.

It had circled back.

That couldn't be good.

I leaped from the boat into the water and powered myself deep.

Just as the *Isla Marie* exploded.

I surfaced.

Thankfully, I'd made it deep enough to escape the destruction. Debris floated everywhere and I felt a swift current that would take it all, including me, out to sea. Quite a mess I'd managed to get myself into and I wondered how much of it had been intentional on the players' part.

Stephanie Nelle. Jansen. Coleen Perry.

And a guy named Valdez.

Stupid me assumed that Jansen had been either harmed or incapacitated. What was the saying? *Fools rush in where angels fear to tread.* And this fool had certainly done that. Had Jansen set me up for a kill?

I tried to swim back toward Loggerhead, but for every few yards gained, the current reclaimed that much and more. A piece of debris floated by and I retrieved it, using it for flotation, which allowed my arms and legs to rest. I'd swum more today than in the past two years.

I quickly drifted away from land.

Hopefully, some of the local residents beneath me weren't out looking for an easy lunch. If so, there'd be little I could do to dissuade them.

An engine broke the silence.

Not a plane. A boat.

I'd been hoping the park service personnel at Fort Jefferson would come to investigate. After all, how many things blew up around here?

I saw a craft headed my way.

But not from the east where the fort lay. This one came from the west side of Loggerhead.

An inflatable.

Like the one from before.

Anything had to be better than wearing myself out and drowning in the open sea. Particularly considering my only exercise was jumping to conclusions. So I waved my arms and attracted attention. The buzz of an outboard came steadily nearer, then eased up toward me and I saw two men inside.

The divers from the wreck.

Nothing about this was going to be good, but what choice did I have? I took some comfort from the fact that if they wanted me dead they'd just leave me in the water.

I swam over and grabbed the inflatable.

Something hard slammed my head.

Thoughts flickered as my brain became dazed with pain.

Then the world vanished.

CHAPTER NINE

I OPENED MY EYES.

I hadn't taken a shot like that since some touch football that got out of hand two summers ago. My head hurt. Where was I? On a boat? Had to be considering the engine roar and a familiar shifting of up and down.

My woozy brain reverberated with all the possibilities.

Just as I'd thought back in the water, nobody here wanted me dead.

Not yet, anyway.

Slowly, the room around me began to take shape. I lay on a bunk, the smelly berth nothing fancy. I pushed myself up and sat on the edge. My first day on the job had definitely been interesting.

Footsteps bounded down a steep set of stairs and a man entered the cabin. He was dark and gaunt, narrow-hipped and rawboned, not a pinch of surplus flesh anywhere on his bones. His face was angular, deep-lined, with a hawkish nose and long black-and-silver hair slicked down close to his skull. An abundant salt-and-pepper beard concealed a thin mouth. What caught my eye were his slender fingers, the nails manicured, a gold ring set with a ruby glimmering from his left hand.

"I am Juan Lopez Valdez. Where is my 1933 Double Eagle?"

He spoke with authority, the perfect English laced with a Spanish drawl. I assumed this was the same Valdez that Coleen Perry had mentioned.

"I don't have it."

"Ms. Perry kept it?"

I nodded. "It was hers. Or her father's, as she pointed out."

He seemed to believe what I was saying. I assumed my clothes had already been searched.

He motioned.

"Let's walk on deck. It's stuffy down here, and you look like you need some air."

I followed him up and saw that we were plowing through blue waves, not a speck of land in sight. The sky had totally cleared. Bright, hot, uncompromising sunshine streaked down. The rear deck was crowded with diving equipment.

"You came here to salvage the wreck?" I asked.

He propped himself against the outer rail and folded his bony arms across his chest. "That was my intention, after the storm cleared. But when we saw your boat, we moved faster. Senor Malone, we have a serious problem. I do not have my files or the coin."

Another new tidbit.

Not *documents* as Coleen had described.

Files.

"How do you know my name?"

He reached into his back pocket and removed my wallet. He opened the wet leather and found my military ID. "Lieutenant Commander Harold Earl Malone, currently at Naval Station Mayport. Judge Advocate General's corps. I'm familiar with that base. I visited there many years ago."

I decided to go with the obvious. "Before the boat exploded, a seaplane arrived. Your files went off in it. Your coin is still on Loggerhead with Coleen Perry. Unfortunately, I'm not in the loop on either of those."

"Except that you forcibly retrieved my files from the wreck. But for you, I would have them."

There was that. "Where are we going?"

"South. Where it's much safer."

That meant Cuba.

"When I agreed to this exchange," he said, "I made the mistake of thinking time had changed things. But I should have known better."

The dots started to connect.

The files were to be traded to Coleen by Valdez for the coin, and all was good until the seaplane arrived. Might as well give this guy more bad news. "I think a guy named Jim Jansen has your files. And there must have been quite a few. That case was heavy."

He shook his head. "A precaution I took, adding lead weights to the inside. If there were problems I did not want that waterproof case being taken by anyone. Better to let it sink to the bottom. But you're right about Jansen. He's been wanting my files for a long time. Now I seem to have provided him the perfect opportunity. With your assistance, of course."

I didn't like how he kept drawing me into something I knew zero about. So I pointed out, "I think Jansen wanted me dead."

That seemed to get his attention. "Go on."

"There were remote-controlled explosives on the boat. That seaplane came back to set them off, with me on board."

"Do you have any idea what you are involved with?"

"Not a clue."

He laughed.

And I didn't appreciate it.

"I believe you, amigo," he said. "I truly do. How would you like to redeem yourself?"

I actually would, but I didn't think that opportunity should come from this man. "You tried to kill me, too."

"That's correct, especially once I realized Jansen was on that boat."

"You were there?"

"Of course. He and I had words through the rain. When I decided to shoot him, he decided to leave."

None of which Jansen had reported to me.

He rummaged through my wallet and found my driver's license. Thankfully, it was from Georgia. Active-duty military personnel were not required to change their driver's license every time they relocated. Mine did not expire for another two years. The address on it led nowhere. Nothing else in my wallet was personal. Stephanie Nelle had told me to remove anything that qualified. So Pam's photo, which I always kept, was gone. Only my military ID, driver's license, State Bar of Georgia membership card, a Visa card, and some cash remained.

"Are you married?" he asked.

Like I was going to admit that. "Never had the pleasure."

"Women can be such trouble," he said. "I've had three wives, and divorce can be bothersome. That's why I killed mine." The declaration came in a matter-of-fact voice. "So much easier."

I tried to read his brittle eyes, but registered not a clue. He found my bar membership card. I carried it because a lot of the civilian jails required proof I was a lawyer. Many times my clients would initially be held by the locals, my first task being to secure their release back to military custody.

"I'm assuming you're some kind of Navy attorney. But if you were working for a private firm, what do you think would be your hourly rate?"

"Four hundred fifty."

Wishful thinking, but it sounded good.

And for some reason I wanted to impress this man.

"I can have someone killed for much less than one hour of your hypothetical time."

Valdez's eyes, tiny pinpricks of white surrounded by the darkest irises I'd ever seen—like black currants—told me that he was not given to exaggeration.

"Jim Jansen is a liar and a thief," he said. "He stole from me and, as you say, tried to kill you."

"So go find him."

"Oh, I shall. But I cannot worry about him at the moment. What I want is the coin I was promised."

"Coleen Perry has it."

"And the park rangers have her. She was arrested once they came to the explosion site. She is being held at the fort, as is my coin."

"What do you want me to do?"

"Steal it back."

"Not interested."

He shrugged.

"Then I'll simply dump you over the side and be done with this."

CHAPTER TEN

I STOOD AT THE RAIL AND STARED OUT AT THE OCEAN.

Two days ago I was a JAG lawyer, bored to tears. Then I shot a cheating wife, got arrested, and became a Justice Department recruit, which led to divers aiming spears at me. A supposed ally tried to blow me up, and now Juan Lopez Valdez, from of all places Cuba, wanted to shove me over the side. Since I was unarmed, outmanned, and on a boat in the middle of nowhere, his threat could not be ignored.

"You do realize that I'm not all that good with this intrigue stuff," I said. "Look where I am. Captured."

"Ah, amigo, you sell yourself short. My men told me you handled yourself quite skillfully in the water." He found a fresh panatela and lit it up. "And let us not forget that you are the one who took my files from the wreck. But for you, I would have them and be on my way home with the coin."

Incredibly, there was some twisted logic to his argument, which did not make the sour taste of failure, hanging thick in my mouth, any easier to swallow. I could spar, feinting and stalling, and try to buy time. But for what?

I decided to work with this guy.

At least until something better came along.

*　*　*

The bricks of Fort Jefferson appeared on the horizon. Valdez had doubled back and again found the Dry Tortugas.

"We will anchor south of the fort," he said. "You can take the inflatable to the island. Get my coin and return it to me, and our business will be concluded. Any ideas on how to make that possible?"

I actually had been thinking on just that. "I need my wallet."

He handed it over. "By the way, you were correct. Jansen is not your friend."

"Tell me something I don't know."

"Be careful who you decide to trust. You have no idea what you are involved with, so you certainly have no idea who you can depend upon. Whether you realize it or not, I am all that you have at the moment."

Which wasn't comforting.

"I simply want the coin. Bring it to me and we will never see each other again."

Still not comforting.

"I realize that you could easily go ashore and escape. So let me tell you something about me. I've always been a collector, but not of things. I like facts, which I savor and accumulate like old men keep stamps or coins. I say this so you will know that I am a man of great patience and, I assure you, I am good at what I do. Jansen can attest to that fact. So if you double-cross me, amigo, I will first learn all about you, then I will come and kill you. The fact that I reside in Cuba is not an impediment. I say this not from braggadocio but only so that you will not make the mistake of doubting me."

I beached the inflatable in the shadow of the fort.

Up close the red-yellow walls were massive, a formidable obstacle to any would-be attacker. Over sixteen million bricks had been used, each one shipped from the mainland. The hexagon shape ensured that every cannon had a clear field of fire. Three sides fronted the ocean, the remaining three a strip of island that eventually accommodated coaling stations. Portions of the outer walls and the corner bastions were crumbling, the effect of time, sea, and weather. It had been built to hold four hundred cannons, in three hundred open-vaulted casements, among two thousand arches. It cost a fortune and was never finished, the whole thing rendered obsolete with the invention of large-caliber rifled cannons, capable of penetrating thick masonry walls.

Two seaplanes were beached to my right. No boats rested at the main dock. Visitors were out enjoying the clear, calm water just offshore where snorkeling seemed to be allowed. I headed for the fort's sally port entrance at the end of a wooden bridge that crossed a saltwater moat. Odd that a fort, surrounded by ocean, would need a moat, but it actually made sense since it kept attacking ships from approaching too close. A stone counterscarp, which worked like a perimeter sidewalk, acted as an additional outer barrier.

Barracks, powder magazines, officers' quarters, and storehouses once filled the interior parade. Now only grass, a few trees, and ruins were there. A different sense of perspective came inside, where the walls, arches, and colonnades blocked the horizon, concealing the fact that there was ocean all around. I imagined a time in the 1850s when the army utilized machinists, carpenters, blacksmiths, masons, general laborers, prisoners, and slaves to construct the fort. Officers brought their families, and enlisted personnel their wives. In all close to two thousand people once lived on this barren splotch of sand, their entire existence precarious.

Like my current situation.

I was looking for the park service office. I should find someone in authority, tell them the truth, and have them contact Stephanie Nelle. Surely there were sea-to-land communications. That was definitely the smart play. But a part of me believed Valdez. He was not a man to cross. And his point about who to trust was a good one. Even more important, I wanted Jim Jansen and I wanted to find out what was going on. Coleen Perry seemed the best route to achieve both of those objectives.

To my left I spotted a door marked PARK HEADQUARTERS. I entered and was greeted by an eager young man in a service uniform. The Spartan office had been built right into the brick casements.

"My name is Malone. I understand you have Coleen Perry in custody."

I'd decided on a direct approach, seeing if I could get a few minutes alone with Coleen before anyone thought things through.

"You mean the lady we found on Loggerhead? Yeah, we have her."

"Why do you have her?"

"She was trespassing and had a gun."

"What kind of weapon?"

"Excuse me, what's your interest?"

I was wondering when the guy would break my momentum. "I came to meet with her and was told you'd detained her. I also happen to be a JAG lawyer." I found my wallet and showed him my State Bar of Georgia card and military ID.

"This lady, is she in the military?"

"Active duty." I circled back. "You said she had a gun. What kind of weapon?"

The young man looked befuddled, unsure what to do. I'd learned from dealing with countless subordinates on military bases that the easiest way to get what you wanted was to act important.

"We have a real situation," I said. "Ms. Perry came here on a sensitive military assignment, which is why she was armed. A boat exploded off Loggerhead today, did it not?"

"We think so. That's where everybody is. Out investigating."

Good to know. "That boat blowing up is all part of an ongoing military investigation. Where is Ms. Perry?"

He pointed at one of two doors on the far end of the office. Each was small, with little headroom and a barred glass window. "Locked in there. We don't have a cell, which is a little ironic since this whole place used to be a prison. I'm keeping an eye on her."

One more time. "Where's the supposed weapon she had?"

"You act like there wasn't one. There was. I have it."

"Show me."

He acted a little indignant, as if he needed to show me that the gun existed. Which was exactly the reaction I wanted. Subordinates also liked to prove to those above them how right they could be. He walked over to a cluttered wooden desk and opened a drawer, removing the same 9mm automatic that Coleen had pointed at me earlier.

I approached and held out my hand. "Let me see it."

Incredibly, the idiot handed it over. I examined the weapon and noticed no magazine. So this guy wasn't as dumb as I thought. "It's unloaded. There's no law against carrying an unloaded gun."

He reached into the drawer and found the magazine.

"Let me see it," I demanded.

He hesitated, then handed it over.

Now we were cooking.

Since some of my superiors liked to accuse me of being a loose cannon, I decided it was time to start acting like one. I snapped the magazine into the weapon, chambered a round, and aimed the gun straight at him. "I'm assuming you can open the door to that room?"

The young man's eyes went wide.

"Never had a gun pointed at you before?"

He shook his head.

"It's not really a problem unless—" I cocked the hammer. "—I do that."

The click added an exclamation point to my observation.

"If I even hiccup this could fire."

He seemed to get the point. "Mister, could you put that thing down? Really. Please. Put it down."

"Do what I asked."

This time he backed his way toward the door, fumbling in his pant pocket and removing a key, which he worked into the lock.

I motioned with the gun for him to open the door then enter.

Inside was a small, windowless space, not much larger than a walk-in closet, with more brick walls, that also served as an office. I caught the surprise on Coleen's face and quickly shook my head, signaling for her to keep quiet. She was handcuffed to an exposed pipe that ran from ceiling to floor beside a desk.

"Unlock her," I said.

He found another key and opened the cuffs. I motioned for him to take her place and he quickly began to cuff his wrist to the pipe.

Coleen watched in disbelief.

I motioned for us to step out into the other room.

"What are you doing?" she whispered.

"Getting you out of here. Where's the coin?"

"That's what you really want. Not to help me."

"Look, I just met Valdez. He's here and not happy. He wants his coin."

"I thought you worked for him?"

"I never said that. You just assumed." We needed to get moving. "Where's the coin?"

"They took it."

Why couldn't this be simple? I stepped back to the doorway and asked the young ranger, "The lady had a gold coin. Where is it?"

"Are you a thief? Is this a robbery?"

I aimed the gun straight at him. "One more time, then that's it for you. Where's the coin?"

"Okay. Okay. It's over in the staff quarters. One of our historians wanted to look at it."

"Tell me where."

He did. "You're in big trouble, mister. Real big trouble."

Didn't I know it. The list of felonies was growing by the minute. And all federal, too. My CO would not believe his good fortune.

"The Coast Guard and FBI are on the way here," he blurted out.

That caught my attention.

"Talk to me."

"They radioed a little while ago. The FBI is flying to get her and should be here anytime. You'll get yours then."

Maybe not.

After all, I was one of the good guys.

And they could be my salvation.

CHAPTER ELEVEN

I LED THE WAY AS WE RUSHED ACROSS THE PARADE TO THE FAR side of the fort, the gun tucked at my waistband beneath my Jaguars T-shirt. Hearing that the FBI was on the way added a new dimension. Sure, Jansen was suspect but that didn't mean everybody was crooked. I could make contact with those agents, explain the situation, and they could talk with Stephanie Nelle. If they moved fast, the Coast Guard could even detain Valdez before he left American waters. But I could see that Coleen Perry was not happy at the prospect of having more federal agents around.

"I assume you don't want the feds to know what you're doing," I said. "Considering that it's illegal to have that Double Eagle."

"Who are you?" she asked.

"Right now I'm the idiot risking my hide to save yours."

"I saw you leap off that boat before it blew, and when those men knocked you silly. The plane that flew by, right before the explosion, was the same one from before. I noticed the ID numbers."

We kept moving across the short grass, following a defined sandy path that bisected the parade.

"What was your name again?" she asked.

"Cotton Malone. Here from the Justice Department."

"Are you new at all this?"

That one hurt. "Does it show?"

"Only that you're young, and I'm guessing you don't have a clue what you're into."

"You're not exactly Ms. Experience," I pointed out. "We're probably about the same age."

"Except I'm not some hotshot Justice Department guy. Let me give you a piece of advice, Mr. Cotton Malone. The FBI is not your friend."

At least one retired agent fit that bill, but I wasn't ready to lump everyone into that category. "Care to explain?"

"Not at the moment."

The young ranger had pointed us toward some freestanding buildings on the parade's far side. Behind them, arches in the tall brick had been filled in with wooden walls and windows, creating enclosed staff quarters where there had once been only open casements. A few visitors loitered about on the coarse grass taking photos. More people ambled through the casements above, revealed in the arches that surrounded us on all sides.

We made it to a set of wooden stairs, which we climbed fast, finding the door we wanted at the top marked RESIDENCE AREA DO NOT ENTER. We ignored the warning and passed through into a long corridor that bordered the exterior wall. A welcome breeze slipped though the open casements. A series of doors stretched down an interior wooden wall to our left. I found the correct door and lightly knocked. No answer. One more time. Same result. I gripped the knob and turned. Probably little reason to lock anything around here. How much crime could they have?

I eased open the door.

The small space beyond was lightly furnished with a cotlike bed draped with a knitted spread, dirty clothes piled on the floor, a cluttered desk, and a small bureau. A screened window facing the interior parade hung open.

And then there was the falcon.

Standing on a perch, wings ruffling from our unwanted intrusion.

"You don't see that every day," Coleen said.

No, you didn't.

Neither of us moved.

"The coin is on the desk," I said, noticing the plastic sleeve.

The peregrine continued to ruffle its wings, like a warning that screamed, *Stay away.* Its sinister-looking eyes remained locked on me.

"Falcons don't attack people, do they?" she asked.

Like I was a bird expert.

I decided to go for the coin. But the bird seemed to read my mind and pounced, springing from its perch, feathers ruffled, talons extended. No shrieks or calls, just a steady beating of wings as it flew toward us. We shielded our faces with our arms and I hoped the damn thing would head out the door.

But it stayed.

Thankfully, it did not touch either one of us and landed back on the desk, near the coin. A silent, ominous pall fell over the room. If I didn't know better I would have assumed it knew what we were after. A small closet opened to my left, near the bed. We didn't have time to duel with this creature, but I also had to respect its abilities. Truth be told, birds made me nervous. I wasn't a fan. And I'd never actually faced one down before, eye-to-eye.

"I'm going to deal with it," I said. "When I do, you get the coin."

Carefully, I eased closer to the bed and grabbed the quilted comforter, noticing that it was thick. The peregrine's cold eyes followed my every move. I told myself that its beak and those talons could do some damage.

So be careful.

"Okay, let's see what you got," I said, keeping my gaze locked on the bird.

I jerked the comforter upward.

The bird flew from the desk and swept toward me, this time emitting a sharp shriek. I grabbed the other side of the spread and brought it up and over the falcon, smothering it inside the folds. There'd only be a few seconds where I'd have the advantage, so I used those wisely, tossing the quilt and the bird into the closet and shutting the door.

"Aren't you the clever one," she said. "Like a matador with a bull."

I heard the falcon freeing itself with more shrieks, its beak pecking at the door.

My heart raced. "Let's go."

Coleen grabbed the coin and we fled the room, heading back down the stairs, my eyes alert for both danger and opportunity. Far across the open parade I saw three men enter the fort through the sally port, all dressed in park service uniforms.

They turned and headed for the main office.

"That's going to be a problem," Coleen said.

To say the least.

We'd never make it out the main portal before they burst from the office and headed this way. So I decided to go high and went back up the stairs, this time turning away from the living quarters and rushing down one of the brick casements. Arches appeared every few feet and we were careful as we made our way around the fort, toward the sally port below us and the only way out. Loose scree and chipped brick were everywhere, as were masonry mounds in the floor that threatened like speed bumps. All of the heavy iron shutters, which would have shielded the exterior arches so the cannons could be reloaded, were gone, exposing the open sea, which stretched in a delft blue to the horizon. Calm had returned after the storm.

"What are we doing?" she asked.

"I'm not sure, but at least we're above them."

In the distance came the familiar drone of a seaplane. We stopped at one of the arches to watch a blue-and-white Cessna drop from the sky and land not all that far from Valdez's boat, which remained anchored about two hundred yards offshore. The plane taxied for the beach, but not before I caught the ID numbers.

1180206.

"That's the same one from before," she said.

Which meant no salvation.

The plane swung around, its prop facing out, then it reversed thrust and beached the pontoons.

The engine switched off.

The passenger door opened and Jim Jansen hopped down to the water's edge, as did another man from the rear seat. The pilot remained inside. The two new players headed toward the fort's main entrance. Below, I heard shouts, and we eased over to an interior arch and watched as an older ranger and the young man I'd subdued ran across the parade toward the living quarters. Another ranger took up a guard position at the sally port. This was now a damned-if-you-do-damned-if-you-don't situation.

My mind raced.

Amazingly, Coleen Perry stayed calm.

Now it was clear how the "FBI" was close enough to get here.

Fool me once, shame on you. Fool me twice—

That's just being an idiot.

I'd been wondering how I could get out of here with minimal questions and avoid Valdez at the same time.

Now I had a way.

I eased back to the exterior arch and pointed at the boat. "Valdez is out there. And as you say, the FBI down there is not our friend. You game to leave here?"

Since I was her only play on the board, the answer was not in doubt.

"How?" she asked.

I pointed to the new seaplane.

"Can you fly?" she asked.

"What do you think?"

She stared down at the clear moat twenty feet below us. The tide seemed to be in, as the water level was high. I also caught sight of a rather healthy-looking barracuda hovering in the clear water.

"How deep do you think it is?" she asked.

Apparently she'd surmised what we had to do.

"Only one way to find out."

And I leaped off.

CHAPTER TWELVE

I HIT THE WATER FEETFIRST, FOUND THE GRASSY BOTTOM ABOUT six feet below and pushed up. Coleen splashed down beside me and rebounded, too. The salt water felt like a hot bath. Surely the barracuda had been sufficiently spooked to have swum far away. We quickly made our way to the brick counterscarp and climbed out.

Wasting no time, we hustled around the east side of the fort, water dripping from our clothes, back toward where the bridge spanned the moat along the south perimeter. Jansen and the other man were nearly across the wooden bridge to the sally port, headed inside. I fled the counterscarp and angled toward the beach. I still had the gun, but it had just taken a warm dousing. Sometimes they worked afterward, sometimes not. Three seaplanes were now beached, but our best bet was the one that had just arrived. I knew the keys for its ignition were still there, as was the pilot.

Double-crossing Valdez could be risky, but there was no way I could actually deal with the guy. Coleen had the Double Eagle and she wasn't about to give it up. Besides, the son of a bitch would probably shoot me dead the minute I delivered the coin.

So screw him.

Everyone said I was a maverick.

Okay. Time to be one.

We made for the beach and used the other two planes for cover as we approached the Cessna. I kept glancing back toward the fort and hoped everyone there was busy trying to figure out where we might be. I halted my approach behind the second plane.

"Wait here and keep a lookout behind us."

I approached the Cessna from the rear, on the pilot's side, and wrenched open the door, which clearly surprised the man sitting behind the controls.

I aimed the gun straight at him.

"So you did make it off the boat," he said. "We couldn't tell for sure."

Not a hint of surprise, or shock, or even a denial, just a flat-out admission that they'd tried to kill me.

"Get out."

"You're making a big mistake. This isn't your fight. Go back to JAG while you still can."

"It became my fight when you tried to kill me. Get out."

"What are you going to do? Shoot me?"

No, but I did smack the butt of the gun into the side of his head, which sent him reeling over toward the passenger seat. Violence was becoming easier for me with each attempt. While he was still stunned I grabbed his left arm and yanked him from the plane. Coleen had abandoned her post and rushed up alongside. The pilot splashed into the shallow water lapping the beach and she added to his misery with a kick to the face.

"Feel better?" I asked.

"Much. We've got company."

Over her shoulder I saw Jansen and two rangers running across the wooden bridge. They were a hundred yards away, which should offer us enough time.

"Get in," I said, climbing into the pilot's seat and starting the engine.

It revved quickly, enough so that I could throttle up and power away from the beach out into the lagoon.

I heard gunshots.

More power and we moved farther from land.

"Give me my gun," she said.

I handed it over.

She popped open the passenger-side door and returned fire as I turned the plane so her side faced the fort. As we continued to taxi I studied the instruments. Nothing unusual. Standard issue.

More gunfire came from shore.

She curled back inside and slammed the door. "Get us in the air."

We were now far enough out in the bay to be safe from any bullets. Valdez's boat sat five hundred yards away, but I wasn't going anywhere near that, either. I turned toward the east so the breeze I'd noticed on shore would be to our back. I throttled up the engines and sent the pontoons skimming across the surface. The controls tightened and I gripped the yoke in a hard embrace. I only needed a few hundred feet before the wings caught air and the plane lifted. No rotating or climbing, just a rise, as if in an elevator. Not bad, if I did say so myself. Certainly no tougher than landing a fighter on a pitching carrier deck, at night, which I'd done several times.

I banked into a long turn, eased off on the throttle, and adjusted course toward the northeast. The sky had turned a soothing cobalt blue with only a few puffs of scattered clouds. Fort Jefferson, the Dry Tortugas, Jim Jansen, and Juan Lopez Valdez all lay behind us. I checked the fuel gauge and saw that we carried three-quarters of a tank. I'd flown many a Cessna and knew that the range on a full tank was around 850 miles. I had no intention of heading for Key West—that would be the first place Jansen would look. What I needed was to contact Stephanie Nelle and now I could do that by radioing to shore, with someone there placing a call.

Coleen was busy checking out the cabin, seeing what was behind us.

"What did the case look like that you brought up from the wreck?" she asked.

I told her.

She sat back in her seat. "We hit the jackpot. It's sitting in the back."

I couldn't help but smile.

Lady Luck had finally dealt me a good hand.

I was alive, in a plane, with the case, the coin, and a radio.

All in all, not a bad first day as a special operative with the Justice Department.

CHAPTER THIRTEEN

I REACHED FOR THE RADIO, BUT COLEEN STOPPED ME.

"You can't do that," she said. "They'll be listening, and you do realize this plane can be tracked."

Of course, but thanks to my fighter-piloting days I had a few ideas on how to minimize that problem. I had already decided to vector toward Florida's western Gulf shore. The Cessna's range was enough to get us to Tampa, but I saw no reason to fly that far north. Jansen had probably already radioed the mainland and alerted the appropriate folks, and Coleen was right: We were surely being tracked on air traffic control radar. The trick would be to land quick and then get away before they, whoever *they* might be, could find us on the ground. The Everglades stretched fifty-plus miles up Florida's southwest coast. Landing anywhere along that wilderness would be easy, offering perfect isolation and plenty of places to hide, but it would also be difficult to traverse without a boat or car.

"I was thinking of heading to somewhere between Naples and Fort Myers."

She shook her head. "Can you make it to Lake Okeechobee?"

That was miles inland, toward the center of the peninsula, a massive expanse of fresh water that drained into the Everglades.

"We can get there, but there's a lot of land between the lake and the coast. Somebody along the way is going to want to know who we are and where we're headed."

South Florida was notorious for drug trafficking, and an unidentified aircraft not responding to radio requests would raise nothing but red flags The situation would only escalate if Jansen called in reinforcements. I had not, as yet, mentioned the former agent to her.

"Does the name Jim Jansen mean anything?"

She stared across at me and shook her head.

"That's the guy who brought me in the boat, then left in the plane and tried to kill me. He was also the one shooting at you from the beach."

She still held the gun, in a way that I noticed wasn't casual or with any apprehension. Instead, it signaled someone familiar with firearms.

"Are you a cop?" I asked.

She nodded.

I should have been surprised, but she'd handled herself under pressure like someone with training. "Is this official?"

"Personal. It concerns my father."

"Why didn't you tell anyone back there at the fort you were a cop?"

"I was debating that when you showed up to rescue me."

I caught the touch of sarcasm.

"Who is your father?"

"The Reverend Benjamin Foster, of the Christian Faith Baptist Church, Orlando, Florida."

"How does Valdez know him?"

She reached into her pocket and found the coin. "This is yours. But those files in the back are mine. That was the deal I made with Valdez."

She slipped the coin into my shorts pocket.

"I don't work for Valdez," I pointed out.

She shrugged. "A deal's a deal. And I don't want that coin anymore."

I decided now was not the time to tell her that I wasn't about to allow her to keep that waterproof case. Though I had no idea what it contained, it apparently was important enough for Valdez, Jansen, and this woman to all want it. I already knew Stephanie Nelle wanted it, and what better way to impress my new boss than by delivering the coin *and* the case? But something told me outsmarting Coleen Perry was not going to be easy.

"Where are you a cop?"

"Orange County Sheriff's Department. Orlando. What do you do?"

"Until yesterday, I was a Navy lawyer. Now I'm not sure what I am. Bait, I think."

Jansen's duplicity still bothered me and I wondered how much information Stephanie Nelle had also withheld. Out the window I saw only ocean. We were still miles away from the Florida coast.

"See if there's a chart anywhere."

She searched the compartments and found one.

Thank goodness. Dead reckoning would have eaten up a lot of fuel. "What's at Lake Okeechobee?"

"I have relatives. I was headed there tomorrow."

That would have been after she made the deal with Valdez and had the files in her possession. But things had changed. As they had for me, so I assessed my options. Landing anywhere on the coast could be a problem. Lots of people and police. Okeechobee had people, too, but it was off the beaten path and its rural location would offer a measure of privacy, one that might be advantageous. The problem was that landing anywhere near where we were ultimately headed would be like dropping a trail of bread crumbs.

So I made a decision.

"We're going to set down away from your relatives," I told her. "Then head that way."

The fuel gauge was near empty as Lake Okeechobee came into view. I'd dropped down low once we'd found the Everglades in the hope of staying off any prying radar. So far, no radio contact had been made and no other planes or helicopters had been spotted.

The lake was enormous.

About forty miles long and thirty wide. Over seven hundred square miles of pristine water, the second-largest lake in the continental United States. A mecca for fishermen and water sports enthusiasts. It also served as a divide among five counties, which meant a ton of local law enforcement from every direction.

"Head east," she said.

I stayed low and followed her instruction. A highway ran north to south, near the eastern shore.

"That's U.S. 441. Track it north."

I banked left and kept going, glancing at the fuel gauge, realizing that we needed to get down soon.

A town came into view.

"Port Mayaca," she told me.

A string of houses began to populate the shoreline like islands in a chain. Huge oak trees draped with vines shielded most of them. A few alligators basked in the sun on the shore.

"My family's place is five miles farther north."

That's all I needed to know.

I reduced the throttle and began to descend. Most of the lakefront properties had docks and any one of them would do. I swung around and dropped out of the bright sky, the plane wobbling in the warm afternoon air currents. I kept the nose high as we gently kissed, then skipped off the flat water. We bounced a few more times then settled on the surface, the pontoons jolting us to a stop. I used the engine to glide across the lake, approaching one of the docks, then killed the prop and glided toward shore.

Coleen opened her door and hopped onto the dock.

I released my harness and climbed across the passenger seat, jumping over to the aluminum deck. A rope was there, tied to one of the vertical supports, and I used it to secure the plane. Then I reached back inside and retrieved the waterproof case, which I immediately noticed was much lighter. Those weights Valdez had mentioned were gone. That meant Jansen had opened the container. But something remained inside. I could feel it shifting back and forth.

"I need a phone," she said.

We left the dock and headed for the house, which appeared to be unoccupied. No vehicles sat in the drive. No sign of anyone. Heat and humidity had settled all around us like a moist blanket. Buzzy, circling flies prospected our sticky skin. Coleen peered in through the glass of the back door.

"There's a phone in the kitchen."

Before I could say a word, she used the gun to break the glass, then reached in and opened the lock. Now burglary could be added to my growing list of crimes. I decided to stay outside and keep watch, but I could hear her talking on the phone. I laid the case on top of a picnic table, near a swing set. Time for me to find out what this was all about.

I released the latches.

"Don't do that."

I turned.

She had the gun aimed straight at me.

"You going to shoot me?"

"If you don't close that lid, that's exactly what I'm going to do."

CHAPTER
FOURTEEN

"I was nearly killed for what's in this case," I said. "I want to know for what."

The gun stayed aimed at me.

I stared into her eyes, which were brown and hard, wondering what was torturing this woman. She was troubled, of that I was sure. But I wasn't backing down. "I'm here for the Justice Department. And whether you like it or not, you're not in control."

"You have no idea what I'm capable of."

"You're a cop. That's all I need to know. You don't shoot people for no reason."

And I was right.

She lowered the weapon. "All right, let's both take a look."

Sounded like a plan.

I turned my attention back to the case.

She exited the house and approached the picnic table. I opened the lid to see several file folders lying inside. They were definitely old, a faded green, edges tattered. Two words were printed in thick black marker on the cover of the top one.

BISHOP'S PAWN

They meant nothing to me. So I asked, "Do you know what that refers to?"

Two sounds broke the silence almost at the same time. A distant siren and the basso beat of rotors through air. I glanced up, stared out over the lake, and in the far distance saw a black dot in the afternoon sky.

Helicopter.

The siren had to be the local police.

"We need to get out of here," she said.

She didn't have to tell me twice.

I slammed the lid shut and snapped the latches in place. With the case in hand, we rushed around to the front yard. The house was set back from the highway, among trees at the water's edge. A detached garage stood off to the side. Coleen ran toward a window in the garage's side wall and gazed inside.

"There's a pickup truck."

"Do it."

She smashed the window, opened the sash, and climbed inside. A moment later the garage door rose and I saw an old Chevy. I ran to the driver's door and opened it, sliding the case across the front bench seat. Coleen climbed in on the passenger side. I knew what had to be done, so I reached beneath the steering column and found the ignition wires. This truck was plenty old enough that it could be hot-wired. I'd learned, as a kid, working on my grandfather's onion farm, how to get a truck going out in the middle of nowhere. I located the three wires, tore them from their connectors, and found the two that triggered the starter.

The engine coughed to life.

I twisted them together, slammed the door closed, and settled in behind the wheel. Perhaps somebody had noticed our arrival and sent a welcoming committee, none of whom I wanted to meet. I backed the truck from the garage and we sped away. The house and the trees blocked our exit from the lake side, but the chopper was still a long way off. The sirens seemed closer but we managed to find the highway and head north without spotting anyone. I decided to slow my speed so as not to attract attention, as it was unclear from which direction the sirens were approaching.

But we passed no police cars.

I kept driving north.

I stopped the truck in a Dairy Queen parking lot, nestled safe among other vehicles.

"Coleen," I said to her. "I'm not your enemy."

"You saving my hide at Fort Jefferson doesn't make you my friend, either."

"But it ought to buy me something."

She smiled.

For the first time.

"You said you're a lawyer. Have you been one long?" she asked.

"About six years. I've only been a Justice Department agent, though, since yesterday."

"Why do you think this guy Jansen wanted you dead?"

"I don't know. But I intend to find out."

Then a thought occurred to me. "They'll know we used the phone in that house. Your call can be traced."

"I didn't make one," she said.

"I heard you."

"All show, just for you. I planned to take you down outside, then leave with the files. I was just about to do that with a smack to the back of your head when we heard the sirens."

I stared back out the windshield. "Once again, what is Bishop's Pawn?"

I'd sensed back at the house that the words were not unfamiliar to her.

"It was a classified FBI operation that ran from mid-1967 to the spring of 1968."

"How do you know that?"

"My father told me. It was part of COINTELPRO."

That acronym rang a bell.

Reading was my passion. I devoured books and, thanks to my eidetic memory, I never forgot a word. J. Edgar Hoover had always been a fascination. Lauded as a saint and savior in life, since his death in 1972 we'd come to learn that he was neither. His legal abuses had become legendary, COINTELPRO perhaps the pinnacle of FBI corruption.

The Counter Intelligence Program started in the 1950s to combat a supposed communist threat within the United States. But it morphed into something far more ugly, eventually infiltrating a variety of political groups. The Socialist Workers Party, KKK, Nation of Islam, and Black Panthers all were targeted. But so were more benign groups like the Puerto Rican independence movement, feminist organizations, and anything that advocated left-of-center positions, especially antiwar protesters. Its goal? *To expose, disrupt, misdirect, discredit, or otherwise neutralize any threat.* To accomplish that it routinely relied on burglaries, opening people's mail, forged documents, having people fired from their jobs, planting fake news articles, even encouraging violence between rivals. It wasn't until 1971 that it was finally exposed, thanks to a group of citizens who burglarized an FBI field office in Pennsylvania, stealing every file and sending them to journalists. That led to a congressional investigation—the famed Church Committee, named for its chairman, Senator Frank Church—which officially identified all of the abuses.

Another siren could be heard, approaching from the south. A moment later a Martin County Sheriff's car raced by on the highway, lights flashing.

"I really do have family here, on the lake," she told me.

"We're not going to be able to get far in this truck," I pointed out. "If they're looking for us, which we don't know for sure, it won't take them long to find the owners of that house and learn what kind of vehicle they kept in the garage."

"Good thing we don't have to go far."

I fired the engine back up.

"Do you have any idea what kind of operation was part of Bishop's Pawn?"

She stared across the truck's bench seat, and for the first time I saw pain in her eyes.

"I think it might involve the death of Martin Luther King Jr."

CHAPTER
FIFTEEN

WE DROVE FARTHER NORTH ON U.S. 441 AROUND LAKE Okeechobee.

Her comment was troubling. I tried to learn more but all she'd offer was that Valdez had mentioned to her during their calls that Bishop's Pawn also concerned the King assassination.

"I was hoping to learn more today when I met with him," she told me.

Which explained all the questions about Valdez back on Loggerhead.

We rode for a while in silence. Finally, she directed me off the highway, down a dirt lane to another house set among a necklace of live oaks, cypresses, and palms. This one was rambling, wood-sided, and ranch-style, fronting the shore. A dark-colored Toyota coupe was parked off to the side. I had a million questions and I desperately wanted to read the files in the waterproof case, but I opted for patience, deciding that ears open and mouth shut might bring me answers faster.

I figured we were about five miles away from where I had landed the plane. Too close for me, but I doubted anyone would be looking here. Why would they? Unless they could connect whoever owned this house to Coleen. What I needed was a phone. Pam owned a cell phone, but I hadn't moved in that direction. Not yet, anyway. People being able to find me wherever I might be wasn't appealing. When I left the base I didn't particularly want to be found. But this new gig with Justice seemed tailor-made for more instant communication. Trouble was, the phone Pam owned only worked here and there. Lots of dead zones in and around Jacksonville.

And the things weren't cheap.

The front door to the house opened and an older black man emerged. He was dressed in a neat, single-breasted suit that accentuated his thin frame. His face was handsome and fleshed out, dark hair fading to gray at the edges. But his eyes, a firm coal black, radiated unquestioned authority.

"Who is he?" I asked.

She did not look pleased.

"My father."

I learned that the weekend house belonged to Coleen's in-laws. Her husband was a lawyer who worked with an Orlando firm. I was a little surprised about the marriage, as she wore no wedding ring. Her father—the Reverend Benjamin Foster—seemed reserved, as he'd said only a handful of words since we arrived. She was clearly annoyed by his presence.

"I told you to leave this alone," Foster said to her.

"You have no right to ask that," Coleen shot back, her voice rising.

"I have every right." His tone was not much above a whisper. "This is not your concern. I told you that, more than once."

"It is my concern. I want to know what happened."

"I told you what happened."

She glared at him. "No. You told me what you wanted me to know."

"You went to meet Valdez?" her father asked.

She looked surprised. "How did you know that?"

"Tell me everything that happened," he asked, ignoring her question.

She shook her head.

He faced me. "Will you tell me?"

Why not.

I introduced myself and explained my Justice Department connection. The older man listened to my story without saying a word. I could see that Coleen did not appreciate my frankness. When I finished, he said to her, "You will stay here. I have to speak with this gentleman in private."

Coleen started to argue, but he raised a hand. "You don't want to try my patience any more than you already have."

She nodded, seemingly surrendering to his parental will.

The older man pointed at the waterproof case.

"Bring that with us."

We left the house in Foster's Toyota with him driving. The case with the files rested in the trunk. We headed south down the highway to Port Mayaca, where U.S. 441 intersected with State Road 76. Foster turned onto 76, paralleling one of several human-made canals that drained into the lake, and drove a few miles east to a cemetery. He turned off the highway, through an open gate, and parked the car. The land was spacious and tranquil. Tall palms and bushy trees dotted the well-kept grass. No funeral was in progress and no one was around.

We stepped from the car.

A leafy scent filled the warm moist air.

"I used to come here when I was troubled," Foster said. "But I haven't been in a long time."

"Does that mean you haven't been troubled?"

"Quite the contrary. Of late, that seems all I've been."

He'd brought me here for a reason, so I decided to allow him the luxury of coming to the point when he was ready.

"Do you know about the 1928 hurricane?" he asked me.

"I'm not from Florida. I'm a Georgia boy. Born and bred."

"The storm came on September 16, a Category 4 with 140-mile-per-hour winds. It hit the lake and destroyed a levee, which flooded all of the surrounding low-lying communities with twenty feet of water. Can you imagine? Twenty feet underwater. This place was totally segregated in those days. The east shore was for whites, the south and west, nearer the Everglades, for blacks. Most of the dead were black, migrant farmworkers who lived in those low-lying western communities. Over three thousand died." He paused for a moment. "That was a horrible thing. But what happened after was much worse."

I wondered how that could be.

"It was warm weather, so the bodies began to decompose in the swamps. The whites forced the black survivors to recover those bodies. The ones who worked were fed, the others either starved or were shot. Coffins were scarce, so only the bodies of white victims were allowed to be buried in the cemeteries. The black victims were piled on the side of the roads, doused with fuel, and burned. The local white authorities bulldozed 674 black victims into a mass grave in West Palm Beach. That grave was never marked. The site was later sold and used as a garbage dump, a slaughterhouse, and a sewage treatment plant. Only recently has it been repurchased and the sacred ground protected. I helped make that happen."

I didn't know what to say.

"Here, in this cemetery, is another mass grave of those black migrant workers."

He led me across the cemetery to a stone marker.

IN MEMORIAM
TO THE 1600 PIONEERS IN THIS MASS BURIAL
WHO GAVE THEIR LIVES IN THE 1928 HURRICANE
SO THAT THE GLADES MIGHT BE AS WE KNOW IT TODAY

"Here they rest, a testament to another time. But I wonder, Lieutenant Malone, have things changed all that much?"

"Of course they have," I said.

"Do you believe that?"

"Your in-laws live on the east shore now."

"And how do you know they're not white?"

"If that's the case, then things really have changed."

He grinned. "Perhaps you're right. A travesty such as what happened in 1928 would not happen today. At least not in the same way. Society has learned to be—less obvious—with its prejudice."

I didn't want to touch that one, and he went silent for a few moments.

"I appreciate you helping my daughter escape from Fort Jefferson," he said to me. "She is too impetuous for her own good."

I found the Double Eagle in my pocket and handed it to him. "She said this is yours."

"Please, you keep it."

"It belongs to you."

He shook his head. "It belongs to the devil."

That was a weird observation, but I respected his wishes and re-pocketed the coin.

At least I'd offered.

"Did my daughter read any of the files in that case?"

I shook my head. "We never had the chance."

"That's good. I want them destroyed."

"Is that why you made the deal to trade for the coin?"

"I didn't make that deal, Lieutenant Malone. Valdez contacted me and asked for a trade. I refused."

"Did you know him?"

He shook his head. "Never met the man. But he knew me, or enough about me that I listened to what he had to say. I was shocked he even knew I had the coin. I didn't realize that Coleen had listened in on my conversation. She went behind me and learned Valdez's phone number. She then made contact and made the deal on her own."

Things were beginning to make more sense.

"My daughter and I have discussed many things about my past of late. She's thirty years old and curious. I've never talked much about the old days. But apparently I've said enough to drive her curiosity." He paused. "She found my hiding place for the coin. More of that police officer in her coming out, I suppose."

I could see he was troubled by her initiative.

"Those files were better off in Cuba," he said. "Where they've been for the past thirty years." He paused. "I honestly never thought I would be addressing this issue again."

"The death of Martin Luther King Jr.?"

He tossed me a curious glance. "What else did Coleen tell you?"

"Precious little. We saw a name. Bishop's Pawn. She told me that Valdez mentioned it might deal with the assassination."

A look of concern filled Foster's face. "You said the files were not read."

"That's all we saw. Those two words. Then we had to leave."

"Did she say anything else about Valdez?"

I realized he'd brought me here to learn what he could, so I shook my head and turned the tables. "Did you know King?"

He nodded. "I traveled at his side for nearly five years. I was a young man, just out of the seminary, assigned to my first church in Dallas. Martin came to my home one evening and tried to recruit me for the movement. I told him no, that wasn't for me. The next day I heard him preach. He spoke for an hour, chastising the black middle class for refusing to fight for its own race. His words were powerful. They hit home. I decided he was right. So I became a disciple and stayed by his side until Memphis."

The extent of what this man had witnessed compelled me to ask, "What was he like?"

He smiled. "Fiery, with an ego. Like most of us, he craved recognition, adulation, respect. More than anything, he wanted people to listen to him. And they did." Concern again filled the older man's face. "Now you tell me, what precisely is your involvement here?"

"I was sent to retrieve that case from the wreck, thinking only the coin was inside. But then things took a 180-degree turn. I'm not exactly sure what I'm doing here now."

"Who sent you?"

I decided to be honest. "A woman named Stephanie Nelle, who works for the Justice Department."

"I know Jim Jansen," he muttered. "He's a terrible man."

Foster drifted away, his gaze out over the graves, as if he was seeking their guidance. I left him to his thoughts.

"People know little to nothing about what really happened in Memphis," he finally said. "There were only a few of us there, at the Lorraine Motel, that evening. None of us saw the moment when the bullet hit.

There's no Zapruder film memorializing Martin's murder. It lives only in the tattered memories of those of us who were there."

"Which might explain why your daughter is so curious."

"I'm sure it does. There are many books on the subject. Nearly all of them written by conspiratorialists, who know nothing of the truth. No Warren Report was ever prepared on Martin's death. A congressional investigation came decades after the fact, and resolved nothing. They found no evidence of any conspiracy. Instead, they concluded that Martin was killed by a lone gunman. The killer caught. He confessed, pled guilty, and was sentenced to life. And that's what he served, dying in prison just a couple of years ago. Case closed."

I was intrigued, and asked the only thing I could.

"So what really happened?"

CHAPTER
SIXTEEN

APRIL 4, 1968, LOOMED COOL AND CLOUDY IN MEMPHIS. ON THE CITY'S INDUSTRIAL *south side, the Lorraine Motel, a local fixture, sat quiet among former cotton lofts and old brick warehouses, five blocks south of Beale Street, not far from the Mississippi River.*

On that day Room 306, which oddly was situated on the second floor, was occupied by Martin Luther King Jr. and his closest friend in the world, Ralph Abernathy. The Lorraine was their favorite Memphis hangout. It was black-owned and family-operated, hosting the likes of Count Basie, Otis Redding, Ray Charles, Aretha Franklin, and Louis Armstrong. A room came for $13 a night, but not for King. The owners never charged him. In fact, King and Abernathy had stayed in Room 306 so much that it had acquired the label of the King-Abernathy suite. But the room wasn't all that much. Just a simple, wood-paneled rectangle with twin beds, a TV, some contemporary furniture, and a phone.

Memphis was turning into a national problem.

Two black, union garbage workers had died in a tragic on-the-job accident after being forced to work in bad weather. Those deaths triggered a citywide strike that quickly escalated into a race struggle, since all of the sanitation workers were black. King came to town on March 28 and spoke to 15,000 people at a union rally. He then led a march down-

town that quickly turned violent, shocking him. It also called into question his leadership. He was deep into planning a massive Poor People's March on Washington, DC, for the summer of 1969, and the media began to wonder about the wisdom of such a huge demonstration. To prove that he could lead a peaceful gathering, King had returned to Memphis.

April 4 was hectic.

A second march down Beale Street was being planned, but the city of Memphis had gone to court and obtained an injunction halting any further demonstrations for the next ten days. That was usually not a problem. King had ignored injunctions before, considering the state judges who issued them just part of the problem he'd come to combat.

But this one had come from a federal court.

A first.

Dodging it demanded far more finesse, since federal judges were among the few consistent allies the civil rights movement possessed.

All afternoon on the fourth King had seemed distracted, not as focused as in days past. Most attributed it to a head cold he'd contracted. But anxiety also hung in the air over what was happening in federal court, as the lawyers were trying to overturn the injunction. A little after 6:00 P.M. King and his entourage were scheduled to have dinner at a local minister's home. A feast of roast beef, candied yams, pigs' feet, neck bones, chitlins, and turnip greens. Soul food. All King's favorites.

And that time was fast approaching.

At 5:00 P.M. one of King's chief lieutenants, Andrew Young, arrived in Room 306 with good news. The federal judge had modified the injunction to allow for a limited demonstration on April 8, four days hence. There were conditions, but none oppressive, and the news immediately put King in a much better mood.

He retired to the bathroom to shave and ready himself for dinner.

At fifteen minutes before six o'clock, after dressing in a clean shirt and tie, he left the room and walked out onto the balcony.

I listened to Foster as he told me about the day Martin Luther King Jr. died. This was not some secondary account from a book, the words filtered years later by an author.

"I was there," he said. "At the Lorraine, with Martin and the rest of the fellows. Abernathy, Young, Jesse Jackson. We were all so bright-eyed and idealistic."

"What did you do for King?"

"I worked for the SCLC. We all did back then."

The Southern Christian Leadership Conference grew out of the 1957 bus boycott in Montgomery, Alabama. An alliance of black ministers and leaders designed to provide the civil rights movement a spiritual basis for change. King was its president.

"Martin used me like a traveling secretary. I kept things in order." Foster stared out across the cemetery. "He was not the most organized of people. He needed a lot of managing."

"You admired him, didn't you?"

He didn't immediately answer me.

"I can still see him on that balcony, at the Lorraine."

King leaned against the railing and enjoyed the cool Tennessee evening. The Memphis police had offered him a full security detail, but he'd refused.

I'd feel like a bird in a cage, *was his standard reply.*

His safety had always been in jeopardy. In 1958 a black woman stabbed him in the chest, nearly killing him. In 1962 a white power fanatic struck him in the head. In '66, during a march in Chicago, a rock hit his head. He'd faced tear gas, police dogs, cattle prods, water cannons, his house had been firebombed, and he'd been burned in effigy too many times to count. But never had he employed bodyguards. In fact, no one close to him carried any weapon. His children were not even allowed to play with toy guns. Violence attached to anger was totally alien to him, and to him nonviolence was much more than a catchphrase.

King stepped back into Room 306 and found his black silk suit jacket. "Are you comin', Ralph?"

"In a second."

Abernathy stood in the bathroom getting ready for dinner.

"I'll wait outside for you."

King stepped back onto the balcony with his jacket on, once again leaning on the railing. There he stood for a few minutes as a crowd began to gather below. Solomon Jones, his driver for the night, cranked up the Cadillac to warm it up.

Jesse Jackson appeared below.

He and King had not seen eye-to-eye much of late, the two strongly disagreeing on the direction of the civil rights movement. A classic clash of young and old. Brash against patience. But tonight King was conciliatory, glad Jackson would be joining them for dinner. The younger man wore an olive turtleneck sweater and leather coat, in stark contrast with the dark suits and ties of the older men. One of those present began to chastise Jackson on his clothes, but Jackson had the perfect retort.

"All you need for dinner is an appetite."

Which King liked, agreeing and laughing at the observation.

The banter continued, King standing on the second-floor balcony, his rich voice booming downward, the others looking up. He was like a preacher holding court with his flock. Everyone seemed relaxed, a stark contrast with the day's legal tension.

Six P.M. arrived.

The people below began to head for the Cadillac. King stayed on his perch, waiting for Abernathy to come out of their room. There was more chatter about the evening, then Solomon Jones told King that he might need a topcoat, as the evening was turning chilly.

"You really know how to take good care of me," King said, still leaning on the railing.

He found a pack of cigarettes and fished one out.

Then he turned for the door to Room 306.

"I was standing below," Foster said. "With Jesse and Andy Young. We all heard it. It didn't really sound like a gunshot, more like a firecracker or a car backfiring in the distance. None of us thought much of it, until we looked up."

The bullet entered the right side of King's face, leaving through the jaw and puncturing his fleshy neck.

The impact staggered him backward.

Blood spewed onto the balcony.

He grabbed for his throat with one hand and tried to grasp the railing with the other. But his efforts failed and his legs buckled, dropping him spine-first to the concrete, his legs out at odd angles, his shoes caught in the railing. Blood continued to pour from his body with each heartbeat, soaking his head and shoulders in a sea of red.

The cigarette remained clenched in his hand, now crushed.

His arms settled out to either side.

"We were all hiding behind the cars in the parking lot," Foster muttered. "Then Ralph ran out on the balcony. That's when I headed up. Martin was lying there, with his arms out, like he'd been crucified. That was my first thought when I rushed up." His voice cracked. "That they crucified him."

"Why are you telling me this?"

"Because, Lieutenant Malone, I have to trust someone, and you, whether I like it or not, are all that I have to choose from."

CHAPTER
SEVENTEEN

I FOUND THE COMMENT BOTH STRANGE AND TROUBLING. WHY would this man trust me at all? We were perfect strangers. And I was from the government. Then it hit me. I should have realized before. But come on, this was my first full day on the job.

"You've spoken to Stephanie Nelle," I said.

"She came to see me yesterday. Apparently, she'd learned about Valdez's contact with me. She knew about Coleen's deal, the coin, and the files. That's how I knew what Coleen had done. She also told me about you. I had no choice then but to become involved."

All troubling to me since none of this had been passed on by my new temporary employer. Instead, I got an ex-FBI agent trying to kill me.

"I'm here for Coleen," Foster said. "But also because I want those files destroyed. No offense to you, Lieutenant Malone, but I was hoping you might fail and all of this would remain at the bottom of the ocean."

"Sorry to disappoint you. Mind telling me what Stephanie explained?" I paused. "Especially since you're trusting me and all."

He caught my sarcasm.

"She seems to have a problem with the FBI. Which I can understand. I remember when it was the most corrupt organization in the United States. During Hoover's time it routinely spied on all of us, violated our privacy, even engaged in active character assassination of Martin. It did everything we despise as Americans."

I was not ignorant of that history. "That was another time and place."

"Which doesn't excuse it. Especially since I was a victim of their abuses."

"All of that ended with the Church Committee. The legacy of J. Edgar Hoover is in the toilet."

"He should have died in prison."

"What does that have to do with here and now?"

"Remnants of that corruption remain, which you and Stephanie Nelle now find yourselves in the middle of."

News to me. "Does that involve the death of Martin Luther King Jr.?"

"That's not for me to say."

I was working at a huge disadvantage. Not only thanks to Stephanie's silence, but because I knew precious little about the King assassination, other than what I'd read in books, newspapers, and magazines. Foster was right. Conspiratorialists abounded on what may or may not have happened, which was no different than the tragic murders of both Kennedys. Anytime a public figure was suddenly gunned down, the word *conspiracy* immediately became attached. Congress had not helped matters, either. Twice it investigated the King assassination, concluding that James Earl Ray pulled the trigger all by himself. But true to form, it also hinted at a possible broader conspiracy—without offering a shred of proof.

"It's important to me that my daughter never reads those files you obtained."

"Can I ask why?"

"Call it the wish of an old preacher."

Not an answer. But I didn't really expect one. "That's not a problem. Those files are going to Stephanie Nelle."

"I would prefer we burn them."

"I can't do that."

"What are you, twenty-eight? Twenty-nine?"

"Something like that."

"A lieutenant in the United States Navy, who has no idea what he's dealing with."

"I catch on fast."

"I hope so. Because the men you're dealing with will kill you."

Those words grabbed my attention.

But before I could probe further a car entered the cemetery from the far side and cruised toward us down one of the graveled lanes that bisected the many graves. A dark-blue, late-model Taurus with tinted windows. I reacted to the potential threat, but Foster grabbed my arm.

"It's okay. I was expecting him."

The vehicle wheeled to a halt, the driver's-side door opened, and a man emerged. Short, well built, with dark restless eyes set deep in a sunburned face. His grayish-brown hair was trimmed close and at odds with a thick beard. He took a few steps toward us, then stopped.

"You couldn't leave this alone, could you?" the man said.

"My daughter is the cause of this. Not me."

"You need to know he called me. He knows all about what's happening with Valdez." The man's voice alternated between highs and lows. "Valdez contacted him, too. You should have left this alone. They're not going to let it rest. All these years have passed, but they're still out there. They haven't gone away."

"This gentleman here is from the Justice Department," Foster said. "I've also spoken to his superior. You're right. This is not going away."

"Are you deaf? He's active again, Benjamin. And all because Valdez decided to come north from Cuba."

The voice had risen in anger.

"Valdez is apparently in financial trouble," Foster said. "That's why he wanted to deal the files for the coin. I told him no. My daughter is the one who made the deal, behind my back, unbeknownst to me. I'm as upset by this as you are."

The guy stretched out his arms. "And yet here I am, just as you wanted. Are you crazy? You know what you're dealing with. Have you forgotten? *They said one to another, behold here cometh the dreamer, let us slay him and we shall see what will become of his dreams.*"

Foster gave a slight nod of his head. "Genesis 37:19–20."

"What became of his dreams?" the guy asked.

"That's not for me to answer."

"It seems to me you're the only person in the world who can answer that question."

These two men had experienced something together.

Something not good.

"All I wanted was to live out my retirement in peace," the man said. "To go fishing. I never wanted to deal with this bullshit again."

Thirty feet separated us from him.

"I haven't ever been able to let it go," the newcomer said. "I think about it all the time." The voice had drifted lower. "What about you, Benjamin. How's your conscience?"

"Not good."

The man pointed a finger. "You shouldn't have called."

"You're the only one I could have called."

"If this is all such a problem," I said, entering the conversation, "why are you here?"

A sadness crept into the man's eyes. "Because a long time ago I did a lot of bad things I regret."

"I've prayed many times to the Lord for both our forgiveness," Foster said.

"Has it helped?" I asked.

Foster shook his head.

"They want you, Benjamin," the man said.

"You do realize," I said, "that if they're looking, you might have led them straight here."

He pointed again at Foster. "That's exactly why he called me. We good, Benjamin?"

"We're good."

The man retreated to his car and left.

I suddenly felt like bait again. "Is that true? You wanted him to lead them, whoever they are, to you?"

Foster said nothing.

He just stood and watched as the car sped from the cemetery.

"Who exactly was that guy?" I tried.

"He once worked for the FBI."

I was beginning to see the bigger picture. These men were involved in something that had lain dormant for a long time. Something that had been roused by the files I'd retrieved. Something that Juan Lopez Valdez, Benjamin Foster, and the guy who was just here knew all about. But apparently Coleen Perry had been in the dark, enough that she went behind her father and made a deal with Valdez, one that people who used to work for the FBI clearly did not like.

A thousand thoughts swirled through my brain.

In the conventional world, law enforcement should be immediately involved. All of this should be turned over to the proper authorities. But I was now working in a universe with different rules. Look at how many laws I'd broken over the past twenty-four hours. Eventually I would come to know that the mission was all that mattered. Sure, never hurt an innocent, but also never let a few laws get in the way. That was precisely how the other side played, so what was good for the goose was even better for the gander. But on this day I was still riding on training wheels.

"We should return to Coleen," Foster said.

I didn't disagree. But Foster had never answered my question. "Do you want them to find us?"

He faced me. "Of course not. That would be foolish."

His denial was not reassuring. I circled back to something he'd mentioned earlier. "How do you know Jim Jansen?"

"We were acquainted many years ago."

"He tried to kill me."

"Which is not surprising."

He said nothing more and walked toward the car.

I followed.

He tossed the keys for me to drive. We both climbed inside and I swung the wheel hard left, gunning the accelerator, heading for the highway. Cars passed us, but none seemed overly interested and there was no one following.

We rode in silence for a while.

Finally, I tried again. "That guy could have led people straight here."

"As you could have, in that plane."

If that was the case, then why had *they* not made a more definitive move? Apparently the helicopter and police activity earlier had nothing to do with me or Coleen.

We approached the driveway for the house and I turned left, speeding down the sandy lane. A new vehicle was parked out front with Florida plates from Orange County.

"Lock the car doors," Foster said.

I got it.

That way no one could get to the case in the trunk.

We headed for the house.

On the front porch, Foster eased close to my left ear and whispered into it. Then he brushed past and stepped through the door. I hesitated a moment, a bit shocked at what he'd said to me, before following. Inside I discovered the car belonged to Coleen's husband, who introduced himself as Nate Perry, attorney-at-law.

Nate was eager-eyed, sharp-featured, and white, with thin dark hair that hung to his shoulders. Maybe mid-thirties. He seemed a volatile combination of self-confidence and lack of polish—a sense of rough and smooth that might explain what Coleen saw in him, since she was a little like that herself. Even more telling was his handshake. Soft and moist. Which always raised red flags with me. Being in the military I was accustomed to hard, firm grips. Most annoying was that he smiled incessantly, his tone sometimes at variance with his gestures.

And he liked to talk.

Which raised a warning.

My grandfather taught me that the smartest chickens in the coop rarely clucked.

"Lieutenant Malone—" Nate said.

"Cotton. Please. You make me feel old."

"That's an old southern nickname. How'd you get it?"

"It's a story too long to tell right now. I'm more interested in why you're here."

He seemed a little taken aback by my inquiry, but in my newfound state of justifiable paranoia I wanted to know.

"That's real simple, *Cotton*. My family owns this house."

"Tell me something I don't know. Why are *you* here?"

"He's the one who ratted me out to my father," Coleen said. "That's how he knew to come. Nate was to meet me here tomorrow."

"Lucky for us all," Foster said. "we came early."

I doubted luck had much to do with any of that.

"I came to read Valdez's files," Nate said. "I understand you have them."

I ignored the observation and gave the room a once-over, noticing the light, airy furniture and white-pine-paneled walls, which you didn't see much of anymore. Everything seemed appropriate and in its place. Even Benjamin Foster, who stood with his shoes unscuffed, suit unrumpled, the shirt and bow tie as crisp as when he'd put them on this morning.

I allowed Nate's declaration about the files to hang in the air and, staring at Foster, I imagined his index finger wagging at me like a metronome.

I heard again what he'd whispered to me outside.

Before we entered.

This house could be bugged. Careful with your words.

CHAPTER EIGHTEEN

MY THOUGHTS RACED BUT HELD NO FORM.

To my tired senses, the revelation that the house might be under electronic surveillance dragged behind me like a lure for hounds. Was Foster serious? Or just trying to rattle me? How would he even know such a thing? And if so, why didn't he want anyone else to be alerted to the fact? Stephanie's silence and Jansen's duplicity were one thing. But this guy was quite another. I definitely had my hands in more than one cookie jar.

Which wasn't good.

Particularly given that I wasn't a fan of cookies.

"We want to read those files," Nate said again. "I know people who would love to know what they say."

"What people?" I asked.

"Nate was involved with *King v. Jowers*," Coleen said.

I knew about the case, which had made the news last December. A civil action filed by the heirs of Martin Luther King Jr. against a man named Loyd Jowers. It started when Jowers appeared on television and openly claimed to have been part of a conspiracy to kill King that involved both the government and organized crime. He owned a restaurant just below the rooming house from which James Earl Ray supposedly fired his shot. But according to Jowers, Ray was not the triggerman. Instead, Jowers claimed to have hired a Memphis police officer to fire the fatal shot. Jowers was supposedly paid $100,000 for the effort by a friend in the mafia. Why was never explained, and conveniently that friend had since died. He then spiced things up by claiming that the government played a big part, alleging that a special forces team also had been dispatched to Memphis to kill King.

But Jowers beat them to it.

The whole story stretched beyond the fantastical.

Still, the King family seized the opportunity to finally have a public airing of their doubts and sued Jowers in Memphis civil court for wrongful death.

"The whole trial was a joke," Nate said. "There was four weeks of testimony. Seventy-plus witnesses. Jowers took the Fifth when he testified, but his lawyer conveniently stipulated that all of his previous comments to the media could be admitted as evidence. What lawyer in his right mind would do that? The Memphis DA had already said that he had no intention of reopening the assassination case, so Jowers could lie away without fear of any consequences. You can count on one hand the number of times anyone objected to anything. It was a scripted show designed to air out a preestablished point of view. Nothing adversarial about it. The King family believes there was a government conspiracy. They think James Earl Ray is innocent. A patsy. So that's what the evidence showed. In the end the jury did their part, finding unanimously that Jowers killed King as part of a conspiracy that involved not only other people, but also the government."

"The family went before the cameras afterward," Coleen said, "and told the world, *See, we were right. Ray didn't pull the trigger. It was a conspiracy.* But that trial proved nothing."

Foster stood quiet during the discussion. I glanced his way and asked, "Is that your opinion? Was that case a joke?"

"Jowers was an opportunist, looking to sell his story for money. The jury's verdict merely provided him with much-needed credibility. It upped the price for his story. Thankfully, he died a month ago and will not profit from his nonsense."

I heard what they were all saying. Trials only worked if there were two opposing sides, each presenting a differing view of the facts in an adversarial way, which an impartial jury would then decide between.

Collusion produced nothing but what the colluders wanted you to hear, the verdict inevitable unless the jury saw through the subterfuge.

"I was there," Nate said. "The judge and the jurors constantly fell asleep. Hell, I had a hard time staying awake myself. It was all a rubber stamp on the King family's belief that there was a government conspiracy."

"Tell us about Juan Carlos Valdez," Coleen asked her father. "And those files I went to the Dry Tortugas to get."

"I should have never spoken to you about anything," Foster said.

"What did you expect me to do?" she asked. "Just forget about it?"

Foster's warning that the house might be bugged again rang through my brain. Which made me wonder. Was he playing to the gallery? Had the guy back in the cemetery been right and Foster wanted Jansen and company to find him?

"Valdez contacted me," Foster said. "Not you. You should have respected my privacy instead of listening in on my calls and searching my house."

I knew what he meant. "Where did the coin come from?"

"I stole it a long time ago."

"That's all he ever says," Coleen said. "From what I've read it may be the last 1933 Double Eagle outside a museum. And my father stole it, then hid it in a drawer. Bullshit."

Nate faced his father-in-law. "Why are you the only one allowed to know the truth?"

They all waited for more.

But Foster seemed off in another place.

"I was there," he finally said. "None of you saw what I saw. Felt what I felt. When I rushed up those stairs to the balcony, it was like the world had come to an end."

The hole in King's right jaw was the size of a fist. Blood poured out in rapid spurts soaking both King's clothes and the balcony's concrete. He was still alive, but his breathing seemed labored. He tried to speak, but no words would form.

"It's all right," Abernathy told King. "Don't worry. This is Ralph. Can you hear me? Are you in pain?"

No reply.

King's skin had turned ashen and seemed clammy and cold. He stared off into the sky, seeing nothing, but perhaps everything. Andy Young and Jesse Jackson had finally rushed up the stairs, too. A Memphis policeman appeared with a towel, which he wrapped around the wound to try to check the bleeding.

Young pressed for a pulse and shook his head. "Ralph, it's all over."

"Don't say that," Abernathy screamed.

Someone brought out one of the hotel bedspreads and covered King. Not as a corpse, but still as a living being. Chaos exploded below. People appeared from their rooms, most crying, praying, and cursing. There were wails, pleas, and accusations. Firemen and helmeted police arrived with weapons drawn.

"Where did the shot come from?" one of the cops yelled up.

Those standing watch over their leader—Young, Abernathy, and the others—all pointed toward the northwest, across the street, past a bushy knoll, at a two-story, brick rooming house. A photographer below captured the moment as their index fingers extended outward.

A siren could finally be heard and an ambulance arrived.

By 6:15 King made it to the hospital.

Fourteen minutes had elapsed since the shooting. He was taken straight into an operating room, his clothing quickly cut away.

The massive wound was no longer bleeding.

"Me and Ralph," Foster said, "watched as they tried to save him. But the whole side of his face was gone. They kept telling us to leave, but Ralph made it clear that we were staying. By now he didn't trust anybody, especially white people."

A thoracic surgeon, heart surgeon, pulmonary specialist, renal specialist, and several general surgeons came.

But the neurosurgeon made the call.

The bullet had damaged the jugular vein and windpipe, severing the spinal cord, then shattering into pieces when it ricocheted off the vertebrae, finally embedding in the left shoulder blade. A lot of important nerves had been irrevocably severed.

"He's alive, but barely. It would be a blessing if he did go. The spine is cut and there is awful brain damage. He could only survive in a vegetative state. He's permanently paralyzed from the neck down."

A respirator kept forcing air into the lungs.

Monitors showed a weak heartbeat.

The doctors decided to try a cardiac massage and a shot of adrenaline. But neither had any effect. Finally, the monitors showed no heart function.

Abernathy walked to the table and cradled his old friend in his arms. They'd been together a long time.

King's inhales grew farther apart.

Then stopped.

At 7:05 P.M., sixty-four minutes after being shot, Martin Luther King Jr. died.

"We just stood there," Foster said. "Ralph kept holding him. I bowed my head and prayed. But our dear friend, our leader, was gone."

Foster seemed to be drifting, wandering, roaming through memories only he understood.

But I had a job to do.

"Do you know what Bishop's Pawn means?" I asked.

He nodded. "The FBI bugged our cars, hotel rooms, telephones, even our homes. We knew they were listening, watching, making files. They never called us by our real names. They had code names for all of us. Andy, Ralph, Jesse, me. We learned about them much later, when those FBI reports became public. Martin's code name was Bishop."

"And Pawn?" Nate asked.

He shrugged. "I have no idea."

I might have been young and inexperienced as a field agent, but I knew a liar when I saw one.

He was good. I'd give him that.

But he was still a liar.

CHAPTER
NINETEEN

I ALLOWED FOSTER THE LUXURY OF HIS LIE.

At least for the moment.

"Lieutenant Malone," Foster said. "I want to speak with my daughter and son-in-law in private. After that, I'll speak with you again. I'm hungry. How about you go and get us all some food."

A shower would also be welcome. Unfortunately, I had no change of clothes and still wore the saltwater-soaked shorts and Jaguars T-shirt that I'd donned this morning. My clothes and toiletries were back in my car on the dock at Key West. So why not? It didn't really matter if these people vanished. I had the coin and the files. Mission accomplished.

Maybe that was exactly what Foster wanted me to do.

Disappear.

I left the house and drove Foster's Toyota fifteen miles south to Pahokee, a moderately sized town of stuccoed buildings bleached from the sun, where I found some jeans and a green pullover shirt at a second-hand store. I picked up a few toiletries and ordered four take-out pizzas at an eatery I spotted. The trip also allowed me to make a call, which I did, collect, from a gas station pay phone.

To Stephanie Nelle.

I narrated the day's events, leaving nothing out, with an even tone and a military completeness.

"I'm sorry about what happened," she said. "I had no idea about Jansen. I was referred to him. Which raises more issues that I have to deal with, here, internally."

"You have some kind of revolt going on?"

"You could say that. It goes back to COINTELPRO."

There was that acronym again.

"It took fifteen presidents, fifty years, and an act of God to end Hoover's reign and finally dismantle his godforsaken FBI," she said. "Over a thousand agents once worked COINTELPRO. Many of them remained with the bureau long after 1972, when Hoover died. And those men didn't change. They just became better at what they did. I was told, though, that Jansen was not one of them."

"Somebody lied to you."

"I see that. But thanks to you, we came away with the files and the coin. Are they safe?"

The waterproof case remained in the Toyota's trunk, within my sight a few feet away. The coin in my pocket.

"They're fine."

"I prefer you not read those files," she said. "They're classified."

"How's that possible? They came from Cuba."

"Just return them to me, please."

"So you knew all along there were files waiting in that wreck?"

"I did. But there was no need for you to know that."

"Except, in the past few hours, people have been trying to kill me over them."

"Just bring them to me."

Looking back, that was the first of countless orders Stephanie Nelle would give me in the field. That one came in the same authoritative voice I ultimately learned to both detest and respect. She would say that I ignored her more times than I obeyed, and she might be right. One thing I knew then, though, was that before I handed anything over I planned to read every damn word in those files. My curiosity meter had tilted off the charts. Too much had happened over the past twelve hours for me to just blindly hand things over. That impetuousness would ultimately serve me well during my time as an intelligence operative, but I can't say that it didn't occasionally lead to trouble.

"Cotton, our job is to keep this under control. Understand?"

"There's a whole bunch you're not saying."

"Welcome to my world."

I chuckled. "Okay. I get it. Shut up and do the job."

"You do learn fast. There's no need to stay there. Foster and his daughter are no longer part of this. Leave now and bring the files and the coin back to Mayport. I'd send some help, but I didn't do so good with choosing that the first time. I'll leave it to you this time."

Fair enough.

I hung up the phone and made a second call to Pam, to let her know I was okay. She knew nothing of my new assignment, the first of innumerable times I would keep her in the dark about my professional life. National security and all that other bullshit. The trust between us was gone, and sadly time would only make things worse. I hurt her. Bad. And each day I felt anew the force of her emotions. Was she vindictive? Probably. But I'd given her good reason. She'd been hurt and she was hurting me back. I accepted her anger because I thought it was all part of making amends. What I wouldn't learn until many years later was how calculatedly she ultimately exacted her revenge, planting and tending my pain as carefully as one would work a garden.

I stood outside the gas station, biding my time while the pizzas were being made. The town loomed quiet, except for a steady breeze tickling the treetops. The sun was dissolving to orange in the western sky, far out over Lake Okeechobee, the dusky air still oven-warm. Shadows had begun blurring into one another like a growing stain on the concrete.

My watch read nearly 6:00 P.M.

Time for me to head north to Jacksonville.

About a four-hour drive.

The Fosters would have to find their own dinner. They were no longer important to this mission. The Toyota could be returned to Foster tomorrow. More of that rules-don't-apply-to-me mentality I was beginning to appreciate.

I hopped into the car and drove farther south to where US 441 veered east toward the Atlantic Ocean. I turned and a sign informed me that I-95 lay thirty-five miles away. Everything Foster had told me about the 1928 hurricane still stuck in my brain. Incredible that such atrocities actually happened right here. What had Martin Luther King Jr. said? *The ultimate measure of a man is not where he stands in moments of comfort and convenience, but where he stands at times of challenge and controversy.*

Amen.

A car approached from behind.

Fast.

A few hundred yards ahead the highway became four-lane in both directions. But here there were only two. The car sped past in the opposite lane, then cut back in front and lit its brake lights. I slammed my right foot onto the brake pedal and slid to a stop. In my rearview mirror I saw a second car behind me.

Doors flew open. Four armed men emerged.

One of whom was Jim Jansen.

I was yanked from the car.

"You should have done yourself a favor and died on that boat," Jansen said.

Two of the other men began a search of the Toyota. It took them only a few moments to find the waterproof case in the trunk. The fourth man kept a weapon trained on me while Jansen patted me down. In my jean pocket he found the coin.

He stared at it through the plastic sleeve, pleased.

"A total disaster. That's what this is," Jansen said. "All thanks to Cotton 'James Bond' Malone. Special Justice Department operative. You proud of yourself?"

"I left you stranded at Fort Jefferson."

"That you did."

He pounded a fist into my gut, which doubled me over.

I gathered my breath and tried to steady my nerve. The other two men grabbed me by the arms, pinning them behind me, slamming me chest-first into the side of the Toyota.

Handcuffs were clipped to my wrists.

Cars were approaching from the west.

I tried to steady my breathing.

"Let's get out of here," Jansen said.

CHAPTER TWENTY

As messes go this one had to be an eleven on a ten-point scale. I was back in the rear seat of a car with my hands cuffed behind my back, exactly how I started in Jacksonville thirty-six hours ago. Only this time, instead of going to jail, I was headed north on U.S. 441 to God knows where.

Jansen sat in the front seat and had not said much of anything. I wondered what had happened to the Fosters and company, but realized that I'd only be told what he wanted me to know. A sinking realization had taken hold. Benjamin Foster had definitely wanted this to happen. Is that why he alerted me to the possible house surveillance? To throw me off guard? To make me think him a friend? Then he sent me off to get food, with the files conveniently in the trunk and the coin in my pocket. Straight to Jansen. I was actually getting pretty good at being bait.

Still, I thought I'd try, "You do know that I reported in to the Justice Department."

"Ever heard of Jimmy Hoffa?" Jansen asked.

I got the message, and with the Everglades just a stone's throw away it would not be all that difficult to accomplish.

"We saw you make a call," Jansen said. "But agents disappear all the time. It's an occupational hazard. Which explains why pains in the ass like Stephanie Nelle recruit young, stupid hotshots like you."

Good to know.

We passed a lot of citrus groves, sugarcane fields, and cattle pastures before finally crossing under Interstate 95, cruising farther east into downtown West Palm Beach. From its inception the town had always lived in the shadow of Palm Beach, its more glitzy neighbor across the Intracoastal Waterway. One was created for people with money, the other for those who worked for the people with money. I'd visited both a couple of times, this side of the water reality, the other side like going to Mars. I saw that we were headed straight into outer space as the car veered right and drove across the bridge.

Tall palm trees lined the main avenue like sentinels keeping watch. We stopped at an intersection, then turned north on the old A1A highway that bisected the narrow spit of island north to south. Past a stretch of churches and high-end businesses, houses appeared.

Big ones.

"We headed to your mansion?" I asked Jansen.

He shifted in his seat and turned around to face me. His right arm came up with a gun that he nestled to my forehead.

Then he cocked the hammer.

I will say, the experience was unnerving. Never had I felt a weapon that close to me, being held by a man who clearly wanted to pull the trigger. Making it worse, my hands were cuffed behind my back so there was nothing I could do about it.

"I'm looking forward to killing you," he said.

"Just not yet, right? Somebody higher on the food chain wants me delivered in one piece?"

His silence confirmed I was right.

"It's a bitch to be a peon, isn't it?" I asked.

He released the hammer and withdrew the gun, then turned back around in his seat. I exhaled, realizing I'd been holding my breath a long time.

We kept driving, traffic moving like blood through a clogged artery. The ocean was no more than a hundred yards off to the right, but invisible, shielded by the trees, the mansions, and some unbelievably well-groomed, towering hedges. There must have been some local ordinance that encouraged everyone to grow theirs thick to the sky.

Here and there the road nestled close to the shore. Old money hummed a loud and obvious tune. Side streets radiated every couple of hundred feet in defined blocks and we turned down one, a narrow lane that passed between more houses, these not as large as their oceanfront companions, but nonetheless impressive.

We finally stopped at a two-story brick Colonial with a portico supported by columns that reminded me of the White House. More tall hedges screened the front yard from the street. We stopped in a forecourt, enclosed on three sides by a stone balustrade topped with urns. Flowers filled the lavish beds among more shrubbery.

Waiting at the front door was a man with neatly clipped silver-gray hair and a face as smooth and rosy as a child's. He wore a pair of tortoiseshell glasses. I was led from the car. Our footsteps made rasping sounds on the soft stone steps as we entered a vestibule dominated by a curving stairway of gray marble that reached up to a second-floor balcony. I was waiting for the queen or the president to descend amid a flurry of trumpets. A crystal chandelier burned bright. We walked across a floor inlaid with black marble highlighted by—of all things—the seal of the FBI.

Glasses led the way to a pair of carved wooden doors that opened into a spacious library. But a quick perusal showed it was in name only, the shelves stocked with the kind of nondescript leather bindings that interior decorators used to make a room appear important.

Scores of framed photographs dotted the walls, all of the same man posing with others. I caught Ronald Reagan, George Bush, Warren Burger, J. Edgar Hoover, Robert Redford, Charlton Heston, and Walter Cronkite. Most mere poses in an office or at some gathering. Others while holding drinks. One on a golf course, another a sailboat. But at the center was always the same man looking equal to whomever he was with. His hairline progressively lightened and receded through the years but was always immaculate. I had a sense of an indexed life, collected and stored right here on this trophy wall. The whole room seemed a suffocating display, overloaded with nostalgia, like stepping back in time with someone who lived around their possessions.

A cluster of wingback chairs and a sofa, all in creamy leather, dominated the center of the room atop a hardwood floor covered with a pale-blue rug. Fading sunlight managed to find a way in through the curtained French doors. A man rose from one of the chairs and waited for our escort to bring us to him. The face was identical to the man in the pictures, but a small potbelly had grown against the tall, commanding frame. He was pushing seventy easily, but the hard and uncompromising expression from the photos remained. He wore fashionable wire-rimmed spectacles with a fawn-colored sport coat, vintage jeans, and shiny penny loafers, which gave him the air of an aging academic, the persona surely not random.

My eye caught a clock on the wall, which read 7:10 P.M.

"Uncuff him," he ordered.

Jansen complied.

"My name is Tom Oliver."

His attire, impeccable posture, and poorly restrained confidence came straight out of the FBI manual. But not his manners. No hand was extended for me to shake, which was fine by me.

"Please, have a seat. You and I need to speak. Alone."

Jansen and the other guy got the message and left, closing the door behind them. Oliver assumed a position in one of the wingback chairs and reached for a pipe on the side table, lighting it up, puffing out acrid smoke. I had already caught its lingering odor in the air.

"Do you know who I am?" he asked me.

I sat. "Not a clue."

"I worked for the FBI my entire career in law enforcement, retiring a few years ago as deputy director."

"I'm so happy for you."

"Is this amusing to you."

My patience was reaching its end. "What's not amusing is your lapdog out there, who wants to kill me. And the fact that I've been kidnapped and brought here against my will."

"I doubt it was all against your will. After all, you are on a mission."

"You know who sent me."

"I do. Which is why we're talking, instead of your corpse floating in the Everglades waiting for the alligators to eat it."

He gave a grunt of satisfaction at his threat, his words and wealth seemingly enough for me to believe him.

"Let me guess," I said. "You married money. Because a career FBI agent couldn't afford the power bill on this place."

He reached for a drink on the side table and swirled the clear liquid in the glass, then downed it in curious little sips.

"My wife's family has owned this house for generations."

I knew that this guy was going to be nothing more than a mine of misinformation. Every movement was measured, calm, and resolute. His goal was to suck in far more information than he let out. Best guess? The subject of the hour was Stephanie Nelle. He knew about her, just not enough. So why not corral the new guy, stick a gun in his face, then drag him into this sorry excuse for a library and wait for him to crack.

Yeah. Good luck with that plan.

I'd rather take my chances with the gators.

The study door opened and Jansen appeared.

"They're here."

Oliver nodded.

"Are we having a party?" I asked.

He grinned, still trying to rattle me.

"Something like that."

CHAPTER TWENTY-ONE

JANSEN LAID THE WATERPROOF CASE ON THE HARDWOOD FLOOR A few feet from where I sat. Atop it rested the 1933 Double Eagle inside its plastic sleeve. That coin was certainly making the rounds. Jansen left again, closing the library door behind him.

"He's well trained," I noted. "You do it yourself, or send him to obedience school?"

"Are you always so disrespectful?"

"Only to those I really like."

"Your new friends have arrived," Oliver said, ignoring my humor. "Foster, his daughter, and her husband."

Good to know.

Like with Desi and Lucy, the reverend had some *'splainin to do.*

"Did you make a deal with Foster?" I asked. "To get that case and coin?"

"Reverend Foster understands the gravity of this situation. He wants this contained, as I do. I'm hoping we can all come to an understanding and end this matter quickly and quietly."

"You have the files, which makes you and Foster happy. You have the coin, which will make Valdez happy. What will make Stephanie Nelle happy?"

Oliver laid his drink down and continued puffing the pipe.

"Without the files or Valdez, she has nothing but a bunch of unsubstantiated talk. I'm trying to keep this at that level and avoid the taking of any *drastic* measures."

"Which would only bring more attention. Better we ramble like idiots on things we can't prove."

"Something like that."

I wanted to know, "Were you listening in at the house by the lake?"

He shook his head. "For what? No need."

"Because the guy who came to the cemetery was your bird dog?"

"He once worked for me, if that's what you mean."

Foster did not want the files inside that case seen by Coleen. So he'd used the situation to reverse what she'd managed to set in motion, allowing Jansen to be led straight to the files. But why not just destroy them himself? Why involve Jansen at all? Only one answer made sense. This guy wanted to see them first.

"What's Bishop's Pawn?"

"How much of the files did you read?"

"Enough," I lied, trying to alter the situation.

"That operation is classified. But it was something of great concern to this country."

"That's what this is about? We're concerned for the country? You're retired. That's not your problem anymore."

"This country will always be my concern. I started with the bureau in 1959, back when the Soviet Union and communism were our greatest threats."

"And how many communists did you find? Never mind. I know the answer. Not enough to get excited over." I paused. "If any at all."

"You have no idea what we faced."

"Actually, I do. I can read. The threat of a communist infiltration was total bullshit, used by guys like you to keep a job and further your own paranoia. The CIA, which actually dealt with communists, determined that King was no threat to national security whatsoever. Yet the FBI decided otherwise. Did you really think that the Soviet Union was behind the civil rights movement? Trying to destroy us from within?"

"Stanley Levison was a member of the Communist Party of the United States."

I knew that name. A close friend and confidant of Martin Luther King Jr., he was a white lawyer from New York who helped draft some of King's most famous speeches and organize events. He also raised money for the SCLC. True, history noted that Levison had once been a member of the Communist Party, but he ceased all connection to it long before he and King ever became linked.

"Levison was called to testify before the Senate Committee on Internal Security," Oliver said. "Parts of that testimony are classified to this day."

"What does that have to do with the price of tea in China?'

That's what my mother used to ask me when I tried to bullshit her.

"There was a genuine concern that Levison might influence or manipulate King into causing widespread political unrest," Oliver said. "That was standard operating procedure for communist organizations back then. They wanted to bring this country down. King himself was on the FBI Reserve Index. People to be detained in the event of a national emergency."

"King was no communist."

"We don't know that."

"Yes. We do. You used that nonsense to justify illegally wiretapping not only Levison and King, but too many other people to even count. The sad part is even both Kennedys and Lyndon Johnson allowed that to happen. They all three loved getting the inside scoop on people, including King. Not a one of them ever told Hoover to stop. All of you were crazy as hell."

"Easy for you to say, sitting here now, reaping the rewards of our caution."

I'd had enough. "Stanley Levison was a progressive liberal who believed that the blacks of this country were getting screwed. And by the way, they were. He stood up for what he believed and helped the man at the tip of the spear do his job. J. Edgar Hoover hated King and everyone associated with him. That's a fact. So Levison became a target. It's just that simple. I agree, it was a different time with different values. But that doesn't make what you did right."

This guy was getting on my last nerve.

"I've heard your criticisms many times before. They don't affect me. We did our jobs. I make no apologies."

I recalled something else I once read. "There was an internal FBI report, from 1963, I think, that concluded the civil rights movement was not communist-controlled. I've read parts of it. Hoover would not accept that report, so its author changed the conclusion and instead proposed targeting the SCLC by COINTELPRO."

"I wrote that report."

The revelation took me aback.

"Hoover was brash, brilliant, full of self-esteem, cocky as a rooster, and totally amoral," he said. "I agree, he institutionalized totalitarianism within the FBI. He was in total control. I witnessed that control for many years. In some respects that was good."

I could not imagine how.

"Presidents, congressmen, cabinet officers. They all thought the FBI was their own personal police force to be used on their enemies. But we were anything but that. Partisanship was strictly forbidden. Hoover worked hard to keep us out of politics. We were then, and still are, an investigatory agency, not a police force. Big difference."

"That didn't prevent Hoover himself from using his agents like the police."

"There is some truth to that. We worked in a vacuum with no oversight from the executive or legislative branches. That wasn't intentional. It simply happened over time, thanks to Hoover's longevity and the reputation he forged as someone who didn't require supervision."

"A big mistake."

"Yes. It was. Hindsight is always twenty/twenty."

"As long as it's not viewed through a filter."

"Again. I agree. Hoover became dangerously autonomous. None of us challenged him. And for good reason. He convinced Congress to exempt the FBI from civil service laws. So every agent's future rested entirely in his hands. Disagreeing with Hoover was the worst thing you could do. Believe me, I know."

"That's why you rewrote the report?"

He nodded. "My career would have been over. Hoover believed King to be an immoral, lying hypocrite. He hated the man. So everyone else within the FBI was required to hate him, too. I knew what he wanted to hear. Once a policy was set by Hoover, it could not be undone. You either played ball or went home. Your choice. I chose."

"The whole 'I was just following orders thing' went by the wayside at Nuremberg."

"This country was different then. The public supported the FBI. They loved Hoover. He was their hero. There was a respect for law enforcement that's gone today."

"All thanks to people like J. Edgar Hoover, who certainly did his part to make people distrust the police."

"Again, I can't disagree with those conclusions. Hoover built an empire. He worked mainly in secret and masked his actions behind a totally crafted public image that he went to great lengths to create. But you're right, he waged a war on civil liberties and, unfortunately for Martin Luther King, by the time the civil rights movement came into existence, Hoover was at his zenith."

My anger was growing. This guy was no moralistic saint. Repentant. I knew his type. Official vigilantes. Self-appointed Boy Scouts of the heartland with their perfect suits and brush-cut hair, possessed of values and beliefs that could justify anything, telling you precisely what you wanted to hear while driving a knife into your back.

"You personally knew there was no connection between communism and King, yet you went ahead and tried to destroy him."

"We tried to destroy a lot of people. But Hoover and King's relationship was different. King had the audacity to openly question the FBI's own civil rights record. He pointed out there were no black agents and he leveled that there was a southern bias, on our part, with investigations. He was right on both counts, by the way. Hoover forbid the hiring of blacks and we did cater to southern law enforcement. We could not have functioned without good relationships with the local police. Those southern cops hated King and everything he stood for. When it came to choosing between civil rights protestors and the cops, that was no choice at all."

I was going to enjoy kicking this old man's butt. And I intended on doing just that. I was rapidly becoming real comfortable with a devil-may-care attitude. But the presence of Foster and the Perrys added a level of complication. So I decided to keep fishing while this guy was still nibbling at the hook.

"In '64 King attacked Hoover again on the communist angle," Oliver said. "His quote was that there were as many communists in the civil rights movement as there were Eskimos in Florida. That's when Hoover held his famous press conference and called King the most notorious liar in the country. After that it was total war for Hoover. My marching orders were clear. Destroy King."

"What was your role in COINTELPRO?"

"I was head of domestic intelligence. I ran the entire counterintelligence operation under Hoover. Then I headed its dismantling, after he died."

At least I was speaking to the man at the top. "Only it's not dismantled, is it?"

"That depends. As far as active and current? It's gone. Times have changed."

"Yeah. People actually try to follow the law now."

"But as to guarding against threats from the past? We must remain vigilant to those."

I motioned to the case. "Like what's in there?"

He glanced at the waterproof case. "I truly believed that Juan Lopez Valdez was dead. He hasn't been heard from in over twenty years. Instead, he's not only alive, but went to the Dry Tortugas to meet with Benjamin Foster's daughter and bring her documents that should no longer exist. I assure you, Lieutenant Malone, nothing good would have come from anyone seeing what's inside there."

"Then it's lucky for you I came along and screwed everything up."

He gestured with the pipe. "There is an element of fortuitousness in your presence."

"Along with a pain in the ass?"

He chuckled. "Oh, yes. Jansen wants to kill you."

"Let him try."

"You're an interesting man. A young naval officer. Fighter pilot. Law school graduate. JAG lawyer. Now a special operative with the Justice Department, whatever that means. And all before you turn thirty."

"I'm having my résumé printed, can I include you as a reference?"

I could see I was getting to him. This guy was accustomed to giving orders, then people bowing as they backed from the room to follow them. But he'd heard two words that he hadn't wanted to hear.

Bishop's Pawn.

My lawyer sense told me he was now more than a little annoyed. Killing me remained a problem. Others knew about me, and he was no longer running with the big dogs. He didn't call the shots. Instead, he was retired, living here in Shangri-la with his marble FBI emblem in the entrance hall floor, dependent on people still in positions of power to cover for him.

Those were the ones Stephanie Nelle was after.

The folks in DC whose strings this guy pulled.

So I decided to get with the plan and help her out.

"Why am I here?"

"I was hoping we could solve this problem together. I know what Foster wants." He pointed at the case. "Those to be burned. I get that. People are motivated by a variety of reasons. Ideology, passion, duty, loyalty. Some by personal gain. What do you want?"

I nearly smiled. He'd brought me here to bribe me.

Something thudded into the door loud enough to grab both my and Oliver's attention. He rose from his seat and rushed across to a desk, where he withdrew a weapon.

"Stay here."

You wish.

He headed for the door.

I snatched up the coin from the top of the waterproof case and pocketed it, then I cut Oliver off, planting a solid right uppercut that sent the bastard down. I then relieved him of his gun and mocked him.

"You stay here."

I opened the door.

Jansen lay on the floor.

CHAPTER
TWENTY-TWO

I BENT DOWN AND CHECKED.

Jansen was still breathing, but he'd taken a pop to his head, a fresh gash marking the method of attack. I came alert and stared down the corridor toward the entrance hall. The man in the glasses who'd escorted us inside lay sprawled on the terrazzo. Apparently, somebody unexpected had arrived.

But what about Coleen, her father, and her husband? I decided there was no choice, so I called out, "Coleen?"

"In here."

I heard the voice, muffled, as if through a closed door, coming from ahead. Three doors down I found them, but the knob was locked.

"Stand back," I said.

I pounded my right foot into the wood. Two more kicks and the jamb gave way.

I stepped inside.

"Something's happening here," I told them. "And it's not good."

Then I realized.

The waterproof case was back in the library.

"Follow me."

We returned to the room to find Oliver still on the floor, the waterproof case gone, the French doors leading out to the terrace open.

"Get in one of the cars out front and get out of here," I told Coleen.

"I'm going with you," she said, then she faced her husband. "Take Dad and go. Do you have your cell phone?"

Nate shook his head. "The guy back there on the floor in the hall took it."

I understood Coleen's point, so I rushed back inside and searched Jansen, finding the unit.

"When you get away," she told Nate, "call us on your phone."

Nate nodded.

"Let those files go," Foster said. "They're not worth all of this."

"I can't," Coleen said.

I agreed with her.

"I demand you listen to me, Coleen."

"We're way beyond that," she told him.

I grabbed Foster by the arm and led him away, whispering into his ear, "Go, or I'll tell her what you did to get us here."

I could see the threat registered.

The older man nodded his acquiescence.

"You and I will talk privately later," I muttered.

We all raced from the house, rounding one side and following the towering hedges back to the driveway entrance.

Several parked cars waited.

"One of those hopefully has keys in it," I said. "Take it."

Foster and Nate headed off.

Coleen and I left the grounds and found the street beyond the hedges. To my left I saw two men moving east, toward the ocean, carrying the waterproof case. They were nearly a hundred yards away, too far for the gun, and besides, I didn't want to draw any attention that might bring the local police.

An engine cranked behind us, and a moment later one of the cars with Nate driving sped from the house. I motioned for them to turn right. Nate hesitated, seeing the two men with the case farther down the street. I knew what he was thinking.

He had a car.

We didn't.

"We'll get it," I told him through the closed window. "Get your father-in-law out of here."

He turned the car right and disappeared down the street.

Coleen was already running toward the two other men.

I followed.

One of them glanced back and saw her. They increased their pace. So did I. I saw them cross the street at the end of the block and trot down a narrow, sandy footpath, then disappear into the oaks and palms that separated two of the estate properties. A posted sign noted that the trail was for public beach access. A wall ran down the right side guarding the perimeter of a huge house that rose among the trees. A fence protected the private property to the left.

Coleen crossed the street and headed for the trail.

I ran faster.

A shot popped ahead.

Coleen was unarmed, which meant she was taking fire. I crossed the street and plunged into the foliage, following the sandy ground through the trees. Coleen was huddled against the trunk of one of the thicker oaks. The two men were near the trail's end, where daylight and the sound of surf signaled ocean.

I knelt and sent a bullet from Oliver's gun their way.

It thudded into the sand at the end of the trail just as the two men crested a small dune and disappeared from sight. I ran ahead since the path was clear and found the dune. The sand beyond was thick and soft, slowing their forward progress. Fifty yards past them, where the waves crested at the shoreline, an inflatable boat waited. Daylight was waning, but enough light remained to see everything clearly. This part of the island seemed the realm of the wealthy. More private. Less crowded. No one was on the beach. I dropped to the sand, using the dune for protection, and fired again, intentionally sending the bullet to the right of both men.

"The next shot will be into one of you," I called out, telling them there was nowhere to go.

They stopped.

"Leave the case."

Coleen came up and lay belly-first beside me. I kept the gun trained. One of the men held a pistol. He moved to raise the weapon and I fired another round at his feet.

"Drop the gun."

He did.

I'd already noticed a large boat about two hundred yards offshore, similar to the one Valdez had been using. But there was no way he could be here. His boat was back in the Keys. My guess was that these guys worked for him and had been previously dispatched to keep an eye on Oliver.

"Leave the case and go," I said again.

They hesitated so I stood and aimed the gun.

"I can shoot you both. Right now. Doesn't really matter to me."

They turned and headed for the inflatable, trudging through more soft sand. Coleen and I headed for the case. She opened the container and made sure the files were still there.

"Tell Valdez to go back to Cuba," I called out. "This is over for him."

Coleen stood beside me and we watched as they pushed the inflatable into the surf and left.

"You handled that like a pro," she said with a grin. "Aren't you full of surprises."

We fled the beach and headed back down the public trail to the street. It seemed quiet at the far end of the block where Oliver's house stood. Probably because they were all still unconscious. Palm Beach proper was left, toward the south, a few miles away, past some of the most expensive real estate in the world. To our right, only a few hundred yards away lay the northern tip of the island. I decided the shorter route was the smart play, so we walked until the road ended. Across a narrow saltwater channel I saw more land populated with more lavish condominiums. No bridge made a connection from here to there. A small park stretched to our left, which came with a boat ramp. I knew Coleen wanted to read what was in the case as much as I did. And since there was no way to exclude her, I gestured toward one of the picnic tables.

Daylight kept fading, now only a rim of orange on the western horizon, a lurid glow that highlighted the ever-graying darkness of the clouds scurrying low overhead.

We sat.

And read.

CHAPTER TWENTY-THREE

July 16, 1967
Federal Bureau of Investigation
Internal Security-C
For CIP Supervisor Only

Contact has been established in Montreal with an
individual who shows promise. He identified himself to our point of contact operative as ERIC S.
GALT. Fingerprints revealed that name to be an alias
for an individual who was in the eighth year of a
20-year sentence at Missouri State Penitentiary for
armed robbery when he escaped on April 23, 1967.
Currently GALT is an active fugitive in Montreal
seeking a passport and passage to South Africa or
South America. He spends a large amount of time at
the local docks trying to secure work on an international freighter. GALT may have possibly robbed a
local brothel a few days ago. We would like to proceed with further checking. Depending on your decision relative to that request, we can alert the
local authorities of his presence for capture.

July 19, 1967
Federal Bureau of Investigation
Internal Security-C
For CIP Supervisor Only

In reply to your specific inquiries, GALT is forty-one years old, slender, fair-skinned, clean-shaven, with black hair flecked with gray at the sideburns, worn oiled and straight back. Psychiatric records have been obtained from the Missouri prison system. They note he is not mentally ill, but is a "complicated individual." He possesses a sociopathic personality and is severely neurotic. Perhaps even a pathological liar. IQ noted at 106. He suffers from undue anxiety and has clear obsessive-compulsive concerns about his personal health, bordering on a hypochondriac. He's noted as introverted, distracted, and rarely returns a gaze. He's a career criminal with multiple convictions of burglary and armed robbery, having served 13 years in four different prisons. Our point of contact operative notes he rarely tips servers, never laughs, and is overly paranoid about police (understandable, given he is a fugitive). Records indicate he was born in Alton, Illinois, raised Catholic, growing up in Ewing, Missouri, during the Depression. His current main motivations are money. He is not a member of any radical group, but admires the Nazis and would prefer an America free of Negroes and Jews. His personal motto is "never let the left hand know what the right is doing."

I glanced up from reading.
Both reports were signed by James Jansen, SAIC.
Special agent in charge.
All of the documents inside the three file folders within the

waterproof case were photographs. Not photocopies. Actual pictures of documents.

Which made sense.

In the late 1960s copiers existed, but they were rare. Duplicates then were more commonly produced by using carbon paper.

"Valdez seems to have taken pictures of Jansen's file," I said to Coleen.

The pages seemed in chronological order. Field reports to people higher up the FBI ladder. I knew that the bureau was legendary for its records thoroughness, particularly at that time in its existence, with Hoover still in charge. Everything then had been meticulously written down. Of course, that was pre-Watergate, pre–Church Committee, when no one in the FBI ever thought those documents would become public record.

We lifted out another page.

October 25, 1967
Federal Bureau of Investigation
Internal Security-C
For CIP Supervisor Only

After six weeks my assessment is that GALT ranks higher than the other three candidates currently being vetted. He fits nearly perfectly the psychological profile we are seeking. In his discussions with our point of contact operative, he's revealed a burning desire to better himself, to be somebody. As with the other three candidates, a simulated field test was approved. Our point of contact operative promised money and travel papers if GALT would smuggle two packages across the Canadian border into Detroit. We considered this a low-risk operation. If he failed he would be caught, discovered a fugitive, and returned to prison. Nothing could be traced back to us, as he knows little to nothing about the point of contact operative. The

actual package smuggled contained illegal pharma-
ceuticals. GALT successfully accomplished both smuggling tasks, though, showing a remarkable tenacity
under pressure.

Based on those successes, GALT was asked if he
wanted to perform additional smuggling trips from
Mexico back into the United States. He agreed, provided he was paid a sufficient amount of money. A
$5,000 figure was agreed upon and GALT left Mon-
treal, traveling to Alabama where he was given additional money to purchase a two-door, hard-top
white Mustang with Alabama license plates. Funds
were also paid to him for living expenses. He requested, and was provided, a revolver but was told
to keep it in the Mustang.

On October 19, GALT drove to Mexico, ending up in
Puerto Vallarta. He has occupied his time there
with various activities. He bought a camera and began photographing a local prostitute named MANUELA
MEDRANO with an eye to perhaps creating and sell-
ing pornographic pictures. We've allowed this diversion to continue as it keeps him occupied. He
has now developed a fondness for MANUELA, who is
being paid by our point of contact operative to be
with GALT. From her, we learned that his sexual relationships with women are shallow and fleeting.
He also likes to read spy novels, especially Ian
Fleming. He fancies himself a "man of action."

October 27, 1967
Federal Bureau of Investigation
Internal Security-C
For CIP Supervisor Only

An incident occurred last night at a local Puerto
Vallarta cantina known as Casa Susana. GALT and

MANUELA MEDRANO were present drinking and listening to music. A few tables over six Americans became rowdy. Two were white, four Negro. They'd apparently just come into town on one of the yachts in the harbor. One of the Negroes, under the influence of alcohol, stumbled into GALT as he walked past and grabbed MANUELA'S arm to break his fall. GALT took noticeable offense and shouted obscenities, including the repeated use of the word "nigger." GALT then approached the table with the remaining Americans and shouted more obscenities, most directed at the Negroes. None of the remaining five seemed to want to challenge him, so he sat back down with MANUELA.

Twenty minutes later one of the Negroes approached and tried to apologize. GALT exclaimed new insults, including further use of the word "nigger." Then GALT left the cantina, returning a few minutes later with the revolver from his Mustang, concealed inside his pant pocket. Shortly thereafter, the six Americans left the cantina. GALT started in pursuit, telling MANUELA that he intended to kill them. She managed to talk him out of doing that, telling him that the police would be making their rounds soon. His extreme paranoia about the police has not waned, so he backed down. All of this was reported by MANUELA. She also stated that GALT has proposed marriage to her several times, but she has rebuked those attempts. Two days ago he became so agitated with her refusals that he threatened to kill her. She ended her relationship with him and quit our employ. We recommend bringing GALT back to the United States, to a more controlled environment.

I was amazed at what I was reading.
If this was a forgery, it was damn convincing.

All had remained quiet a mile or so to the south of us. No sirens. No police. Nothing. The day was fading rapidly into an ever-dwindling twilight, the sun gone on the western horizon, making it increasingly difficult to read.

A car approached and I came alert.

But it was only a small pickup towing a boat, which the driver backed down the concrete ramp into the water.

Somebody was going night fishing.

Coleen reached for another page.

And we kept reading.

```
October 28, 1967
Federal Bureau of Investigation
Internal Security-C


    I concur with your recommendation. Bring GALT
back to the United States. I suggest Los Angeles
for a temporary location. Keep his confidence and
dependency high. You are authorized to expend what-
ever funds necessary to maintain his availability.
Future course is still uncertain, but could arise
with little to no advance warning. I recommend that
you continue to explore and encourage the asset's
natural biases and prejudices. It is vital that all
contact remain only through the point of contact
operative. Nothing should link back to you in any-
way. If anonymity is broken, both GALT and the point
of contact operative are to be immediately termi-
nated.
```

This one bore no signature.

It came from higher up *down* to Jansen below.

The newly honed investigatory part of my brain said this was all a scam, played out by Juan Lopez Valdez to get his hands on a coin worth millions of dollars. What had Reverend Foster said to the guy in the cemetery? *Valdez is apparently in financial trouble. That's why he wanted to deal for the coin with his files.* But the lawyer part of my brain was not convinced. And I could see that Coleen shared my doubts.

"These memos are for CIP eyes only," I said. "That has to mean Counter Intelligence Program. COINTELPRO."

I wondered if the CIP supervisor referred to in the memo headings was Oliver himself. The man had admitted he was in command back then.

We thumbed through more of the images, killing a little more time until darkness fully enveloped us. Then we'd find a way off this island.

One page caught our interest.

Longer than the others.

More detailed.

From Jansen.

```
March 16, 1968
Federal Bureau of Investigation
Internal Security-C
For CIP Supervisor Only


    GALT has been present in Los Angeles since Novem-
ber 19, 1967. He was told to stay in the city until
needed for further smuggling activities into Mex-
ico. Funds have been continuously provided, allow-
ing him to pursue more activities. During the past
four months he has attended bartending school, ex-
plored again the possibility of working in the por-
nography business, taken dance lessons, and enrolled
in a correspondence locksmithing course. Without
our knowledge he began seeing a local clinical psy-
chologist, DR. MARK O. FREEMAN. We covertly obtained
the doctor's file, which contained little to noth-
ing in the way of new information, then we maneu-
vered GALT into ending that relationship, playing
off his fears and paranoia of the police.
    GALT has also been active in the GEORGE WALLACE
presidential campaign, becoming a member of the
```

American Independent Party. He has been working the streets, going door-to-door for the Wallace-for-president effort. Over the past few weeks he has identified himself more and more with Wallace's racist ideals and has clearly revealed himself as an ardent segregationist. White rule and apartheid appeal to him. He has repeatedly talked of wanting to emigrate to Rhodesia and help fight for the white-rule cause. He is impressed and influenced by J. B. STONER and the National States' Rights Party. He now subscribes to the *Thunderbolt,* the party's newsletter, which openly calls for violence against minorities and the expulsion of all Negroes from the United States. He refers to MARTIN LUTHER KING JR. as Martin Luther Coon, mimicking the label STONER utilizes. His comments of late reflect a deep-set resentment at the attention many Negro leaders receive in the media.

One further note. GALT underwent plastic surgery to alter his nose, offering little explanation as to why. Disturbingly, he was dissatisfied with the initial results, so he removed the bandages and remodeled the nose himself before the cartilage set. He's also frequented a hypnotist, but nothing substantial occurred from that association.

"You do understand who they're talking about," Coleen said.

I got it. "James Earl Ray."

"He went by the name Eric S. Galt in Canada, Mexico, and back in the United States. What Ray said at his trial makes sense now."

I waited for her to explain.

"Thirty-six hours before his trial began, Ray pleaded guilty to murder and was sentenced to ninety-nine years in prison. Toward the end of the sentencing proceedings, he interrupted the judge and objected on the record. He said he freely pleaded guilty to murder, but did not agree with comments made by Attorney General Ramsey Clark and

J. Edgar Hoover. His words at the time were odd. He said, *I don't want to add something on that I haven't agreed to in the past.*"

I was confused, since the statement made little sense.

"After killing King," she said, "Ray went on the run from April 4 to June 8, 1968, prompting the largest manhunt in history. Yet he made it to Canada, to England, to Portugal, then back to England where he was finally caught. Clark and Hoover both proclaimed to the world that Ray acted alone. No conspiracy. Case closed. The prosecution relied heavily on those statements during Ray's sentencing hearing. But Ray said he did not agree with them. The judge pressed him on what he meant and he said, *I mean on the conspiracy thing.* Now I see why. There actually *was* a conspiracy." She paused. "A big one."

I watched the guy with the boat work a winch and drop the keel into the water. It was about a fifteen-footer. V-hulled. Open deck. High-sided. Good for the ocean. He tended to it with affection, tying the bow rope to a piling and easing his truck and trailer out of the way.

A lot was happening. Much more than I'd been told about yesterday by either Stephanie or Jansen. The idea had been to retreat here until dark, then make our way off the island.

Now I knew how.

CHAPTER TWENTY-FOUR

I ROSE FROM THE PICNIC TABLE AND WALKED OVER TO THE GUY with the boat, who was locking up his truck.

"Headed out for some fishing?" I asked.

"Looks like a good night for it."

The saltwater inlet between here and the next patch of land over, Palm Beach Shores, was about a hundred yards across, the water calm and still. A damp breeze was working in from the east that felt good, but had so far done little to tussle the surface. Out over the water two squawking seabirds fought in midair for a fish.

"I was wondering," I said. "How about I contribute twenty dollars to your gas and you give us a lift across to the other side?"

He gave me a cautionary look.

"It's not a problem," I said, adding a chuckle. "We're not on the run or anything. We just need a lift."

"That your girlfriend?" he asked.

Explaining would be far too complicated, so I lied. "She's mine, though sometimes she doesn't see it that way."

He grinned. "I've got one of those, too."

I fished out a still-damp twenty from my wallet and handed it over. Then I returned to Coleen and told her we had a ride. We gathered up the files and quickly stuffed them back into the waterproof case.

We climbed aboard the boat with the case and our driver revved the outboard, backing away from the ramp. Behind, in the park, headlights cut a swath through the growing darkness. I glanced back and saw a car come to a stop near the concrete ramp. But it wasn't towing any boat. The door opened and Jansen emerged.

"Malone," Coleen said.

I turned and followed her pointing finger toward the far shore, where another car had arrived.

Two men stood waiting.

Seems like I would have learned what being bait felt like, but once again we'd stepped right into their trap.

Then the driver leaped from the boat.

"Get down," I yelled to her, realizing what was coming.

The men on both sides of the channel drew their weapons and fired our way. We dove to the deck. Bullets ricocheted and tumbled past, leaving a whirring sound in their wake. I belly-crawled forward and seized the helm, whipping the wheel hard right, increasing the throttle, and heading toward open ocean that lay about five hundred yards to the east.

More shots came our way.

But none of the rounds found us.

The outboard was now fully revved, the bow planing as we skipped across the narrow inlet. We were far enough away now that the shooters were not a threat. A sloping jumble of boulders to our right extended a hundred-plus yards from the beach out into open ocean, the jetty blocking the currents into the inlet and providing a relatively safe harbor west of the park. A few fishermen were standing atop it. We motored past the jetty's end into open ocean.

"That was way too easy," she said.

And I agreed.

"They knew we were there," she said. "Why not just take us?"

The answer to that question appeared off our starboard bow. The boat from earlier, the one the two guys in the inflatable had returned to, had shifted position and was now much closer to the jetty. In the scant few rays of light left I saw the inflatable tied at its side and men climbing down into it.

"They made a deal," I said.

The idea had been to get us out here, with the coin and the files, leaving us to Valdez's men. Tom Oliver had apparently determined that was the quickest and easiest way to solve his problem. How the deal had been made so fast after Valdez's attack on Oliver's house was hard to say. But it clearly had. And we'd been maneuvered into stealing a boat and coming right to them.

The inflatable swung away from the larger vessel and headed our way.

"We need to get out of here," Coleen said.

I swung the wheel left and vectored north, paralleling the coast of Palm Beach Shores. High-rise apartments and condominiums lined the way, lights dotting the buildings up many stories. Beaching the boat and making a run for it seemed the smart play, but we'd never make it to shore before the inflatable overtook us.

At least I had Oliver's gun.

I glanced back.

The gap was closing between us and the inflatable.

A crack rang out.

Rifle fire from the inflatable.

"Stay down," I yelled to Coleen.

Another pop and the windscreen to my left shattered.

That was close.

And a lucky shot from a pitching boat to another pitching boat in near darkness.

Running no longer seemed the right move.

"Take the wheel," I told Coleen.

She grabbed hold.

"Slow the throttle," I said.

"For what?"

"Do it."

I'd tried maybe seventy-five court-martials. My job always was to represent my client and obtain the best result possible. Sometimes that was for the military. Sometimes that was for the accused. That was the thing about JAG. You worked both sides. When representing the accused, most of my colleagues took winning to mean "how much punishment can I avoid," since nearly every defendant was guilty of something. I never cared for that concession. I wanted an acquittal. A not guilty. An "I'm sorry, we made a mistake and should have never charged your client in the first place."

That's what I liked to hear.

So I learned to take a stand.

And stick with it.

I read once that nothing takes the place of persistence. Damn right. Not talent. I know a lot of lousy lawyers with talent. Not brilliance. Hell, unrewarded genius was almost the norm. Not education, since the world was full of smart derelicts.

Nope.

Persistence wins.

And like Einstein said, *You have to learn the rules of the game, then you have to play better than everyone else.*

So let's play.

Our boat slowed.

I found the coin in my pocket.

The inflatable closed the gap between us.

I stood at the stern and held the coin up high, out over the water, the outline of the square plastic sleeve clear and distinctive, even in the dim light.

"Lower the rifle," I hollered.

There was hesitation, so I made it clear, "You want me to drop it? You can shoot me, but I'm still going to drop it. Good luck finding it in this water, in the dark."

These were acolytes. Hired help. If Valdez himself had been here I'd probably have to rethink this ploy. But with these guys their number one job was to please the boss. So far today they hadn't had much success—they'd already lost the files. I could hear Valdez now. *Don't come back without my coin.*

And I was right.

The rifle lowered.

The inflatable kept closing, its motor now in idle.

Thirty yards away.

"Hit the throttle and go like crazy when I tell you to," I whispered to Coleen, keeping my lips still.

"Just say the word."

Twenty yards.

"I give you the coin and you go away," I yelled to the shadows in the inflatable.

"*Sí*, senor. You give the coin. We let you leave."

Right. They came all the way out here, after being tipped off by a group of retired feds, just to get the coin? Sure, that's what these guys wanted. But the people who'd supplied all of that intel wanted us dead, and the files we had either back in Cuba or at the bottom of the ocean. Otherwise they'd never make it out of American territorial waters.

I stood still, Oliver's gun held tight in my hand, masked by my right thigh. All attention was on the coin. I felt like a magician working an illusion with misdirection.

Ten yards.

"Come and get it," I said.

The inflatable hooked left, now leading with its long side, the idea to gently bump against our boat.

I braced myself and whispered to Coleen, "Now."

She gunned the throttle.

The outboard sprang to life from idle.

Water churned up from the props.

The guys in the inflatable were momentarily surprised and I used that instance to raise my gun and send four rounds into their craft, making sure to puncture holes in the bow, midsection, and stern. Those things were tough and versatile, but not invincible.

The men scattered with each round.

Our boat bolted away.

I watched as they tried to give chase, but they were having trouble staying high in the water.

No way to catch us now.

Eventually, the thing would flounder.

Sure, they had their main vessel.

But we'd be long gone in the dark before they could ever give chase.

CHAPTER
TWENTY-FIVE

WE CRUISED NORTHWARD FOR OVER AN HOUR. THE NIGHT loomed clear, warm, and cloudless with a great wash of stars. Thankfully, the boat came with full gas tanks. Maybe the idea had been to set it ablaze with our corpses and the files on board, the thought of which sent a chill down my spine.

I was navigating by dead reckoning, in the dark, and figured we were now at or near Jupiter Island. No sense going any farther, as I was unsure of the cruising range. So I turned west and passed through an inlet into the St. Lucie River, following its twisting path to what was labeled a municipal dock operated by the city of Stuart. The time was approaching 10:00 P.M. Day one as a special agent for the Justice Department was drawing to a close. There'd been ups and downs, but I was in one piece and still had the coin and the files, which had to count for something.

We left the boat and walked from the waterfront into town, which seemed a colorful collection of clapboard and shingled buildings. Only eateries were open. I carried the waterproof case, the coin safe in my jean pocket, the gun tucked at my spine beneath my shirt. A bar and grill, Rick's Oyster Dock, was doing a brisk business.

"Let's eat something," I said.

Coleen didn't argue.

We stepped inside and found a table that fronted one of the sides open to the night, overlooking the river.

"Order some food. I like oysters, fish, shrimp. Don't care. Just get lots of it and some sweet tea to drink."

"Where are you going?"

"I have to make a call."

And I took the case with me.

I doubted she was going anywhere without those files, so I was fairly certain she'd be there when I returned. On the walk over from the dock I'd noticed a pay phone outside the entrance to a motel next door to the restaurant. I used it to call Stephanie Nelle.

Collect.

She answered like she'd been waiting for me. I explained everything that had happened since a few hours ago, omitting only, for the moment, my exact location and the little I'd read in the files.

"I want you to stay put," she said. "I'm sending people to get you."

"No," I told her.

"Cotton, this is just like the military. I give the orders, you obey them."

"You have a problem," I said. "It apparently involves both former and current members of the FBI. I've managed to attract the attention of at least half your problem. Let's play this out and see where it leads."

I was truly embracing my new role as bait.

"I can take Oliver and Jansen into custody," she said. "Your testimony alone is enough to convict them of kidnapping and aggravated assault."

"And that's all you're going to get. What about your issues at the FBI and within Justice? And there's more going on here than you think."

"You want to explain that?"

"Not at the moment. You're just going to have to trust me that there is much more involved. I need some time to see where this leads."

"I want those files," she said.

And I was beginning to see why. "I'm going to ask you something and I want you to tell me the truth. I know I have no way of knowing if you're lying, but could you humor me and give it a shot?"

"Go ahead."

"Do you know what's in those files?"

"I really don't. But I've read an old FBI intelligence assessment that speculates about what might be there. Juan Lopez Valdez is a former asset of both the FBI and the CIA. He may even still do some work for the CIA. I don't know. Officially, he's attached to the Cuban secret police, but he's a man for hire, with no loyalties other than to himself. There are people here who want to know why, besides the coin, he chose to contact Foster. And those files could provide the answer."

"They do."

"You've read them?"

"Enough to know this is not going on *60 Minutes*. This gets its own one-hour, prime-time special report."

"Cotton, listen to me. You've been doing this for all of one day. You've done a great job. I really appreciate the effort. But let me handle this from here on."

"You've yet to say a word to me about *you* talking to Benjamin Foster."

Silence reigned for a few moments.

"It wasn't necessary for you to know that. But I had to judge the man for myself."

"He set me up to take the fall with Jansen and Oliver. He wanted them to take the files. He was able to do that, thanks to you."

More silence.

"You wanted me out here because you said you liked the fact that I didn't play well with others and I improvised. It's bad enough that you gave me half the story, which led me into a trap. So how about you let me do this my way now."

"And you're not going to tell me a thing?"

"Let me play this out. If it leads nowhere, I'll bail and turn it all over to you."

This was the beginning of a pattern that would mark our relationship for many years to come. Sure, it was flawed, but we came to accept that rarely did either of us tell the other everything. My working relationship with Stephanie Nelle ran smooth but never straight. It also delivered results because we both possessed an iron purpose, and we were good at what we did.

"What do you want me to do about Tom Oliver?" she asked. "My inclination is to arrest him."

"Leave him be. Give 'em a long leash."

"And if that leads straight to you?"

The prospect of that was not encouraging, but I knew the correct answer to her question. "I'll handle it."

She didn't like the situation, but finally agreed to my conditions.

"One day," she told me. "That's all I'll give you."

"Fair enough."

"Keep in touch."

I ended the call.

I stood for a moment and listened to the noise emerging from the restaurant where I'd left Coleen. The tinkle of laughter, the clink of glasses, the dozens of meshed conversations. Streetlamps pushed weak yellow light down over the black asphalt. I debated whether to make the next call, but decided it was the right thing to do.

I dialed my house.

Pam answered.

"I wanted to let you know I'm still okay," I said to her.

"You sound tired."

"It's been a long day."

"Where are you?"

Stephanie had instructed me that no one was to know my mission or my whereabouts. "You know I can't say."

"How convenient. Too bad you didn't have that excuse before."

I closed my eyes and bit my tongue. I'd become accustomed to her not-so-subtle reminders of my infidelity. "I assure you, I'm on the job and it hasn't been fun."

"And what you did before *was* fun?"

"That's not what I meant, and you know it. I called to tell you I'm okay and that I love you."

"Both are always nice to hear. When will you be home?"

Never did she return those three words. Not once since all that had happened had she uttered them to me. More of my punishment. "I don't know. But I'll try to keep in touch."

"Are you lying to me, Cotton? Again?"

Looking back, it was foolish to think that I could ever make amends. When you're barely thirty, cocksure of everything, you tend to think that all can be made right.

But it can't.

"I'm not lying to you, Pam. I'm working. Something important and hush-hush. You're going to have to understand."

"I understand, Cotton. I understand perfectly."

And a click signaled she was gone.

I hung up the phone.

That call had been a bad mistake.

I returned to the restaurant where Coleen had ordered a seafood feast. I laid the waterproof case on the booth's bench and slid in beside it, opposite her. Sure, I was here with a woman, but this was anything but sexual.

"Check-in with your parents? Let them know you won't make curfew?"

"I do have a boss. And she's not happy with all this."

She held up her cell phone. "I tried Nate. No signal. These things are worthless."

I chuckled. "Exactly why I don't own one."

We dug into the shrimp, fish, and oysters. I had a few hundred dollars and the credit card Stephanie had provided, on a Justice Department–secured account she'd told me. I shouldn't be hesitant to use it. No way anyone could track its use. Only her, she'd said. Which didn't provide me with any great measure of comfort.

"I've been thinking about what we read," Coleen said. "Those reports confirm the common knowledge of Ray's whereabouts before the assassination. He did go to Alabama, then Mexico, ending up in L.A. in the fall of 1967."

"Which may not be meaningful," I said. "The King assassination has been investigated to death by everybody and their brother. Those documents could have been tailored to the facts, not the other way around."

"There's something you don't know."

Those were five words no lawyer ever wanted to hear. They always spelled disaster with a capital *D*.

"My father told me some things a few weeks ago. Things he's never spoken of before. I suspect that my mother might have known bits and pieces, but she never said a word. That was her way. Sadly, she died years ago. I'd basically given up hope that my father would ever open up. But finally, just recently, he talked to me about Martin Luther King Jr."

I munched on a piece of fish and waited for her to explain.

"He told me about COINTELPRO and the FBI surveillance of King and everyone around him."

Which Foster had mentioned to me, too.

"He also told me that there were spies within the SCLC. Paid informants who ratted King out to the FBI."

I was curious. "How did he know that?"

"It was his job to find them."

CHAPTER
TWENTY-SIX

I KEPT EATING THE FISH WHILE ALSO DIGESTING WHAT SHE was telling me.

"I've read many books," she said, "on Hoover, the FBI, and King. It's something Nate and I have in common."

"And the fact your father was there made it even more interesting."

She smiled, as a proud daughter should. "It was a thrill to see his name in those books. He was even mentioned in declassified FBI reports. A lot of those are now public record. It's amazing how much Hoover hated King. He called him the burrhead." She shook her head. "The sad part is that King, in many ways, made it easy for Hoover. He had a weakness for women. My father told me all about it."

I listened as she explained how King had possessed a string of mistresses across the country, in town after town. The FBI first learned about it from a DC party that happened at the Willard Hotel, in January 1964. Nineteen reels of tape revealed how King liked to use raunchy language, that he smoked, drank, and told off-color jokes. More tapes from other hotels revealed more of the same, including the affairs themselves.

"Hoover believed that King's moral lapses could be used to discredit him," she said. "Not only in the eyes of his hardcore, black supporters, but whites, too. He wanted to release transcripts of the tapes, but LBJ said no. And even the great J. Edgar Hoover had to think twice before defying the president of the United States. But he did defy him. Instead of leaking the tapes, in December 1964 he had an anonymous package mailed to King's home that contained some of the worst sexual recordings along with a typewritten note."

That note would later come to light during all of the FBI abuse hearings. A shocking narrative that the FBI itself had to officially acknowledge had been sent.

King, look into your heart. You are a clergyman and you know it. You are a colossal fraud and an evil, vicious one at that. King, like all frauds your end is approaching. You could have been our greatest leader. But you are done. Your honorary degrees, your Nobel Prize (what a grim farce), and other awards will not save you. King, I repeat, you are done. The American public will know you for what you are, an evil, abnormal beast. King, there is only one thing left for you to do. You know what it is. There is but one way out for you. You better take it before your filthy, abnormal, fraudulent self is bared to the nation.

The package was opened by Coretta King, who was not happy about the revelations. The incident definitely placed a strain on the marriage. And was there a suggestion of suicide? Or was the *but one way* simply to have King step down from any leadership in the civil rights movement?

Historians continue to debate that point.

"The ploy had the opposite effect," she said. "Coretta King would not allow the FBI to intimidate her. Nor would she allow her husband to be silenced. No matter what he might have done to hurt her. My father was there. He told me what happened. Coretta displayed a remarkable patience. It's incredible to think that the FBI would do what it did, but it illustrates how much Hoover hated King."

I thought I would see if she knew what Foster had been unwilling to tell me. "Did your father ever mention a man named Jim Jansen?"

She shook her head. "That was the name on the memos we read."

"He's also the guy who tried to blow me up and shot at us when we left Fort Jefferson in that floatplane."

I could see the revelation surprised her.

"My father never mentioned the name. He told me, though, that people in the SCLC were concerned about King's infidelity. Its revelation would have hurt the movement. King tried to justify it by his travel schedule. The loneliness of being on the road. He told my father that he was away from home twenty-five days a month. Women were his form of anxiety reduction."

"It seems reckless," I said. "He knew the FBI was watching, particularly if your father was charged with finding their spies."

"Certainly by January 1965, after that package arrived at his house, King knew the FBI was watching. Only the FBI had the resources to gather those recordings. King hated Hoover for sending those, so he asked my father to look into things. He told me they found three spies. One was even the treasurer of the SCLC, which came as a shock."

I reached for one of the fried shrimp. "Was anything done about it?"

"He didn't tell me. I have no idea. I was hoping Valdez and what he had might answer those questions."

"You had no inkling that this involved the assassination when you made the deal."

"Not until I talked to Valdez. I was at my father's house when he first called. I listened in to my father's side of the conversation, without him knowing, and heard enough to realize there was a connection. I was able to get a detective I know to pull my father's phone records. Illegal as hell, but I could feel something was wrong. I found the Double Eagle in my father's bedroom, hidden in a jewelry box. Then I called Valdez back and made my own deal."

"What did he tell you?"

"Enough for me to go to the Dry Tortugas. He also warned me that the FBI could be a problem and not to trust any of them. He mentioned no names. He just told me to keep it all to myself and proceed with caution. He would explain more when we met."

Which had not happened. "What about what we read?"

"That's what's eating at me. My father told me that after the package of tapes came to King's house, things actually cooled off between King and the FBI. During '65 and '66 the FBI kept up its smear campaign, but they were much more subtle. No more in-your-face dirty tricks. Then in April 1967 King came out against the Vietnam War and everything boiled over again. King was also planning a huge Poor People's March on Washington, DC, for the summer of '69. Hoover was petrified of that happening. I read in several books how he wanted new wiretaps, but the attorney general turned him down."

I connected the dots. "The dates of the memos we read about Ray's recruitment started in July 1967."

She nodded. "The timing is right. We know now that during 1967 Hoover simply ignored the attorney general and wiretapped King on his own, with no authority. But what if he did even more beyond that?"

Indeed. What if?

"I know from Nate that the King family is convinced James Earl Ray didn't kill anybody. They think the FBI, or the CIA, or the military pulled the trigger."

Which was exactly what the *Jowers* jury in Memphis had ruled last year, finding that Ray fired the shot, but the government itself had been part of an active conspiracy to kill Martin Luther King Jr. Of course, that outcome had been predetermined and manipulated by the trial's participants. The pages we'd read earlier, though, were another matter. The FBI had clearly been on the lookout for someone special. *An asset.* And they found what they were looking for in Montreal, eventually sending him to Alabama, then to Mexico, and on to Los Angeles.

"You told me Ray was in L.A. at the end of 1967," I said.

She nodded. "Still posing as Eric S. Galt. I need to read the rest of the documents in those files. I know a lot about this. I can place them in a historical context for you."

"Not tonight," I said. "We're going to eat our dinner, then get some sleep. There's a motel next door that doesn't look busy. We should be able to get a couple of rooms."

"Then what?"

"We'll deal with this in the morning."

Two rooms were available and I paid for them with the government credit card. I had no choice. My cash was limited and I might need it on the road. If she hadn't before, Stephanie Nelle would now know exactly where I was located. I hoped she'd be true to her word and give me my one day, as promised.

In my room I undressed and took a shower, locking and barricading the room door. The waterproof case came with me into the bathroom, never leaving my sight.

But all remained quiet.

Coleen was a few doors down the hall.

The clock beside the bed read 11:40 P.M.

I lay on the bed in my boxers and stared at the container. The Double Eagle sat beside Oliver's gun on the nightstand. I was tired, but I was also curious. Many times I'd used my eidetic memory to recall word for word what a witness had said during a trial. It also allowed every detail of my prep file to stay right at the edge of my thoughts, available for use in an instant. I'd grown accustomed to an abundance of information.

Time to add some more.

I opened the container.

And read.

There were more memos between Jansen and his boss, then replies, all geared toward the pre–April 4, 1968, activities of Eric S. Galt. There were details of a March 29 trip to Birmingham where Galt bought a Remington .243-caliber rifle with a scope, along with ammunition, signing the sales slip Harvey Lowmeyer. He paid the $248.59 bill in cash. In those days nothing was required to buy a weapon, not even identification. The so-called point of contact operative had been in Birmingham and examined the rifle, determining that it was not powerful enough. So Galt returned to the store the next day and exchanged it for a Gamemaster .30-06 with a scope. One of the memos noted that the scope allowed for 7x magnification of the target and provided a wide field of view. A magnesium fluoride coating enabled shots to be taken in low light, even in the late dusk. The second rifle was more expensive and Galt paid the difference in cash.

I counted the photographic images in the files.

245.

And as fascinating and eye opening as most of the pages were, there were a few that genuinely shocked me.

CHAPTER
TWENTY-SEVEN

July 28, 1967
Federal Bureau of Investigation
Internal Security-C
For CIP Supervisor Only

A confidential source who has furnished reliable information in the past reports a private conversation with MARTIN LUTHER KING JR. The topic was the ongoing racial riots in Detroit. At present the toll from that riot is 43 dead, 1,189 injured, over 7,200 arrests, and more than 2,000 buildings destroyed. KING blamed the situation on Congress, who has consistently refused to vote a halt to, as he described, "the destruction of the lives of Negroes in the ghetto." He equated the ongoing violence in terms of race saying that "white affluence amid black poverty will never lead to racial harmony." He pointed out that Negroes know that a society able to plan intercontinental war and interplanetary travel is able to plan a place for them. For Congress and white society in general to do little or nothing is as inflammatory as inciting a riot, so the current state of violence should not be any surprise.

August 11, 1967
Federal Bureau of Investigation
Internal Security-C
For CIP Supervisor Only

A confidential source who has furnished reliable information in the past reports a private conversation that occurred at the Fairmont Hotel, San Francisco, California, between MARTIN LUTHER KING, JR. and RALPH ABERNATHY.

KING discussed the American Negro's present situation and stated that there has never been any real commitment by white people concerning "black equality." He emphasized that racial injustice is the "black man's burden and the white man's shame." Riots are the natural result of intolerable conditions. Another cause of riots, in KING'S opinion, is Congress, which he considers hypercritical and insensitive. He blames legislatures across the country (and especially Congress) for failing to pass fair housing bills; labor unions for keeping Negroes out of unions; and the white clergy for remaining silent. He warned they should all be careful as "a destructive minority can destroy the majority."

He also spoke about President JOHNSON, who he says is more interested in winning the war in Vietnam than winning the war on poverty. He stated that Congress is more concerned with rats than Negroes since it at least proposed a bill (which failed to pass) that would have provided aid to inner-city rat infestations, while doing absolutely nothing about fair housing for Negroes.

August 14, 1967
Federal Bureau of Investigation
Internal Security-C
For CIP Supervisor Only

A confidential source who has furnished reliable information in the past reports that MARTIN LUTHER KING JR. has been suffering for the past few weeks from a growing mental depression. The July racial riots in Detroit and Newark weigh heavy on his mind. His diminished mental state has been aggravated by physical exhaustion, the result of nearly constant traveling over the past decade.

KING was not comforted by the fact, as was pointed out to him, that the vast majority of blacks in Detroit and Newark did not participate in the rioting, perhaps demonstrating the effectiveness of his policy on nonviolence. The source reported that KING has stayed quiet and subdued since July, speaking more about the Vietnam War than usual. The source stated that the war, to KING, was now more serious than anything else in the world. He deplores the war for wasting national resources and unnecessarily destroying lives and society. In his opinion the conflict has isolated the United States morally and politically and scarred the image of the nation. Even worse, it has directed attention away from civil rights. KING stated emphatically that attention must be drawn back to civil rights.

The source reported that KING remains concerned about the FBI and Hoover. He knows they are still watching him but hopes that things stay relatively civil. He feels that his relationship with the president, though troubled, is enough to ensure that Hoover will be kept under control. Attorney General RAMSEY CLARK is regarded by KING as both a

personal friend and a friend to the entire civil
rights movement.

August 25, 1967
Federal Bureau of Investigation
Internal Security-C
TO ALL FIELD OFFICES ONLY

The purpose of this new counter-intelligence
endeavor program (COINTELPRO) directed at black
nationalist-hate groups is to expose, disrupt, misdirect, discredit, or otherwise neutralize the activities of black nationalist hate-type organizations
and groupings, their leadership, spokesmen, membership, and supporters, and to counter their propen-
sity for violence and civil disorder.

The activities of all such groups of intelligence
interest to the Bureau must be followed on a continuous basis so we will be in a position to promptly
take advantage of all opportunities for counterintelligence and inspire action in instances where
circumstances warrant. The pernicious background
of such groups, their duplicity, and devious maneu-
vers must be exposed to public scrutiny where such
publicity will have a neutralizing effect. Efforts
of the various groups to consolidate their forces
or to recruit new or youthful adherents must be
frustrated.

NO OPPORTUNITY SHOULD BE MISSED TO EXPLOIT THROUGH
COUNTER-INTELLIGENCE TECHNIQUES THE ORGANIZATIONAL
AND PERSONAL CONFLICTS OF THE LEADERSHIPS OF THE
GROUPS AND WHERE POSSIBLE AN EFFORT SHOULD BE MADE
TO CAPITALIZE UPON EXISTING CONFLICTS BETWEEN COM-
PETING BLACK NATIONALIST ORGANIZATIONS.

When an opportunity is apparent to disrupt or
NEUTRALIZE black nationalist, hate-type organ-

izations through the cooperation of established local news media contacts or through such contact
with sources available to the Director's Office, in
every instance careful attention must be given to
the proposal to insure the targeted group is dis-
rupted, ridiculed, or discredited through the publicity and not merely publicized.

You are also cautioned that the nature of this
new endeavor is such that UNDER NO CIRCUMSTANCES
SHOULD THE EXISTENCE OF THE PROGRAM BE MADE KNOWN
OUTSIDE THE BUREAU and appropriate within-office
security should be afforded to sensitive operations
and techniques considered under the program. No
counterintelligence action under this program may
be initiated by the field without specific prior
Bureau authorization.

March 4, 1968
Federal Bureau of Investigation
Internal Security-C
TO ALL FIELD OFFICES ONLY

For maximum effectiveness of COINTELPRO, and to
prevent wasted effort, long-range goals are being
set:

1. Prevent the coalition of militant black nationalist groups. In unity there is strength, a truism
that is no less valid for all its triteness. An ef-
fective coalition of black nationalist groups might
be the first step toward a real "Mau Mau" [Black
revolutionary army] in America, the beginning of a
true black revolution;

2. Prevent the rise of a "messiah" who could unify
and electrify the militant black nationalist

movement. MALCOLM X might have been such a "messiah;" he is the martyr of the movement today. MARTIN LUTHER KING, JR., STOKELY CARMICHAEL and ELIJAH MUHAMMED all aspire to this position. ELIJAH MUHAMMED is less of a threat because of his age. KING could be a very real contender for this position should he abandon his supposed "obedience" to "white, liberal doctrines" (non-violence) and embrace black nationalism. CARMICHAEL has the necessary charisma to be a real threat in this way;

3. Prevent violence on the part of black nationalist groups. This is of primary importance, and is, of course, a goal of our investigative activity. It should also be a goal of the COINTELPRO to pinpoint potential troublemakers and neutralize them before they exercise their potential for violence;

4. Prevent militant black nationalist groups and leaders from gaining respectability, by discrediting them to three separate segments of the community. The goal of discrediting black nationalists must be handled tactically in three ways. You must discredit those groups and individuals to, first, the responsible Negro community. Second, they must be discredited to the white community, both the responsible community and to "liberals" who have vestiges of sympathy for militant black nationalists simply because they are Negroes. Third, these groups must be discredited in the eyes of Negro radicals, the followers of the movement. This last area requires entirely different tactics from the first two. Publicity about violent tendencies and radical statements merely enhances black nationalists to the last group. It adds "respectability" in a different way.

5. A final goal should be to prevent the long-range growth of militant black organizations, especially among youth. Specific tactics to prevent these groups from converting young people must be developed.

The primary targets of COINTELPRO should be the most violent and radical groups and their leaders. We should emphasize those leaders and organizations that are nationwide in scope and are most capable of disrupting this country. These groups include:

Student Nonviolent Coordinating Committee (SNCC)
Revolutionary Action Movement (RAM)
Nation of Islam (NOI)
Southern Christian Leadership Conference (SCLC)

The specific leaders to be targeted include:

STOKELY CARMICHAEL OF SNCC
H. RAP BROWN OF SNCC
ELIJAH MUHAMMED OF NOI
MARTIN LUTHER KING JR. OF SCLC

CHAPTER
TWENTY-EIGHT

Morning brought clear air and birds bickering outside the window. Daylight streamed into the hotel room, the sky clear and blue, the events of yesterday still fresh in my mind.

After reading everything from the waterproof case, I'd lain in bed for a couple of hours fighting a fool's sleep. Twice I found myself wide awake, nowhere near the murky borderlands of dreams. But eventually I managed a few hours of fitful rest.

I rose from the bed a little before 8:00 A.M. and flexed my shoulders to relieve the early stiffness. In the bathroom I doused cold water against the sleepy numbness on my face. A shave would be great, but I had no razor or shaving cream. A toothbrush and toothpaste would be even more welcome. I called housekeeping and asked for all four, which were delivered a few minutes later. I dressed and was ready for something to eat when a hard knock sounded on the door.

"Malone. Open up."

Coleen.

I did.

She burst in. "We have company."

We both bolted to the window, which overlooked from the second floor the back side of the building facing the river and the dock where we'd left the boat last night. A warm, rosy flush of sunrise lit the ground.

Cruising out in the river was a familiar inflatable. Probably the same one from last night, only now patched.

Three guys were inside.

One face I knew.

"The man in front is Valdez."

Who did not looked pleased.

"He has no fear coming ashore," I noted. "That means Oliver and friends are looking out for him."

"How in the world did he find us?"

She had a point. There were too many places where we could have beached the boat for these guys to come straight here to lovely Stuart, Florida, the Sailfish Capital of the World, as the sign at the dock proclaimed.

Only one explanation made sense.

A leak on Stephanie Nelle's end that made its way to Tom Oliver.

The inflatable eased close to one of the docks.

The three men hopped ashore.

I gathered up the case and the gun. The Double Eagle was tucked safe in my pant pocket. Strange how carrying around a multimillion-dollar coin was becoming an everyday thing. I almost regretted not taking Stephanie up on her offer of help.

We fled the room and found the stairwell, descending to ground level, and exiting into a humid morning. We were standing in a small parking lot on the far side of the building.

I had an idea.

"Our boat is the only way out of here," I told her. "We need to get around this building and make it there while they're looking for us."

We headed for the street, avoiding the side of the hotel that faced the water. I'm not sure what Valdez planned to do, but I had to assume that it wasn't going to be good. My guess was that whoever sold us out to Tom Oliver had also learned our specific room numbers. Once again, the decision had apparently been made to let Valdez clean up the mess. Thank goodness Coleen had been vigilant—a trait I should learn to mimic.

We came to the main entrance and were careful when we passed, but the windows and glass doors did not open directly into the lobby, which offered us some protection. We hustled past and headed for the docks, crossing the street, which was light on traffic. I kept glancing back over my shoulder to see if Valdez had noticed our escape.

So far, so good.

Few people were out this early.

We approached the dock entrance.

A car roared in behind us and squealed to a stop. I looked back to see a man emerge from the driver's side. He rushed forward and tackled me from behind. We both slammed into the pavement and I lost my grip on the waterproof case, which clattered away. He had me in a bear hug, squeezing tight, and he was strong for a retired guy. We rolled a few times and I could feel the gun nestled at my waist as it pressed to the pavement. I freed my right arm and elbowed the bastard in his ribs, then a little lower to the kidneys. His grip weakened enough for me to break his hold. I knifed my other elbow into his gut, then rolled off him and pounded my right fist into his jaw. I had no time to linger, so I sprang to my feet but stumbled in my haste, rolling over, scraping my hands and knees.

I looked for the case.

It was gone.

My gaze searched the concrete.

Nothing.

Then I focused out to the dock.

Coleen was in our boat, drifting away, the outboard revving.

She spun the wheel and powered off.

No question where the case had gone.

A voice came from behind me.

"Cotton."

I turned back.

Stephanie had stepped from the car. "Let me handle this."

I was beyond pissed. "No way."

I bolted onto the dock and leaped into the inflatable that had just arrived. It too came with an outboard—not near as much horsepower as the other boat, but enough.

I yanked the cord and fired up the motor.

The man on the dock was starting to stand, still dazed.

I pointed at Stephanie and yelled, "You lied. I still have a day."

She stared back but said nothing.

There were a few other boaters around, all looking on in astonishment at the mayhem. Valdez and his men were nowhere to be seen. I angled the inflatable away from its mooring and headed off in Coleen's direction. A quick look back and I saw the guy on the dock reaching for a weapon. I freed my own gun and fired a round his way, scattering both him and Stephanie.

Which bought me a few seconds of confusion.

More than enough to motor away.

CHAPTER TWENTY-NINE

NOW I HAD A REAL PROBLEM.

The files were gone.

And Coleen's boat had disappeared around a bend in the river ahead, past where two tall bridges littered with cars spanned north to south. I glided beneath them and managed to just catch sight of her wake, headed north, farther up the St. Lucie River. Thank God I caught a peek as I could have easily headed south down the river in the wrong direction.

I angled the steering column and twisted the outboard's throttle to full power. The bow lifted from the water and I sped ahead. Houses, apartments, and condos lined both banks. More houses and a golf course could be seen ahead. I was worried about streets running close to the water's edge, places where Stephanie or Valdez could catch up to us by car.

Coleen had seized the first opportunity she'd found to grab the files and go, leaving me to fend for myself. I suppose I shouldn't have been surprised. I was a total stranger to her. And besides, I'd been a thorn in her side since the moment we met. What was it about partners in work or life? I had a hard time keeping either.

The river widened.

Maybe half a mile across now between the banks. We were headed due north to God knew where. I kept glancing back but saw no one in pursuit.

Stephanie had apparently tracked my use of the credit card, deciding that giving me a little rope was not a good idea. So she beat a trail straight to Stuart, Florida. Who could blame her? A rookie in the field had gone rogue. No reason at all for her to trust me. She knew little to nothing of my capabilities. Still, a deal was a deal. Not to mention that she might have serious security leak within her ranks. The smart play was for me to continue forward. Explanations could come later.

But shooting at my new boss?

That might be a problem.

I sympathized with Coleen's agitation. Her father was someone she surely admired. Once he'd been a warrior in a great struggle, close to Martin Luther King Jr. himself. But his insistence that the past be forgotten was frustrating. I was frustrated by his deliberately leading me into a trap. I could partially understand his duplicity toward me. But to her? Why would he not want to tell his own daughter how he helped change history? And there was one other curiosity. Based on what I'd read last night, I could not understand why he'd want those files burned. On the contrary, it would seem he'd want every word to see the light of day. They revealed truths that the public should know. Nothing was incriminating toward Foster. So far I'd shared nothing with Coleen, thinking I was honoring not only her father's wish but Stephanie's, too. But for the life of me I could not fathom why.

The river began to narrow.

Houses remained on the east side, but marsh appeared to the west, with only a few residences scattered at its far edges toward higher ground. The river's wide-open expanse was gone, the width here more like a canal, the banks tight. Coleen still had a solid half-mile lead, but I had her in my sights. This wasn't so much a chase. More a following. At some point she'd run out of either water or gas.

She veered left.

Now heading due west.

I kept pace, entering some sort of human-made canal. I knew that south Florida was littered with them. A way to divert fresh water inland where it was needed for agriculture and helped with coastal flooding. We passed under a pair of bridges for a highway. Had to be the Florida turnpike. Then, a couple of miles later, another pair of viaducts streaked with speeding cars. Interstate 95. We were heading inland. Subdivisions of single-family homes gave way to flat farmland, stretching as far as the eye could see. Here the canal fed off into a multitude of non-navigable irrigation channels. This was a path to nowhere, and I saw that Coleen realized that, too. She stopped, then leaped from the boat to shore, the waterproof case in hand. I motored up, killed the engine, and jumped onto the low grassy bank. She was waiting for me, her forehead twisted into a scowl and bathed in a light sheen of sweat. She sat on the ground, knees to her chest, rubbing her arms as if she were cold.

"Dammit, Malone. I have as much right to read this stuff as you do. More so, maybe."

We were alone. Nothing but cleared land in every direction, the grass beneath us close-clipped and damp with dew.

"Can't you just go away," she asked me. "Can't you just let me take these files and leave? This isn't your fight. It doesn't concern you."

I heard the anger and frustration and stayed quiet, letting her vent.

"You don't get it," she spit out. "I admire my father more than any man alive. He's been there for me every day of my life. He taught me about right and wrong, good and evil. He showed me how to live. But the one thing he's never spoken about was that day in Memphis. Never. Not once."

I knew the rest. "Until recently."

She nodded.

"And I could tell that he was holding back. He dodged my questions and avoided answers. He finally got angry and went silent. So when Valdez called and wanted to make a deal, one he'd refused, I decided that was my chance. I went behind him and set up the meeting in the Dry Tortugas."

"Why there?"

"Valdez made the choice, and I wasn't in a position to argue."

"There's more happening here than just you and your father," I pointed out. "There's some kind of current corruption going on inside the FBI. What's happening to us is bringing that to light. That's why I'm here."

"I don't give a damn about the FBI. They can all go to hell. I want to know what happened to Martin Luther King Jr. and what my father has to do with it."

I suddenly realized something. "You can't discuss this with your husband, can you?"

"To a point. For Nate this is about changing history. Like me, he came along long after King was dead. We grew up in a different world. It's not perfect by any means, but it's not the 1960s, either. Nate's a good man. Don't get me wrong. He loves me. But he's a fourth-year associate in a law firm with a long way to go before he's a partner. He's got a black woman for a wife, which shouldn't matter. But we all know it still does. He volunteered to work with the King family in the Memphis civil trial. My dad made that happen. He's still close with the family. But Nate was more errand boy than lawyer. He thinks my father knows things, and he wants to be the one to discover them. He wants to change history. Make a name for himself. But this isn't about him. It's about me and my father. So no, I can't discuss this with him."

"So I got nominated?"

She looked up and for the first time smiled. "Something like that. You seem to be my only choice."

Exactly what her father had said to me.

"I never thought all this would happen," she said. "I had no idea. I was going to trade the coin for the files and pick Valdez's brain. Simple as that. But after I found that coin in his drawer, I did some research and learned all about it."

"I imagine that was a shocker."

"To say the least. Which created even more questions I knew my father wasn't going to answer."

"So you opted to give Valdez a try?"

"It seemed like my only play."

I walked closer and crouched down before her. Her anger seemed to have passed. She appeared more defeated now.

"Have you heard from Nate?"

She shook her head. "He hasn't called, which is troublesome."

"I read every page of the files last night," I told her.

Her eyes burned into mine. I knew what she wanted to hear.

"It does change history. If it's real."

"I want to read it all, too."

I would eventually come to learn that there were moments in every intelligence operation when only one course was available. Blind risk. A point when you had to place your trust in something that would otherwise be senseless and hope for the best. In later years I both lived for and feared those moments. But right now I needed an ally, not an enemy. And Lincoln was right. *Do I not destroy my enemy when I make them my friend?*

"Okay," I said. "You can read it all. But we still have to establish that what's inside this case is real, and not something Valdez manufactured."

"How do we do that?"

"I have an idea. But I need your help to make it happen."

CHAPTER THIRTY

I LISTENED AS COLEEN USED NATE'S CELL PHONE TO CALL Orlando and the Orange County Sheriff's Department. Back in the cemetery at Port Mayaca, when the guy Foster had taken me there to meet drove off, I memorized his Florida license plate. I didn't know at the time whether the information would be important, but I realized last night that it was now vital.

That guy knew things.

And he was former FBI.

What I needed was a name and address, and now I knew that I couldn't contact Stephanie Nelle for help. But a sheriff's deputy? All she had to do was ask one of her friends to run the tag. Cops did it all the time, as did military police. Thankfully, the phone had a signal out here in the middle of farm country, albeit a weak one as the conversation appeared to be cutting in and out with a lot of *can you hear me*'s.

She ended the call.

"The car belongs to a Bruce Lael. He lives in Melbourne. You gonna tell me who he is?"

"Your father brought him to Port Mayaca."

And I told her what happened.

"He wanted Lael to lead Jansen straight to us."

She seemed astonished. "For what?"

"My guess is, when you opened this can of worms, he saw it as the only way to close it. So he calls Lael, who calls Oliver. Then he sends me to get food, with everything in the car. He didn't want any harm to come to you, and he doesn't want you reading what's in that case, so he sent me out to be caught."

She glanced at the container as if it were a holy relic. "What the hell is in there?"

"Enough to raise some serious questions about who really killed King and why."

She sat silent on the damp grass and I allowed her a moment with her thoughts. The sun was rising, becoming hotter by the second.

"Melbourne is about two hours north of here," I said. "When we passed under I-95 a mile or so back I saw there was an exit just beyond the canal. I say we head there and see if we can bum a ride north."

"We could wait for Nate to call. I'm a little surprised he hasn't by now."

I shook my head. "We have to do this without your father. He won't want us to find this Bruce Lael. No way."

"You still haven't explained why not."

Because I didn't know. None of it made sense. But hell, I'd only been an investigator for all of one day.

"How long have you been a cop?" I asked her.

"Four years."

"You like it?"

"I like what I represent. A little color in blue is good for everyone."

I smiled. "So you're a trailblazer. Like your father was long ago."

She stood and brushed the moisture from her clothes. "I'm a good cop."

And for the first time I heard the pride of a daughter trying to earn the respect of her father.

We walked back to the boats.

I carried the waterproof case. She seemed resigned to our uneasy truce. We left the inflatable and took the other boat back to the I-95 overpass. From there we walked through a neighborhood of boxy, single-family homes to a busy street, with exits on and off the interstate, that accommodated gas stations and a truck stop. It took only half an hour to find one of the long haulers willing to take us north to Melbourne. The rig's main cab came with a sleeper compartment. I sat up front and chatted with the driver while Coleen occupied the sleeper, flicking through the files, reading every page. Every once in a while I glanced back and caught the surprise on her face.

Which I could understand.

It took just under two hours to make it to the Melbourne exit, where we thanked the trucker. I offered some money, but he refused. At a gas station I found a pay phone and learned the number of a Melbourne cab service. A car arrived a few minutes later and took us east, toward the coast, and the address we had for Bruce Lael.

Twelve years as a Magellan Billet agent would eventually teach me that people nearly always left trails. It's human nature. Paper ones. Pictures. Bread crumbs. Doesn't matter. There's something. But I felt reasonably safe that no one could have possibly tracked us to this point. We'd made it away from Stuart with no one on our tail and I had laid down not a single speck that anyone could follow. Once we found Lael's house, though, that could all change. It was entirely possible Oliver had the guy under surveillance. Of course, once Lael had served his purpose and led Oliver to Lake Okeechobee, they may have abandoned him. But then again, maybe not. So I had the taxi driver drop us off about a mile from the address, learning from him directions the rest of the way.

I paid the driver and we walked down the quiet street, the air filled with the sweet, sticky smell of freshly mowed grass. The houses were small, single-story, concrete-block rectangles, most with tile roofs and painted either white, pale blue, or yellow. Lots of tall trees signaled that the neighborhood had been here awhile. An enormous brown-and-white dog bounded across one of the front yards, charging with a canine friendliness, a light in its eyes, paws upraised, tail flailing like a whip. Coleen showed the animal a little attention, but it quickly lost interest and padded away.

The address we sought was at the end of a long street, another ordinary sort of place, one of the white-painted houses. The same dark-blue, late-model Taurus with tinted windows and the correct Brevard County tag sat parked on the street, the short driveway filled with a flat-bottomed bass boat on a trailer.

We walked to the front door and I knocked. It was answered a few moments later by the same man from the cemetery.

He appraised me with a careful gaze.

But his words sent a chill down my spine.

"What took you so long?"

CHAPTER THIRTY-ONE

BRUCE LAEL SEEMED LIKE A MAN WHO STILL BREATHED THE PAST. He wore a pair of dirty cargo shorts, a loud Hawaiian shirt, and tattered flip-flops. His house cast a measure in simplicity, everything neat and orderly. The living room reminded me of the one at my grandfather's house back in Georgia, complete with an upholstered sofa, high-backed chairs, flat beige walls, and a brick fireplace. The cool rush from an overhead AC vent was particularly welcome.

"Were you expecting us?" I asked.

The warm grin slipped from his face. "You're with the Justice Department. I figured you'd eventually run me down and come for a chat."

"You didn't seem real happy back in Port Mayaca?"

"I did what Foster wanted."

"Leading Jim Jansen straight to me?"

The guy nodded. "I thought it was nuts, too. But that's what he wanted."

"You do everything he wants?"

I could see he did not appreciate my sarcasm.

"I don't want those files going anywhere near Washington, either. I saw the wisdom in involving Oliver. He'd take care of things." He paused. "And I don't give a crap about you."

I noticed he hadn't offered us a seat or anything to drink, which meant this was going to be a short conversation. So I came to the point. "What is it you and Foster know about the King assassination?"

"Aren't you the impatient one. No romance? No dinner beforehand? No foreplay? Just get right to it. Wham, bam, thank you ma'am. You're awful young. How long you been on the job?"

"It's his second day," Coleen pointed out.

Lael looked me over with a grin. "So we got ourselves a genuine rookie."

I did not like the label.

"Tell me, rookie, why would I say anything to you?"

"I don't know. Maybe because you've got a conscience? Unlike Tom Oliver and his group of Merry Men."

"Now, on that we see eye-to-eye. Oliver was a Hoover man, through and through. His whole career was geared to making that creepy bastard happy. We had six thousand FBI agents back then, every one of us expected to cater to Hoover's whims, obey his rules, and satisfy his every need."

"That include you?" I asked.

"If you wanted a long career, that was part of the job description."

"You worked for Oliver?"

"Oh, yeah. In COINTELPRO. I was one of the bagmen."

Which meant he handled break-ins, most of which were done without search warrants. Congress later determined that the FBI routinely engaged in thousands of illegal burglaries as a way not only to obtain information, but also to plant listening devices.

"Our motto was *Do unto others as they are doing unto you.* And believe me, we did. I was assigned to the Bishop himself."

I recalled the code name Foster had mentioned for Martin Luther King Jr. "Did you break into King's house?"

He nodded. "I planted microphones everywhere. In the SCLC offices, King's home, his office, and too many hotel rooms to count. I was good at it."

It was one thing to read about all of those constitutional abuses. But here was a living, breathing participant.

"Did you testify before the Church Committee?"

Lael shook his head. "A bunch of pansies. I may have hated Oliver and Hoover, but I was still FBI through and through. I actually believed what we were taught. To lead a careful and disciplined life. Easy on the alcohol, no drugs ever, and keep your pants zipped as much as possible. Stupid me just thought we ought to obey the law, too."

"Yet you didn't," Coleen said, finally joining the conversation.

"No, little lady, we didn't. But we were the exception. The vast, vast majority of FBI agents did their job, and did it right."

"So what is it you and Foster think about all the time?" I asked, bringing him back to what I'd heard in the cemetery.

"You're the preacher's daughter?" Lael asked Coleen.

"How do you know my father?"

"We met about ten years ago, and we've stayed in touch."

"Are you looking for forgiveness?" I asked.

He tossed me a measured glare. But his answer surprised me.

"Something like that."

"Did you get it?"

"That's none of your business." He faced Coleen. "Does your father know you're here?"

"No," she blurted out before I could lie.

"I didn't think so."

All of this posturing was grating on my nerves.

"COINTELPRO targeted King. That's old news," I said. "There are books filled with unclassified FBI field reports on what you did. Okay, he had mistresses, he liked to smoke and drink. He told dirty jokes. Who gives a crap? I want to know what's really going on here."

"And if I don't say, what then?"

I could tell he was challenging me, trying to determine if I was more than a paper tiger. So I decided to roar. "The next person who comes to see you will have a subpoena to appear before a grand jury. The questions then will be asked under oath. Sure, you can take the Fifth and refuse to say anything, but what do you think is going to happen then?"

I caught the nervous snicker in his breath. My threat had rubbed a sore, which brought a change in mood.

For the worse.

"My answers won't be the Fifth Amendment," he said. "They'll be more direct. Two words that should sum it all up and will let you know exactly what I think of your grand jury. This stuff has lain dead for thirty years, and dead is where it should stay."

"Along with King?" I asked.

He took in my rebuke in silence.

Finally he said, "Who are you to judge?"

"I'm the guy with the badge, asking the questions."

If that had any effect, Lael didn't show it.

"Does either of you have any idea what it was like back then?"

Neither of us answered him.

"I was there, in June '64," Lael said. "I was sent to St. Augustine when all the trouble exploded." He pointed at Coleen. "That's where I first saw your daddy."

"And what did you do to stop all of the violence against good, decent people like my father?" she asked.

"Not a thing. Wasn't my problem. I was there to watch King, and watch I did. I saw the acid being poured in the pool."

That I knew about.

King was arrested in St. Augustine for trespassing at the Monson Motor Lodge. His response came in the form of a "swim-in," where a group of protesters, black and white, jumped into the motel's "white-only" pool. The manager tried to break the protest by pouring muriatic acid into the water, hoping the swimmers would leave. And though the chemical was really no threat—one of the swimmers proved that by drinking some of the water—the image of that white manager pouring acid into a pool full of blacks and whites appeared in newspapers around the world.

Shocking people.

"What did you do when that happened?" I said, mocking him. "Like a good little COINTELPRO agent, you snapped pictures, took notes, and filed reports."

"We were like *Star Trek*," he said, "and the prime directive. There to observe, but never to interfere or alter the course of events."

I shook my head. "You were the damn FBI, and yet you sat back and allowed white supremacists to do whatever they wanted. And that's because J. Edgar Hoover hated Martin Luther King Jr."

"That's pretty much it, in a nutshell," he said. "Different time and place."

My eyes noticed a notepad on the enameled kitchen table. Lying in plain sight. A name written upon it in black ink. Cecelia Heath. Along with what appeared to be a phone number. Odd that a careful man like Bruce Lael would leave that out for us to see. He noticed my interest, but made no effort to collect the pad. Instead he gave a gentle nod. Toward it.

"Did you know Foster searched inside the SCLC for FBI informants?" I asked, not acknowledging the gesture.

He seemed surprised by the question. "Foster tell you that?"

"He told me," Coleen said.

Lael nodded. "Sure, I knew. I bugged his house and taped him many times. We watched a lot of people back then, particularly antiwar protestors, which included King and Foster. We spied on them all."

I needed to steer this man back to what we came for. "Did you know that Juan Lopez Valdez recruited King's killer?"

"And the FBI assisted," Coleen added.

"Really? Sounds like something from the *National Enquirer.*"

"That's not an answer," I said.

He tossed me a glare. "It's news to me. But everything back then was compartmentalized. We were told only what we needed to know to do our job. Jansen and Oliver would not have included me in that loop. I knew a little more than most because I handled the wiretaps. But not all of them. There were other people, besides me, who manned the recorders."

He still had not admitted a thing. "So if you don't know anything, why are you so troubled?"

"Like I said, I knew the reverend from the wiretaps. I reconnected with him years ago to talk about those. We each filled in some of the blanks for the other. Call it curiosity."

"Valdez was working for the FBI," Coleen said. "Surely you taped him at some point."

Lael nodded. "A few times. That's one slimy bastard."

"Did Valdez arrange for James Earl Ray to be in Memphis?" I asked again.

He stood there, arms crossed on his chest like an umpire under attack.

But I caught a look of unfeigned indecision on his chopped countenance. Like he was wrestling with a dilemma. Sizing us up. Making a decision. His eyes drifted again down to the pad on the table, then back up.

"I told your daddy yesterday to leave this alone," he said. "You two should take the same advice."

"Why didn't you just tell him no when he contacted you?" I asked. "Why lead Oliver to him?"

"You're going to have ask him that."

"We're asking you."

"I don't know who the hell you think you are," Lael spit out. "I was an FBI agent before you were even born. You apparently have little to no experience, barging in here, thinking I'm going to break down and confess all my sins. Or that the threat of some subpoena will scare me." He pointed a finger. "What you need to be asking yourself is why did they pick you for this? With all the trained agents available, why go to a rookie?"

I wasn't going to allow this guy to rattle me. "It doesn't matter why. I'm here."

He chuckled. "So you're doing as you were told? Following your orders. Not asking questions. Where have I heard that before? Oh, yeah. That would be me."

I decided to ask something that had been nagging my brain. "You said you taped a lot of people. Yet you made a point, ten years ago, to connect with Reverend Foster. Why him?"

He shook his head. "Not going there. I never crossed Oliver back then and I haven't in the years since." But his eyes again contradicted his words, as did another nod toward the pad. Then he pointed at the door. "Get out."

Neither of us moved.

He reached beneath his shirttail and pulled out a Glock.

"You can walk. Or I'll drag your bodies out after I shoot you. It's legal to kill home intruders in this state."

"That subpoena will be coming," I said.

"I can hardly wait. I'll have my two words ready."

I motioned and we left through the front door, Lael right behind us, still holding the gun, only now his grip was concealed by the wrinkled folds of his T-shirt.

I carried the waterproof case.

"Get on down the street," he said. "Disappear. And don't come back."

No sense arguing any further, so we walked away. I had the name and telephone number from the pad etched in my mind.

"One more thing, rookie," Lael called out.

I stopped and turned.

"Tell whoever it is that sent you that I didn't take that case away from you. Though I should have. That ought to count for something."

I got the message. Just like inside with the name on the pad. He was doing what he could. Maybe he wasn't the total asshole I thought him to be.

"I'll be sure to do that."

"Now get on. I'm going fishin'."

We walked away.

"Were you serious about the subpoena?" Coleen asked.

"That won't be my call. But it sounded good. You saw the name and phone number on the pad? He wanted us to see that, without him saying it."

Was he just being cautious?

Or was something else at play?

The street remained tranquil, the houses understandably quiet for a Thursday workday morning. I glanced back and saw Lael still watching us, standing at the curb, beside his Taurus at the driver's door, one hand on the gun beneath his shirttail. We were fifty yards away, the end of the block another fifty yards ahead, where we would turn and leave the neighborhood.

We kept walking.

Then an explosion rocked the morning.

I whirled around.

Streaks of flame burst upward from the Taurus, blue and yellow and red fusing into one violent tint. Glass shattered into fragments, then a second explosion rocked the car side-to-side.

We instinctively reeled down, shielding our faces.

Flames seared though the car's interior.

Black smoke billowed from the hulk.

CHAPTER THIRTY-TWO

I watched the Taurus consume itself. We were far enough down the street that the concussion effects of the explosion never reached us.

"My God," Coleen muttered.

Lael was nowhere to be seen outside the car.

A few neighbors had drifted out of their front doors, investigating the commotion. I figured we had another five minutes before all hell broke loose. That bomb had obviously been planted between the time Lael returned from Lake Okeechobee yesterday and now, just waiting for him to crank the engine. Our being here could never have been anticipated.

I heard the distant braying sound of emergency vehicles.

They came faster than I thought.

"Let's get off the street," I said.

We hurried into a stand of trees between two houses. I laid the case down and we stood out of sight and watched as a sheriff's car raced by.

I wondered about such a public display with Lael's murder. A lot of attention would be drawn.

But maybe that was the idea.

More sheriff's cars rushed past from the direction we were going.

"We need to go," I said. "We'll head farther down this street, away from traffic, and find another way out of this neighborhood."

We started walking again.

It wouldn't be long before the whole area was cordoned off as a crime scene. I could see that Coleen was shaken. Hell, I was, too. That was another first for me. It seemed my week for them.

More emergency vehicles headed toward the scene. I imagined they'd have a local law enforcement convention here before the day was through. Not too many car bombs went off in Melbourne, Florida. Everybody would want to be part of the action. It wasn't that cops wished for bad things, it was just that something out of the ordinary was exciting. Like TV weather people, who seemed genuinely upset when a hurricane veered out to open ocean, never making land.

We were now a few streets over from the burning car, heading out of the neighborhood.

A car wheeled around the corner behind us.

I turned.

A white Yukon sped our way. Not a police vehicle. Perhaps one of the residents leaving. The SUV slowed as it approached, then stopped. The driver's-side window disappeared down.

"You need to get in," a man said.

My instinct was to drop the case and reach for the gun beneath my shirt. But something about the guy telegraphed that he was no threat.

He displayed a badge. "I'm with the FBI. You need to get in the car."

"Why?" Coleen asked.

"Because we're on the same side. We know about Stephanie Nelle and her investigation. We also know about Juan Lopez Vadez and Tom Oliver. You're out here, bare ass to the wind. I'd say you need a friend."

I couldn't argue with that.

I motioned for us to climb inside.

"Are you nuts?" Coleen asked. "This guy could be working for Oliver."

I walked around and opened the passenger-side door. "Yep. That's right." I laid the case down on the asphalt and found my gun, which I tossed across the hood to her.

She caught it and understood.

Then she climbed into the rear seat.

We drove away from Melbourne, west toward I-95 from where we'd come earlier. But instead of heading south, we went north, for Jacksonville and home. I sat in the front seat because I wanted to be able to look this guy in the eye. Coleen was in the back with the gun, keeping watch and listening. I'd already passed the case over to her, and it rested on the seat behind me. I was hoping that my trusting her with both the gun and the case would count for something in her eyes.

"We learned of Valdez's contact with Reverend Foster, then your contact, Ms. Perry, with Valdez."

"How is Valdez able to prance around Florida like he's a tourist on vacation?" I asked.

"That's thanks to a few problems that remain both within and outside of the FBI. People Ms. Nelle is focused on."

Whether any of that was true remained to be seen. All I knew was that we were headed away from Melbourne and Palm Beach and Coleen had a gun to this guy's back if he tried anything stupid.

I asked a few more questions but received no replies. Our driver told us all would be explained shortly by someone who wanted to speak to us. I was beginning to learn that being a field operative meant making choices. Lots of them, in fact. One thing led to another, then to another, or at least that was the way it was supposed to happen. An agent's job was to make the right choice and keep moving forward. By the time I left the profession, over a decade later, several agents I came to know died from making bad choices. Luckily for me, my mistakes were never fatal.

But they were nonetheless painful.

Like the one I was about to make.

We exited I-95 after a two-and-a-half-hour ride and made our way east into downtown St. Augustine. Whoever wanted to speak to us was apparently there. I knew the hype associated with what was supposedly the oldest European settlement in America. The town was already over two hundred when George Washington became president. The Spanish first settled here, on a narrow strip of land nestled close to the Matanzas River. Another stretch of thin, low-lying island to the east provided beaches as well as shelter to a superb natural harbor that drew not only the Spanish but eventually the French, the English, and pirates.

Its main roads ran north and south, the cross streets at defined right angles east and west, everything on a perfect grid. Many still retained their narrow width, first placed there as a means of internal defense. Most were named for either people or things from the past. Streets like St. George, Treasury, Cathedral, and Francis. Overhanging balconies and high stone walls were common, all of the stunted buildings made of wood, tabby, or coquina. Henry Flagler put the place on the modern map when he built a railroad down the East Coast to Florida. Along the way he constructed magnificent hotels that started the annual craze of the rich coming south for the winter. St. Augustine boasted three of his resorts, all of which were still standing, but only one remained a hotel.

We wound our way into the center of downtown, traffic typically congested for a busy summer afternoon. Past Flagler College we came to Government House, then the city's main square.

The Plaza de la Constitución.

The oldest public park in America.

Once it was a community focal point. A place of progress and protest. Now the tall trees, shrubbery, and tight grass accommodated tourists enjoying the shade. Pam and I visited last Christmas when the trees, and the rest of the city, were illuminated with thousands of tiny white lights.

The SUV eased to the curb.

"He's waiting for you near the slave market," our driver said. "We prefer you not haul that case around in the open. There's a backpack in the rear. Use it."

I made eye contact with Coleen and nodded.

She reached around and found a green canvas shoulder bag. Then she removed the files from the case and stuffed them inside.

"You have to leave the gun," the driver said.

I shook my head.

"It's not a request. No weapons. We don't want any attention drawn to this gathering." The guy paused. "We went to a lot of trouble to set this up in a nice public place, so you'd feel at ease. You're definitely going to want to hear what he has to say."

I weighed the options and made another of those choices.

"Leave it," I told her, then I climbed from the vehicle.

We crossed the street into the plaza.

Coleen donned the backpack.

Concrete walks stretched in several directions beneath the leafy canopy. I caught sight of the olden monuments, the cannons, a wooden cupola topped with a bell, and a Spanish well. We followed one of the paths to an open-air pavilion that had acquired the dubious label of slave market. Whether any slaves were ever sold here was a matter of debate. Waiting out front was a short, thin man dressed in a sport coat and jeans. Perspiration glistened at the start of a receding hairline.

"Lieutenant Malone. Ms. Perry. I'm Dan Veddern."

The guy did not extend a hand to shake.

"I can't say it's a pleasure to meet. You've both been nothing but trouble."

CHAPTER
THIRTY-THREE

I IMMEDIATELY DISLIKED THIS GUY.

He reminded me too much of my current CO. Arrogant. Self-righteous. Moralistic. Little-man syndrome.

"I was forced to come all the way down here to this godforsaken heat and humidity," he said. "Thanks to you two."

"It's the oldest city in America," I pointed out. "Great place to visit."

He tossed me a wiry grin. "I bet that smart-ass attitude really endears you to your commanding officers."

"I learned it in anger management class."

He didn't seem amused at my humor.

"I'm director of the intelligence branch for the FBI."

I assumed we were supposed to be impressed.

"And if Stephanie Nelle had come to me, instead of recruiting you, we wouldn't be here."

The plaza was busy with tourists milling in every direction, taking pictures, pointing out landmarks, enjoying the agelessness. The streets beyond were lined with taverns, restaurants, galleries, and shops. All busy. I liked that we were in public. I didn't like the fact that this guy had chosen both the time and place.

"What do you want?" Coleen asked.

"I assume you've read the files on your back."

Neither of us replied.

"Okay. I get it. I'm the enemy."

He stood close and spoke low. We were positioned off to the side, about ten feet away from the airy pavilion, off the concrete path, in the grass. Nobody paid us any attention.

"You opened a bad can of worms," he said to Coleen. "When you talked with Valdez."

"How do you know she did?" I asked.

"We monitor international calls."

News to me.

"And when the words *1933 Double Eagle* were mentioned," he said, "that grabbed our attention."

"So you can isolate certain words in certain calls?"

"You'd be amazed what we can do."

Probably so, but that discussion was for another day.

"Was Valdez once FBI?" I asked.

"Unfortunately. Before that he was CIA. He was the one who gave them the bad intel on the Bay of Pigs."

I hadn't heard those three words in a long time.

Three days in April 1961. A military invasion of Cuba, carried out by thirteen hundred CIA-sponsored Cuban exiles, which failed so badly it only strengthened Castro's hold, making him a national hero, driving Cuba straight into the arms of the Soviet Union. I recalled a *New York Times* article from a few years back when an internal CIA report on the invasion was finally declassified after thirty-five years. It found that the agency had exceeded its capabilities and failed to realistically assess the risks. Even worse, it had recruited poor field leaders, established no organized internal Cuban resistance, exercised awful internal management of communications and staff, and, overall, lacked a realistic battle plan.

A disaster all the way around.

"In hindsight," he said, "Valdez probably gave them the bogus intel intentionally. He ended up working for Castro in the 1970s and '80s. He was probably playing both sides all the way back to '61. The CIA got rid of him in '62. That's when Hoover picked him up. I'll ask again. Have you read what Valdez brought?"

"We both have," Coleen said.

I could see that development troubled him.

"I keep secrets for a living," he said. "This country has always needed people like me to keep its secrets. You do realize that this whole thing is way beyond classified."

"How are these reports classified?" I asked. "They came from Cuba."

"They were created during an FBI operation known as Bishop's Pawn."

There were those two words again.

"It was part of COINTELPRO."

And the third word of the day.

"Hoover liked everything written down," he said. "And I mean everything. There are reports after reports after reports. Millions of pages from those days. You can't imagine how much paper. We've known for a long time that Valdez managed to get his hands on some of the classified documentation from Bishop's Pawn. How? I have no idea. But he's blackmailed us with it before. Years ago it was cheaper and easier to pay—"

"Than kill him?"

I couldn't resist.

"Not necessarily. But he stayed in Cuba, which made that option more difficult."

"For the FBI?" I taunted. "Come on? You guys have reach."

"We do, which I hope you won't forget."

I received the message loud and clear.

"So we're clear," Veddern said, "if I had been around back then, I would have taken the SOB out. Absolutely. That's the trouble with blackmailers. They never go away." He motioned to everything around us. "Hence, once again, why we're here in this oven."

"Tell us more about Valdez," Coleen asked.

"Why are you so interested in him?"

"I read the files. They're enlightening."

"I bet they are. How do you know they're real?"

"You just said they were," I said.

He pointed a finger my way and smiled.

"How about we dispense with the bullshit and you answer her question," I said. "What about Valdez?"

"J. Edgar Hoover thought himself a master of the intelligence business. Before 1947 he did a good job rooting out Nazi spies in World War Two. But after the war the FBI was supposed to get out of the intelligence business. Spies became the CIA's problem. But Hoover couldn't let it go. He kept his nose in the intelligence business. After the CIA cut Valdez loose, Hoover brought him on to root out home-grown communists. In 1967 Hoover switched him over to Bishop's Pawn. Nearly everything we have on Bishop's Pawn is gone, except for records that detail Valdez's employment history."

I considered the implications of what this man was saying, re-calling articles and books I'd read on the King assassination. Every-one saw a conspiracy. The various theories ranged from the amazing to the fantastical. But this was no theory. If what I'd read was true, the FBI had been an active party to an actual conspiracy to commit murder.

Which reminded me about Bruce Lael.

"We just watched a man being blown up," I said.

"Tom Oliver doesn't like loose ends. But that's the thing about con-spiracies. By definition, they require participants. We were about to bring Lael in for questioning. This meeting was originally meant for him. We assume Oliver found out and decided to move first. I honestly didn't think he'd make a move on Lael, but I've been wrong about Oliver before."

"Arrest him," Coleen said.

"There is a little thing called proof. We're gathering it, as we speak. When you two appeared earlier, I had my agent on the scene bring you here instead of Lael. Of course, we've been looking for you both since we found out what happened on the Dry Tortugas."

"How much of Bishop's Pawn do *you* know about?" I asked.

"What you're really asking is, Did the FBI participate in King's death?" He shrugged. "I can honestly say I don't know the answer to that question. I can also say that there's not a single piece of paper I'm aware of in our files that even hints at such a thing. And I would know."

"Because you're the keeper of secrets," I mocked.

"Precisely."

"But you know that Bishop's Pawn involves King's death," I pointed out. "Valdez blackmailed you before. So whatever you bought back then had to point that way."

He nodded. "It did. The bastard sold just enough to keep them coming back for more. But those documents are long gone, too. I only know what I just said from speaking to an agent, a few years ago, who was there back then. Another keeper of secrets who's dead now."

I knew this guy's type. He craved order.

And all he had right now was chaos.

"I do know Bishop's Pawn was an atypical FBI operation, highly classified. Jansen, Lael, Oliver, and Valdez participated. My guess is James Earl Ray knew the least, on purpose, since the idea seemed to be for him to take the fall when it was all over."

"Ray pulled the trigger?" I asked.

Veddern nodded. "No question in my mind. And pretty damn amazing, really. One shot, from a long way off. And he was no marksman. He'd barely fired a rifle and certainly had no sniper training. But he did it." The guy cocked his fingers to form a gun, then bent his thumb signifying a shot fired. "Right in the head."

It was a tacky gesture, but I assumed that came from dealing with bad crap all the time. People died in the law enforcement business. It was part of the job. Easy to forget that such was not the case with 99.9999 percent of the rest of the world.

"This whole thing is a nightmare," Veddern said. "It's been dormant a long time, but it just keeps coming back for more. We cannot have any public speculation that the FBI may have been involved with the death of Martin Luther King. If Stephanie Nelle had come to us, we could have handled this quietly. There are things involved she has no way of knowing. Instead, she sends you out there to generate a hurricane."

"It is my first assignment," I noted, with a grin.

"Lucky for us."

I caught his attempt at humor.

"We want this to be over," he went on. "We want it contained. Look, everybody knows Hoover kept a slew of secret information on people. It's one of the ways he stayed in power for as long as he did. Thank God, when he died, his secretary destroyed those private files. For days she shredded paper, and bless her soul for doing that. Nothing good would have come from all that crap coming to light. It was better off gone. Over. Done with. And the same is true for Bishop's Pawn. Any and all records of that need to be gone, too."

But something else was bothering me. "You said there were FBI employment records about Valdez that survived. Were they pay records?"

Veddern nodded. "We know he was given a 1933 Double Eagle. And that's not in a record. Someone else from that time reported it a long time ago. Hence our interest when those words were mentioned recently."

"He didn't want cash?" I asked.

"He apparently needed to ingratiate himself with Castro. A lot of people don't know this, but Castro fashioned himself as some great numismatist. Can you imagine? A murdering moron in green fatigues, collecting coins." He shrugged. "I suppose everyone has to have a hobby."

I got it. "And what better way for him to ingratiate himself than to present Castro with the rarest coin in the world."

"Exactly."

But something else swirled around in my brain, and I saw it was bouncing around inside Coleen's head, too. She beat me to it and asked, "How did my father get a 1933 Double Eagle?"

I removed the coin from my pocket.

Veddern stared at the gold piece. "That's another reason why I'm here. We didn't even know, until now, that there was another coin out there."

I could see that Coleen's patience was nearing its end.

"I need to find my father."

"I want to find him, too," Veddern said. "We want to know how and why he has that coin."

CHAPTER THIRTY-FOUR

WE BOTH STOOD THERE.

I knew Coleen's nerves were stretched beyond thin. But Veddern seemed to enjoy her predicament.

Which made me like him even less.

"We need to go," she said again.

I looked at her. "Not yet. It's important we hear what this man has to say."

She stared at me with eyes that swam with fear and alarm.

I could only imagine the thoughts swirling through her brain.

Finally, she nodded, and I faced Veddern. "You had no idea there was a second Double Eagle?"

"That's what sparked my branch's interest in the first place. We were planning on being in the Dry Tortugas. Then the boat sank, so we decided to wait a few days and go down to the wreck. You and Stephanie Nelle beat us to it. Ms. Nelle's mistake was trusting Jim Jansen. If she'd bothered to check with us, we would have told her to steer clear of him."

Roger that.

"Then things just drifted from bad to worse." He held out his arms. "And here I am, in nature's steam room."

"You get used to it," I said.

Veddern stared out over the plaza. "I've been reading some of the old FBI files. Did you know the KKK had a huge rally, right here, on this spot, in 1964? I've seen the film. Scary as hell. In response, there were protest marches around the plaza. Blacks and whites walked in silence. 'Round and 'round. But there was a lot of violence. This plaza became the focal point for the entire war on integration."

I realized what he was doing. The same thing I did to break a witness. Rarely did frontal assaults work, since they tended to telegraph the punch far too quickly. Guerrilla warfare fared much better. Circle around with your questions. Ask easy ones first. Then friendly ones. Be diversionary. Throw in some brittle chatter to distract. And only at the last minute, when their guard lowered, did you start asking what you really wanted to know.

"King called St. Augustine the most lawless community he ever visited," Veddern said. "All the things that man endured. Riots. Rocks. Bricks. Beatings. Insults. And to him, this was the most lawless place of all."

On civil rights, the past had not been kind to St. Augustine. Odd considering that the town's claim to fame was history. It started in 1963 when three local black integrationists were brutally beaten at a KKK rally. One, a dentist, had his hands intentionally broken. The protest marches that followed turned into full-fledged riots with angry rednecks. Andrew Young was beaten while the local police watched. The home King rented at St. Augustine Beach as his local headquarters was burned to the ground.

Emotions ran high.

Everyone seemed to sense what was at stake.

King intentionally chose St. Augustine as the place to remind America about the need for the Civil Rights Act, which in the summer of 1964 was bogged down in the Senate, frozen from passage by the longest filibuster ever. White, southern, supremacist senators wanted to stop that bill. King opted to take his stand right here. He decided protests were the way to break the stalemate, and his took a variety of forms. From his usual lunch counter sit-ins to a wade-in, where a group of black and white students tried to integrate a whites-only beach. When King tried to eat at the Monson Motor Lodge he was refused service and hauled off to jail. A few days later came the famous swim-in, when the motel's owner poured acid in the water. For weeks people were attacked and beaten.

Images of all that hate circulated around the world.

And changed minds.

Twenty-four hours after the swim-in, the eighty-three-day filibuster ended and the Senate passed the 1964 Civil Rights Act, which Lyndon Johnson signed. To test the new law, Andrew Young and a few others reentered the Monson Motor Lodge for lunch. A nervous waitress seated them and served their food without incident. But later that night the restaurant was fire-bombed. A message to all the other local businesses that might have been considering obeying the law, too.

Veddern was right.

A lot had happened right here.

But I also noticed that the Plaza de la Constitución still contained a huge contradiction. Its largest monument was a towering coquina obelisk, topped by cannonballs, dedicated to the local Confederate war dead. To me it resembled a giant middle finger. Not a single reminder existed anywhere of what happened here in the summer of 1964. It would not be until 2011 that a civil rights memorial was finally erected, one that faced the old Woolworths where four black teenagers were arrested, and spent six months in jail, for simply trying to order a hamburger and a Coke. Not surprisingly, it took a change to the city code to make the monument happen, as memorials to events that occurred after 1821 were inexplicably banned.

"What about my father?" Coleen asked. "Tell me what you know about him."

Veddern pointed at the coin I still held. "I was actually hoping you could tell me."

She didn't reply.

I slipped the coin back into my pocket. "Tell us what you know."

He shrugged. "Are you asking if he was a spy for us? The FBI had informants all over the SCLC, the Progressive Labor Movement, the Congress of Racial Equality, and the Student Nonviolent Coordinating Committee. That's how a lot of inside information made its way to Hoover's desk. I can say that I've never seen any report that mentions your father as being part of that. In fact, nothing on Bishop's Pawn, outside of Valdez's blackmail, has ever surfaced." He pointed at the backpack. "Until now. I was involved with both congressional investigations into the King assassination. I'm the bureau's recognized expert on that event, so I would know."

"Provided you're telling us the truth," she said.

My gaze swept the plaza and the border streets. People moved everywhere, as did cars, trollies, and horse-drawn carriages, the *clip-clop* of their hooves on the pavement as monotonous as a clock ticking. Veddern was definitely not here alone, so I was trying to assess any threats while Coleen held his attention. Veddern was trying hard to be the guy on the white horse, but I wasn't ready, just yet, to play the trust game. Particularly given the two men who loitered toward the far end of the plaza, near Government House. Definitely not tourists.

I decided to do a little diverging myself.

What I'd read last night was fairly specific on the lead-up to the assassination, but not so much on what happened afterward. So I asked *the bureau's recognized expert,* "Did the FBI help Ray escape Memphis?"

"Why do you ask such a thing?"

I reiterated what some of the memos had stated, adding, "Ray fired the shot, then fled the rooming house. He was supposed to get in his car and leave town. He was carrying the rifle, rolled inside a bedspread, out on the street and saw a couple of Memphis police cars. For once in his life he panicked and ditched the bundle in an entryway. What he didn't know was that someone was inside that store, so the rifle was found quickly and that same somebody saw Ray drive off in a white Mustang. It should have been an easy matter to catch him before he made it far. What's the old saying? You can't outrun the radio?"

"I know what you're getting at. It's part of the official assassination file."

We listened as he explained that less than ten minutes after the shooting, the Memphis police put out an alert for the Mustang, driven by a well-dressed white male. Twenty-five minutes after the shooting, reports placed the Mustang heading north out of the city. Then, thirty-five minutes after the shooting, a car chase began to be heard across local CB radio. A 1966 Pontiac was apparently in hot pursuit of a fast-fleeing Mustang. The voice broadcasting the report said the Mustang was being driven by the man who shot King. The Memphis police tried to establish two-way communication with the Pontiac, but the voice on the other end would not reply. The chase seemed to be happening on the east side of Memphis, the shooter apparently making a run for the Tennessee hill country. The Memphis police dispatched cruisers. Roadblocks were erected. The highway patrol alerted.

And then things turned even stranger.

The Pontiac's driver reported over the radio that the Mustang was shooting at him and that his windshield had been hit. The police asked if the driver could see the Mustang's license plate and, for the first time, the man replied saying that he feared for his life getting that close.

Then the transmissions ended.

Nothing more was heard from the Pontiac.

"Reports from the official assassination file quote interviews with people who listened to the exchange on CB radio. They all said the voice was incredibly calm for someone in a high-speed car chase with shots being fired at him. And it was odd that he wouldn't identify himself. The guy was willing to risk going after the Mustang, but not willing to tell the police who he was. Then there was the S-meter. One person listening noticed on his own CB radio that the signal strength never diminished, even though the transmission came from a moving vehicle. The signal stayed constant. That meant it was coming from a stationary source."

"But no one paid attention to those details," I said. "They were all caught up in the moment and thought they had the killer."

"That's right."

I began to connect the dots with what I'd read. "COINTELPRO may have been a lot of things, but those guys weren't stupid. On the one hand they engineered the killing. On the other, they sat back and allowed the rest of the FBI to organize the largest manhunt in history to find Ray."

"Which was easy for them to do," Veddern said. "Within the bureau only Oliver, Jansen, Lael, and Hoover knew about Bishop's Pawn, and probably only Oliver and Hoover knew it all. There have been countless investigations into King's death. Lots of innuendo. Speculation. Guesses. But nothing has ever pointed to the FBI. They did know how to keep a secret back then. Hoover publicly proclaimed that the FBI would stop at nothing to find King's killer. That was the reputation he'd forged for *his* bureau. It's what the public expected from him. Ray should have made it to Rhodesia, out of reach, long before the FBI ever closed in. My God, he was on the run for two months. But when you pick an idiot for a job, you have to expect idiocy, and that's what they got."

"But why plead guilty?" I asked. "Why didn't Ray just rat them out?"

"Nobody knows. He had a great defense for trial. No discernible motive. No fingerprints of his in the rooming house. No prints found in the car he was driving. No ballistics report that established the rifle was the murder weapon. Even worse, an FBI accuracy test on the rifle showed it consistently fired both left and below the intended target. Ray was not a marksman, and knew little to nothing about guns. The only eyewitness to place him at the scene was blind drunk at the time, and never made a positive ID until years later. It was a defense lawyer's dream."

Veddern pointed another finger my way.

"Once the FBI publicly identified Ray as the killer, which was about two weeks after the assassination, Hoover made sure the bureau focused on Ray, and Ray alone. I've read every directive issued at that time. The field offices were ordered to stay on Ray. No conspiracy was ever investigated."

I knew something this man didn't. "Right before his trial, word was sent to him that once George Wallace was elected president, he'd be pardoned. Ray was a strong Wallace supporter and believed them. That's why he agreed to plead guilty."

I could see that was news to him.

"That actually makes sense," Veddern said.

"Three days later," I continued, "his narcissistic personality took over and he recanted. He realized that he was the man of the hour. Everyone wanted to hear what he had to say. So he talked. And talked. And talked. So much that no one, other than conspiratorialists out to make a name for themselves, ever listened to him. He became the perfect smoke screen."

"Yes he did," Veddern said. "In the decades since, the mafia, racists, segregationists, the Klan, communists, labor unions, the military, left-ists, the government, and the Memphis police have all been implicated in theories to kill Martin Luther King Jr. I'm wagering, though, that those files you have from Valdez are an entirely different matter."

His tone had grown more serious, and I assumed the attempt at reasoning was ending. His words were driving toward a point.

He pointed at Coleen.

"I want them. Now."

CHAPTER THIRTY-FIVE

I REALLY, REALLY DIDN'T LIKE THIS GUY.

But I knew to keep cool.

"This can't escalate beyond what it already has," Veddern said. "We thought it was containable when the boat sank. But Stephanie Nelle managed to find herself someone who resurrected the problem."

"I'll take that as a compliment," I said.

"Don't. But you can redeem yourself. Hand over those files and the coin and walk away. Mission done."

"Without those, there's no proof of anything," Coleen noted.

"Exactly my point. Did you hear me? This. Has. To. End."

"I don't work for you," I said.

"A fact I fully realize. Look, I understand. Tom Oliver has been a problem for a long time. He's old school, rising up in the ranks from a field agent to deputy director. Along the way he oversaw a lot of our departments. COINTELPRO was just one of many. He has a lot of friends in the bureau that owe him lots of favors. He thinks of the FBI like in the old days, when Hoover was there, when they could do whatever they wanted. And though retired he still has friends in high places, friends the attorney general wants to expunge. We want those people gone, too. But we prefer to clean our own house."

"Just like the fox cleans the henhouse?" I asked.

"We're not all bad," Veddern said. "Most of us do our job the right way."

"And yet you've known about Bishop's Pawn and never said a word."

"I know little to nothing about it, and I have no proof of anything."

I pointed at the backpack. "You do now."

"Those files, and Juan Lopez Valdez, should have stayed in Cuba."

"We've both read them," I pointed out again.

He shrugged. "So what? You'll be just two more crazies expounding wild theories with nothing to back them up."

"I want to know more about those FBI spies," Coleen said.

She kept coming back to that subject. Like a bird dog on a scent.

"I told you all I know," Veddern said. "And I'm not being evasive. Just honest. The documentation on all of that no longer exists."

Which I could see made Coleen even more anxious to find her father.

"You're going to have—"

Veddern's body suddenly lurched.

Odd.

Then he shuddered.

I stared at the man and saw first puzzlement, then pain, and finally fear fill his eyes. A small hole appeared at his right shoulder, from which dark rivulets began to seep.

He grabbed for the wound, then dropped to the grass.

I lunged for Coleen and we both hit the ground, scrambling for the pavilion's protection, huddling close to a thick stone pillar. Hard to say for sure, but the shooter could be atop one of the taller buildings across the street, on the other side of the pavilion. The bullet had definitely come from that direction.

Another round skipped off one of the stone pillars and thudded into the grass.

Yes, the shooter was behind us, testing our shield.

No sound was associated with the firing, which meant the rifle was sound-suppressed. People had begun to notice Veddern and the blood. A scream and shouts of *oh my God* echoed. The afternoon crowd began to scatter, like ants from the mound. That confusion could work in our favor. As would the trees.

"Let's go."

We sprang to our feet and joined the chaos, bolting from the plaza to the street, which was only a few feet away, weaving our way through the congealed traffic, using the cars for protection. A round ricocheted off the sidewalk just a few feet way. As I suspected, the trees in the plaza were now blocking the shooter's aim. But most likely, here and there, we would be visible through the canopy.

We rushed past the shops.

People were beginning to notice what was happening across the street and the panic spread. None of them realized they were also in the line of fire.

And that bothered me.

We needed to disappear.

Past the traffic I saw the two suspect men from earlier in the plaza hustle across the street on an intercept course. They had no idea there was a separate shooter. For all they knew we'd taken Veddern down.

"You see them," I asked.

"I'll take one. You the other."

I liked the way she thought.

The two men angled their approach so they would find the sidewalk about twenty feet ahead of us. I'm not sure what they expected, but what they got was a tackle from Coleen and a fist to the jaw from me. My guy fell back against a parked car at the curb. The people around us reacted to the fight and began to flee. I didn't give my guy time to react, planting my curled, hard knuckles into his face, then reaching beneath his jacket for a shouldered weapon. I removed the gun as he slumped to the pavement. Coleen was on her feet, having driven her man to the concrete hard enough to knock him out.

She, too, had a gun in her hand.

We both stuffed the weapons at our spines, beneath our shirts, and kept moving, turning right, heading down an even busier path. I knew where we were. St. George Street. A pedestrian-only way lined with olden buildings that housed an eclectic array of galleries, shops, and cafés, running right through the center of downtown to the old city gate. Being the middle of a summer afternoon, there were a lot of people in shorts, T-shirts, and flip-flops—which helped hide us, but they also made it much more difficult to determine any new threats. I heard sirens and realized the local authorities were about to arrive on the scene. My eyes scanned back and forth, studying faces.

"Do you know where we're going?" I asked Coleen.

"Not really."

That was encouraging.

Behind us the two guys we'd taken down on the sidewalk were nowhere to be seen. We kept hustling forward, excusing ourselves, delving deeper into the pedestrian-only quarter. I knew that this part of the old town was a warren of narrow lanes and even narrower alleys. Some car traffic was allowed, but not much. Ahead of us, through the crowd, I saw a tall, angular, gaunt man with a beard standing in the center of the street.

Juan Lopez Valdez.

We stopped.

Then I felt something hard touch my spine. I stole a glance over my shoulder and saw the two men from Palm Beach who'd tried to steal the files. One behind me, the other Coleen, both with guns to our backs. I noticed that Coleen recognized them, too.

Both of our weapons were discreetly taken away.

Valdez beckoned with a friendly wave and we all four walked forward.

"Are you hungry?" he asked as we came close.

Strange question.

He pointed to a restaurant over his shoulder and said, "Shall we?"

CHAPTER THIRTY-SIX

W₉ ᴇɴᴛᴇʀᴇᴅ ᴛʜᴇ Cᴏʟᴜᴍʙɪᴀ—ᴡʜɪᴄʜ ɪʀᴏɴɪᴄᴀʟʟʏ ғᴇᴀᴛᴜʀᴇᴅ Cuban cuisine. Pam and I had eaten there a couple of times.

"With what just happened," Valdez said, "you both need to be off the street."

"Your doing?" I asked.

He nodded. "A favor to Oliver. He's not in the best of moods, particularly considering you managed to escape this morning. He decided a message needed to be sent. I was here. So he asked me to send it. But we do have a common interest." He pointed at me and Coleen. "You two. Thankfully, Oliver learned of Agent Veddern's presence, so we drove up."

"Veddern was here to take Bruce Lael."

Valdez nodded. "I know, and I would have shot them both if that had happened. But luckily, you two appeared, providing new opportunities."

"Oliver's got problems with his own people," I said.

"Far overdue, if you ask me."

We approached a hostess station and Valdez asked for a table for three. It was midafternoon, past lunchtime, but the place remained reasonably busy. The two guys behind us continued to stand close, keeping their weapons concealed within their shirttails. Making a move would endanger not only us but everyone around us, so I decided to sit tight. Looking back, I've always been amazed at my patience that day, especially considering my lack of experience and the threat level.

We were shown to a table on the second floor. Valdez instructed his two men to wait below and keep an eye on the exits. The restaurant's interior cast a measured Spanish feel with colorful tiles in bright yellows and blues, a faux garden of a place where ferns and potted palms accentuated the sense of being outdoors. The main dining room resembled an enclosed two-story patio-courtyard, complete with a working fountain at the center. A skylight high overhead added light and ambience. Our table was near the railing on the second floor overlooking the fountain.

"I must say," Valdez noted, "I've never eaten here. But I have visited the Columbia in Tampa. Their version of Cuban cuisine is reasonably good."

"What do you want?" Coleen asked.

"Such hostility," he said. "You should be grateful. Outside is about to be crowded with police. A downed FBI agent is going to attract attention."

"Is he dead?" I asked.

"I certainly hope so. That's what Oliver wanted. It seems he and Veddern are not the best of friends."

"Is Oliver always so reckless?" I asked.

"More desperate at the moment. He has a lot to keep contained. He thought it could be done in Stuart, but you both managed to get away. Was the confrontation at the dock your people trying to stop you?"

"More my people not keeping their end of a bargain."

He chuckled. "That I can appreciate, amigo."

Obviously, Stephanie Nelle had not seen Valdez.

"Murder is a serious crime," Coleen stated.

"I agree. Which is why Oliver wanted me to deal with things. I would have handled it differently, but at the moment I have to please Oliver. We have a mutual problem." He pointed at us. "You two. I'm hoping we can come to an understanding and end all this."

A server approached and left menus, promising to be right back.

"I was electronically listening to your conversation in the plaza," Valdez said. "You've both read the files and you, Lieutenant Malone, have my coin, so let's have a meal and I'll answer all questions for Senora Perry that Veddern avoided. The ones about your father. I don't suffer from the same lack of knowledge that Veddern possessed. I was there in 1968. Then you will give me my coin and we can be done."

The server returned.

"If you don't mind," Valdez said. "I'll order for the table."

He perused the menu and selected several different entrées, which the server assured were all excellent choices. Coleen and I just sat, our gazes meeting occasionally as we both assessed the situation from differing perspectives. She seemed intrigued by what she might learn. I was more concerned with getting out of here in one piece—with the files and the coin.

Valdez pointed to the green backpack, which Coleen cradled in her lap. "Those photographs are all I have left."

"How'd you get your hands on that stuff?"

"Jansen was always sloppy. He trusted me far more than he ever should have. He and I were quite friendly back then."

"Which you took full advantage of," I asked.

"It's my nature. I can't help it. Jansen should have known that." He pointed again at the backpack. "Of course, I don't like being cheated."

"You've gone a long way to make sure a bargain is a bargain," I said. "You must really need money."

"I am in short supply at the moment. I was thrilled to learn, when I called Reverend Foster, that he still had his coin."

"How did Castro like the one you gave him?"

"He was quite pleased."

"Lucky for you the FBI had one available."

"That was one of those fortuitous things. Jansen was my handler and mentioned how they'd surreptitiously found two of the rarest coins in the world during one of their infamous break-ins. Since they were obtained illegally, Oliver opted to keep them. Returning them to the Treasury would have only raised questions. When I was asked to perform my services for Bishop's Pawn, I named my price. One of the coins."

"I don't give a damn about any of that," Coleen blurted out. "Just give him the coin. We have the files. And let him tell me about my father."

"You and your father both said the coin was mine now," I reminded her.

"Give him the damn coin."

"You can't be that naive?" I asked.

She seemed puzzled.

Then it hit her.

Oliver and Valdez had teamed in Palm Beach to kill us both out on the water. Sure, Valdez wanted his coin, but Oliver wanted the files. No matter what Valdez had just said, his job was to retrieve both.

"I'll give him the files," she made clear.

That I did not want to hear.

"When you called me," Valdez said to Coleen, "I was direct. I mentioned the words *Bishop's Pawn* and I told you a little about the FBI. I even advised you to stay away from them. Which, as it has turned out, was good advice. We made a deal. I honored my part." He faced me. "I told you when we first met, Lieutenant Malone, that I may be the only person in this world you can actually trust. I meant that."

"Yet I double-crossed you anyway."

The server returned with water and bread for the table. I decided, what the hell, and enjoyed a few bites. I figured it was going to take a few minutes for the food to come, so why not learn what I could. The time would also give me a chance to decide how to handle Coleen's shifting allegiances. I sat straight and strong in my chair, and tried to project an image of all business and gumption.

"I've had few opportunities to ever discuss this," Valdez said. "I'm sure Senora Perry is anxious to know the truth."

"I am."

I wasn't, given what her father wanted, so I asked, "Tell us about James Earl Ray."

"Quite a personality. He so wanted to be important."

"He got his wish."

Valdez nodded. "That he did. He thought himself such a big man. Through the years, I've read several of the books Ray published while in prison. Quite the writer. I must say, though, the picture they paint is nothing like the man I knew. He wanted the world to think he was an innocent patsy, used by others." He shook his head. "Ray was a sadistic racist, through and through. He hated blacks, especially ones who thought themselves important. He really hated King. He also had little regard for women. He wanted to be a pornographer. I gave him money to buy a lot of expensive cameras. When he was in Mexico he took many racy pictures of women. They were terrible. Disgusting. Overt. Obvious. Nothing about them sexy or provocative. That was Ray. Overt and obvious. It was easy to get him to do what I wanted."

"Why was it necessary to kill King?" Coleen asked.

He shrugged. "I have no idea. Jansen passed the order on to me to have Ray do it. I assumed that came straight from Oliver and Hoover. No low-level field agent would have ever made that call. I simply did what they wanted."

"You were the mysterious Raoul," I said. "The one Ray ultimately blamed everything on?"

"It was the name I used with him."

"So why didn't Ray rat you out when he was arrested?"

"He did, once he realized they'd lied to him about everything. But by then no one cared. He was just a murderer trying to get out of prison, saying whatever he could in order to make that happen. Blaming whoever he could."

"Was he that stupid?" I asked.

Valdez chuckled. "That and more. He was the perfect person to pull the trigger. He was capable of doing it. He *wanted* to do it. He relished doing it. And he loved the attention he received afterward. Ray was a career criminal. Prison was home to him. To live the rest of his life behind bars, while still being important? That was more than he could ever have hoped for as a free man. The amazing thing is that so many people listened to him in the years after."

Coleen remained anxious. The files lying in her lap were important, but not nearly as important to her as her father.

She'd give them away in a heartbeat.

I was going to have to do something.

And fast.

So I discreetly assessed the local geography. Six tables surrounded us down our side of the second floor. Half were occupied. Below, the ground-floor dining room was crowded, nearly all of the tables busy.

Servers moved about in all directions. A soft murmur of conversation filled the air. In the bottom left corner, on the ground floor, I spotted the kitchen entrance where trays of food came and went through a swinging door.

Okay. I had the lay of the land.

Only one question remained.

What to do next.

CHAPTER THIRTY-SEVEN

THE WHOLE THING SEEMED UNREAL.

I was sitting at a table in a restaurant with the man who arranged for the murder of Martin Luther King Jr. Not a seed of doubt existed within me that Valdez was the real thing. A downed assistant director in the Plaza de la Constitución and a dead former FBI agent in Melbourne further proved that point.

"I don't get it," I said. "Why do you want this whole thing exposed to the world? It's been thirty years. You surely realized that could happen when you traded those files for the coin."

The leathery face broke out in a wiry grin. "Maybe it's time the world knew the truth. Why not?"

"It implicates you in a conspiracy to commit murder."

He shrugged. "Where? My name is never mentioned anywhere. Jansen always referred to me in his reports as the *point of contact operative*. Even if somehow I am implicated, I'll be back in Cuba, far away from your justice system. I imagine Castro will be pleased to learn that the American government is not opposed to assassinations. My value to him will only increase. Hypocrisy has always been an American affliction. Have you ever heard of Operation Northwoods?"

I shook my head.

"It happened in 1962, after the Bay of Pigs. It called for the CIA to secretly sponsor acts of terror against the United States, then blame it on Cuba as justification for a war with Castro. The military loved the idea. So did the CIA. They were talking about bombings and hijackings. Many of your citizens would have died. President Kennedy rejected the idea, which was a smart move. I had already alerted Castro to what they were planning."

"I can see why the CIA wasn't happy with you."

"It just proves that the United States does not own the moral high ground. It also shows that your government was paranoid and desperate, capable of anything. Even the murder of a civil rights leader."

"It wasn't our government. It was a few fanatics who misused their positions of power."

I watched Valdez shift in his chair. Coleen, too. This was like trying to keep frogs on a wheelbarrow. There wasn't much I could do about Coleen, but I could tempt Valdez. I removed the plastic sleeve from my pocket and laid it on the table.

"It's worth what?" I asked, pointing. "Eight million? Ten million?"

"At least," Valdez said. "There are buyers out there willing to pay for the privilege of owning the last one known to exist outside a museum."

"But you didn't figure on Oliver still being in the picture, did you?" I asked.

"Stupid me assumed that time had rendered it all forgotten. Only a handful knew that Bishop's Pawn even existed in the first place. I was told the FBI's files on it were destroyed after Hoover's death."

"Which only upped the value of your stash of documents," I pointed out.

Valdez nodded. "A fortunate occurrence."

Unfortunate for him was our government's newfound ability to listen in on international calls.

"Thank goodness Oliver is still negotiable," I said.

Valdez chuckled. "More like out of options. I seem to be all he has to work with on matters like this."

"Give him the coin, Malone," Coleen said. "I don't want to change the world. I don't want to rewrite history. I just want to know what my father did to earn a 1933 Double Eagle."

I caught sight of our server approaching from the far side of the second floor, toting an oval tray loaded with our lunch. She swung around and stopped to my right, flicking open a wooden stand upon which she gently balanced the tray. She was just about to start doling out the entrées when I pivoted off my chair, securing the coin within my clenched left fist, sweeping my right hand under the tray. I brought it up and over, depositing an assortment of hot Cuban food right onto Valdez.

He reeled back from my assault.

Coleen just sat there.

I slipped the coin into my pocket and grabbed the table with both hands, upending and sending it Valdez's way, too, which shoved him and his chair down to the floor.

The server stood in shock.

"This guy has a gun," I yelled. "Everyone run."

I then stuck my head out over the second-floor railing and screamed, "There's a guy up here with a gun. Get out of here. Now. Hurry. Go."

People both on the second floor and below contemplated my warning for a millisecond, then began to spring from their chairs and rush toward the exits. I was hoping the confusion would be enough to allow us to avoid the two men with guns below.

"We have to leave," I said to Coleen.

"I'm staying."

"We have to go. I'll get you answers, but not here."

Valdez was beginning to rouse from his predicament.

"You're not getting this coin from me," I made clear to her.

And she seemed to realize that *would* place her in dire jeopardy if she stayed.

She rose from the chair and we headed for the stairs.

Other patrons from the upper floor came with us, no one dawdling, everyone wanting nothing more than to flee the building.

At ground level it was chaos.

People rushed for the outside.

The two men with guns were nowhere to be seen.

I avoided the three main exits and turned right toward the kitchen door I'd noticed from above. The ground-floor dining room was nearly vacant. I glanced up to see Valdez still struggling to raise the heavy table off himself, the server helping. We passed through the swinging door and into the kitchen, where the panic had not quite taken hold. I decided to toss a little gasoline on the fire.

"There's a guy out there with a gun," I yelled.

The cooks and a few of the servers did not have to be told twice. They all headed for a door at the far side that, I hoped, led to daylight.

And it did.

We came out to the back of the building and a small parking lot. More of the old town's narrow streets bordered the open space along with rows of clapboard houses. If we hurried we could disappear before Valdez, or his two men, realized where we'd gone.

We both saw the trolley at the same time.

One of those long, open-aired vehicles, orange and green and fashioned like a choo-choo train, it was intended for visitors who wanted to be driven around to the city sights. Its tail end had just passed the restaurant parking lot, heading away, down the street. We rushed ahead and leaped onto the last car, taking a seat. The driver fifty feet away was droning on about the historic sights we were passing. I glanced back and saw Valdez, standing in the street, his clothes stained by the food shower.

"Senora Perry," he called out. "I never was able to say that your father sends his regards. I'll be seeing him shortly."

Valdez raised one of his fingers, as if to add some accusing emphasis to a seemingly casual remark. Coleen heard the words and I saw the concern in her eyes. We both got it. Valdez had Benjamin Foster. Which changed everything. I knew what she wanted us to do.

Go back.

"We can't," I said, motioning to the backpack. "If Oliver gets those files, they'll never see the light of day."

I've always been amazed how easily I made that decision considering what was at stake. In the years that followed I would make a zillion similar tough calls, some that even cost people their lives. Each one would be agonizing, but none would ever measure up to that first one.

"I get that," she said. "I got it back in the restaurant. You go. Find out what you can. Keep the files and the coin. I'll take my chances that these files are more important than I am. Oliver will surely want to deal." She handed over the backpack and fished Nate's cell phone from her pocket. "Hold on to this. You may need it."

Then she hopped off the moving tram to the street.

I turned back to see her waiting on Valdez, who was marching toward her.

The trolley turned a corner.

Should I jump off, too? Go back and help her? No. The mission came first. All I could hope was that she was right and Valdez and Oliver would do nothing until they could obtain the files and the coin.

The tram kept moving, picking up speed.

I left it a few minutes later at a crowded intersection, slipping off to the sidewalk while the driver waited for the red light to change. I was back near the main plaza and I could see a litany of emergency vehicles, their lights flashing in the bright sun, still busy at the scene where Veddern had been shot.

I needed some privacy to assess my options.

I noticed a large Spanish Revival–style building not far away, identified as the Lightner Museum. Originally one of Henry Flagler's flagship hotels, it once contained the world's largest indoor pool. Now it was a massive antiquities museum housing an eclectic collection of 19th-century art and décor. Some people called it Florida's Smithsonian.

I recalled what else was inside.

So I hustled around the building to its west side and followed the walkway to a side entrance. Through a dim, cool corridor I stepped into what was once the hotel's indoor pool. Now it housed the Café Alcazar, which Pam and I had visited. White-clothed tables dotted the gray, weathered cement. Three stories of railed balconies rose above from where guests had once leaped down into the cold water. Now those floors were part of the museum. Only a few of the tables were occupied. A pianist played, the soft, tinny music echoing through the cavernous space. What made the spot appealing was that it was entirely inside, with no windows. I needed a few minutes in relative safety to catch my breath.

And to think.

Coleen had told me to keep going. That meant finding the person named on Bruce Lael's pad.

I sat at one of the tables.

A server approached and, to buy time, I ordered a glass of iced tea.

I couldn't call Stephanie Nelle. She probably wasn't all that happy with me at the moment. This had escalated into something way beyond anything I'd ever imagined. My thoughts traced back over the last day and a half, which seemed like a lifetime. A man had just been shot. Another man had been blown up. Now Coleen and her father were in jeopardy.

Everything seemed to depend on me.

I sat for a few minutes and tried to connect the dots, but my thoughts spun uselessly. Much later in my career I would learn to embrace the constant fear, unceasing tension, and unrelenting insecurity. That unsettling combination of nerves, alertness, and weariness. At this moment, though, I was only just becoming acquainted with their presence. What I knew for sure, even then, was that I could not afford any rebellion inside myself.

Nothing that might trap me in a dilemma.

Had these men conspired to kill Martin Luther King Jr.? Were the conspiratorialists right? Did the wrongdoing stretch all the way up to the director of the FBI? A new sense of vibrancy, mixed with unease and dread, swept through me.

I had to keep going forward.

But I needed transportation.

I could call Pam. Our house was less than an hour away. But I wondered what she'd think if she knew I'd been traveling across the state with a woman. Would she think me as weak as I'd once been? Would she take out her fears on me with caustic and damning comments? More hateful words? I was beginning to believe that relationships never lasted. Pam and I had been together ever since I joined the Navy. Neither one of us had dated many others. We chose each other. I'd resolved never to repeat my mistake. I'd learned something during my dalliance into adultery. I hadn't liked anything about it, which probably explained how I was caught. I'd realized the mistake almost immediately, knowing that I loved my wife. So I'd ended things fast, but not before Pam learned what had happened. The old cliché was true. The spouse always knew.

No.

Pam was not an option here.

The server returned with my tea.

I sipped the cold liquid and tried to calm down. A wince of shame swept through me. I should have gone with Coleen. Maybe I should just turn this all over to Stephanie Nelle. Her resources far exceeded mine. But this was my operation. My chance to show that I could make things happen. I recall vividly how, on that day, my driving ambition seemed cloudy in its outlines, but precise in its parts. Was I being selfish? Probably. But what rookie wasn't a little bit self-centered?

And really, really blind.

Remember that mistake I'd made?

Its presence had yet to be felt.

But it was about to.

CHAPTER THIRTY-EIGHT

I RODE OUT OF ST. AUGUSTINE ON HIGHWAY 16, HEADING WEST toward Green Cove Springs. Originally, all I had was a name from Bruce Lael's pad.

Cecelia Heath.

And a telephone number.

Luckily, it included the area code.

So I borrowed the house phone at the Café Alcazar and called a friend I'd made at the Naval Criminal Investigative Service in Jacksonville. Thankfully, he was at his desk and helped me out, linking an address to the telephone number. The Orange County Sheriff's Department used that capability when Coleen had called, and NCIS had it, too. The address he provided was located in Starke, a small community in central Florida, about fifty miles from St. Augustine. Its claim to fame was twofold: a National Guard base and the Florida State Prison. I then found a local taxi company that agreed to drive me the fifty miles for $100. Luckily, I had that amount in my wallet.

I sat in the backseat of an old Chevy Impala converted into a cab and drank my iced tea, which I'd switched into a to-go cup. The sweet, cold liquid ran down my throat and felt good, spreading relief to all channels in my body. I thought about the questions Coleen would have for her father. Why had he been given a 1933 Double Eagle? And yet he never cashed the coin in. Holding on to it for over thirty years. If Valdez had not made contact, and Coleen hadn't gone behind his back, no one would have ever known.

I realized exactly what she was thinking.

Valdez had been paid with a coin. Her father had been paid with a coin. We knew what Valdez had done to earn his payment. He'd recruited, encouraged, then made sure James Earl Ray went to Memphis.

But what had her father done?

The cab kept heading west down a twisting lane of asphalt, through stands of hardwoods and pines and farmland. I appreciated the fact that the driver stayed silent. The last thing I needed right now was a chatty Cathy.

Florida wasn't so flat here. There were actually hills, the highway rolling in spots. No palm trees or beaches in sight. Just dense pine forests and verdant thickets that occasionally gave way to agricultural fields. I had no idea who I was heading to see, only that Bruce Lael had wanted me to make the journey. I wondered what it took to live with the fact that you'd participated in the death of Martin Luther King Jr. The man had been a son, husband, father, minister, activist, Nobel laureate, icon. He helped change the face of America, leaving a mark on the entire world. Imagine what more he could have accomplished if he'd lived. No wonder Lael was tormented. But what about Foster? Was he equally tormented? Or had his involvement been something else entirely, something more selfish that he did not want revealed to anyone.

Especially to his daughter.

All good questions.

The cab drove into Starke, a tiny town among a sea of trees, home to about five thousand people. Lots of gas stations, fast-food places, billboards, and power poles. Everything about the place yearned back to a time before tourism became the state's number one industry. No flashy neon or high-rises, just quaint and walkable. The address I had was Greek to both me and the driver, so we made a stop at a 7-Eleven and learned directions. We found the house a few miles outside the town limits on a rural, two-lane blacktop, not far from the state prison. I paid the fare and climbed from the cab into the afternoon's humid gloom.

A dirt lane led from the highway about fifty yards through pal-
metto spikes and scrub trees to a white brick house with reddish-brown
shutters. The drowsy caw of a crow offered me a greeting. No name
appeared on the mailbox, only an innocuous route number. I opened
the box and was pleased to see envelopes addressed to either Cecelia or
Cie Heath.

Apparently I was at the right place.

I walked ahead, following a low chain-length fence hidden under a
bank of honeysuckle.

The crack of gunfire broke the silence.

A bullet plucked at the ground to my right, scaring the crap out of
me. I stopped, a hard knot of apprehension knotting my muscles.

"Who are you?" a woman's voice called out.

I stood there, with the backpack in one hand, focusing on the house
and an open window under the front porch.

"I came to speak with you. Bruce Lael sent me."

"You have a name?"

"Cotton Malone."

"Walk down the drive. Real slow. And keep those hands where I can
see them."

I did as ordered, realizing that I'd been shot at more during the past
twenty-four hours than ever in my entire life.

"Are you Cecilia Heath?"

"I prefer Cie," she said, pronouncing her name *See*. "Why are you
here?"

I came close to the porch steps and could see the rifle barrel in the
half-opened window.

"Stop there."

"Bruce Lael is dead," I told her.

No reply.

So I drove the point home.

"Tom Oliver blew him up with a car bomb."

Still silence.

But the rifle disappeared.

Then a small, sparrow-sized woman emerged into the porch shade, the screen door banging back on its hinges. She was in her late sixties or early seventies, mouth wide, face slightly squared off, her cheekbones framed by an unruly mass of gray-brown hair. She held the rifle angled down, her face and eyes as flat, dark, and expressionless as stone. I stood in the afternoon sun, watching her.

"How did you know Lael?"

"We were married fifteen years."

"Do you know Tom Oliver?"

She nodded.

"I was his secretary, for nearly thirty."

She invited me inside where the air was thick with the waft of nicotine. She did not relinquish the rifle. I could tell she was wary of my presence. I told her again who I was, who I worked for, and why I was there. Her last name was different, so I asked, "You and Lael were divorced?"

"For a long time. My second husband died a few years ago."

"Lael wanted me to come find you. Do you know why?"

"What's in that backpack?"

"Classified files from Cuba that detail an operation called Bishop's Pawn."

She smirked. "Those are two words I haven't heard in a long time."

"Did you work for Oliver when it happened?"

She nodded, but studied me with a calculated gaze. This woman had apparently been a career civil servant. I decided to play a hunch and found a few of the memos that had been sent from Washington back to the field and showed them to her.

Her perusal was short.

"I typed those," she said.

"You must have typed tens of thousands of things. How do those stick with you?"

"You don't forget plotting to kill the greatest civil rights leader in the country."

Hearing that admission shocked me. Everyone else had beat around the bush. Not this woman. "Why didn't you ever tell anyone?"

She shook her head. "Because when it happened I was a racist and a bigot. I hated every colored person in this country. My boss, and his boss, hated them, too."

She glanced back at the memos in her hand.

"The summer of '67 was full of race riots. So many people died. Black militants were on the rise, antiwar protestors were everywhere. We believed communists were behind it all. Who else could it be? Martin Luther King took his marching orders straight from the Kremlin. It made sense. Sure. Why not? Part of a national fear that people today just don't understand. Back then, most of the country believed we had to stop the spread of communism in Southeast Asia. When King publicly came out in '67 against the Vietnam War, that made him even more of a danger. Mainstream white America became terrified of King. So when Hoover decided to kill him, I frankly could not have cared less. Good riddance."

But I sensed something in her. "That's not you anymore, is it?"

"A little, maybe. I'm still no flaming liberal. But I'm not a racist or a bigot anymore. Thirty years teaches you how wrong you can be. What did King himself say? *The arc of the universe is long, but it bends toward justice.* He was right."

"And yet you've still stayed silent?"

"What am I supposed to do?" Her voice rose. "Nobody would believe a thing I said." She motioned to the memos. "You're the only one with written proof. What are you going to do?"

"Are you willing to come forward now?"

"And do what?"

"Corroborate what's in these files. Like you just said, you typed some of them."

"What are you, some kind of lawyer?"

"Not today." I recalled what Oliver himself had told me about compartmentalizing, and how no one knew it all but him. "How did you know what happened? Oliver surely didn't include you in the loop on the main goal."

She tossed me a glance as she considered the obvious strain of in-credulity in my voice.

"No, he didn't tell me a thing," she said.

I was puzzled.

Then I heard movement from another room and someone entered the den.

"I told her," Bruce Lael said.

CHAPTER THIRTY-NINE

I CAME TO MY FEET FROM THE CHAIR. "YOU LOOK GOOD FOR A guy torched in a car bomb."

"Your visit interrupted my diversion," Lael said.

"A bit dramatic, wouldn't you say?"

"I actually got the idea from Oliver himself. He paid me a visit a few days ago. He and I have never seen eye-to-eye. He told me that it would be a shame if my car exploded one day, with me in it. So I decided, what the hell, why not?"

"And the point?"

"It draws a lot of attention, which will slow him down and give me time to disappear from both him—" He paused. "—and your subpoenas."

"I'm going with him," Cie said. "Tom Oliver is not going to let this lie. Valdez has opened a firestorm, aggravated by you."

"I'm glad to see you got my message," Lael said. "I was wondering if it struck home."

"Contrary to what you called me, I'm not some dumb-ass rookie."

"You keep telling yourself that. Confidence is good in the field. You're going to need it."

"There was no body in that car?"

Lael shook his head. "Nope. Just one big bang. It's been a few hours so they certainly know by now I wasn't inside. The locals are wondering what the hell is going on. Oliver is probably shaking his head. The idea was just to buy me some time and slow Oliver down." He pointed a finger at me. "I made some calls right after Reverend Foster called me. The bureau has an active investigation going on Oliver. An internal corruption probe. But the Justice Department is involved, too, separately, headed by a lawyer named Stephanie Nelle. You work for her?"

I nodded, deciding to be honest. "An FBI administrator named Dan Veddern was shot in St. Augustine. Valdez did it."

"Shooting the head of the intelligence branch takes balls."

"You don't seem surprised."

"It takes more than that to shock me."

I said, "There are a lot of questions about why people in the FBI are so curious about a 1933 Double Eagle and a man named Juan Lopez Valdez, who made it to the Dry Tortugas from Cuba. Did you help the FBI get its hands on two 1933 Double Eagles?"

Lael smiled. "I found them during a COINTELPRO burglary around 1963, I think. I can't really remember. They came off a mafia connection. We stole them to generate a civil war within that family, and we got one. They killed each other faster than we could have prosecuted them. Oliver kept the coins. Turning them in to the Secret Service would have raised a pile of questions that nobody wanted to answer. So we just held on to them. We collected lots of cash and valuables that way. It became a private reserve fund. I knew that Valdez and Foster were paid with those coins."

"You recorded the transaction?"

He nodded. "Not Valdez. But I did Foster. Oliver wanted everything memorialized. His way of making sure Foster never went public. But the coin was an insult. Payment, yet not. He'd have to liquidate it somehow, which Oliver knew would be tough."

"Was Foster an FBI informant?"

He didn't immediately answer me. Finally, he said, "I'm going to take the Fifth on that one. Ask Foster."

I added that to the list of questions for later. "Veddern said they were about to take you into custody."

"Which is another reason for the big bang. I was tipped off by

Oliver that Veddern was coming. His way of showing me we were all on the same side. Veddern's problem was in underestimating Oliver. That's a mistake I don't plan to make. Oliver was the world's greatest kiss-ass. All he wanted was Hoover's constant approval. He told that SOB exactly what he wanted to hear, and did exactly what Hoover wanted. Then after Hoover died he turned on him, and managed to stay around for twenty-five more years. He knows where a lot of skeletons are buried, literally, and he still has friends in high places."

"Where are you two going?"

Cie shrugged. "Far away from here. Hopefully far enough that Tom Oliver, or the FBI, won't consider us a threat anymore."

"They'll go looking for you."

"Sure they will," Lael said. "But I'm real good at being a ghost."

I was curious. "Was it as bad, back in the '60s, as FBI history says it was?"

"Worse," Cie said. "We had little to no oversight. Congress and presidents were terrified of Hoover. No one wanted to cross him. Ever hear of Jean Seberg?"

I listened as she told me about the actress, whoses donations to the NAACP, Native American groups, and the Black Panther Party placed her squarely on the subversive radar, so Hoover turned COINTEL-PRO her way. They created a false story that her white husband was not the father of her unborn child, but that instead it was the product of an affair with a Black Panther. The article appeared in both the L.A. *Times* and *Newsweek*. The stress and trauma from that supposed revelation caused Seberg to prematurely lose the baby. In defiance, she held a funeral with an open casket to allow reporters to see the infant girl's white skin.

But Hoover didn't stop there.

COINTELPRO conducted years more of surveillance, break-ins, and wiretapping on Seberg, all of which happened not only within the United States but in France, Italy, and Switzerland where she lived for most of her life. Progressively, she became more and more psychotic until, at age forty, she killed herself.

"Six days after she died in 1979," Cie said, "the FBI confirmed publicly everything I just told you. *Time* magazine did a big article. 'The FBI vs. Jean Seberg.' I remember the outrage. People couldn't believe the FBI would do something like that to a private citizen. Of course, Hoover was dead and gone by then. Oliver okayed the release of the Seberg file as a way to distance himself from Hoover. He was trying to survive the Church Committee, and he did. Little really changed, though. COIN-TELPRO was officially dismantled, but its activities kept going, just in different forms, and much more quietly."

"This is something entirely different," I pointed out.

"How do you figure?" Cie asked. "Same people. Same rules. Same thing. Do you think King was the only person they killed?"

I wondered how much this woman knew, but realized this was not the time or place.

"Can I take a look at those files?" Lael said.

I didn't see the harm and it might lead to more information from him. So I handed over the backpack.

"This is a lot easier to carry than that case you were hauling at my house," Lael said.

"A gift from the FBI."

"What do you mean?" Lael asked.

"We switched it out before meeting with Veddern. Our FBI escort gave it to me."

I saw Lael's eyes light up and the look of concern he tossed toward his former wife.

"What did I do wrong?"

"Get your suitcase. Now," Lael said to Cie. "Hurry."

Lael himself sprang from his chair and gathered up a duffel bag on the far side of the room. Cie raced into another part of the house, emerging with a suitcase in hand.

I had no idea what was happening. "What's going on?"

"They didn't give you that backpack to be friendly. It's tagged. It has to be. They can track it."

I'd only seen such things in the movies or on television. "They really can do that?"

"Absolutely. We have to get out of here. You may have screwed up everything we planned." Lael faced Cie. "What do you think? Leave it here?"

She nodded.

Lael unzipped the backpack and removed the files, stuffing them into his duffel bag. Then he tossed the backpack across the room and said, "Let's go."

We rushed out the back door and headed for a detached garage. Inside sat a shiny Chevy pickup. Lael tossed his duffel bag and Cie's suitcase in the bed and we all climbed into the cab.

"You drive, rookie," Lael said.

I noticed that Cie had brought her rifle.

I heard the sound of a car arriving outside, then the screech of tires as it braked hard on the loose ground.

Doors opened, then closed.

Lael motioned for silence.

We crept to one of the garage windows, this one offering a view toward the front of the house.

The two men from the plaza, the ones Coleen and I had coldcocked, were here.

CHAPTER FORTY

"They're Veddern's men," I whispered to Lael and Cie.

We stayed low and out of sight, not making a sound. All of the doors into the garage were closed. The two visitors seemed to be deciding whether to enter the house. A deep and leaden silence reigned.

"They know the backpack is still inside," Lael whispered. "They're going in to find it. You can count on that."

"Which gives us time to get out of here," I said.

"You got that right."

I noticed that the garage door opened with an electronic motor. Which could take forever. I saw Lael was considering that dilemma, too.

"We'll pop the release to the motor," he said, "and I'll roll it up fast. Once I have the door headed up, start the motor and I'll hop in. Cie—"

"I know. I'll be ready."

Cie and I crept over to the truck, and I quietly eased open the driver's-side door.

"They're about to make their move and go inside," Lael reported from the window.

I settled in behind the wheel and she handed me the keys. I readied the ignition and noticed her rolling down the passenger-side window, leaving the door itself half open.

They're inside, Lael mouthed, shifting from the window to the front of the truck and hopping up on the bumper, reaching for a rope that hung from the metal ceiling track on which the garage door ran. Every garage had a release lever that allowed the door to be manually opened and closed. If not, what would you do when the power went out?

Lael released the door from its track.

Then he climbed down and grabbed hold of a metal handle, glancing back my way.

His look said it all.

Ready?

I nodded, my fingers on the keys, foot on the accelerator.

He lifted the door upward.

It rose, exposing the light of day. I fired the engine and moved my right foot to the brake, shifting the automatic transmission into drive. Lael hopped into the cab and closed the door.

"Hit it, rookie."

I revved the engine and we roared from the garage, heading for the drive out to the street. We passed the new vehicle and Lael pushed back in his seat, allowing Cie to aim her rifle across him, out the window. She fired three times, taking out two tires in the process.

That should slow them down considerably.

In the rearview mirror, through a plume of dust rising in our wake, I saw the two guys rush from the house. We found the highway and I turned left, heading west, away from Starke. A van appeared to our right, slowing at the drive. I cut it off by speeding ahead.

The van braked to a stop.

I increased speed.

Lael and Cie were staring out the rear windshield.

In my mirror I saw the two guys from the house run out into the highway and leap into the van.

"That's not good," I muttered.

"No. It's not," Lael said.

The van sped our way.

We had a half-mile head start, but that might not mean a thing. The gleaming blob in the rearview mirror kept growing in size as it approached.

"You ever done this before?" Lael asked.

218 | STEVE BERRY

"On my grandfather's farm all the time."

He shook his head. "Lot of good that's going to do us."

I drove with a sense of urgency, forcing attention on my hands and feet, my eyes flicking back and forth, watching the mirrors, then what was ahead.

The road ran straight as a ruler.

Where was a state trooper when you needed one.

"They're coming," Cie said.

At least we had the rifle.

The van sucked close to my bumper. I gave the engine more gas, but the van stayed near. Then it veered into the other lane and pulled abreast. I decided why outrun it and let off the gas, allowing our speed to slow, dropping us back behind the van.

"That'll work," Lael said.

The van veered back into our lane and its rear doors suddenly swung open.

We all saw the gun at the same time.

I swung the wheel hard left, into the oncoming lane. Away from the gun, but right into the path of a vehicle coming straight at us.

An eighteen-wheeler.

The van seemed to see the approaching truck, too, dropping speed and trying to hem us in in the wrong lane. I had no choice but to hit the brake and slow, so we could drop in behind the van, but the move was going to allow the eighteen-wheeler to close the gap between us even faster.

Timing was everything.

I popped the brake, slowed the truck, then veered right into the correct lane just as the eighteen-wheeler swished by, its horn blaring.

"Not bad," Lael said.

We were now back behind the van with our original problem.

Men with guns ahead of us.

The rear doors swung open again.

But Lael was ready.

He hung his head and arms out of the passenger-side window with the rifle in hand, firing twice.

The van swerved into the opposite lane to disrupt our line of fire.

No cars were coming from ahead. Trees and fields lined both sides of the rural highway.

"Can you take out one of the tires?" I asked.

The speedometer showed we were moving at 75 mph. The van had started weaving back and forth between the two lanes, the men inside probably readying for more shots of their own. Lael stuck his head and shoulders back out the window, along with the rifle, and tried two shots that missed. I decided I'd had enough and floored the accelerator, speeding us up so that when the van veered left into the opposite lane, I brought the truck parallel to it, then I jerked the steering wheel left, slamming the truck into the van.

Once.

Twice.

A third time, adding even more speed to the thrust.

The van vaulted the highway and plowed a path into a field, bumping and weaving before settling into soft earth.

Lael let out a yell.

We kept barreling down the highway.

CHAPTER FORTY-ONE

I FOLLOWED THE DIRECTIONS CIE PROVIDED. WE EVENTUALLY found U.S. 301 and turned south, driving thirty miles to Gainesville, home of the University of Florida. Neither Lael nor Cie had much to say. Cie led us through town to the Greyhound bus station. I parked out front and we walked inside.

"This is where we leave you," Lael said. "We'd planned on a different route. But that won't work anymore."

"I'll say it again. You two are the only ones who can verify any of this."

Lael unzipped his duffel bag, removed the files, and handed them over. "This is your problem, rookie. Not ours. We're done."

"You're just going to let this all fade away," I asked.

"Better than us dying," Cie said. "You have no idea all the bad things COINTELPRO did. It was so much more than Martin Luther King. Tom Oliver wants all that to stay buried, and I agree. You need to take a lesson from us and let this lie. Give those damn files to whoever you have to give them to, then forget any of this ever happened."

"I can't do that."

"Sure you can," Lael taunted. "It's real easy. Nobody is going to believe you anyway. They'll just say those files were fabricated."

"That's where you two come in. It's called corroboration."

Lael wrapped an arm around my shoulder. A friendly gesture. "Listen to me. There's nothing here. You can't prove a thing. Let it go."

The bus station was crowded, typical probably for a college town. I'd only ridden on a Greyhound once, years ago when my mother and I traveled from my grandfather's farm in middle Georgia to Atlanta for the weekend. *An adventure,* she'd called it. I was eleven, my father gone by then. I remembered every minute of the entire weekend.

"Where are you going?" I asked.

"Better you don't know," Lael said. "But it'll be somewhere that Tom Oliver, you, and the FBI will have a hard time finding."

"Keep the truck," Cie said. "You're going to need it more than we do, since I don't suspect you're going to take our advice and give this up."

"Valdez has Foster, his daughter, and his son-in-law. And Oliver is still out there. I'm the only one who can deal with that."

"Now, that's some new information you kept close to the vest," Lael said. "Another piece of advice. Being the hero is great. There are rewards. But when you tug on Superman's cape, expect him to tug back. Oliver has resources and reach and he's on high alert. Everything he's worked to accomplish could unravel. He lives that rich high life now off his wife's money. He doesn't plan on spending the rest of his time in jail. So he's prepared to do anything, and I mean anything. Are you?"

I didn't answer him.

But it was a fair question.

"I saw a lot of agents in my time," Cie said. "I became pretty good at judging them. You need to turn this over to the professionals."

Now, that one hurt. "I can handle it."

She chuckled and looked at Lael. "Another hotshot. How many did we know?"

"You can change history," I said to her.

"And get myself killed in the process."

"You have to realize something," Lael said. "We didn't know anything about anything at the time. I knew some, thanks to the taping I overheard. More than most, in fact. But I didn't know it all. Cie, here, learned a lot from me, and I learned things from her. When I made contact with Foster years ago, I learned some more, as he did from me. But

I never had the whole picture, and I liked it that way. I know just enough to get me either jailed or killed."

There was nothing more to be said. These two were about to disappear. Fine. Good riddance. I had a job to do. "Go find your bus. I'm out of here."

And they walked off.

No farewells, no handshakes, no words of comfort or encouragement, just a blunt parting of the ways.

I headed outside for the truck with the files, disgusted by the whole situation. At the time their attitude was both puzzling and annoying. But twelve years later when I left the Magellan Billet, I felt the same way. I'd done my time. Served my country.

And survived.

It was someone else's turn.

"Rookie."

I turned to see Lael, outside, trotting my way.

He approached and stopped. "I wanted you to find Cie for a reason. I've become quite the cynic in my retirement. But when you've done the kind of things I did for a living, for as long I did them, it's unavoidable. Your view of the world changes. Your morals change. Your conscience changes."

He reached into his pocket, removed a cassette tape, and handed it over.

On it was written a date.

March 31, 1968.

"I recorded that myself, in Atlanta, from inside a motel room. It's a conversation between Jansen and Foster. The original went to Oliver as part of COINTELPRO. But I made a copy. It's the only thing I ever copied. A few years ago I transferred it from the old reel-to-reel tape to cassette. You'll understand everything once you listen to it. I was going to burn it, but Cie just told me that would make what we did even worse." He paused. "She's right."

I could see he was bothered.

"I was like Cie. I hated blacks. I really hated King. Why? I couldn't tell you now. So I had no problem, then, doing what I did."

"And now?"

He shrugged. "I wonder what in the world I was thinking. I broke into people's homes and businesses and planted bugs. I recorded what they said and listened to every private word. I thought I was doing the right thing. Protecting America. But I wasn't." He pointed at the cassette. "That's the only copy that exists. Cie has kept it all these years. That's why you and I had to come to her. It's your problem now, rookie. Make the right call, okay?" He paused. "Cie and I have been divorced a long time. She remarried. I never did. Truth be told, she's the only woman I ever loved and she knows it. Maybe we can have a few years together, in peace, and forgive ourselves."

I stared at the cassette.

Over the following decade I came to learn that the second rule of the intelligence business was to always know your opponent. The first was to identify your friends.

And this man had just become the latter.

"Good luck to you," I told him.

A small wisp of a smile formed on the corner of his lips.

He tossed me a casual salute then walked off, disappearing inside the bus station. I never saw him again, nor did I ever learn what happened to him or Cie. Hopefully, they found those few years of peace.

I climbed into the truck and noticed that the music system came with a cassette player. I was parked under the shade of some tall oaks, so why not. I laid the files on the front seat beside me. The coin was still in my pocket along with Nate's cell phone.

I popped the tape into the machine.

And pushed PLAY.

CHAPTER
FORTY-TWO

Jansen: What happened in Memphis? That was a full-fledged riot. The police had to use Mace and nightsticks. A sixteen-year-old boy was killed, fifty more injured. Four thousand National Guardsmen had to be called out to keep order. What a mess.

Foster: The march turned uncontrollable. We were moving along, like always, then a group of militants appeared and started smashing store windows. After that, it just became worse. King wanted to stop them, but the locals were worried about his safety. They took us out of there. People are angry in Memphis. Really, really angry. They're not interested in nonviolence anymore.

Jansen: This just proves our point. The Bishop talks that peaceful protest crap, but he can't deliver on that anymore. The press filleted him for that riot. Finally, we're getting somewhere with him. For the first time, a march led by Martin Luther King Jr. turned violent by the demonstrators themselves.

Foster: You need to know. There's also a division forming within the SCLC. A meeting yesterday turned nasty. King walked out and told them all to go to hell. Most everybody wants to head off in a new direction. Jesse Jackson is probably breaking out on his own soon. Hosea Williams has been attacking King more and more. The Black Panthers are on the rise. Everything is changing.

Jansen: Did you see what LBJ said about the Memphis march? He offered no defense of King. None at all. But he did denounce what happened and laid the blame on the black leaders. LBJ isn't King's pal anymore.

Foster: King wants to go back to Memphis in a few days.

Jansen: Does he now?

Foster: Nobody else wants to go back. Jesse Jackson thinks Memphis is too small for King. Andy Young is ready to move on. Even Levison wants to stay away. But King told them he has no choice. He has to go back and lead another march. He says it will be his Poor People's Campaign, planned for DC next summer, in miniature. He'll show the country that he can lead a peaceful, nonviolent protest. No one agreed with him. He became really agitated and lost his temper. That's unusual. Then he stormed out of the meeting.

Jansen: So he's having problems with his own people. That's even better to hear. He's been on a self-destructive path for a while now.

Foster: Why don't you stop hedging with me?

Jansen: What are you talking about?

Foster: I'm not a fool.

Jansen: I never said you were.

Foster: You just treat me like one. We've been at this for months now. I know what you're doing.

Jansen: We pay you for information. What we do with it is none of your business.

Foster: I've watched King for years. I've been right there every step. Hoover's right. He's immoral. He's also a liar. He tells all of us to toe the line, but he does whatever he pleases. He says money isn't important, but he wants for nothing, while we get paid next to nothing. I'm tired of it. I don't give a damn about this civil rights crap. Who the hell cares? I'm not interested in changing the world. I'm tired of being sprayed with fire hoses and attacked by dogs. They're never going to give me a Nobel Prize. I. Don't. Care. All I want is money. What do you want?

[PAUSE]

Jansen: We don't want a martyr.

Foster: You won't get one. You people have tape after tape showing what King does with women. I heard the recordings you sent to his house. I know about all those women, along with others you don't know about. Release those tapes and you won't have a martyr. People will know King for the barnyard dog he really is.

Jansen: What will happen if he's killed?

Foster: There'll be violence of a magnitude never seen before in this country. Cities will burn.

Jansen: You really think so?

Foster: Everything is ready to explode. I just told you that the SCLC is on the verge of collapsing. Nonviolent resistance is over. America will burn, then it will all fade. If you handle it right, King will be remembered for what he is. A lying, cheating husband who can't be trusted. And I'll be rich.

Jansen: You're a coldhearted bastard.

Foster: I'm just being real. I'm a black man in a country full of hate. Some of what King says makes sense. But the price to be paid to get what he wants is too much. Too many are going to be hurt or die. White people aren't going to share their world with us. Not without a fight. I don't want to pay that price. I don't care about civil rights. I care about money. I figure if I get enough from you, it won't matter that white people hate me.

Jansen: How much do you want?

Foster: A million dollars.

Jansen: You can't be serious.

Foster: Don't push me, or I'll ask for two.

Jansen: And what do I get for that kind of money?

Foster: I'll make your job real easy.

[PAUSE]

Jansen: What do you have in mind?

Foster: He's headed back to Memphis. He'll be at the Lorraine Motel starting the afternoon of the third.

Jansen: Why wait three days? I can have it done here in Atlanta right now.

Foster: No. Do it in the turmoil in Memphis. A white man kills Martin Luther King while he fights for the rights of black garbage workers.

Jansen: Who said anything about a white man?

Foster: If it's not, then you're a damn fool. It has to be a white man.

Jansen: I prefer to choose the place.

Foster: Good luck with that, since if you do I won't be providing any information to help. Ever thought about Kennedy's death? Oswald didn't need informants. They published the president's whole schedule in the newspaper, days in advance. All he had to do was show up. There's no schedule printed for

King, and things change constantly. My job is to keep up with those changes and get him where he needs to be. I'm your only source on that. I can help, or hurt you. Make a choice.

[PAUSE]

Jansen: *All right. We'll do it your way. But you're sure? You're ready to send the Bishop to his death?*

Foster: *You don't have to keep asking me that. It's clear we both know what we're doing. They're sending lawyers to federal court on the third and fourth to try to lift the injunction preventing another march. King will stay in Memphis until they get that done. Room 306. There'll be plenty of opportunities on the fourth to make this happen. Be ready. I'll call and provide you the best one.*

Jansen: *Memphis it is then.*

The tape ended.

I popped it from the machine and stared at the cassette.

A confidential source who has furnished reliable information in the past.

A fancy way to keep a trusted source's identity secret. I'd seen similar language in many NCIS reports. No wonder Benjamin Foster didn't want Coleen to know anything about this. He'd set Martin Luther King Jr. up to die.

All for a 1933 Double Eagle.

I looked again at the date on the cassette. March 31, 1968. Three days before the assassination. Bruce Lael had lived with that knowledge a long time. No wonder he'd made contact with Foster. I could only imagine what those talks had been like. I was truly amazed at Foster. To hear him talk, he'd been at King's side for years. He was there in the hospital when the man died. He cast himself as some civil rights warrior.

I sat in the truck.

Something buzzed in my pocket.

Nate's cell phone had come alive.

I removed the unit and answered.

"You ruined my clothes," Valdez said.

Like I cared. "Stuff happens."

"That it does. I have Reverend Foster, his daughter, and his son-in-law. I want my coin or I'll kill them."

"How about I just give your files back?"

"Too late for that. Reverend Foster would like to speak with you."

A moment later Foster came on the line.

"You and I need to talk. In person," Foster said.

I agreed. We did. "How's that possible?"

"Valdez says he will make it happen."

Like I was going to trust that. I stared out the windshield at the bus station. My mind raced.

"Do you have a car?" I asked.

"I did. But you took it."

"Sorry about that. Can you get another one?"

I heard Foster speaking to Valdez.

"Yes. I can get a car," Foster said.

"All right, here's what I want you to do."

CHAPTER FORTY-THREE

I SAT IN THE TRUCK AND ATE A BURGER, STILL TROUBLED BY WHAT I'd heard on the cassette. Foster had told me that it would be more than an hour before he appeared. The time was approaching 3:00 P.M., that hour about up. I'd told Foster to drive to Gainesville and find the bus station. I knew this site was secure. All I had to do was make sure it stayed that way, up to and including Foster's arrival. The experience with the backpack had taught me a lesson. I didn't plan on making the same mistake twice, and my caution was compounded by the fact that Valdez and Oliver were definitely working together.

That meant anything might happen.

Including the possibility that this was a trap.

I had told Foster to drive here and that a ticket would be waiting for him at the information desk inside. He was to take the designated bus when it arrived. Of course, the idea was to get him in and out of the station without attracting attention or alerting any tail that might be on him. I'd already reconnoitered the bus station, noting all of the exits, and I'd positioned the truck two addresses down from the depot in the parking lot of a strip mall busy with traffic. There was a path from here to a side exit in the bus terminal that could work as a discreet way for Foster to disappear.

Not foolproof.

But what was?

At least I was trying to stay ahead of things.

The burger had tasted great. I hadn't eaten a meal since last night. For me, stress brought a loss of appetite. When I tried a case I'd go days without eating much of anything. Once the verdict came in, my appetite always returned, and usually with a vengeance. I was beginning to see that the same malady occurred as a field agent.

I sucked more of my lemonade through the straw.

It seemed I was now the proud owner of a relatively new Chevy pickup. But I doubted we'd be together for long. That was another thing about my new temporary career. Few physical or personal attachments ever lasted.

From where I was located I had a clear view of the depot's main entrance and parking lot. I'd been watching everything carefully and had neither sensed nor seen nothing out of the ordinary. I kept reminding myself that Valdez was only allowing this gesture as a way to locate me.

So I'd taken even further precautions.

At a Mail 'N More I passed on the way to get the burger, I rented an onsite storage bin with a combination lock. I also bought a couple of oversized manila envelopes. The coin stayed in my pocket, since it might come in handy. It meant little to me, but everything to Valdez. So I decided to keep my options open as far as it was concerned. Cars came and went from the bus depot. Nobody seemed even remotely suspicious. Finally, a pale-yellow Camry entered and found an empty space.

Benjamin Foster emerged.

The car he was driving could definitely be tagged. After all, it came from Valdez, supplied surely by Tom Oliver. Another car entered the lot and parked on the far side beneath the trees. My eyesight was excellent and I could see two forms inside.

The tail I was expecting.

Foster disappeared inside the terminal.

Both car doors opened.

Jansen and Oliver stepped out.

I felt honored. Batman and Robin themselves had come.

There'd only be a few moments. The ticket that Foster would

receive at the information booth contained a note that instructed him to leave the building through the side exit to his left.

It also told him not to be obvious or in a hurry.

I revved the truck's engine and cruised through the lot, toward the dry cleaner next door, which sat between the strip mall and the bus terminal. It had a drive-through lane that faced the side exit from the depot. The key was to time this just right.

Oliver and Jansen were headed for the terminal's main entrance. Foster had been inside about two minutes. More than enough time. Oliver and Jansen were still thirty feet from the front doors when Foster emerged from the side exit. I wheeled from the dry cleaning's drive-through line and came to a stop, the passenger-side window already down.

"Get in. Fast," I yelled.

Foster hustled over and hopped inside.

I could no longer see the front of the terminal, but I had to assume Oliver and Jansen were inside, looking for Foster. Once they didn't see him in the main lobby, they'd check the bathroom. Only then would they realize he was gone.

Which should be ample time.

Foster settled into his seat.

I drove from the dry cleaner and turned left, heading off down the street, keeping watch in the rearview mirrors.

No one was following.

"We have much to discuss," Foster said.

I agreed.

"Nate and I were taken a few miles outside of Palm Beach," Foster said. "Like they were waiting for us."

"Valdez and Oliver are definitely working together. Before you say a word, though, there's something you need to listen to."

I hit PLAY on the radio and watched as Foster listened to his conversation with Jansen from thirty-two years before. When it was over, I stopped the cassette. I wanted him to know that this was going to be a no-bullshit conversation.

I knew it all.

"Where did this come from?" Foster finally said.

"Bruce Lael kept a copy. He gave it to me."

"Coleen said you found him. But he's dead?"

"Nope. That was all for show. He is long gone, now, though."

Foster pointed at the player. "Jansen is prepared to give me the original of that taped conversation in return for Valdez's files. Do you still have them?"

I reached beneath the seat and displayed two manila envelopes, thick with contents. "Right here."

Then I stuffed them back beneath me.

He still hadn't said a word about the recording. I assumed everything seemed unreal, distant, too dreadful to contemplate. My instincts told me to stay cautious. Nothing had been proven and nothing would be until I could unearth names, times, and dates. The minutiae. Which always told the whole story. Sure, I had feelings and emotions on what I knew so far, but those rarely led to victory. Winning demanded good judgment, steady discipline, and perfect timing.

"The files are bad enough," he said. "But you understand now why Coleen cannot hear that recording. Why she has to let this go."

"I get it. But I'm a different story. I know the truth."

I kept heading south out of Gainesville.

"Coleen has read the files," I told him.

I saw the concern on his face.

"But they say nothing about you. They only refer to an unnamed confidential informant. I'm assuming that was you."

After hearing the tape, it was the only thing that made sense.

He nodded. "Martin was the Bishop. I was the Pawn."

CHAPTER FORTY-FOUR

"I KNOW EXACTLY WHO YOUR SPIES ARE," FOSTER SAID TO JANSEN.

They were sitting inside a Krystal hamburger joint in Macon, Georgia, fifty miles south of Atlanta. This was their first face-to-face meeting. Contact before had always been by phone, Foster calling a number Jansen had provided to report information. A few days later a mailed envelope would arrive at a post office box, filled with hundred-dollar bills. The rules were clear. No envelope, no more information.

"As if I'm going to admit or deny anything to you," Jansen said.

Foster rattled off four names.

The look on Jansen's face confirmed that he was right.

"King told me to search out our ranks for any problems. He knows you have people there watching him. I searched and found those four. Fortunately for you, I haven't told King what I learned. Not yet anyway. I'm figuring that silence is worth more than a few hundred dollars."

"I'm not saying any of those people work for us."

"Okay. That's not a problem. I'll report their names to King. He'll fire all four and that will be the end of it. You can then start recruiting a new set of eyes and ears."

Jansen held up a hand in mock surrender. "All right. I get the point. You're calling the shots here. How did you ID them?"

"It wasn't that hard. They're not good at what they're doing."

"And you are?"

"I'm still here, working for King. He trusted me to find the spies. That means he doesn't suspect me at all. So yes, I am that good."

"Cocky is what you are."

"I'm still waiting for an amount from you on what you think I'm worth."

Jansen seemed to consider the matter, then said, "Five thousand."

"Twenty."

"Since I have no choice, okay."

"Send it the usual way."

"Why do you do this?" Jansen asked.

"White people think that all Negroes worship at King's altar. We're just mindless followers. That's not the case. A lot of black people out there have suffered to make a name for Martin Luther King Jr. They didn't get Nobel Prizes or invites to the White House. They don't hang out with celebrities or appear on television all the time. They just get beat up, arrested, then beat up some more, all while he lives the life of a hypocrite. You don't see what I see with King."

"I know enough to hear what you're saying."

"I owe a lot of people money. I barely make my rent with what the SCLC pays me. I need what you pay me, and more. So I want you to do something. Pass a message along to the men above you. The ones who tell you what to do. Ask them if they're willing to go all the way with King."

I listened as Foster told me about his face-to-face meeting with Jansen somewhere around the first of October 1967. In my mind I placed it in context with the reports I'd read from Valdez. That would be about the time James Earl Ray, posing as Eric S. Galt, was sauntering around Puerto Vallarta.

"Were you feeling them out?" I asked.

We were parked inside the municipal limits of a little town called Micanopy, about fifteen miles south of Gainesville, a lovely place from another time full of majestic live oaks dripping with moss. The main street came with a grand red-brick Greek revival mansion, complete with Corinthian columns, that housed a local historical society. The rest of the quaint old buildings supported a profusion of shops and eateries.

One caught my eye.

O. Brisky Books.

"I was definitely feeling him out," Foster said. "I suspected that they were planning something. You could tell. They were always anxious. I'd helped one of the spies they were already utilizing, providing him access to information he could never get otherwise. That was passed on, which led to Jansen making contact and recruiting me. But once I discovered all three of the other spies, I used that to up my value."

"When did they answer you? About how far they were willing to go."

"We met again. About a month after. This time in a motel room outside Atlanta."

"I posed your question," Jansen said. "To the people above me. Their answer is yes, they are more than willing to go all the way. We want King removed from any and all positions of leadership."

"That's not what I meant, and you and they know it."

"You want him dead?"

Foster nodded. "And don't look surprised. You've checked me out. You're the FBI. You know all about me. I'm a guy with a divinity degree that means little to nothing. My chances of ever becoming any more than I am now are next to zero."

"And you think killing King is a smart move?"

"I think it could be a profitable move. For me. But let me tell you how it's also good for you. There's something I've heard the Bishop say more times than I can count. He calls it the parable of the tent. There was this king who sought refuge in a tent with a hundred of his subjects. The problem was, none of those hundred people got along. They always fought among themselves. One day ten of them made the king mad, so he banished them from the tent. The next day ten more did the same thing and they were banished. The following day twenty more were tossed out. Finally, one of the king's advisers spoke up regarding the wisdom of throwing all those people out. "They're on the outside now, working against you," was the warning, which was a good one. The king laughed it off by pointing

out that those forty people couldn't agree on anything. All they did was
fight among themselves. Not true, his adviser said. They all agree on one
thing. They don't like you."

Jansen seemed to consider that statement.

"That's your problem summed up," Foster said. "Negroes love to fight
among themselves. They can hardly agree on anything. King knows that,
so he uses the parable of the tent to keep them united in the one thing they
all agree on. They hate the white establishment. So the only move you
have is to take him out."

Foster told me when that conversation occurred. November 1967.
I slipped it into its proper historical place. Ray/Galt was back in the
United States, cocooned in Los Angeles, where they kept him until
March 1968. Then he drove across the country, ending up in Atlanta
by the end of the month.

"Did Jansen ever actually say they were planning to kill King?"

"Never. Not until the conversation you have there on the cassette,
which was just days before. Prior to that we played cat and mouse on
the subject. Both of us knew what we were talking about, but no one
spoke the words."

"To make this work," Jansen said, "we have to track his movements. I
need precise details. This is not something that will happen immediately.
Nobody wants to get caught. We have to plan this out."

"I get it. I can provide everything. He moves around a lot. The man
never sits still, and his schedule changes by the hour."

"Your job is to keep us posted. We have to build a model of his move-
ments. How he interacts with crowds, the people around him, how he
travels, where he stays, who he sees. It's all important."

"That's what you pay me for."

"I gave him that information over the next several months," Foster
said. "Every detail on our movements. From November 1967 to April 4,
1968. I was never told directly what they were doing with it."

I knew.

At least in part.

From one of the reports in Valdez's files, dated March 28, 1968.

> Since March 18 GALT has been traveling by car from Los Angeles to Atlanta. A confidential source who has furnished reliable information in the past reports that KING is currently in Alabama. Yesterday, GALT was diverted to Selma, Alabama. KING was scheduled to make an appearance there to drum up recruits for his 1969 Poor People's Campaign in Washington, DC. GALT was sent there to evaluate KING in public and determine any vulnerabilities. Unfortunately, KING never made it to Selma. He was delayed in Camden, Alabama. The source alerted us to that fact and GALT was sent to Camden, 38 miles away, where he attended KING'S event and made his assessments. On March 23 GALT drove to Atlanta. For the past four days GALT has reconnoitered the city and identified both King's home and the Ebenezer Baptist Church.

My analytical brain plugged that memo into the time line with the cassette's recorded conversation. The report came three days before the face-to-face with Foster. Then, on March 31, 1968, they all decided that King would die in Memphis sometime on April 4.

"Lieutenant Malone," Foster said. "I'll say it again. You must see why I can't allow Coleen to learn any of this."

Part of me was disgusted even talking to this man. He was a willing party in a conspiracy to commit murder. Add to that the victim had been a leader, a hero, an icon. Even worse, he seemed to only care what Coleen would think. Which was not in doubt. But I needed this man to keep talking. So I played along.

"I get it, loud and clear. But, Reverend, this toothpaste is out of the tube. It's going to be hard to keep this a secret anymore."

He shook his head. "Coleen doesn't know any of this. Just you, me, Lael, Oliver, and Jansen. Valdez suspects, considering I had the coin, but he doesn't know for sure. We can keep this secret. Just give them the files."

Most of the dots had connected.

One remained.

"On the recording you asked for a million dollars. Yet they gave you a 1933 Double Eagle. How did that happen?"

CHAPTER FORTY-FIVE

WE SAT IN THE TRUCK, WITH THE WINDOWS DOWN, BENEATH THE shade of a stately oak. The June day was warm with little breeze. The bustling metropolis that was Micanopy, population 450 according to the welcome sign out on the highway, churned along at a quiet pace.

I watched as Foster struggled with his thoughts.

"You have to understand," he said. "I was only twenty-three. Barely out of divinity school. Martin recruited me before I was ever assigned a church. I was young, brash, and, in some ways, terribly arrogant. We all were some combination of that back then. It seemed necessary in order to endure what we had to endure. Four years I traveled across the country with him. So many protests. So many marches. Poverty was everywhere. It seemed the Negro's fate to always be poor. Most had little to no chance of doing anything meaningful with their lives. A few managed success, but the vast majority were beat down and held in their place by a system that refused to yield. I wasn't one of those who thought we should burn the country down in a violent revolution to change things."

"You just wanted to be rich." I mocked him with words from the tape.

He nodded. "I was foolish with money. I loved to bet on horses, dogs, sports, you name it. And I wasn't good at it. But it was an outlet. I liked nice clothes, fancy cars, good beer. In short, I liked to spend money. But what twentysomething-year-old doesn't?"

"What did you think would happen once King was dead?"

"I didn't care. None of that mattered to me. I only wanted my million dollars."

"But you got a coin."

He nodded. "A final insult from the white establishment."

"What is this?" Foster said, examining the gold coin Jansen had laid on the table.

"A 1933 Double Eagle. It's worth millions of dollars."

"How many millions?"

"Four or five at least. It's actually the last one known to exist."

"Why are you giving it to me?"

Jansen shrugged. "Sell it. Some buyer somewhere will pay you for it. Just be careful and don't get caught. It's actually illegal to own that coin."

"I don't want it. We agreed on a million dollars. Cash."

"And I just paid you more with the coin."

"That was not our deal."

"Look, Foster. There's no way we can give you a million dollars in cash. The moment you go to put that in a bank, red flags would rise everywhere."

"I have no intention of putting that money in a bank."

Jansen waved off the observation. "We can't risk anything being traced back to us. This has to be a clean break. You did your part. We did ours. We had this coin, which no one knows about. There's no trail back to us, besides your word. But you would have to implicate yourself in a conspiracy to commit murder in order to involve us. Besides, no one would believe you anyway. Trust me, preacher, we have erased all connections to you. There's not a piece of paper that even hints you ever existed. It's all gone. So take the damn coin. Sell it. And be grateful."

"You're a lying bastard."

"And you're the guy who sold out Martin Luther King Jr. for money. Which one of us is worse? You're lucky we even gave you the coin."

Foster picked up the gold piece. "Millions, you say?"

"Yep. I'm told it's the most valuable coin in the world."

"After he gave me the coin," Foster said, "I never saw or spoke to Jansen again, until yesterday."

"If not for Valdez and his pictures from Jansen's file, it would be all gone. Too bad for them it's not."

And I brought out the two thick manila envelopes again.

"They want those and the coin," Foster said, "in return for Coleen and Nate. They told me that if we can't make a trade, Nate and Coleen will go back to Cuba with Valdez and I'll never see either of them again. Do you still have the coin?"

I patted my jean pocket. "Safe and sound."

And I also still had Cie's rifle, whatever good that would do me.

"We have to give them what they want," Foster said. "Oliver said he'd give me the original of the recording you have here."

"Is that why you sold me out in Port Mayaca?"

"We were brought to Oliver's house for appearances. Once you and he talked and everything was secure, we would have all been released and I would have the original recording. Everything over. It seemed like a smart move."

"Except that Valdez had other ideas."

"That caught Jansen and Oliver off guard. So they've sent me to try one more time. They want this to go away as much as I do."

But I didn't.

I was now privy to a conspiracy that would shock the world.

"J. Edgar Hoover sanctioned the death of Martin Luther King Jr. Surely you can see that I can't let that go."

"What good comes from exposing it now?"

"Jansen and Oliver will go to prison."

"As will I, and I'll lose a daughter in the process."

"That inevitability was set in motion a long time ago, when you made the deal with them."

"I never sold the coin."

"Why not?"

"Never could find a buyer."

I smiled. "I thought you were broke. In debt. I thought you wanted to be rich. Tell me the truth. Why didn't you sell it?"

"The last year of Martin's life was truly difficult for him. He lost the president's ear when he came out against the war. He'd already lost the ear of many young blacks, who no longer believed nonviolence was the way for change. His marriage was in trouble. The SCLC swirled in civil war. He stayed depressed, tired, and despondent. Even his health was failing. He was overweight, smoked terribly, and drank too much. Doctors had told him he had the beginnings of serious heart disease.

"Black people were tired of being beat up by racists and thrown in jail, offering no resistance. They'd had enough of symbols. Even worse, many whites soured on Martin because of his shift on the Vietnam War. They accepted him as a spokesperson for civil rights, but not as an antiwar advocate. By April 1968 Martin was not the same man who'd stood at the Lincoln Memorial five years earlier and proclaimed *I have a dream.*"

I could hear the torment and regret in his voice.

"After his death, though, everything changed. It was amazing. The world began to listen again. It was as if he were still alive, at the height of his influence, his message loud and clear. He became relevant again. Hoover never discredited him. How could he? The man had been shot down in his prime. His image remained inviolate. He became a martyr. Only years later, when historians started culling through declassified FBI records, were Martin's personal weaknesses finally exposed. But by then none of it mattered. He wasn't a martyr anymore. He'd become a saint. A savior. How could I cash in on that?"

Maybe because you helped kill him? But I kept my thoughts to myself. Foster was right about one thing, though. Coleen and Nate were the priority.

"Where did you drive to Gainesville from?" I asked.

"A commercial building outside of St. Augustine, near an outlet mall. Valdez told me they would be leaving there just after I drove away. I have no idea where they are now. He gave me a telephone number to call, after I spoke with you, to arrange the trade."

"I still don't get why he let you leave."

"He wanted me to broker a deal, but I refused to do that anywhere near Coleen or Nate. This had to be face-to-face, just like when Jansen recruited me. Valdez knows that destroying those files and that recording is more important to me than anything. All he wants is the coin. Jansen and Oliver are a different matter. But strangely, we all have a similar goal."

"They followed you to Gainesville."

"I assumed that would be the case. What you had me do in the bus depot was to throw them off?"

I nodded. "And it worked."

No one had followed us.

My mind was racing.

I was assessing all of my options, which weren't many. One thing I knew. I couldn't tell Foster that there was no way I was relinquishing the files. The coin? Who cared? But the files and the cassette? Those were going to Stephanie Nelle. Yet to get Foster's cooperation, I would have to lie.

This guy shouldn't mind that, though.

He seems to have forged an entire life based on a lie.

"I have an idea," I said. "How we can help Coleen and Nate and solve your problem, too."

CHAPTER FORTY-SIX

DAN VEDDERN HAD THE RIGHT IDEA WHEN HE MET WITH COLEEN and me in St. Augustine's main plaza. Lots of people. Activity. Plenty of distractions. I decided that though it had been the right idea, there wasn't enough of all three for what I had in mind. So I opted for Disney World. If I was going to confront Jansen, Oliver, and Valdez, the place to do it was where there were thousands of people, a security presence, and too many witnesses for any of them to try anything foolish.

Foster and I drove from Micanopy south to Orlando. The trip took about ninety minutes. Just before reaching the entrance to Disney World, I stopped and called Valdez, at the number he'd provided Foster, using Nate's cell phone, its battery about on its last leg. Thankfully, the call went through and the meeting was arranged. I'd waited as long as possible before making contact so that this time I could control the high ground.

Foster and I parked the truck in a massive asphalt lot and took a replica steamboat across the lake to a dock outside the Magic Kingdom. There were three ways to get to the park: the boat, a monorail, and a bus. I opted for the boat so I could see in all directions. Twilight had arrived and darkness was coming. The time was approaching 8:00 P.M.

And it was raining.

Not hard. A steady mist that actually felt good mixed with the summer heat.

I paid for two admissions at the ticket gate using Stephanie's credit card. It didn't really matter whether she found me now or not.

This was about to be over.

One way or another.

I carried the two manila envelopes, sealed tight with tape. To protect them I bummed a plastic Mickey Mouse shopping bag from one of the vendors and handed the protected bundle over to Foster. I could see he felt better just holding those envelopes.

I was a little disappointed that there were no security checks to get inside the park. I'd been hoping for more. But people just walked right in through the turnstiles. That meant Oliver and company would most likely come armed. I was working at a disadvantage without a weapon. Cie's rifle would do me no good here. But sometimes you just had to play your cards as dealt. I was hoping this would go smoothly. I didn't want to place anyone here in jeopardy. But I kept telling myself that Oliver wanted the files, Valdez the coin, and Foster the recording and his daughter and son-in-law.

Nobody wanted a spectacle.

I had no idea where Valdez was located when I called, but I was sure we were way ahead of him. He'd told me on the phone that he would be there by 9:00 P.M. The park was on summer hours, open until midnight.

We headed into the Magic Kingdom.

Brightly lit topiary shrubs arranged as Mickey Mouse greeted us at the entrance. Through a covered breezeway we came up to ground level inside a town square adorned with manicured grass and pruned trees. Overhead the whistle of a train could be heard as it entered the station we'd just passed beneath. An array of pastel-colored, Victorian-style buildings surrounded us, creating the vision of a midwestern American town, circa 1900. The lilting strains of Disney tunes filled the damp air. Everything looked like a movie set, the perfect image of a perfect town. I decided higher was better, so we climbed some stairs to the train station depot and stood under an elevated porch that overlooked the square below. The rain continued to fall in a light drizzle, but the crowds didn't seem to mind. I assumed little to nothing ever stopped the fun here. Both breezeways into the park from the main gates were visible, one left, the other right. Foster and I stood at the railing.

"The incredible thing," Foster muttered, "was that it all happened over nonsense."

He'd offered little to nothing on the trip south, so I waited for him to explain.

"In '62 Martin told the press that the FBI was biased toward southern police. He said the FBI was a white organization that catered to white police. Blacks stood no chance with them. He also wondered why there were no black FBI agents. Hoover took great exception to all that. He never allowed anyone to criticize *his* FBI. Right after Martin made those statements, Hoover tried to set up a meeting to clear the air. This was the first encounter between Martin and Hoover. Hoover had subordinates call the SCLC office to make an appointment for them to meet. The people there took the messages and passed them on, but Martin never called back. Hoover took that to mean he was being shunned. Put off. Ignored. But that was not the case."

Foster shook his head.

"Martin was just bad about returning calls. He never did. Not to anyone. We all had to stay on him to make sure he called folks back. It was just his way. We now know that Hoover took that omission as a personal insult. Everything between them started after that."

"Why do you call him Martin?"

He stared back at me.

"You always refer to him as Martin. Not King. Or Bishop. Or anything, other than his name. Except on the tape with Jansen. There you called him King."

That was the lawyer in me. Listening to a witness. Noticing details. Especially inconsistencies.

"I did a terrible thing," he said, his voice barely audible. "I was so self-centered. So selfish. Martin saw that weakness in me early on."

"The money problem?"

He nodded. "That and my ego. I think the only reason the bookies didn't break my legs was because I was close to Martin. He and I talked about that a few times. He was such a forgiving man. Not a bone of hate in his body. I always thought it ironic how we both had weaknesses, only different."

"If you didn't care about the movement, why did you join?"

"It seemed like something exciting. An opportunity to be more than what life seemed to be offering me. I went to divinity school because that's what my mother wanted me to do. I joined the movement as a way to avoid a life as a preacher. I was hoping things would change. That there would be more opportunities. And there were. I became an informant for the FBI. I told myself that I didn't care about the world. About people. About anything, other than myself. Andy Young wanted me gone. Abernathy didn't like me, either. But Martin was in charge, so I was allowed to stay."

"You haven't answered the question, and you just called him Martin twice more."

"It's my way of humanizing him. Making him still real to me. An illusion that somehow we have remained friends." His sad eyes were near tearing. "But he's dead and I'm not."

"Nor are you rich."

He shook his head. "That's true. I never sold the coin because I was frightened. Finding the right buyer might have exposed me. Might have exposed the FBI. Those were dangerous men, who were not beyond killing people. I decided to stay in the shadows. To let it go. So I tossed that coin into a box, where it stayed until Coleen found it."

"What about all those debts?"

"I paid them off with the money Jansen gave me."

"Your wife never knew any of this?"

"Nothing. We married the year after Martin died. Coleen came along the year after that. My wife knew little of what I did before I met her."

"Coleen thought she might have known."

He shook his head. "I've kept this to myself for a long time, and I intended on taking it to my grave. All of this happening now is like a nightmare. Please tell me that you can keep this contained."

I had to maintain the lie.

"That's the plan."

We kept watch below, me to the left, Foster to the right. The two breezeways that led up from the turnstiles on the other side of the train station were the only paths into the Magic Kingdom. Our spot offered the perfect vantage point to see both, without being seen from below. Disney's famed Main Street stretched out before us, lit to the gloomy evening, Cinderella Castle in the distance, maybe a quarter mile away. A flood of people came and went in the light rain, most sheathed in plastic ponchos, their faces filled with excitement. I was hoping the weather might work to our advantage.

Below, to my left, I saw Oliver and Jansen enter the grounds. A quick turn of my head to the right and there were Valdez and Nate.

But no Coleen.

"Where is she?" Foster asked.

I gently pushed him back from the railing, so we'd be out of sight from below. We were not alone on the covered porch, as others had fled here to avoid the rain. We took refuge behind one of the wooden columns that supported the ornate roof.

Oliver and Jansen rounded the town square, staying on the left side of Main Street. Valdez and Nate followed on the right. Shops lined both sides all the way to Cinderella Castle. I'd told Valdez to meet me at the statue that stood at the far end of the street. I knew about it from visiting here once a long time ago as a kid. My one and only venture to the land of Disney.

"Stay here," I told Foster. "They've kept Coleen back as insurance to make sure this goes right. That's okay. I'm keeping you and those envelopes back as our hole card."

He nodded in understanding.

"Just stay put until I come back for you."

He grabbed my arm. "Get her and Nate back. Unharmed. Please."

"I will."

Many times, I've been wrong in my life.

But never more so than at that moment.

CHAPTER FORTY-SEVEN

I DESCENDED TO GROUND LEVEL AND HUSTLED ACROSS THE TOWN square, crossing the wet pavement and entering the first of the many stores lining Main Street. I remembered from my previous visit as a kid that the shops drained into one another so it wasn't necessary to go out of one, then back into the next. A clever marketing tool to keep people inside buying, it now provided me with a way to stalk my targets without being seen.

I zigzagged around display racks and merchandise counters, aiming my gaze to the right and out the doorways and glass storefronts. I was keeping pace with Oliver and Jansen on the sidewalk. There was no way for them to see me unless they stopped and entered one of the stores.

I chose the rendezvous point with a purpose. The bronze statue of a waving Walt Disney holding hands with his creation, Mickey Mouse, sat in the center of the park, just before the castle, at a busy crossroads. There should be plenty of people, though the rain might have thinned the crowd.

Occasionally, I caught sight of Nate and Valdez on the far side of Main Street, staying parallel to Oliver and Jansen. They were all being cautious, which I expected. Looking back, I'm ashamed at my arrogance. I'd been a field agent for all of two days and I was making life-and-death decisions like I was a pro. Even worse, I was doing it with a cavalier attitude of a lawyer thinking that the worst that could happen was I lost the case. Sure, my client might stay in custody, or be taken off to prison, but I still get to go home.

Not here.

Losing came with the direst of consequences.

I kept moving.

Oliver and Jansen came to the end of Main Street and I entered the last shop, creeping over to the open doorway and watching as the four men regrouped and walked straight toward the Disney statue. I caught the waft of popcorn and cookies, which seemed oddly out of place with what I was facing. The rain remained a steady drizzle. People here had ditched umbrellas, nearly all of them draped in plastic ponchos with Mickey Mouse logos. My four targets had utilized neither, opting to just get wet. They stopped at the statue, which stood on a low dais surrounded by flowers. I exited the shop and stepped into the rain. Darkness had arrived with the suddenness of a drawn curtain.

Valdez saw me coming.

"No files or Foster?" he called out.

I came close and stopped. "No Coleen?"

The Cuban shrugged. "What can I say? I'm not trustworthy."

"You okay?" I asked Nate.

He nodded. "I'm fine. Coleen's okay, too."

"Where are the files?" Oliver asked.

"Safe from the rain."

"Odd choice of a place to meet," Valdez said.

"Not really. I like Mickey Mouse. And all these tourists should keep us all under control. The last thing we want is attention, right?"

It had to be a little odd, though. Five grown men, standing in the rain, no umbrellas, chatting with one another. Discouraging was the fact that I hadn't seen a single security guard or policeman in the past several minutes.

"What now?" Jansen asked.

I caught his contempt.

"You do what I tell you and we'll all get out of here with what we want."

"Who died and put you in charge?" Jansen asked.

"He is in charge," Valdez said. "He has my coin and your files. Why don't we give him a chance to produce both so we can end this."

"I agree," Oliver said. "But I have an added problem. The FBI has become focused on me, and I don't intend to spend my retirement in jail."

"You should have thought about that before you had Martin Luther King Jr. and Dan Veddern killed," I said.

I caught the shocked expression on Nate's face.

Oliver pointed a finger at me. "That's exactly what I'm going to hear, over and over. I didn't kill anybody. I didn't order anybody killed."

I pointed at Valdez. "That's not what he said."

"Is that true?" Oliver asked.

Valdez nodded.

I'd already decided to keep quiet about the copy of the recording Lael had provided me. That was my ace in the hole. "Do you have the original recording Foster wants?"

Oliver fished a small spool of the old reel-to-reel tape from his pocket. "Right here. You have the files?"

I nodded. "Yep."

"But you don't intend to give them to us, do you?" Valdez asked.

"You know how to get them, and the coin. Where's Coleen?"

"She's here, in the park," Valdez said. "Just not with us. I can have her brought to wherever, as soon as we conclude our business."

"Bring her here," I said.

I watched as Valdez reached back, thinking he was looking for a phone or radio in one of his pant pockets.

Instead a gun appeared.

He fired two shots into Nate's chest, the bangs loud and out of place. Nate collapsed, falling back against a knee-high stone wall that encircled the statue, ending up sprawled spine-first over the railing and into the flowers encircling the dais, his legs dangling up in the rain.

Valdez then tossed the gun to me.

Instinctively, I caught it.

The bastard smiled.

I gripped the weapon, aimed it straight at him, and pulled the trigger.

Just clicks.

Again.

More clicks.

"Only two rounds," he said. Then he pointed and yelled, "He has a gun. Run. Everyone. He has a gun."

Bastard.

He was mimicking what I'd done to him at the Columbia, only this time there really was a gun. Jansen reacted, reaching for his own weapon beneath a jacket. Oliver stepped back, out of the way. The people around us had already heard the shots and could see Nate's body lying in contorted angles at the base of Disney's statue.

Shouts rose, fast and anxious.

People scattered.

I tossed the gun away and ran.

CHAPTER FORTY-EIGHT

NOTHING ABOUT THIS WAS GOOD.

I had badly underestimated Valdez and Nate paid the price. Naively, I'd thought that no one wanted to make a scene. I'd wisely not displayed the coin in my pocket, keeping its whereabouts a mystery. I knew Valdez wanted the coin and Oliver the files. But Valdez seemed to play by a book that contained no rules.

I raced across the wet concrete, glancing back over my shoulder to see Oliver and Jansen rushing my way, all of us weaving a path through the chaotic crowd. Thankfully, Foster was safe, back near the main entrance, a long way from this trouble. I negotiated a wooden bridge and passed through an elaborate timber gateway labeled ADVENTURELAND. What happened back at the statue had not filtered to the people this far away yet. Everyone was still enjoying the attractions, moving in all directions through the drizzle. Buildings lined the concrete path to my right, trees and foliage to the left. I had no idea where I was going. This was a big place. Surely, plenty of exits. I could find one and just leave. I had the coin and the files. But there was still the matter of Foster and Coleen. They both needed my help, and I'd never run from a fight. Not then. Not now. Not ever. The one saving grace was the coin in my pocket.

But would that keep Valdez at bay?

Another quick glance over my shoulder and I saw Oliver pressing my way, but no Jansen. I kept going. Buildings stayed on my right, a potpourri of Asian, African, and Middle East architecture arranged in a calculated disorder. I caught the sounds of drums and squawking parrots. I rounded a ride that dominated the center of the pavement in front of me and angled left. I passed the Jungle Cruise attraction, crowded with people, and spotted what looked like an old Spanish-style castle that housed Pirates of the Caribbean.

Then I saw Jansen.

Past the Pirates building, waiting for me where the pavement curved right and began to head out of Adventureland. Somehow he'd managed to double around and hustle ahead of me. It had to be from the other side of the buildings. I'd spotted more crowds through a couple of breezeways that linked this side with the other. Apparently, Jansen had been here before.

I banked left and passed through a collection of baby strollers parked outside the Pirates ride. I zigzagged through them and hopped over the last row, pushing through a wet hedge and finding a concrete walk that paralleled the Pirates building. This was not an area where the public ventured.

Both Oliver and Jansen were still on my tail.

Ahead I spotted a high barbed-wire fence with a gate leading out. Padlocked.

To my right, a metal door opened from the side of the building and a man emerged. Probably an employee working on the Pirates ride. I found my wallet and held it up like a cop would, displaying credentials.

"Malone, from Human Resources," I said, as I brushed past. Then I stopped, reached back, and grabbed the inside handle.

"Where are you going?" he asked me.

"To fire someone."

I closed the door.

Outside I'd noticed that there was no way to get inside without a key card passing through an electronic reader. I could only hope that the guy I'd just bamboozled wouldn't open it for Oliver and Jansen.

I stood inside a lighted, air-conditioned room that held a long metal table with chairs around it. On the wall hung a schematic of the building showing the waterways that wound through the interior carrying visitors on their way through Disney's version of the 18th-century Caribbean. A whiteboard seemed to be for work assignments. I made a quick survey, spotted where I was currently standing, and plotted a route through the building to the nearest exit—which, to my delight, seemed outside the park's fence.

Perfect.

I heard the door lever behind me being turned.

I rushed to the other exit and left.

The corridor beyond was dimly lined with a series of closed metal doors. From behind them I heard the murmur of a familiar song. *Yo ho, yo ho, a pirate's life for me.* I was apparently behind the scenes, in the attraction's maintenance corridors, a quick way to get from one place to another without anyone knowing the better.

I hustled forward.

Rumblings came from the other side of the doors, which sounded like cannon fire, and kept repeating. The door I'd entered from behind me opened. Jansen appeared. He held a gun. I darted for the next door, yanked it open, and lunged through.

More cannon fire thundered.

A shot rang out.

The bullet pinged off the door as it slammed shut on its spring-loaded hinges. A short walkway led onto a galleon, complete with sails, masts, and rigging. The music rang louder. The source of the explosions became clear: cannons on the ship "firing" on the visitors' boats passing by on the water below. More cannons returned fire, in a mock battle, from a fortress on the other side of the dark, cavernous space, each blast accompanied by a burst of flame. Explosions from beneath the water tossed geysers upward, creating cannonball breaches. Cool air simulated a brisk ocean breeze. A robotic captain on the ship led the assault, shouting threats while brandishing a sword. More animatronic figures created the illusion of an anxious crew. I looked around and could see there was no escape off the galleon. I moved to the railing and glanced over the side.

Only water below.

The door behind me opened.

I darted right and hid behind a cabin that rose from the deck. I peeked around the side and saw Jansen creeping across the walkway and onto the ship, gun in hand. I waited until he was on the deck then pounced, kicking the gun from his grasp. He whirled and cocked his right arm back, but before he could land a fist I planted my head into his chest. We hit the deck hard and rolled toward a row of animatronic crewmen who faced toward the water. Electrical cables snaked a path across the deck, out of sight to anyone not on the galleon, and I wondered about the voltage.

We rolled, tight in each other's grasp.

I shoved Jansen off me.

He sprang to his feet.

More cannons fired.

I stood.

He egged me on, motioning toward himself with his upstretched fingers. "That all you got, Malone?"

He stood near the rail, beside the ship's captain who was ordering the cannons to be fired at will toward the boats below. I decided to oblige Jansen and rushed toward him, burying my shoulder into his chest and wrapping my arms around him like a linebacker leveling a quarterback.

Momentum drove us forward and over the rail.

We fell.

The cannons extended out from the hull, readying themselves for another round. We plunged downward. Jansen led the way and his right rib cage slammed into one of the protruding barrels.

Then it "fired."

Which was not all sound effects. Real flames erupted from the barrel's end, probably thanks to propane.

Jansen screamed.

His body shielded me from the few seconds of heat, but I caught a little singe to my arms. We rebounded off and splashed into the water. My grip on Jansen released. The water was cold and only chest-deep. Jansen came to his feet and lunged for me, slipping his arm around my neck from behind in a lock vise. A boat passed by a few feet away, loaded with visitors.

The pressure increased.

He was strangling the breath out of me.

I jabbed my right elbow into his side, the one that had struck the cannon, hoping some damage had been done.

And it had.

He winced in pain.

His grip released enough for me to break his hold and shove him away. But Jansen knew how to handle himself. He pushed off the concrete bottom of the waterway and launched himself at me. I had twenty-plus years on him in age, but the guy could fight. The people in the boat were mesmerized by what was happening.

Cameras flashed.

To them we were an exciting live-action part of the show.

Jansen tried to swing a fist my way but I stopped the jab and planted one of my own, which only seemed to enrage him. I had already felt metal rails beneath the water, surely a track that guided the boats on a designated path through the attraction. Here it veered close to the galleon for the cannon attack, then swerved to the far side toward the fake fort.

Jansen was not backing off.

He kept coming.

Another boat emerged into the hall.

Looking back I'm not sure what happened, but something snapped inside me. Up to that moment in my life I had never intentionally harmed anyone with, as the law says, *malice aforethought*. But up to that point I had only been a lieutenant in the United States Navy and a lawyer for the Judge Advocate General's corps. For less than two days I had been a special operative to the Justice Department. People had been continuously trying to hurt me, for one reason or another.

Enough was enough.

I pounced on Jansen and grabbed him by the throat. His arms came up in an attempt to shove me away. I brought my knee into his gut, the water cushioning the blow, but enough force remained to get his attention. He resisted, which sent us careening through the water.

I faced toward where the next boat was coming and could see it approaching, the people inside fixated on our brawl. The robotic captain in the galleon continued to yell orders for the cannons to fire at will.

And they did.

More thunder and fire erupted from the hull. Explosions from beneath the water shot up a few feet away, most likely pneumatic from compressed air. Jansen was not letting up. I could feel the metal track with my right foot. The boat kept coming toward us at a steady pace. I decided to use it to my advantage.

Ten feet away and closing.

Jansen's eyes were filled with rage.

He'd come to kill me. No question.

Five feet.

I still had his throat in tight lock, which allowed me to swing him to the left just as the boat arrived, the mass and speed of the hull pounding into the back of Jansen's head with a sickening thud.

The people glancing down were shocked.

One woman screamed.

I yanked Jansen back and let go.

He floated still in the water.

CHAPTER FORTY-NINE

THE BOAT PASSED.

People sitting at its stern stared back in astonishment. I left Jansen in the water. He was not my problem anymore. More boats appeared as I sloshed my way toward the far side. I hopped up to dry ground and found myself in a town square where a hapless soul had been captured and was being repeatedly dunked in a well as animatronic pirates kept asking him the location of the town's treasure. I sought refuge behind the well and noticed that though it appeared solid, it was only foam board painted to seem like stone. At least I was out of sight from the boats.

My breathing was quick, short, and hard.

I willed myself to calm down.

The first wave of people who saw me and Jansen fall from the galleon would surely report a problem when they came to the end of the ride. Security would then come to investigate. But that wouldn't be for a few more minutes and I really didn't need the hassle of being arrested. I decided not to hang around and darted to my right into the buildings that backdropped the scene, hoping to find an exit door behind the fake town. The music continued to play and the lyrics were beginning to get on my nerves.

Yo ho, yo ho, a pirate's life for me.

I hustled through an open archway and found a metal door leading out, similar to the one on the galleon. My breathing had calmed. My clothes dripped with water. I left the Caribbean and reentered another of the bland hallways, this one stretching left and right in a straight line. A stairway began its ascent a few feet to my right. I was deciding on which way to go when I heard movement from the left.

Someone turned the corner.

Oliver.

He saw me and reached beneath his jacket. I knew what was coming. To turn away and head down the corridor would be foolish. He'd have a clear shot. Instead, I leaped for the stairway and headed up, two steps at a time. I came to a platform where the risers right-angled. I kept climbing and found myself above the main ceiling, in a spacious area lined along its perimeter with metal catwalks. Electrical cables ran in all directions along with ductwork. Everything was open, the two sides of the building connected by a single, mechanized catwalk on a track that moved left and right. I was out of sight to anyone below. The music continued to blare, dulled only by the thin acoustical ceiling that separated this service area from the attraction beneath. Low-level amber lighting lit the entire space. I could use the crosswalk and find the other side of the hall, but if Oliver came up he was going to have a clean shot. Since I was making this up as I went, I decided there was no choice.

I raced ahead.

Adrenaline surged, carrying with it fear and vigilance. But also a whisk of excitement, that sensual chill of danger that I would at first find enticing, but eventually come to resent.

Halfway across I heard, "Malone."

I stopped and turned back.

"You're proving really difficult," Oliver said, his gun aimed at me.

"Yo ho, yo ho, a pirate's life for me."

"You think this a joke?" He stepped onto the catwalk. "You saw what Valdez is capable of. He shot that young man with no remorse."

"I noticed you didn't bother to take him down or arrest him."

"Where's Jansen?" he asked.

"Probably dead."

"You've had quite the first mission, haven't you?"

He stopped about twenty feet away. I'd halted about three-quarters of the way across the catwalk at a panel attached to the platform. From a quick glance at the buttons it appeared to control the platform's movement back and forth.

"I had a lot of agents, like you, work for me. Young hotshots, eager to make a name for themselves, prepared to take chances."

"Like Jansen."

"Exactly. Jim always wanted to please. He was good, though, at following orders."

I realized that the only two reasons he hadn't shot me yet were the files and the coin.

He had to have *both*.

Which I commanded.

Since we were all alone, I decided to ask, "Why kill King?"

"Hoover gave that order. Not me. I just did what the old man wanted. Valdez was willing to make it happen, and Ray was supposed to disappear into Rhodesia."

"Where he would have been killed."

"Definitely. He was told he'd be paid for what he did once he made it to Africa."

"Since paying him beforehand, if he was caught, would smack of conspiracy."

"Absolutely. Valdez was already there, waiting on him. His body would then have been returned to DC. Killer found by the FBI. Hoover does it once again."

"Things didn't work out, did they?"

He shrugged. "Ultimately, they did. No money was found on Ray. Nothing pointed anywhere, but to him. Hoover got the credit for catching him. Then his narcissistic personality took over and he lied so much no one gave him a thought."

I'd been thinking, so I told him, "Hoover hated the civil rights movement. He thought it all a communist plot. But in reality, he was just a racist, pure and simple. He wanted black people kept in their place. And he was intuitive enough to realize that if the movement went violent the country would want it stopped. Whites who'd supported King would flee him. There'd be riots. Deaths. Destruction. It was King's nonviolent methods that had traction. Images of rednecks spitting on calm, young blacks sitting at a lunch counter were never good for the segregationists. Stay the course and King's way might just ultimately work."

Oliver nodded. "The riots did happen after King died. The militants tried to change the course. But King's legacy proved stronger than Hoover thought. The civil rights movement kept going, pretty much as King would have wanted. Still, we did have more control after that. King had been a pain in the ass for a long time. Both Kennedys aligned themselves more with him than with Hoover. JFK even warned King we were taping him. With King gone, things were easier."

His eyes looked tense, the muscles around them taut, his cheeks flushed with blood. I had to keep telling myself that this man traded in misery. How careful must he be not to be trapped by his own lies? For so long Oliver had basked in power, a shrewd and experienced operator, tough, sure of himself. Now he was running scared, everything dependent on a loose cannon from Cuba and a rookie from the Justice Department.

I said, "It would've all stayed buried, if not for Valdez and Foster."

"I need Valdez to go away, and he won't without the coin."

The gun remained aimed at me.

I'd managed a few quick glances at the control panel and spied the switches that activated the movable walk. We stood in the center of the building, seventy-five feet of air on either side of us, the crosswalk capable of traversing the entire length. This guy had spent a lifetime containing problems. He'd been head of COINTELPRO, one of the most corrupt organizations the U.S. government ever created. He was certainly immoral, more likely amoral. What Oliver didn't know was that Bruce Lael had sold him out. I'd heard the cassette. I knew the truth about Foster. All I had to do was survive and I could take this bastard, Jansen, and Foster down to the mat for the ten-count.

"Where are the files?" he asked.

"Foster has them."

And with any luck he was still hidden away at the train station near the park's main gate.

The walkway was a latticework of aluminum with lots of openings.

I stared down, as if assessing the situation, but what I was really interested in was the controls to my left. I saw a red, a green, and an orange button. I decided red was bad.

Push the orange and green.

"You're going to take me to Foster," he said.

I nodded.

Then my left arm swung over and my palm slammed the two buttons. Motors came alive and the crosswalk quickly shifted left, then one side dipped lower than the other and I realized the buttons were for lateral movement and vertical attitude, the catwalk capable of assuming differing positions depending on what needed to be done.

Oliver's arms went skyward in an attempt to regain his balance but the catwalk had shifted from flat to about a thirty-degree angle. I gripped the control panel, which allowed me something solid to hold on to. Oliver had only the low railing that ran the crosswalk's length. I moved to hit the buttons again and stop all movement, but it was too late for Oliver. He dropped over the side and smacked into the acoustical ceiling, which offered little resistance, his body plunging through, falling another forty feet. Unlike Jansen, he did not find the water. Instead, he pounded into the concrete flooring of one of the pirate displays.

A dark pool of blood welled outward.

I locked away the bad thoughts that were racing through my brain and hit the buttons. The catwalk stopped moving. I had traveled laterally about thirty feet from where I started. I worked the orange button and brought the thing level. Time to go and fast. I could hear people below in the boats, voices raised in fear and concern.

But the damn music just kept playing.

One thought raced through my mind.

The reel of tape Oliver had displayed back at Disney's statue.

I had to get it.

I fled my perch and found the walk on the other side of the building. I spotted an exit and quickly descended stairs similar to the ones I'd used to climb up. This was rapidly gestating into a huge mess, one that I was going to have a hard time explaining to Stephanie Nelle, especially after my rebellion in Stuart. I came to ground level and stepped into another service corridor. This one only went one way, deeper into the attraction, about fifty feet, one exit out on the right, another at the far end.

I reached for the handle of the nearest door and swung the metal panel inward. It led into another of the faux town scenes, this one complete with animatronic wenches being sold at auction. I entered behind the female figures and decided the thing to do, once I got the reel, was to hop into one of the boats and head for the exit, acting like one of the visitors. Hopefully, no one would rat me out, or at least not until I could slip away.

Oliver lay a few feet away.

I sidestepped the mechanical women and ran over, pretending to see if he was all right. People in the boats were watching. I faked a check for a pulse.

"Is he dead?" someone called out from the boats.

I ignored the question and stuck my hand into his pant pockets, finding the reel, which I pocketed.

Time to get the hell out of here.

"He's dead," I called out, readying myself to hop into the boat.

Something slammed hard into my right hip.

CHAPTER FIFTY

I HIT THE CONCRETE FLOOR AND REALIZED THAT JANSEN HAD returned from the dead. On the way down we'd taken out two of the skirted wenches, each tied to the other with a hemp rope. The robots broke from their underlying supports with a spray of electrical sparks, the two heavy figures tumbling toward the end of the dock and the water, taking down a mechanical goat along the way. We rolled across a couple of concrete risers. Jansen's arms were wrapped around me and he maneuvered himself on top, releasing his grip and delivering a fist to my jaw.

Which hurt.

He'd apparently survived the earlier encounter and watched as Tom Oliver died from his fall. He must have crossed over the arched bridge that spanned the waterway. He was damn strong for a man past sixty. I flipped him off me and hopped to my feet. Jansen rebounded quickly. A gun appeared in his right hand. I kicked it away. The auctioneer kept droning on about the women for sale. A sign proclaimed TAKE A WENCH FOR A BRIDE.

Jansen lifted one of the barrels adorning the dock and hurled it my way. I dodged the projectile, which bounced off the concrete and collided with another animatronic figure. The gun lay to my left and I could see that he was searching for it, too. More boats passed, the waterway here narrow from one side of the hall to the other, the scenes connected by the arched bridge loaded with animals and characters, beneath which the boats passed into another building. Employees or security should be appearing any moment. I couldn't be around when that happened. I had to deal with Coleen and her father. Jansen, too, surely did not want to be taken into custody.

"I'm going to kill you," he spat at me.

And I believed him.

His face had gone white, teeth bared, eyebrows furrowed. We both crouched forward, circling, looking for chances. He kept his left fist cocked back like a southpaw. I landed a sharp jab to his cheek that sent him back on his heels. Before I could take advantage of the moment he attacked with that left, but I dodged the punch and thumped him with a hard right uppercut to his midbody.

He backed away.

I saw more boats with people passing in the water. He lunged forward and grazed my cheek with a fast left and a right to my ribs. I gave him a solid jab to the face, my knuckles tight. Sparks kept flying from where the two animatronic figures had been torn from their supports. You would think this stuff ran on low voltage, but apparently that was not the case. I told myself to be careful with the open wires, especially since Jansen kept nudging me in their direction.

I searched for the gun.

Which I spotted a few feet away.

"You'll never get to it," he told me.

He swung and missed with a right. I managed to grab his wrist and land a fist of my own into his left kidney. He broke away and darted toward one of the characters, this one brandishing a pitchfork.

Not a facsimile.

Someone had thought that an actual pitchfork would work just fine.

He thrust the blade my way.

I seized a moment and snapped his head back with a stiff jab to the right eye. He went into a rage and grasped the pitchfork with both hands, swinging it in a desperate attempt to make contact with me. I retreated, dodging the swishing metal tips, which were not dulled. He began to stumble, maybe stunned and hurt from the blows. Blood poured from one nostril. The first wave of visitors had to have made it to the end of the ride by now and alerted the staff about what was happening inside the attraction.

This had to end.

Now.

But Jansen suddenly looked restored.

"It's over," I told him.

"Because you say it is? You're nothing." His voice was rising. "Nothing at all. We gave our entire lives for this country."

"You killed him," I said.

"I did as I was told," he yelled. "I did my job."

He'd quickly transitioned from patriot to "loyal employee," his conscience searching for anything to justify reality. For him this had gone from search-and-find to an outright suicide mission. Of course, Valdez had narrowed the options when he chose to gun down Nate Perry. Oliver was dead. Valdez was God knew where. Jansen was the last man standing.

I recalled my boot camp training in hand-to-hand.

Keep your mouth closed. Clench the neck and jaw. Protect the stomach. But careful with hitting the other guy's face, especially the forehead. You can break a bone in your own hand.

But I'd never been one to follow the rules.

He stopped his flailing with the pitchfork.

I grabbed his upper right arm and sank an uppercut into his gut. Then I slammed my forehead into his.

We met with a crack.

Everything blinked in and out.

My brain spun.

I was near the end of the fake wharf at the water's edge, fighting to regain my equilibrium. Jansen was having a problem with balance, too. He staggered backward, still holding the pitchfork, his arms flailing as he fought the vertigo. He tried to stay on his feet. More blood poured from his nose. Three barrels stood to my right. I shook off the fog in my brain and reached for one, hurling it toward Jansen. He raised the pitchfork to block the impact, but the barrel was solid wood and crashed into him, driving him farther back. He hit the pavement among the animatronic figures, finding the spot where the two skirted wenches had been torn away.

Sparks exploded.

He screamed.

I realized what was happening. The exposed electrical conduits had connected with his wet clothes, completing the circuit. The barrel lay atop him, pinning him down. His body shuddered, arms and legs extended outward. His screams rose, then faded as the life ebbed from him.

He lay still, in silence.

I stared over at him.

Another boat of people approached.

"You. Stop. Stay right there."

I turned and saw three men dressed in security uniforms on the other side of the waterway, running my way. They were headed for the arched bridge, and it would only be a few moments before they were on me.

I grabbed the gun still lying on the concrete, then fled the wharf back into the fake buildings and found the metal door through which I'd entered. I headed left and saw that the corridor was long and straight. The guards could easily find me, so I headed back up the stairs to the service area. I ran across the catwalk to the other side, then down, careful at the bottom to make sure the coast was clear. Seeing no one, I turned right and hustled to the end, where a door opened into the attraction's lighted, main entrance.

I eased the door open and peeked out.

People were being channeled away from the building. Someone was yelling that the attraction was temporarily closed. The crowd was contained within nylon safety barricades that usually formed an infuriating zigzag back and forth, but were now set for a full-scale exit. I tucked the gun at my spine, then slipped out and ducked beneath one of the retractable straps, melting into the crowd and following the surge out of the building to the open pavement of Adventureland.

I'd made it out.

CHAPTER FIFTY-ONE

WHAT HAD JUST HAPPENED WAS ONLY NOW BEGINNING TO REGISter. Two men had died, both of whom had been trying to kill me. I still had the coin in one pocket and Nate's cell phone in another, though I doubted that thing would be working after its bath off the galleon. I was also armed, which brought some comfort, but not much. I decided to head for Foster, who should still be back near the main entrance at the train station. But walking there, out in the open, might not be the smartest move.

No telling who else was on the lookout.

Once I was outside the Pirates building, beyond a stand of trees and foliage, I heard the churn of an engine and realized the train tracks were nearby. Something in the back of my brain reminded me that the train encircled the entire park to form an outer perimeter, offering a way to get from one side to the other without walking. I saw a park employee assisting visitors and asked where the nearest station was located. She directed me to Frontierland, where I arrived just as the train was slowing into the station. I hopped aboard and rode in the open car all the way around the park, stopping a couple of times for more passengers. I was moving farther away from Pirates of the Caribbean by the second, which could only be a good thing.

The rain had slackened to no more than a few sprinkles.

Ahead, I spotted the station above the park's entrance, back over Main Street and the town square, where I'd started. I left the train and walked through the station onto the covered porch that overlooked the town square. People were sitting among the covered deck's benches.

But no Foster.

Instead, sitting alone was Juan Lopez Valdez. Both arms outstretched on the back of the bench in a welcome.

"I've been waiting for you," he said, motioning.

I walked over and sat beside him. Both of us kept our gazes out into the misty night.

"Oliver and Jansen?" he quietly asked.

"Dead."

"From you?"

"I helped."

"Killing two ex-FBI agents. What will your superiors say?"

"What did yours say when you did what you did?"

A moment of silence confirmed that he knew what I meant.

"They said good job. I spoke to Hoover directly, in fact."

"That was unusual."

"To say the least. But he asked to speak with me."

I waited for more.

"Oliver took me to Hoover's house, in the middle of the night. What a strange place. Every room was packed with antiques. So many you could barely walk. There were rugs on the floor and throw rugs on top of the rugs, which I've always thought really odd. Everywhere there were photos, paintings, cartoons, etchings, even busts, all of Hoover. The house was a shrine to himself. And there I was, standing in the middle of it."

The lawyer in me had to ask, "What did he want?"

"My assessment of Eric S. Galt or, as he knew him, James Earl Ray. This was about three months before the assassination, maybe late January 1968. I told him that Ray could do the job and, if needed, also take the blame."

It was weird discussing this, but my job was to gather information. "Did he say why he wanted King dead?"

"He rambled on about communism, how King was involved with the

Soviets, and how Moscow was trying to topple the American government. I listened to him, but it was all a lie. Something he told himself to rationalize what he was doing. He killed King because he could. He hated change and considered civil rights dangerous. He particularly hated, as he called them, 'uppity Negroes who do not know their place.'"

"Did he personally order the kill?"

Valdez nodded. "I made him. I looked him straight in the eye and told him that I wanted him to say the words. If not, then he could find another way."

"Was Oliver there?"

"Not in the room. Outside. Hoover and I spoke alone, which is the only way he would have made that admission. I spent an hour listening to his speeches. He liked to talk. But in the end, I only wanted to hear the words."

I waited.

"He told me to kill the burrhead."

I closed my eyes and shuddered at the implications. If not for the files I'd read, and hearing Oliver and Jansen and Bruce Lael's tape, I might not have believed this psychopath.

But I knew he was telling the truth.

"He told me to make it happen, then make sure Ray died so his corpse could take the blame."

"You do realize that you're no better than he was."

"Unlike the dead director, I've never pretended to be anything other than what I am."

"There was no need to kill Nate Perry."

"It seemed the only way to get your attention. Let's be honest with each other, you had no intention of voluntarily giving us anything. You want to keep it all to show to your superiors."

"Why not shoot me, instead of Nate?"

"Oliver would not have been happy. He wanted those files. And I needed Oliver's help to get out of the country." He paused. "But things have changed, haven't they? That's no longer possible, and you still have my coin."

"Where are Coleen and her father?"

"My man found Foster here, waiting for you. I now have them both."

"I'm taking you down."

He chuckled and shifted his arm from the top of the bench to my shoulders. "Amigo, if I don't return exactly ten minutes from now, both father and daughter will have a bullet placed in their heads."

I heard sirens in the distance.

The local police were converging on a double murder scene at Disney World. That meant plenty of backup to take this man down.

But not in the next ten minutes.

I considered the threat level from his words and determined it to be high. Killing Nate had proven to me that Valdez was prepared to do anything. The number of people left to corroborate the tape I still possessed was dwindling. Lael was gone. Oliver and Jansen dead. That left two. Foster and the man sitting beside me. The one who set the killing up, and the other who made it happen.

"Nine minutes," he said.

I didn't move.

The gun still nestled at my spine was somewhat reassuring.

"A few years ago," he softly said, "there was a man in Havana I was ordered to eliminate. Castro loves to kill people, too. I was paid a worthy amount and told to make sure that nothing linked back to the Dirección General de Inteligencia. But they wanted it to happen in public, the death noticed. Something to send a message. So one day I followed the man to the street market. He wandered through the booths, talked to vendors, and bought some fruits and vegetables. When he finished shopping, he turned down a small alley that connected one of the busier merchant streets to the next. I was waiting in a doorway. He strolled by, bags in both hands, and I slit his throat. One swipe with a knife. Quick, deep, silent. He drowned in his own blood right there on the cobbles."

I glanced to my right.

In his now open palm rested a knife, closed for the moment, that had been there the whole time.

"You see, I could have already killed you."

His eyes were bitter with an almost unsensing animal gaze. He had the look of a thug, pure and simple. We sat at the far end of the covered porch, all of the other benches to our left, so no one could see the knife, that hand toward the outer railing.

"Seven minutes," he said. "I was quite serious about that time, and my man will not disobey my order. He knows the price to be paid for that."

I stood. "Let's go."

He came to his feet.

"I suggest we hurry. It's a long walk and time is running out."

CHAPTER FIFTY-TWO

HE WAS RIGHT ABOUT THE WALK.

We retraced our previous path down Main Street, then turned right and headed through Tomorrowland, swinging around to the back side of the park where a section had been cordoned off, under construction. An eight-foot-high wooden wall separated the park from the work site, decorated with elaborate Disney murals. Valdez headed for a gate that opened through the wall, a wooden door with a simple keyed lock.

"It was easy to pick," he said as we headed through and he closed the panel behind us.

I understood his problem. He would have preferred to leave the premises with both Coleen and Foster. But that might have proven a problem. Coleen came in willingly. Doubtful she'd leave that way. And Foster would only cooperate to keep her safe. Exiting the Magic Kingdom would not be easy. It required either a bus, monorail, or boat, all loaded with people, and the walking distances were impressive. Too many things could go wrong, so he'd chosen to take a stand within the gates.

I looked around. Some kind of new attraction was being built. There were piles of bricks and wire mesh fashioned into various shapes, like boulders, stacked one on top of another, awaiting mortar. A ladder leaned against one of the unfinished walls. No ceilings. Lights from the park spilled in from overhead, illuminating the scene in a dim glow. Everything was also wet from the rain. Coleen sat on the damp concrete, her back to an unfinished wooden wall, her hands bound behind her. Foster was in the same position to her left. One of the men from the inflatable boat back in the Dry Tortugas stood guard with a gun. Coleen's and her father's legs were unrestrained, but they were both gagged with strips of duct tape. The two manila envelopes I'd left with Foster lay in the preacher's lap.

Valdez relieved his man of the gun and told him to leave.

"Now it's just us. Oliver and Jansen are dead." He motioned at Foster with the gun. "That leaves only me and you."

I doubted Foster was going to say a thing about the cassette he'd listened to on the way here. That was the last thing he wanted Coleen to know about, and Valdez had no idea the tape existed. I'd left it in the truck, still in the player, protected by locked doors among a zillion other cars in a vast parking lot.

"First off," Valdez said. "I need the gun you have."

He was looking at me.

I hesitated.

He clicked the hammer of his weapon into place and aimed it straight at Coleen. "Surely you comprehend what I'm capable of."

Absolutely. So I reached back and found the gun.

"Bring it out holding the barrel," he said.

I did as ordered and handed it over. He tossed it away, gone in the debris.

"This entire situation has been a problem," he said. "Just a simple trade. That's all I wanted. Instead, we've had nothing but turmoil."

My sense of humor had dulled. "You're a murdering bastard."

He nodded. "I am that. But people have long had a need for my services, your own government one of those."

I glanced over at Coleen. As Valdez focused on me I saw her arms tense, her shoulders shift. She was working on her bindings, trying not to draw attention, and perhaps having some success. Her eyes told me to keep him occupied.

"You never wanted any credit?" I asked Valdez.

"My ego requires no such stroking. I prefer compensation."

"You told us back in St. Augustine that you read all of Ray's books. You found him. Recruited him. Encouraged him. He really had no idea he was being used?"

Valdez shrugged. "Not even a hint. It was easy to push him along. Hate filled him. As did the need to be somebody. He just lacked opportunity, which I provided. I read those books with a smile on my face. Nearly every word in them was a lie. Until the day he died he unknowingly did exactly what we wanted."

I could see that Coleen was still working away, trying hard to keep her arms and shoulders still.

"Why not just kill him afterward, like Ruby did to Oswald?" I asked.

"I would have, if he'd made it to Africa. But not only did Hoover want to kill King, he wanted the credit for capturing the killer. He told me that when we met that night, in his house. Nobody then could accuse him of prejudice toward King. But that capture had to be a corpse. Jack Ruby, to his credit, never explained why he killed Oswald, and died quickly in prison. Ray, on the other hand, lived a long time and could not keep his mouth shut. Thankfully, he was a pathological liar."

I was keeping him talking, buying Coleen time, but I was worried about the choice of subjects. We were drifting closer and closer to forbidden topics. Foster's eyes pleaded with me not to raise any questions about him. But I was more concerned with what Valdez was about to do. He had not brought us here to chat.

Valdez flicked the muzzle of his weapon toward Foster. "Get those envelopes."

A tingle of apprehension ran down my spine.

I walked over and retrieved them.

"Open them."

I tore open the sealed flaps and removed the stacks of paper inside. Each sheet was blank.

He chuckled. "I thought as much. I knew you wouldn't bring that information along. I told Oliver, but he didn't believe me. You still have my files."

I nodded. "Stored away safely."

At the Mail 'N More in Gainesville, Florida, stashed in a locker I'd rented, paid for six months in advance, where no one would ever find them.

"How did you plan to make a deal with Oliver?" he asked me.

"I didn't."

He chuckled again. "You have balls, I'll give you that. I watched as you stole that seaplane in the Dry Tortugas, double-crossing me. That took nerve."

He stepped away from me and walked over toward where Foster and Coleen sat on the dirty concrete. I noticed Coleen stopped all movement and sat still. Valdez crouched down in front of Foster, unconcerned that he'd turned his back on me, as if he were taunting me with a challenge. I may have been a rookie, but I was no fool and did not take the bait, deciding to wait until the odds were a little better.

He reached down and tore the tape from Foster's mouth. "There's something I've been wanting to ask you. Something your daughter asked me. What did you do to get that Double Eagle?"

Foster said nothing.

But Coleen's eyes were unmistakable.

She wanted to hear the answer to that question, too.

CHAPTER FIFTY-THREE

I waited for Foster to reply, wondering how he intended to do so.

"For an operation like Bishop's Pawn," Valdez said, "Jansen had to have reliable and continuous information. He was directing me with great care, wanting Ray in a given place at a given time. I moved him around like a player on a chessboard. Each move calculated, and King was right there, every time. Jansen's field reports talked about a reliable confidential source he used repeatedly. Was that you?"

"I loved Martin Luther King. I admired him more than any man I'd ever known. I still do to this day. I never would have betrayed him."

I listened to the words, amazed at the sincerity of the lie.

"I stood side by side with him in the marches," Foster said. "I was there, working to change the country. The FBI was working to destroy us."

Valdez pointed a finger. "But they knew everything King was doing days in advance. I had Ray actively stalking King from the end of March until April 4. I was told precisely where to have him in Memphis at a precise time. Six P.M. In the bathroom of that rooming house. With a clear line of fire to the balcony outside Room 306 at the Lorraine Motel. How would Jansen have known that?"

"You should have asked him those questions," Foster said.

"I did. Several times. He told me nothing."

I noticed how Valdez kept his back to me, continuing to dare me to make a move. Or maybe he thought me incapable of challenging him? No matter. I was more concerned with Coleen and what she might do. I liked the idea of her freeing herself, but I preferred a co-ordinated attack.

Valdez reached over and ripped the tape from her mouth.

"What has your father told you?" he asked her.

"You never answered him," she said to her father. "Why do you have that coin?"

An element of anger and pleading had entered her voice.

Foster said nothing.

She glared at Valdez and asked, "You never told us back at the restaurant, how did you know my father had the coin?"

"Jansen told me shortly after I was paid mine."

I saw the surprise on Foster's face.

So did Valdez.

"Yes, Reverend, I've known about you from the beginning. I just never knew your exact role, or why it was worth paying you a Double Eagle. Recently, when I came into a need for money, I decided to locate you." He motioned at Coleen with the gun. "And if not for you calling me back, I would have never known that coin still existed."

Valdez stood and stepped back my way.

Coleen quickly worked her shoulders and arms again, still fighting with the bindings to her wrists.

"Where is my coin?" Valdez asked me.

I ignored his question.

"Why can't you answer me?" Coleen suddenly said.

Both Valdez and I looked her way.

She was staring at her father. "Why can't you tell me the truth? You're a man of God. Is not being honest with your daughter important to you? Why do you have that coin?"

Foster kept silent, feigning and stalling, seemingly trying hard to avoid a damaging admission. Finally, the older man said, "Being honest is the most important thing in my life, Coleen. I have never lied to you."

"But you worked with the FBI, didn't you?"

"My job was to find the spies within the SCLC. I did that."

Not an answer, but realization dawned in her eyes. "But you didn't tell anyone about what you found, did you? That's why they paid you. To keep silent about their sources?"

"They would have paid a few thousand dollars in cash money for that," Valdez said. "Not a Double Eagle. Your father had to do much more for that coin."

"Lieutenant Malone," Foster said to me. "Surely you knew Oliver and Jansen were not going to be satisfied with blank pages. How did you plan to make a trade with them?"

I got the message. Change the subject.

"He didn't," Valdez said. "He's young and eager to please. His superiors want those files and he intends to deliver them."

"You placed us all in jeopardy," Foster said. "Coleen especially."

He was right, but that was a chance I'd been prepared to take. Now I wasn't quite so sure. This had not played out as I intended, but with Oliver and Jansen gone there might be another way to get us all out of here alive. I hadn't mentioned the coin. Valdez had no reason to believe it was here.

Time to use it.

But before I could play that card, Coleen leaped to her feet.

Valdez's attention had been momentarily on me, but he turned at the sudden movement. She was fast and agile, springing his way in just a millisecond. Perhaps she sensed, as I did, that Valdez intended on killing us all. Why wouldn't he? That way there'd be no trail, nothing left linking anything that had happened over the past two days to him. But Valdez was a seasoned pro. A trained operative accustomed to tight situations. Sure, she had thirty years on him in age, but time had not dulled his reflexes.

He swung the gun around and fired.

"No," Foster yelled.

The bullet hit her square in the chest.

I reacted and started to pounce, but he whipped the weapon back my way. Coleen grabbed at her midsection, struggling to breathe. Blood spewed from her mouth with each exhale. Her eyes changed from rage, to concern, and finally to fright. I could do nothing but watch. Foster tried to come to his feet, but having his hands bound behind his back made it difficult. She looked my way, her expression pleading for help. Then her eyes rolled skyward and she smacked facedown to the concrete.

Foster's face was filled with shock.

Valdez's attention alternated from Coleen to Foster.

A rage I'd never felt surged through me. Uncontrollable. One that canceled all fear and focused everything on one thing.

Attack.

I dove at Valdez.

CHAPTER FIFTY-FOUR

AT THE SAME INSTANT OUR BODIES MADE CONTACT, MY RIGHT hand grabbed for the gun. Valdez reacted to my assault with a moment of awkwardness, enough for me to take him down. I wondered if anyone heard the shot and, if they had, if it would raise any alarm. Loud noises were the norm at an amusement park, and this one had come from an obvious construction site.

We hit the pavement.

I lifted, then slammed the hand with the gun several times into the concrete, which caused it to clatter away. Valdez shoved his way off me and scrambled for a pile of rebar, gripping one of the remnant pieces and coming my way. I caught sight of Foster struggling to crawl toward Coleen, who still had not moved or made a sound. Valdez swung the piece of iron at me, trying to make contact. I dodged the swishes, retreating, eventually running out of real estate and hitting one of the walls. Valdez lifted the iron bar and tried a vertical blow, which I managed to avoid.

I kicked him in the chest.

Which sent him staggering back, but he found his balance and decided to just whirl the rebar at me. The projectile spun through the air and caught me hard in the thigh, thankfully not with one of the sharp ends, which could have done some damage. Instead it was a horizontal smack.

Which hurt like hell.

I dropped to the ground.

Valdez fled.

I made myself stand.

Adrenaline surged through me. The pain that had been there a moment ago went numb. I knew that was an illusion, but I embraced it. I rushed over to Foster and freed his hands, bound by duct tape.

"Deal with her," I said.

My eyes probed the shadows and, near another rubble pile, I spotted the gun, which I grabbed before racing after Valdez.

I heard the wooden door through which we'd entered open, then bang shut. I approached and passed through, back into the park, catching sight of Valdez weaving through the crowd. The storm had blown itself out, but the warm air felt as if it were filled with invisible steam. People seemed to be enjoying the wet summer evening, the rain nothing more than a minor nuisance.

Valdez was headed toward a carousel where the choice of routes varied. He could go left or right. No way could I take a shot. He passed the carousel and banked left toward Cinderella Castle, lit to the night in all its glory. A breezeway bisected the towering structure. I realized that on the other side was the central hub and Walt Disney's statue where all this had started. Nate's body would still be there, as would be police, and security. Valdez seemed to sense that, too, as he angled right and stayed on this side of the castle, far away from any commotion on the other.

We kept moving, passing more attractions.

It's a Small World. The Haunted Mansion. The Hall of Presidents. We came back into Frontierland and he suddenly disappeared into one of the breezeways I'd seen earlier that connected over to Adventureland.

I kept running, about thirty yards behind him.

I passed through the breezeway and caught sight of Valdez as he zeroed in on the Jungle Cruise, entering a wooden pavilion that looked like some kind of African outpost, where a line had formed for folks waiting their turn at the ride. I could see lights and water on the other side of the olden-looking structure and heard the rev of engines as boats arrived and departed.

I kept up my pursuit, rushing inside and watching as he vaulted a wooden railing. He'd avoided the queues to the left and negotiated a part of the interior that had been roped off, not being utilized at the moment for crowd control. I ducked under one of the black nylon straps and dodged the décor of tools and gear, heading to where I had last seen Valdez. At the railing I saw him on one of the canopied boats cruising "upriver," deeper into the attraction. The banner atop the boat's canopy identified it as the *Nile Nellie*. Another boat was being loaded with visitors to my left. More people waited to be off-loaded in boats behind it. I doubted any of these craft were built for speed, so overtaking Valdez did not seem an option. I rushed over to one of the safari-suited attendants.

"That boat that just left," I said to him. "How can I cut it off and get to it?" He tossed me a puzzled look so I decided to make myself clear. "I'm a federal agent. I need to get to that boat. Now."

On the run over I'd tucked the gun beneath my shirttail and considered using it to make my point clearer. But my stern tone seemed to grab the young man's attention. He pointed across the narrow waterway.

"The river winds in a big circle back to here. Through those woods and you'll get to the boats anywhere they may be along the track."

"Is there a way out of the park through this ride?"

He nodded. "Beyond the fake jungle is a service road, near the railroad tracks, that leads out. But you'd have to get off the boat."

Valdez surely wouldn't know that, but he might discover that fact once he fled the boat anywhere along the way.

I couldn't allow him to escape.

A narrow wharf cordoned off the boats as they arrived at the pavilion. A wooden walkway, about two planks wide, stretched across the water to the "jungle" on the far side. I sidestepped the visitors, hopped onto one of the boats that had just emptied, balanced myself on the benches, then leaped off on the other side, finding the walkway and rushing toward the foliage. I pushed my way into the ferns and shrubs, heading up a short incline among tall trees, and realized this was a berm that shielded one side of the ride from the other, offering privacy during the experience. I could hear boats churning along beyond the greenery, their engines alternating between bursts of speed and slow cruising.

I crested the berm and pushed through more ferns and shrubs. The foliage was thicker along the edges, which made sense as that would be the most noticeable part to the people on the boats. Here, on the other side of the sight line, concealed trails led in all directions, service routes like the corridors back in the Pirate ride. I could hear water falling and the guides as they entertained people in their boats over PA systems.

I spotted the *Nile Nellie*.

A man was tossed over the side near the bow. He hit the water with a splash and I saw that Valdez was now driving the boat, revving its engine and picking up speed. But, as I'd assumed, there were limits on the boat's abilities. He seemed to be trying to steer the craft closer to shore, but it stayed out in the center of the "river," surely tracked like those in the Pirate ride.

I heard a commotion behind me.

Men yelling and others saying, "He went up that way."

Apparently security had arrived. Perhaps even the police, too, given what had happened earlier.

In just a few moments they would find me.

Valdez seemed to realize that the boat's maneuverability was limited. He fled the craft, hopping into the chest-deep water and wading his way toward the far shore and an animatronic display of animals. The bank beyond was clear and open, angled upward to another berm lined with vegetation. On the other side might be that service road the attendant had mentioned. There he could find a way out of here with nobody the wiser. I was hemmed in among the trees and the darkness.

Valdez had no idea I was there.

I heard thrashing behind me.

Whoever was coming would be here in a moment.

Valdez exited the water, walking up among the mechanical lions, giraffes, and zebras.

About a hundred feet away.

I reached for my gun.

To that point I'd never once, in my entire life, had the urge to kill someone. But I desperately wanted to end Juan Lopez Valdez's life. The only thing that stopped me was the knowledge that he was a critical witness in a diabolical conspiracy. One part of me wanted him dead, the other screamed that justice demanded he be taken alive.

"Fan out and find him," I heard a voice call out from the plants behind me.

And not all that far away.

I stood just off one of the trails, at the water's edge. Warm beads of sweat trickled down my forehead. Valdez shook the moisture from his clothes and turned to head up and out of the attraction.

I aimed the gun, steadying it with both hands.

The navy had taught me how to shoot. My proficiency with a firearm was rated above average. If I called out to tell him to stop, the pursuers behind me would be on me. They'd take my gun and Valdez would get away. He might also ignore the command and use the many robotic animals that dotted the far rocky shoreline for cover, easing his escape.

But if I said nothing—

I couldn't allow him to just slip back to Cuba and pay no price for all that he'd done.

Not only for King.

But for Coleen and Nate.

He was moving away.

Farther into the gloom.

I had to make a decision.

"There, I see him," I heard a man call out.

Do it.

I pulled the trigger.

The round smacked into Valdez's spine, jerking him forward. He turned around toward me, searching for the source of the attack.

I fired again.

Then again.

Both slugs found flesh.

Valdez collapsed.

I lowered my weapon.

"On the ground," an excited male voice yelled behind me. "Now. I won't tell you again."

I assumed the man was armed, so I dropped the gun and raised my hands, allowing my knees to fold to the dirt. There I lay as he pounced, cuffing my hands behind my back.

Just like when all this had started.

Forty-eight hours ago.

What seemed like an eternity.

CHAPTER FIFTY-FIVE

I WAS LED BACK TO THE CONSTRUCTION SITE IN HANDCUFFS, uniformed policemen holding on to each arm. Thank God this was in a time before cell phone cameras or I'd probably have become an instant Internet sensation. DANGEROUS CRIMINAL NABBED AT MAGIC KING-DOM. As it was, all I had to endure were the stares and parents huddling their children close. I wondered why I wasn't being taken away from the park. After all, I'd just shot a man dead.

Juan Lopez Valdez was no more.

Good riddance.

I would not shed a tear over his demise. But it was the first time I'd ever actually killed someone in cold blood, and I'd be lying if I said it didn't affect me. Sure, Oliver and Jansen both died. But those were self-defense, heat of the moment. With Valdez I'd simply pulled the trigger. I'd heard guys in the navy talk about killing. It wasn't as easy as people thought. It bothered them, too. As it should. Yes, sometimes it had to be done. But that didn't mean it was ever easy. I would think about what I'd done for many months, never regretting the decision but always mindful of its consequences. Later on I would kill again. More than I'd ever thought possible. It came with the job. And each time I'd reflect on the pros and cons, convincing myself that it had to be done.

We reentered the construction site.

Coleen's body still lay on the concrete only now covered with a plastic tarp. Her father stood off to the side with an Orange County deputy. Surely they now knew that one of their own had died. To the end she'd been a good cop, doing what cops were trained to do.

Make things happen.

Take charge.

I stood there with my hands cuffed behind my back. The blank sheets of paper I'd used as a decoy were scattered everywhere. The piece of rebar that had bruised my thigh was still there, too. Foster was saying nothing. He just looked dazed, staring down at the ground.

"Valdez is dead," I said to him.

The older man looked up and nodded.

I wanted him to know that justice had been done. An eye for an eye and all that crap. But Coleen was still gone. I wondered if the sorrow etched deep into his face would ever lessen. It already seemed permanent, the enormity of what had been set in motion thirty-two years ago had come to fruition here, amid the laughter and gaiety of what some called the happiest place on earth.

But only sorrow filled the night air.

Stephanie Nelle appeared with an older man in uniform, a bunch of gold stars on his collar. A pin at his left breast identified him as the Orange County sheriff.

"Uncuff him," Stephanie said.

The sheriff nodded to one of his deputies and my restraints were freed. She motioned for us to walk off to the far side.

"You okay?" she asked.

I nodded. "How did you find me?"

"It wasn't hard. Just follow the bodies. The FBI is not happy. The attorney general is not happy. Tell me something that can change all that."

I actually had a mouthful, but I needed to speak with Foster first.

I walked over to him.

Stephanie came with me. The sheriff stayed with his people.

"Reverend Foster," she said. "I'm so sorry for your loss."

The older man said nothing.

Deputies scurried about working the crime scene.

"She was a good police officer," Foster said.

"I've explained all that I can to the sheriff," she said, "and invoked federal jurisdiction. I told him the three of you were working with the Justice Department on a special assignment."

"I would rather you not say that," Foster muttered. "I prefer to have nothing to do with the government."

"Would you rather go to jail?" she asked. "Five people died here tonight."

He glared at her. "I only care about two of those deaths. My daughter and her husband are gone."

I heard what he hadn't said.

That he was to blame.

"What's all the blank paper scattered around?" she asked.

"A bluff that didn't work," I said.

"Do you still have the files?" she asked.

This was the moment. Did I tell her the truth? Yes, I knew enough to set history on its head, but Foster had just suffered a horrific personal loss. Did I compound that by implicating him in the murder of Martin Luther King Jr.? No statute of limitations existed on that crime. He could still be prosecuted and face jail. Between the files and the cassette tape, the proof of his involvement was beyond a reasonable doubt. Ultimately, my career in the intelligence business would show that I had a great ability to hold things close. Secrets became second nature for me. People trusted me. And I never let one of them down. But here, amid the surreal gaiety of the Magic Kingdom and the horror of Coleen and Nate's death, I was confronted for the first time with that dilemma.

Talk?

Or not?

"Valdez didn't fall for it," I said. "I had to hand the files over. One of his men took them away just before he shot Coleen."

Foster did not react to my lie, but something told me he appreciated the temporary deflection. I wanted the opportunity to talk with him privately before I leveled with Stephanie.

"And the coin?" she asked.

I reached into my front pocket and produced it. The small reel of tape was in my back pocket, out of sight to her, and there it would remain.

"Do you plan to explain what happened here?" she asked me, taking the coin.

I nodded. "But not tonight. Let's do this tomorrow or the next day."

"It doesn't work like that, Cotton."

"It does for me."

Foster seemed near tears.

Deputies were finishing photographing Coleen's now uncovered body. No father should have to watch that. He should leave, but I realized that wasn't going to happen. This man had helped kill Martin Luther King Jr. What it had taken for him to live with that wrong for the past three decades I could only imagine. Now he would have to live with the fact that his daughter and son-in-law were dead, too.

And he was certainly at least partially responsible.

"Reverend Foster, one of the deputies will take you home," Stephanie said. "I'll be by to see you in a few days."

"Don't waste your time," he said, the voice filled with sorrow. "I'll have nothing to say."

His gaze met mine and I could read his thoughts, as clear as if he'd spoken the words out loud.

He and I were a different story.

We did need to speak.

"Do you need a ride?" Stephanie asked me.

I shook my head and found the keys in my pocket.

"I have a truck."

CHAPTER FIFTY-SIX

COLEEN AND NATE WERE BURIED THREE DAYS LATER, A LITTLE before noon on an endless, dragging, dreadful day. The funerals were held at her father's modest church in Orlando, a small, bricked, single-nave building with a pointed bell tower. Every pew was filled with mourners, the sheriff's department honoring one of their own with a color guard and a uniformed escort to the cemetery. The sheriff himself spoke. Foster did not officiate. Instead, he sat on the front pew, silent and solemn, a prone figure communing with himself.

I'd returned home from Disney World in Lael's truck. Its presence raised questions with Pam, and I explained that I inherited it from someone who no longer had any use for it. She asked about what I'd been doing, but I deflected the questions, telling her I wish I could tell her but I couldn't. Official Navy business. She actually seemed okay with the explanation, and a lovely dinner at a local seafood restaurant helped ease any of her lingering fears.

I would give anything not to have hurt her.

Thoughts of Coleen and Nate stayed in my mind. Along with the fact that three other men had died. Two I helped, the other I killed my-self. Of course, not a word of any of that could be uttered to anyone. I was only beginning to understand that being an intelligence officer was a lonely profession. Little to no recognition ever came from anything you did, good or bad. The job was only about results.

Nothing else mattered.

I returned to work at Naval Station Mayport and, amazingly, my CO acted like nothing had ever happened. Perhaps it was the fact that the Justice Department had specifically recruited my services. That had the smell of some captain's or admiral's touch, and the one thing my CO could sniff out at five hundred yards in the middle of a hurricane was the sweet waft of command. All my past transgressions seemed to have been forgiven. I resumed my job as a staff attorney and it didn't take long for me to realize that there was no comparison between that and what I'd done for the past few days.

On the way back from Orlando I'd stopped in Gainesville and retrieved Valdez's file photos from the Mail 'N More. The cassette tape had remained safe inside the truck's player. Both items, along with the reel tape from Oliver, were now resting in the lower right drawer of my desk at work. Nobody had a clue I possessed them, which to me seemed the best protection. What to do with them was still up in the air. My assignment called for me to turn them over to Stephanie Nelle.

But I had to speak with Foster.

So I took a personal leave day and drove to Orlando for the funeral. Another lie to Pam quelled any questions she might have had.

Follow-up to what I just did.

I'll be home by nightfall.

Coleen and Nate were laid to rest together in a small cemetery west of Orlando, beyond the sprawl, in what was once orange groves. A perfect bowl of bright blue stretched overhead east to west. About two hundred people came to the graveside service. Foster sat with a few others, whom I assumed were Nate's family, in rickety wooden chairs as the final words were said. Then everyone filed by and paid their respects. Foster remained in a daze, but seemed mindful of each person, shaking their hand, forcing a sad smile, thanking them for coming.

The crowd progressively thinned, everyone leaving the quiet cemetery in cars parked in an orderly line atop the close-cropped grass. Foster lingered, and a few of the older folks in the crowd remained with him. I loitered off to the side, among the other graves, waiting for a chance to speak with him.

Finally, he walked over.

"What have you told them?" he asked.

Right to the point. "Not a thing."

"I knew that about you."

I was puzzled by the observation.

"When I first met you in the house by the lake, I told myself you were a man who could be trusted."

"How could you possibly know that?"

"Forty years of trusting other people."

"Look what price King paid for trusting you."

He nodded. "His life."

"You say that as if it means nothing to you."

"On the contrary, it has ruled my every moment for the past thirty-two years."

"Coleen died never knowing the truth."

"I noticed how carefully you chose your words in front of her with Valdez."

"And you said nothing."

"It seemed the best course. One thing I never did was lie to Coleen."

His words came in a low, soft monotone with little emotion accompanying them. I wondered if he really believed his own bullshit.

"You still have the tape and the files?" he asked.

I nodded. "They're safe. No one knows I have them. I also have the original recording from Oliver."

Which surprised him.

"I took it off his body."

"What are you waiting for?" he asked.

"You."

He seemed to consider my dilemma, then said, "It's not complicated. I was told to find FBI spies within the SCLC. I did, but I sold my silence to Jansen in return for cash that I needed. Then I sold out King, in return for a rare gold coin."

He seemed to be keeping with his official line. "You should be in jail."

He gave a slight nod. "A better fate than everyone else. They're all dead."

"Except Bruce Lael."

"You don't need him. You have the cassette copy and the original tape. All you need is for me to validate those and the files, implicating myself in a murder."

"Those thoughts had occurred to me."

"I'm afraid none of that is possible."

"I'm sorry to hear you say that." I wondered what he expected from me. "I'll have to arrest you."

I'd known this man for less than a week. My opinion of him had ranged from none at all, to sympathetic, to outright loathing, to finally pity. His wife died long ago. His daughter and son-in-law were now gone, too. Certainly nothing about him should demand any compassion. He'd brought all of his troubles onto himself.

But something wasn't right.

My lawyer intuition had been telling me for days that two plus two here did not add up to four. Foster was a man of God. A preacher with a flock. I'd just watched a ton of people shake his hand and hug his neck. Not a perfunctory gesture, expected or required. Those people were hurting, because they knew he was hurting. Many who'd been there had to be members of his church. Nothing but love and respect filled their faces. Either this man was one of the most accomplished phonies in the world, or something else was going on. I'd lied to Stephanie Nelle and kept silent the past three days on the belief that something else was indeed going on.

"It's time you tell me the truth," I said. "No more hedging. We're at the end. I have to make a decision."

He stared back at me with eyes that genuinely considered the request, which came with the tone of a plea.

"People expect me to come to the gathering at the church for Coleen and Nate. It will be over by 5:00. Come to my house at 6:00. We can talk there in private."

He gave me the address, then said, "Truth is defined as sincerity in action, character, and utterance. As Christians we believe that every word in the Bible is true. It is the foundation upon which we live our lives. I have counseled many people in need with what the Bible says about truth. I've always told them that keeping God's word in their heart helps them to know when they are listening to the voice of truth. Now it's my turn to follow that advice. *These are the things that you shall do. Speak the truth to one another; render in your gates judgments that are true and make for peace.* Let us hope Zechariah is correct."

And he walked off.

CHAPTER
FIFTY-SEVEN

I KILLED TIME BY FINDING A CRACKER BARREL AND EATING A late lunch, not getting in a hurry and thinking about the past few days. I called Pam and told her that I would be late getting back and, for once, there was no interrogation. The past couple of days had been good between us. We'd even started talking about having a baby. Both of us wanted a child, and perhaps the time had come. With all of the trouble in our marriage, having a baby had never seemed the solution. But maybe we'd turned the corner and could move on, a child providing some additional glue to keep the pieces together. I liked the idea of becoming a father. My own father died when I was ten, so I grew up with my grandfather. I wanted to make a difference in a child's life. Be there for him or her. Be a part of their growing up. As to my military career, who knew where that was going. My temporary foray into the Justice Department was over. I was back in the navy and a job that I was more and more starting to resent. And I had to fight that. The home front was chaotic enough without work joining in the battle.

A little after 5:30 I left the restaurant and headed toward Foster's house. I stopped at a local convenience store and purchased a city map. Orlando was a big place. Easy to get lost among its many neighborhoods, but I found the house, a modest one-story, brick home in a quiet subdivision. Foster's Toyota wasn't parked in the driveway—probably still in Port Mayaca where I'd left it after Jansen cornered me.

I approached the front door and rang the bell.

The door opened a few moments later and Foster invited me inside.

"I told everyone that I wanted to be alone," he said. "We should not be disturbed."

The house was clean and spacious, the walls papered and ornamented with pictures of Coleen and another older woman, surely her mother.

He noticed my interest.

"I was so proud of her. She was a good daughter. Not a follower in any way. She had a mind of her own, never craving the strength of others."

I also noticed the photos of a much younger Benjamin Foster and Martin Luther King Jr. Some just the two of them, standing together, smiling. Others in the presence of a crowd. A few during a march or a sit-in. One had them being forcibly taken away by police. In another they were behind bars.

"We were both arrested in Mobile," Foster said. "We spent three days in jail together. That was 1966."

"How could you sell him out?" I asked.

"Jansen paid me over twenty thousand dollars to be his spy. In those days that was a lot of money."

"Nobody noticed you had that money?"

He shook his head. "It all went to bookies and car dealers. No one paid me any mind."

That feeling swept through me again. "You're lying."

"Why do you say that?"

"You worked with the FBI and set King up to die. I heard you on the recording. Yet you keep these pictures on the wall? You say King was the man you admired the most. You call him Martin. Then you watched as he was shot down. Either you have no conscience or morals at all, which I doubt, or you're lying."

"Coleen challenged me, too, right here in this room. Of course, she was not aware of all that you know." He paused. "She called me a liar when

I told her that I was given the coin by someone else. Which probably only propelled her to make the call to Valdez even quicker. I handled the situation with her terribly. I've decided to handle this one better."

He motioned and we entered a dining room filled with a shiny mahogany table, four chairs, and a sideboard. The windows, sheathed in opaque curtains, allowed in only a halo of late-afternoon sun. Atop the table sat an old reel-to-reel tape recorder. I hadn't seen one since I was a kid. Cassettes and CDs were the norm now. I noticed that a half-full reel was already threaded to a blank spool.

"I need to explain a few things," Foster said. "Some of which we discussed in Micanopy, some we did not."

I recalled the conversation.

"The years 1965 and '66 were relatively calm for Martin. After the incident with the lurid recordings sent to the King house, the FBI seemed to keep their distance. But when Martin came out against the Vietnam War in April of '67, the FBI again increased their surveillance. Hoover also gradually became terrified of a messiah who might unify and electrify the militant black nationalist movement. Jansen spoke of that to me. Malcom X could have been that messiah, but he was killed. Hoover was deathly afraid that Martin would abandon his obedience to nonviolence and embrace black nationalism, becoming their messiah. Of course, that would have never happened. It ran contrary to everything Martin believed. But Hoover didn't know Martin Luther King Jr."

"That may explain why they wanted him dead," I said. "But it doesn't explain why *you* wanted him dead."

"It actually doesn't explain their motives, either. Martin always sought to work *with* the federal government, not against it. Federal judges were our closest allies. The federal government was all we had in the fight with state and local authorities. Martin was no danger to the United States. He was liberal to moderate compared with Stokely Carmichael, Malcolm X, or Roy Wilkins. Hoover had the situation read all wrong."

"Hoover hated King. It was personal between them."

He nodded. "We know that now. In '62, when Martin questioned the FBI's credibility and motives on civil rights, he made an enemy for life."

Foster pointed toward me.

"But the differing sexual mores between the two men certainly came into play. Hoover was either asexual or homosexual. We'll never know for sure. Martin was pure heterosexual. He loved women. He routinely cheated on his wife, and that repulsed Hoover. To him it showed a man who could not be trusted by anyone. Martin was greatly conflicted by that weakness, knowing it was a contradiction to all he preached. But he accepted the flaw as a human frailty."

I wondered about the point of all this but kept my mouth shut.

"By the fall of 1967, Martin was in dire trouble," Foster said. "He'd been working nonstop for twelve years, and the strain had taken an enormous toll. He smoked, drank, and downed sleeping pills almost every day. His marriage was crumbling, and his criticisms of the Vietnam War cost him valuable allies, which included the president of the United States. He was no longer welcome at the White House. His base of support, which had once been enormous, had eroded. Nonviolence was losing its appeal, dismissed by many blacks as out of touch. George Wallace was running for president, and his segregationist message had begun to take hold. Martin felt frustrated, like all of his work had been in vain. A great depression came over him."

I could see that the memories were painful. Whatever was racking this man's conscience seemed to be finally bubbling to the surface. His expression, tone, even his posture, all signaled that he was telling the truth.

"In January of '68, Martin told Coretta about his love affairs. She'd always known in her heart, even before the FBI sent those tapes to their house three years before, that he'd wandered from the marriage. They'd been steadily growing apart. What many never realized, for all his progressiveness on race, was that Martin was a chauvinist at home. He thought a woman's place was raising children. Coretta desired a more active role. She wanted to be out on the road with him. He lived in the spotlight, which to a degree she resented. Money was also an issue. He took little salary from the SCLC and accepted no gifts of cash from anyone. He even donated the $54,000 he won for the Nobel Peace Prize to civil rights groups. She wanted it kept as a college fund for their children. They never took a family vacation and rarely went out socially together. His life was the movement, but the movement was leaving him behind."

I'd never heard these details before on King.

"When we first met you asked me what Martin was like. I told you *fiery, with an ego. He liked recognition, adulation, and respect.* That's all true. I remember in early '68 when a Gallup poll showed that he was no longer in the top ten of admired Americans. That hurt him deeply. By then, SCLC fund-raising was dropping because of his antiwar stance. Universities began to withdraw their lecture invitations. No publisher was eager to sign on with him. Above all, the civil rights movement had split into two factions. One that favored civil disobedience and nonviolence, the other pushing for more militant acts. It hurt to his core that violence was winning out. By the time we arrived in Memphis on April 3, 1968, Martin was politically dead."

I pointed at the tape recorder. "What is this?"

"In a moment," Foster said. "You must understand some things first."

I nodded, conceding that this was his show.

"You heard on the cassette tape when I told Jansen about the March 30 meeting in Atlanta of the SCLC leadership. Everyone was there. Tempers flared. Martin wanted to go back to Memphis, then on to the DC Poor People's March. Everyone else favored another course. He stormed from the building, angry, more so than I've ever seen. A few hours later he called and said he was going to come by my house. He came, and we spoke for about an hour. He brought a recorder and taped every word."

A tight feeling grabbed my throat.

"He wanted there to be no questions. No misunderstandings. He assumed my house was not being bugged, and it wasn't." He pointed at the machine. "This is the original tape from that day."

He sat at the table.

I did, too.

CHAPTER FIFTY-EIGHT

King: Ben, it's been a year since I stood in the pulpit of the Riverside Church and denounced the war. Three-quarters of America now thinks I was wrong to do that. Nearly 60 percent of Negroes agree with them.

Foster: When have you ever been motivated by public opinion? This whole movement runs counter to everything popular in this country.

King: "You're a preacher, not a politician. Don't overstep." "You're a Nobel laureate with opinions on race relations that people all over the world listen to." "A leader of your people." "Why risk all that by taking a stand on an issue that is irrelevant to your purpose." Those are the questions I've been asked over and over.

[PAUSE]

King: For the past year, I've asked myself the same questions. Was I wrong, Ben? Did all common sense leave me? With all my being I believe the war is wrong. It would have been a sin to remain silent. The worst part, though, is how the war protests have nearly all turned violent. I understand why that has happened. Frustration has brought forth an idea that the solution resides in violence. I simply cannot get across to those young people that I embrace everything they feel. It's just tactics we can't agree on. I feel their rage, their pain. But the system is choking them, and us, to death.

Foster: It can't be the entire system. Parts have worked in our favor. The other parts you can fix.

King: No. I can't. I've tried and look where we are. The reality is we live in a failed system. Capitalism will never permit an even flow of economic resources. A privileged few will be rich beyond conscience, and almost all others are doomed to be poor at some level.

Foster: But we've had successes. Desegregation is happening.

King: I've come to believe that we are integrating into a burning house.

Foster: What would you have us do?

King: It's time, Ben, we become firemen.

[PAUSE]

Foster: No. No. Not that.

King: We've talked about this at length. You knew this day would come.

Foster: I'm not going there.

King: Ben, it's vitally important you listen to me. Don't you think I've considered this in every way possible? I've thought of little else these past few months. Can't you see how hard this is for me? And don't forget, it's not you who's going to die.

Foster: It doesn't have to be you, either.

King: There is no other way. You've seen what we're facing. The SCLC is in peril. I want to keep going, stay the course, go back to Memphis, take a stand on poverty. All of my aides, my associates, my friends, they all have a different opinion. Even you have doubts. There was a time when none of you would challenge me. Not anymore. I'm smart enough to see that the world has changed.

Foster: That's all thanks to you. You changed it. You stood in the face of hate and never retreated. I was there with you in Selma, Birmingham, St. Augustine. You made those victories possible.

King: None of that was done alone. Many people sacrificed themselves in those struggles. I still feel for those three young people in St. Augustine who spent six months in jail for just trying to order lunch. So many people, Ben. More than I could have ever imagined, who gave of themselves.

Foster: It's not time for that.

King: For years now I have heard the word wait. It rings in the ear of every Negro with a piercing familiarity. Wait till next year. Wait till after the election.

Wait until things are calmer. Wait *almost always means "never." I will not wait any longer.*

Foster: *I can't do this, Martin. I won't.*

King: *Hoover is not going to stop. He hates me, you, and everyone in this movement. He has a massive force of men at his disposal, and he cares nothing about the Constitution or the law. We have to attack this problem from an angle he will not anticipate.*

Foster: *They make it all about communism. That's all Jansen talks about. He wants to know anything that might point to a red influence.*

King: *"A drop of red dye, then another, and another, accumulating to stain the whole country." That's how they think. But that's smoke, to conceal the real fire burning in their hearts. They attack us, Ben, because they hate us. They hate us because we are not like them. That's not going to evaporate. There is only one thing that can stop them.*

Foster: *I still can't do this. I won't help you die.*

King: *That's why this entire conversation is being recorded. I want the world to know that you did this because I wanted it done. In no way were you compliant. You did exactly as I asked of you, being the friend that you have been for these past years.*

Foster: *Martin, that doesn't change a thing for me.*

King: *We started this many months ago. We agreed then on what we would ultimately have to do. To make this record complete, I want to memorialize what happened.*

[PAUSE]

King: *I suspected that there were people among us spying for the FBI. People close to me. I asked Ben Foster to investigate and find out if that was true. He did as I asked and discovered at least three individuals who had been recruited by an FBI agent named James Jansen. Instead of compromising those traitors, I decided to use them to our advantage. I asked Ben to make contact with Jansen and maneuver himself into being recruited as a spy, too, using the fact that he was aware of the other three yet had not reported their identity to me. The continued flow of information from those other three served as proof of his good intentions. For several months Ben provided Agent Jansen with additional information about me and our activities, all of which I knew about. Is what I've said, so far, true and accurate?*

Foster: *Every word.*

King: On my insistence, Ben began to steer conversations with Agent Jansen into a darker place. We all have our flaws. Ben is plagued with the sin of debt, so convincing Jansen of his need for money presented little problem. He also led Jansen to believe that he was disloyal to both me and the movement. That he had come to resent me. My lapses with women. My drinking. He considered me a hypocrite. Someone not worthy to be in a position of leadership among the Negro people. He also convinced Jansen that there were others who felt the same way. But he emphasized that there was no way I was going to walk away from the movement. Hoover's slander and personal intimidations would never work. Even the disgusting tapes sent to my home, which my wife heard, and the note that implied suicide was my only honorable way out, would not work. If they wanted me gone, they would have to kill me. Is that a correct statement of what occurred?

Foster: It is, with one change. They were suspicious of my motives at first, wondering why I was doing what I did. But I steadily upped the price for my cooperation, which they paid. Eventually, they came to believe that I was genuine.

King: Because they wanted to believe. No, that's incorrect. They had to believe. I do want to point out that every dollar paid to you by the FBI was used to pay your debts. I approved that action. At present, that totals a little over $22,000. Doing that was necessary in order to maintain the story we created. Ben's carelessness with money, his gambling, are facts that existed before all of this started. It was easy for them to investigate and verify their truth.

[PAUSE]

King: Starting in October of last year and continuing to now, Ben has continued to plant the seed of violence in their minds. This was all done at my insistence. None of this was hard to accomplish. These men already hated deep in their hearts. Do I have a death wish? Not in the least. But I have come to realize that in order for this movement to spring forward, to shift to another phase, I must die. Christianity itself was founded on the death of our Lord Jesus. It took his sacrifice on the cross to spur his followers ahead. I do not mean, nor do I imply, that I am similar in any way to Jesus. Quite the contrary. I am a man filled with sin. But I am determined to win the war that I seem born to wage. I cannot, and will not, allow what I've worked so hard to achieve to be destroyed. It is clear that I cannot accomplish this mission in life. But in death it may be possible.

CHAPTER FIFTY-NINE

FOSTER SWITCHED THE MACHINE OFF.

I sat at the table in shock.

He seemed to sense my quandary.

"Martin wanted to die," he said. "He set the whole thing up."

If not for the tape I would have thought him insane. But King's distinctive voice had made clear those intentions.

"At the time I had so many reservations. You heard me resisting. It was decades later, when FBI documents finally became public, that I realized Martin had been right. In early 1968 Hoover stepped up the surveillance of Martin and again began to fan white fears with smear campaigns. What he was doing became so obvious, the *Washington Post* ran a story exposing it. We now know that in January of '68 Hoover asked for more wiretap authority. But the attorney general said no. So he created another of his slanderous dossiers on Martin to try to convince his superiors of the threat Martin supposedly posed. It spoke of more sexual misconduct and possible communist influences. He circulated that document to the attorney general, the State Department, the CIA, the president, even the military. He was told no again on more wiretaps. But he went ahead anyway. Martin was correct. Hoover was never going to stop."

"But to kill him? For King to want to die? That's extreme on both sides, wouldn't you say?"

"It was a different time in so many ways. A white establishment truly existed then. Hoover existed. Blacks were just beginning to come out from under the clouds of segregation and discrimination. But only baby steps had been taken. Martin's ability to mold public opinion had diminished. The FBI wanted, using Jansen's words, *to knock him off his pedestal.* Before they could succeed, though, he found a way to get ahead of them. I know now that it was the correct path."

I continued to stare at the reel-to-reel recorder and recalled what Valdez had said about meeting with Hoover. When the kill order had been issued.

Late January 1968.

Right in the correct time frame.

"There was something else that worked in our favor," Foster said. "By March of '68 public opinion on the Vietnam War had gone negative. A majority no longer supported the war. That's when LBJ lost the New Hampshire primary to Eugene McCarthy and withdrew from the presidential race. Jansen was really concerned about that. He told me Martin's opposition to the war might no longer be an obstacle. He might even be deemed prophetic. They were scared he could have a resurgence. Martin had me use that fear to move them forward with the assassination."

"Which makes his death wish even more puzzling. He could have weathered the PR storm."

"He'd fought the fight for a long time. He told me the fact that white people might decide that the war was bad for them would mean nothing for the oppression of the black and the poor. He might win on one front, but lose on the other. He believed his death would cut across all of that. And it did."

I recalled what Foster had told Coleen.

I loved Martin Luther King Jr. like a father. I admired him more than any man I'd ever known. I still do to this day. I would have never betrayed him.

"You really didn't betray him," I said.

"I did exactly as he wanted."

"Why did he choose you to do it?"

Foster stayed silent a moment.

Then he explained.

"It has to be you," King said. "Andy, Jesse, Ralph have all been with me for so long. That fact alone would never allow them to be a part of this. They also each have their own agendas, their own paths to follow. They are good, determined men. The movement will need them in the future, and they'll make a difference. But you, Ben. You are lost, and have been for a long time."

"I can do great things, too."

The indignation in his voice was hard to conceal.

"I agree, but there are many different ways in which to do great things. I don't say this with any malice in my heart, nor with any ill intent. But you are not meant to be a leader of this movement. There are captains and there are lieutenants. You are the latter, so your fate will be different from the others'. You have a talent for people, a way of sensing what they think and telling them precisely what they want to hear. But, like me, you are flawed. You're searching, Ben, looking for something in your life. Whether that will be in the pulpit of a church remains to be seen. Maybe this will help you find what it is you are searching for. You've done a good job keeping me pointed in the right direction. I've come to depend on your watchful eye. When I decided that it was time for me to meet God, you were the only one I would want to make that happen."

"I wasn't sure whether to be offended or honored," Foster said. "He essentially called me a con man. But he was right. He knew me better than I knew myself. I could con the FBI because I'd spent my life conning others. I was good at it. Ralph, Andy, Jesse—none of them ever liked me. I was tolerated because Martin liked me. The day after the assassination Ralph told me that my services, as a traveling secretary, were no longer needed. He fired me."

"None of them had any idea what really happened?"

He shook his head. "The old proverb is true. The buyer needs a hundred eyes, the seller but one. Thankfully, Jansen never looked close enough to realize he was being played. Martin used to say I was a little bit of a lion, but more a fox."

I grinned.

"The FBI cut me loose after Martin died, too. They gave me the coin and told me to disappear. That's when I decided to go back to preaching. By then I'd changed. I was a different person. Martin's death made me someone else entirely. A new man, one I came to embrace and like."

I needed more details so I decided to probe. "Why in Memphis?"

"Martin didn't want it to happen in Atlanta. That would be too close to his family. He also wanted to die at a dramatic moment. His death had to mean something. Memphis seemed the perfect place. Tensions were high. The danger real. Looking back, it seems that fate was working with us the whole time. The night of April 3, before he went to sleep, he told me to set it up for the next day at 6:00 P.M. He said he would make sure he was out on the balcony at the Lorraine for several minutes. The perfect target. So I told Jansen where and when and to be ready if the opportunity presented itself. Of course, I knew that it would."

I could only imagine the courage that had taken.

"There was a big rally scheduled for the night of the third at the Masonic Temple. The weather was bad. Rain, with a threat of tornadoes. Martin was battling a cold and was a little depressed, as you might imagine, so he opted not to go. Abernathy went instead to address the crowd, but they wanted Martin. They chanted for Martin. So Ralph called the Lorraine. Martin was already asleep. I answered the phone and, at Ralph's insistence, went to wake him. He was really moved that so many people wanted him to be there, so he dressed and we both went over to the temple."

I was amazed listening to history, seen through Foster's eyes, ingrained in his memory.

"When we got there a huge thunderstorm erupted. Rain pounded the roof. Thunder clapped. It was almost biblical, like a sound effect from a movie. Martin took the pulpit and the place went dead silent. Keep in mind he hadn't intended on coming, so he'd prepared no remarks. He spoke straight from the heart. It was nearly a year to the day since he'd denounced the war and started a public free fall. The last year of his life was about over. He already knew that a white man would gun him down at 6:00 P.M. the next day. Have you ever studied what he said that night? What they now call the Mountaintop Speech."

I shook my head.

Foster stood from the table and left the room for a moment, returning with a book containing the published works of Martin Luther King Jr.

He opened to the right page and passed it to me.

I read.

CHAPTER SIXTY

Something is happening in Memphis.

Something is happening in our world.

And you know, if I were standing at the beginning of time, with the possibility of taking a kind of general and panoramic view of the whole of human history up to now, and the Almighty said to me, "Martin Luther King, which age would you like to live in?" Strangely enough, I would turn to the Almighty, and say, "If you allow me to live just a few years in the second half of the 20th century, I will be happy."

Now that's a strange statement to make, because the world is all messed up. The nation is sick. Trouble is in the land. Confusion all around.

That's a strange statement.

But I know, somehow, that only when it is dark enough can you see the stars. And I see God working in this period of the twentieth century in a way that men, in some strange way, are responding.

Something is happening in our world.

The masses of people are rising up. And wherever they are assembled today the cry is always the same. We want to be free. Now, I'm just happy that God has allowed me to live in this period to see what is unfolding.

And I'm happy that He's allowed me to be in Memphis.

Now, what does all of this mean in this great period of history?

It means that we've got to stay together. We've got to stay together and maintain unity. You know, whenever Pharaoh wanted to prolong the period of slavery in Egypt he had a favorite formula for doing it.

What was that?

He kept the slaves fighting among themselves.

But whenever the slaves get together, something happens in Pharaoh's court and he cannot hold the slaves in slavery. When the slaves get together that's the beginning of getting out of slavery.

Let us maintain unity.

We've got to give ourselves to this struggle until the end. Nothing would be more tragic than to stop at this point in Memphis. We've got to see it through. And when we have our march, you need to be there. If it means leaving work, if it means leaving school, be there. Be concerned about your brother. You may not be on strike. But either we go up together, or we go down together.

Let us rise up tonight with a greater readiness.

Let us stand with a greater determination.

And let us move on in these powerful days, these days of challenge to make America what it ought to be. We have an opportunity to make America a better nation.

And I want to thank God, once more, for allowing me to be here with you.

You know, several years ago, I was in New York City autographing the first book that I had written. And while sitting there autographing books, a demented black woman came up. The only question I heard from her was, "Are you Martin Luther King?" I was looking down writing and said, "Yes." The next minute I felt something beating on my chest. Before I knew it I had been stabbed by this demented woman. I was rushed to Harlem Hospital.

It was a dark Saturday afternoon.

And that blade had gone through, and the X-rays revealed that the tip of the blade was on the edge of my aorta, the main artery. Once that's punctured, you're drowned in your own blood. That's the end of you.

It came out in the New York Times the next morning that if I had merely sneezed, I would have died. About four days later they allowed me, after the operation, after my chest had been opened, and the blade had been taken out, to move around in the wheelchair in the hospital. They allowed me to read some of the mail that came in from all over the states and the world.

I had received one from the president and the vice president.

I've forgotten what those telegrams said.

I'd received a visit and a letter from the governor of New York, but I've forgotten what that letter said.

But there was another letter that came from a little girl, a young girl who was a student at the White Plains High School. And I looked at that letter, and I'll never forget it.

It said simply,

"Dear Dr. King, I am a ninth-grade student at the White Plains High School. While it should not matter, I would like to mention that I'm a white girl. I read in the paper of your misfortune and of your suffering. And I read that if you had sneezed, you would have died. And I'm simply writing you to say that I'm so happy that you didn't sneeze."

And I want to say tonight that I too am happy that I didn't sneeze.

Because if I had sneezed I wouldn't have been around here in 1960, when students all over the South started sitting in at lunch counters. And I knew that as they were sitting in, they were really standing up for the best in the American dream, and taking the whole nation back to those great wells of democracy which were dug deep by the Founding Fathers in the Declaration of Independence and the Constitution.

If I had sneezed, I wouldn't have been around here in 1961, when we decided to take a ride for freedom and ended segregation in interstate travel.

If I had sneezed, I wouldn't have been around here in 1962,

when Negroes in Albany, Georgia, decided to straighten their backs up. And whenever men and women straighten their backs up, they are going somewhere, because a man can't ride your back unless it is bent.

If I had sneezed I wouldn't have been here in 1963, when the black people of Birmingham, Alabama, aroused the conscience of this nation, and brought into being the Civil Rights Bill.

If I had sneezed I wouldn't have had a chance later that year, in August, to try to tell America about a dream that I had.

If I had sneezed I wouldn't have been down in Selma, Alabama, to see the great movement there.

If I had sneezed I wouldn't have been here in Memphis to see a community rally around those brothers and sisters who are suffering.

I'm so happy that I didn't sneeze.

I left Atlanta this morning, and as we got started on the plane there were six of us. The pilot said over the public address system, "We are sorry for the delay, but we have Dr. Martin Luther King on the plane. And to be sure that all of the bags were checked, and to be sure that nothing would be wrong on the plane, we had to check out everything carefully. And we've had the plane protected and guarded all night."

And then I got into Memphis.

Some began to say the threats, or talk about the threats that were out. What would happen to me from some of our sick white brothers? I don't know what will happen now. We've got some difficult days ahead.

But it really doesn't matter with me now, because I've been to the mountaintop.

And I don't mind.

Like anybody, I would like to live a long life.

Longevity has its place.

But I'm not concerned about that now. I just want to do God's will. And He's allowed me to go up to the mountain.

And I've looked over.

I've seen the promised land.

I may not get there with you. But I want you to know tonight that we, as a people, will get to the promised land.

And so I'm happy tonight.

I'm not worried about anything.

I'm not fearing any man.

Mine eyes have seen the glory of the coming of the Lord.

CHAPTER SIXTY-ONE

I'D HEARD THAT SPEECH SEVERAL TIMES. BUT ONLY BITS AND pieces. Highlights. Never this much at one sitting. But reading it now, knowing what I knew about what happened the day after, I was moved in a powerful way. I had to admit, given the context as described by Foster, King's words sounded like those of a man who knew he was about to die. Not in a decade. Or a few years. Or even in a week.

Now.

"He spoke of mortality that night," Foster said. "His own, but only he and I knew the true immediacy. It was an amazing speech. His voice rose and fell in calculated waves, controlling the audience's emotions like a drum major would with a band. Not a note in front of him. Every word conceived as he spoke. There was lots of applause and verbal affirmations. I felt like I was at church on Sunday. When he uttered those last words, *Mine eyes have seen the glory of the coming of the Lord,* he turned from the podium and nearly collapsed into Abernathy's arms. He seemed totally spent. As if he'd completed all he wanted to do."

My mind stood still, blank and bare, but I wanted to know, "Why didn't you just tell Coleen all of this?"

His face collapsed onto itself, retreating behind folds of slackened flesh as the guilt, grief, and regret again took hold. "I couldn't."

"I don't see why not."

He reached for the switch on the reel-to-reel recorder.

"Listen."

King: *It's going to be okay, Ben. Really, it is.*

Foster: *I will have to live with this for the rest of my life. It's not right of you to ask this of me.*

King: *I agree. I have no right. But you're all I have. You're my friend, Ben. My dear friend. We both know that my fate has been sealed for a long time. We all knew that one day some damn fool would kill me. Thankfully, that didn't happen back when we had so much to accomplish.*

Foster: *We still have things to accomplish.*

King: *They'll be done, just not with me alive. I was once the voice of the Negro in this country. That is not the case anymore. Other voices have risen louder. Ones that, sadly, shout destruction and violence. We have to silence them. As Gandhi said,* There are many causes I would die for. There is not a single cause I would kill for. *We have to make sure our folks don't forget that.*

Foster: *Yet you ask me to kill you.*

King: *Yes, I do. And I apologize for that. But if a man hasn't found something he's willing to die for, he isn't fit to live. My cause. My race. They are both worth dying for. I'm ready to be at peace, Ben. Something else Gandhi said has stuck in my mind of late.* First they ignore you, then they laugh at you, then they fight you, then you win. *I'm ready to win.*

Foster: *You have.*

King: *Not entirely.*

[PAUSE]

Foster: *Do you ever want the world to know what you did?*

King: *I've thought on that. So let me say this to those listening to this recording. If physical death is the price a man must pay to free his children and his white brethren from a permanent death of spirit, then nothing can be more redemptive. But that can only succeed if we take the high road. Leave the low road to others. If we stay the course that has already been set, I firmly believe we will see the promised land. Here's my answer to your question. Wait fifty years* *before ever saying a word about any of this. If you survive to that day, make the decision then. My dream is that in fifty years the Negro will be in the promised land. If you come to join me with God before fifty years have passed, then only you and I will ever know what we've done. Take the secret to your grave. In this, Ben, I will trust you and you alone.*

Foster switched off the machine. "I've respected his wish. It's what he died for, so I could not violate that trust. I knew my life, from that day on, would come with conditions. Prudence being one of those. I've kept silent, and that silence included my wife and Coleen. A little over thirty years have now passed on the fifty, and I'm still breathing."

The implications of what I was hearing weighed heavy. But I needed to know more. "Where did King get the idea to use the FBI to make it happen?"

"That was the ironic part. Hoover himself provided the spark. That note he sent to King's house back in '65, which suggested suicide."

I recalled the wording.

King, there is only one thing left for you to do. You know what it is. There is but one way out for you. You better take it before your filthy, abnormal, fraudulent self is bared to the nation.

"Martin eventually came to believe Hoover was right. Death was the only route that would work, but not for the reasons Hoover wanted. That note, though, did convince Martin that Hoover wanted him dead. It's what got him thinking in such a dark direction. Starting in late summer of '67, he had me drop hints and suggestions to Jansen. Test the waters, lead them our way. Finally, as you heard on the cassette, I came right out and proposed it to them. They could have said no. Rejected the whole idea. But they didn't. No one was more shocked by that than me. I was so hoping they would not go down that road."

I saw the stress of the past few days etched into his face.

"Martin and I talked many times about mortality," Foster said. "He meant what he said in Memphis the night before he died. There was something to be said for longevity. He would have preferred to live a long life. But he was smart enough to know when to quit, and persuasive enough to convince me that his way was the right way. So I did what he asked of me."

"He just walked out on the balcony at the Lorraine Motel and stood there to be shot?"

"That's exactly what he did. I was below in the parking lot with the others. When he came out to the railing, I said a prayer. He'd been specifically told not to be out in the open like that. But Martin did what Martin wanted to do, so no one questioned him. The mood that evening was light. Everyone felt good. We'd won in court. The second public march was going to happen. Things were working out. We were all headed to dinner at a local preacher's house. Only I knew Martin would not be coming with us. Two hours earlier, Jansen had told me it was definitely going to happen."

Foster's gaze went distant.

"That rooming house, where Ray found his perch, offered the perfect angle to the balcony at the Lorraine. The bathroom had a straight line of sight, so Ray positioned himself there, standing in a tub, the rifle out the window. One shell loaded. That's all. Just one. The man had confidence."

Or was just an idiot.

Hard to know for sure.

"Martin was leaning over the railing when the bullet struck, his back toward Ray, proving what he'd said the night before at the Masonic Temple. *A man can't ride your back unless it is bent.* Those words flashed through my brain the instant I heard the shot. I also recall him smiling. Just as he turned to go back into his room for a coat. He died with a smile on his face."

Foster pointed at the recorder.

"There's a little more on the tape."

And he switched the machine back on.

King: *I entered this fight when I was twenty-six, and destroying Jim Crow has been a hard battle. I've known since the first day that my life of nonviolence would end violently. Everyone thinks about dying.*

Foster: *You more than others.*

King: *I agree. I've often spoke of it. Probably too much. But they killed Kennedy. They killed Malcolm X. They killed Medgar Evers. They've killed little black children and white reformists. I think about Selma and Jimmie Lee Jackson all the time.*

Foster: I do too.

King: I want to say this to the people listening to this tape. In 1965 we went to Selma to march for voting rights. Jimmie Lee Jackson was twenty-six years old. A farm laborer and church deacon. He marched with us that day to the Perry County Courthouse when the state troopers attacked with clubs. Jimmie saw his mother and grandfather being assaulted and rushed to help them. An Alabama state trooper shot him in the stomach, then they dragged him away so he could be arrested for assault and battery. It took hours before he made it to the hospital. He lingered in terrible pain for nine days before dying. Nine days after that we marched from Selma to Montgomery. Thousands of people came, outraged at the clubs, whips, chains, tear gas, and bullets they'd seen on television being used against defenseless marchers. One of those marching there that day, a white minister and father of four, James Reeb, was beaten to death by an angry mob of whites. A few days later a forty-year-old white mother named Viola Liuzzo was shot dead by several Klansmen. So many have died for this cause. People forget that this movement is stained with blood. I don't want them to forget. Not now. Not ever. How many times have we seen men with rifles, perched in trees, as we marched, just waiting for a chance to take a shot at us? How many bomb threats have there been? Immortality is not gained by how much money you make during your life, or how many houses you own, or how popular you may be. It's gained by service to the poor and lost, the heartbroken and despairing, the hungry and naked. Jimmie Lee Jackson, James Reeb, and Viola Liuzzo knew that. They gave their lives. What they lacked was notoriety. I have that. So my life will now be offered so that none of them will ever be forgotten.

[PAUSE]

Foster: What do you want us to say at the funeral?

King: I want it short with only a brief eulogy. I don't want any mentions of my Nobel Prize or any of the other awards I've been given. Just have them say that I served and loved others. That I tried to be right on the war. I tried to feed the hungry, clothe the naked, and visit the imprisoned. The more hate my enemies spat, the harder I pushed myself. The more they tried to stop me, the harder I worked. End it with I tried, with all my might, to love and serve humanity.

Foster switched off the machine for the last time.

He and I both were visibly wrestling with emotion.

"In the last year of his life Martin experienced a difficult erosion of faith. That halo of abundant confidence, which early success generates in the young and rash, had disappeared. He was approaching forty years old and viewed life with a frantic urgency. I heard Coretta talking to Ralph Abernathy, about a month before Memphis. Even she noticed a change, she said it was like fate was closing in on him."

Hard to hide much from your wife.

Which I should know.

"He told me that people tended to memorialize the dead, and he was right. His death gave an extra meaning to all the others who'd died before him for the cause. None of them were ever forgotten."

What I should do next was no longer clear. I'd come here intending to tell him that everything would have to be revealed. Coleen was gone. No reason existed to keep this secret, except perhaps to keep Foster from jail. But with this new revelation everything had changed. This wasn't a murder. It had been an elaborate suicide, staged to look like a murder.

"King seemed to have thought it all through," I said.

"That was his gift. He had a vision. He'd been the producer, director, and costar in many civil rights performances. Marches, demonstrations, rallies, freedom rides, protests, sit-ins, speeches, eulogies. He organized them with expert precision. Nothing happened by chance. His last production, his greatest production, was his own death."

Foster reached beneath his jacket and brought out a .38 revolver, which he laid on the table.

I pointed at the weapon. "Is that for you or me?"

"Maybe me. I don't know yet."

He hadn't asked me any of the details about what occurred with Jansen, Oliver, and Valdez. I doubted he knew much of what had happened with me and Coleen until we made it to St. Augustine and she surrendered herself.

"Coleen willingly went with Valdez to protect you," I said. "She wanted you to be safe. Now you plan to shoot yourself?"

He shrugged. "I'm tired of living with other people's deaths on my conscience. I'm tired of staying silent. I'm just plain tired all the way around."

No question. This guy had turned the practice of playing both sides against the middle into an art form. And I suddenly realized that the roles had reversed. I was him, to him being King. One would die, the other would keep the secret.

Or would I?

He rewound the tape until one spool was empty, then removed the reel.

"Take this."

He handed the tape over to me.

"You have everything else, you'll need this, too. It's your decision on what to do. I pass the duty on to you. Now get out of here, Lieutenant, and let me die in peace."

PRESENT
DAY

EPILOGUE

I STAND INSIDE THE KING FAMILY HOME AND STARE ACROSS THE dim hallway at Benjamin Foster. I've finished talking about what happened eighteen years ago. I point to the gun at his waist. "Why didn't you pull the trigger back then?"

"Why haven't you told the world what you knew?"

"When I didn't hear about your death, I drove back to Orlando. I was told you resigned as pastor and left town. Where did you go?"

"California, Arizona, Mexico. You haven't answered me. Why didn't you tell?"

"I decided to honor King's wish and keep silent, until fifty years had passed."

Foster motions to the side table. "I see the cassette and the tape reels. What's on the flash drive?"

"The photos from Valdez's files started to turn. Photography in the '60s wasn't what it is today. Before they completely disappeared, I transferred everything to digital. They're on that flash drive."

"It's not the same."

I shrug. "It's all we've got. The originals faded away."

"Like my life. I still miss Coleen every day."

I, too, often think of her and Nate. Both died for the cause. Two more casualties in a social revolution that started in April 1865 and continues to this day.

"I eventually came back home to Florida," Foster says. "My church was quite understanding. They hired me back. I've stayed with them ever since."

"My life also changed. When you vanished, Stephanie Nelle wanted me to find you. But I told her to let it go. I convinced her that the files were probably back in Cuba and you couldn't add a thing. I don't know if she really believed me, but she let it go."

He says nothing.

The King house remains cemetery-quiet, the night outside equally tranquil. Tomorrow, the entire Martin Luther King Jr. Center will be alive with activity. Former presidents Barack Obama and Danny Daniels are coming to speak from the pulpit of the Ebenezer Baptist Church. Many visitors are expected at the epicenter of King's memory. But now, in the wee hours of the morning, it is just me and Foster.

"Stephanie came to see me again about a month after I moved her off your trail," I say. "All hell broke loose inside the FBI thanks to Oliver and Jansen's antics. They cleaned house there and in the Justice Department. No more Hoover cronies anywhere. Finally, the stain was removed. They then started a new unit within Justice to deal with sensitive problems like that. It eventually became much more, expanding its reach around the world. I was its first recruit. The Magellan Billet."

"I learned about that from a friend in government. That's how I found you in Copenhagen."

"If you hadn't, I would have found you. Today is an important day."

I glance at my watch.

12:30 A.M.

April 4 has begun.

"Martin promoted hope and curiosity," Foster says. "History has proven that his memory is secure. So many people grieved when he died. His death became *their* death."

"You were right with what you told Jansen. There were riots coast to coast."

"For a time it seemed Martin's death was the death of hope, progress, and justice. But as he told me would happen, we moved past that.

We settled back down and resumed the fight, leaving the streets and entering politics. Black mayors were elected in New Jersey and Indiana. Andy Young became the first black man from Georgia, since Reconstruction, to serve in Congress. Many more election victories followed. Eventually, a black man became president. Martin would have loved all that."

I ask what I really want to know. "What do you think? Is it time to tell the world?"

"I've thought about that these past few years. The movement opened doors. That's true. Doors that had once not even existed. But that has mainly been for the black elite and middle class. The Civil Rights, Voting Rights, and Fair Housing Acts created a whole list of new freedoms that they were able to take advantage of."

"And the poor?"

"Exactly. The poor. The inner city. The disadvantaged. Little has changed for them. More to the point, they seemed to have become demonized. It's easy to beat up on poor people, and it comes from both sides of the political aisle. Look what Clinton did in the 1990s. He caved to the Republican Congress and signed welfare reform, which did nothing but create even more poor people. The poor no longer have a champion. So they wallow in poverty, with few jobs, even fewer opportunities. It's not hard to see why they decide to kill one another. Black-on-black violence seems epidemic. For me, there's no doubt that Martin's dream remains unfulfilled."

I, too, had thought about that question on the flight from Denmark, knowing that was why I'd been summoned. For eighteen years I have kept the secret, lying to Stephanie, never revealing what I possess nor what I know. Now here I am, inside the childhood home of Martin Luther King Jr., faced with a decision.

"We all made a serious mistake," Foster says. "Myself included. After Martin died, we grieved him into perfection. That was something he never anticipated. The love and respect people felt easily allowed them to elevate him to a lofty perch. Nearly every town in this country has a street or boulevard named for him. His birthday is a national holiday. To criticize him has come to be regarded as treasonous to the black race. Which is odd, considering that, in his life, he dealt far more with criticism than with praise. We all forgot that his faults, and he had many, only emphasized his humanity. His shortcomings, which we all possess, made him real. He was no saint. But he was a savior."

"Why are we here?" I ask.

"I've lived with the pain of my friend's death for fifty years, and the pain of my daughter's for nearly twenty. I don't want to live with either any longer. I did not pull the trigger when you left my house because I made a pledge to Martin. He gave his life and he asked me to give mine, only in a different way. He wanted me to live to see this day. All right. I've kept that pledge. When nothing was ever publicly revealed, I realized that you were keeping that pledge, too."

We stand in silence for a few moments.

"My daughter never had the chance to experience a full life," he mutters. "She never knew the joy of raising a child of her own, and that was all my fault. If I'd only made the deal with Valdez and traded the coin for the files, then burned the files, none of it would have ever happened. But I foolishly thought myself capable of controlling events. I thought I was in charge. I thought my refusal was more than enough. How wrong I was."

I can see where this is headed.

Which has been a long time coming.

"Martin was right about me," he said. "I was never meant to be a captain."

"No. You're a general. He trusted you with the most important decision he ever made. He chose you to make sure it all could be possible. And you didn't disappoint him. You did exactly what he wanted. And look what you became. A husband. Father. Respected minister. He *was* right about you. He knew you better than you knew yourself."

"A part of me wishes I never met him."

I hear the defeatism and know it's over. "Are you ready for me to leave?"

He nods. "Thank you for telling me what happened. I wanted to know. I appreciate you coming. Take the tapes and the flash drive and decide what needs to happen on this fiftieth anniversary. You've done well so far. I trust you to make the right call."

No sense arguing, so I retrieve the four items from the side table and head for the door, my footsteps muffled on a thin rug that covers the hardwood.

"Take care," Foster says.

I stop, turn back, and say, "You, too."

I leave, gently closing the door behind me. The Atlanta skyline looms a few miles away, lit to the night. Sweet Auburn rests quietly around me. I descend the porch steps and find the sidewalk, turning left, straddling Auburn Avenue. A few cars pass on the street.

I hear a bang.

Deadened by wooden walls.

I stop and stare back at the King home.

Benjamin Foster is gone.

To my knowledge I am now the only one left alive who knows anything. Not a word has ever been heard from Bruce Lael. Dead or alive? No one knows. I still hold the cassette, the two reel tapes, and the flash drive in my left hand.

I trust you to make the right call.

I keep walking, crossing an intersection and reentering the grounds for the King Center. I turn and follow the concrete path around to the rear. A large lit pool with fountains separates the buildings. One, the King Library and Archives, holds the largest repository of primary source materials on Martin Luther King Jr. and the American civil rights movement in the world. All of King's papers, along with those of the SCLC and other major civil rights organizations, are there. Preserved for all time. So many had tried to silence those voices, but they failed.

I keep walking—no one else is around at this early hour—following the pool toward its far end. After King died he was carried on a farm wagon, drawn by mules, to a local Atlanta cemetery. Eventually, his remains were moved here, to the institute that bore his name, lying alongside his wife, Coretta. Georgia marble had been used to construct their crypt, which sits in the center of the glistening pool, a timeless acknowledgment of the man's simple southern roots. I stop and stare at the crypt, the white marble lit to the night, and the inscription.

REV. MARTIN LUTHER KING, JR.
1929–1968
"FREE AT LAST, FREE AT LAST,
THANK GOD ALMIGHTY
I'M FREE AT LAST."

Sure, there's been great progress in race relations. The elimination of Jim Crow, the end of separate but equal, school integration, fair housing, equal employment. History has shown that, beyond Abraham Lincoln, Martin Luther King Jr. did more to bring about social change than anyone in American history. His motivations, though questioned during his life, became clear after death. Without a doubt King walked a fine line between morality and politics. But by and large, he'd been successful keeping to the high road. His legacy is exactly as Foster had said. *Hope and curiosity.* I've read many books on his life and work. Along the way I came across something he once said that seems fitting tonight. *A nation or civilization that continues to produce soft-minded men purchases its own spiritual death on an installment plan.*

Benjamin Foster had not been soft-minded.

Instead, he'd assumed an awful responsibility, thrust on him by a man who could not be denied.

I wonder what King would think of us today?

The unemployment rate for minorities hovers at three times that of whites. The net worth of an African American is $6,000, compared with $110,000 for a white. The average medium income for black households stays $55,000 or more below that for whites. An epidemic of shocking deaths has given rise to a Black Lives Matter movement, reminiscent of something King himself would have organized. Poverty continues to reign. Little has been done to combat it, which King surely would have found horribly disappointing.

And not just in America.

But around the world.

There is nothing new about poverty. What is new is that we have the resources to get rid of it.

King's words.

Wise then and now.

I stare hard at the crypt, seeking answers. What would be gained by revealing what I know? Those who oppose King would still oppose him, and those who support him might find their faith challenged. Would they feel manipulated? Used? Or would they recognize the sacrifice he'd made? And that was precisely what it had been. The ultimate sacrifice.

King gave his life, so his message would live on.

And it has.

Every movement requires a hero.

No matter how unlikely or unwilling.

I turn from the grave and see the eternal flame burning behind me. I step close and read the plaque at its base.

> THE ETERNAL FLAME SYMBOLIZES
> THE CONTINUING EFFORT TO REALIZE
> DR. KING'S IDEALS FOR THE
> "BELOVED COMMUNITY"
>
> WHICH REQUIRES LASTING PERSONAL
> COMMITMENT THAT CANNOT WEAKEN
> WHEN FACED WITH OBSTACLES.

That it does.

Many people would agree that history matters. Truth matters, too. But sometimes things are better left unsaid. Revealing what I know would only spread a dense cloud of smoke around an already burning fire, masking the flames themselves.

And that flame cannot be concealed.

To distract in any way from what King helped start seems pointless. Why fuel the naysayers? The work must go one. Sure, battles have been won, but the war is not over. King gave Foster the sole option of deciding what to do when fifty years had passed.

Now that duty is mine.

I toss all four items I hold into the eternal flame.

The two old magnetic tapes incinerate instantly, the cassette and flash drive take a few moments longer. Soon they're nothing but charred, melted plastic. Unrecognizable. Useless.

Before walking away I whisper to King and Foster and all of the other restless spirits who surely roam this hallowed place.

Three words.

That could still have meaning.

"Free at last."

WRITER'S NOTE

The idea for this book has swirled around in my head for more than a decade, but I delayed its writing until 2018 and the fiftieth anniversary of the King assassination. This is also my rookie foray into full length, novel-sized first-person narrative. Always before I've utilized several points of view (usually three to five) to tell the story. This time it's all Cotton, and he and I have become much closer thanks to the experience.

Time now to separate fact from fiction.

This story is a travelogue of Florida, which included Jacksonville, Key West, Port Mayaca, Lake Okeechobee, Palm Beach, Neptune Beach, Melbourne, Stuart, St. Augustine, Starke, Gainesville, Micanopy, Orlando, and Disney World. Of particular note were the Dry Tortugas (chapters 4, 5). If you've never visited, it's definitely worth the trip. There are indeed shipwrecks scattered off the southwest coast of Loggerhead Key (chapter 7). Sadly, Loggerhead no longer appears as described in the novel, since nearly all of its trees were removed by 2001.

A few extra mentions on the locales: Fort Jefferson is faithfully described (chapters 10, 11, 12), including the staff office, grounds, and moat with a barracuda (which I saw firsthand). Seaplanes and boats do come and go from the fort several times each day. O. Brisky Books is there, in Micanopy (chapter 44). With regard to Neptune Beach (just east of

Jacksonville) the Sun Dog Diner (chapter 3) is no longer there, but it did exist years ago. The Bookmark, though, was there then and now, owned by Rona and Buford Brinlee. Since 2003, I've held an event there with the release of each novel. The cemetery at Port Mayaca (chapter 15) is real, as is the memorial to the victims of the 1928 hurricane. A similar memorial also stands in West Palm Beach, Florida (chapter 15). Outside of Florida, the Martin Luther King Center in Atlanta figures prominently into the story (prologue, epilogue), and that includes the King family home, Ebenezer Baptist Church, burial crypt, and eternal flame.

The 1933 Double Eagle mentioned throughout the novel exists. The coin is the rarest and most valuable in the world (worth many millions), and it remains illegal for anyone to either possess or sell one. Nearly all of the missing coins have been accounted for, but nobody really knows for sure how many disappeared in 1933. If you'd like to see one firsthand, visit the National Numismatic Collection either in person inside the Smithsonian's American history museum in Washington, DC, or online. An excellent book on the subject is *Double Eagle,* by Alison Frankel.

Sadly, the FBI's counterintelligence initiative, COINTELPRO, is not a work of fiction. It existed from the late 1950s until 1972. First designed to root out supposed communist influences, it metamorphosed into perhaps the most corrupt and illegal organization ever created by the U.S. government. Its abuses included burglaries, illegal wiretaps, mail openings, slander, libel, you name it, they did it. Bagmen, who handled the burglaries and illegal wiretaps, like Bruce Lael, were on the payroll (chapter 31). Paid informants and spies were also utilized, several close to King (chapters 25, 34). The destruction of Jean Seberg, described in chapter 39, and publicly admitted to by the FBI in 1979, is but one example of COINTELPRO's abuse.

The race riots of 1967 (chapter 38) generated great fear throughout the country. That was when Hoover shifted COINTELPRO toward civil rights organizations. The memos dated August 25 and March 4, quoted at the end of chapter 27, are the actual documents (with the actual wording) that ordered the move.

COINTELPRO's abuses were finally exposed in 1975 by the Church

Committee (chapter 14). Things came to light after the daring burglary of a local FBI office in Media, Pennsylvania, on March 8, 1971 (chapter 14). A group of private citizens stole every file in the office and were never caught. That theft revealed myriad instances of corruption, including COINTELPRO and Hoover's secret files, all of which found its way into the media. An excellent account of that little-known event is *The Burglary,* by Betty Medsger.

Hoover's use of a possible communist influence in the civil rights movement as the basis for his illegal surveillance is historic fact. But that ran contrary to a 1963 internal FBI report (mentioned in chapter 21) which concluded that no such communist influences existed. As described in the novel, Hoover rejected that conclusion, and its author (William Sullivan in reality, Tom Oliver in the novel) changed the report, conforming its findings to Hoover's predetermined (and false) belief.

The accounts of King's assassination, detailed in chapters 16, 17, and 18, are taken from reality. The only addition is the presence of Benjamin Foster. The details of Eric S. Galt's (James Earl Ray's) activities (beginning in chapter 23) from the summer of 1967 until June 1968 are from historical accounts. The only addition was his secret observation and direction by the FBI. The shadowy figure of Raoul (chapter 36) was an invention of James Earl Ray, first mentioned after he recanted his guilty plea in 1968. Through the years the story of Raoul, who supposedly used Ray as a patsy for the murder, changed many times. As did the man's physical appearance. Even the spelling of the name is clouded in doubt. I used *Raoul,* but other variations appear in print. No one knows if such a person ever existed. Here, I made him Juan Lopez Valdez.

It is well documented that Ray purchased a rifle in Alabama (chapter 26), then returned it the next day, exchanging it for a more powerful weapon. Ray ultimately claimed that it was Raoul who ordered the switch. To this day, why Ray made the change in weapons remains a mystery.

Ray did in fact stalk King beginning in late March 1968, traveling to Selma, Alabama, on what appeared to be a reconnaissance mission (chapter 44). He then followed King back to Atlanta, where he kept close tabs. An Atlanta city map found among Ray's possessions after the assassination showed two spots circled. King's home and the Ebenezer Baptist Church.

Ray was no trained marksman, yet the rifle he used to kill King contained but one shell and only one shot was fired, which struck King in the face. The bullet disintegrated on impact, making it impossible to match the slug to the rifle (chapter 34). Whether the rifle found near the assassination, the one Ray bought in Alabama, was in fact the murder weapon has never been determined. And consider this, as noted in chapter 34: Ray possessed no discernible motive. No fingerprints of his were found in the rooming house where he supposedly stayed. No fingerprints were found in the white Mustang he was driving. An accuracy test on the rifle showed it consistently fired both left and below the intended target. And the only eyewitness to place him at the scene was blind drunk at the time, and never made a positive ID until years later.

In addition, Ray's trip out of Memphis bordered on the miraculous, considering the police sweep that occurred immediately after the murder. The false CB radio report of a car following Ray's white Mustang, and a gunfire attack on that car, happened (chapter 34). No one knows who orchestrated such a ploy, but it definitely diverted law enforcement and aided Ray's escape.

Despite one of the largest manhunts in history, Ray managed to stay on the run for two months, finally caught in London's Heathrow Airport. Ultimately, and never explained to anyone's satisfaction, Ray pled guilty to murder on the eve of trial (chapter 34), but recanted three days later, starting twenty-one years of ranting in which he maintained his innocence and alleged a grand conspiracy. All of the groups detailed at the end of chapter 34 have, at one time or another, been implicated in those conspiracies.

Nothing has ever been proven.

The Southern Christian Leadership Council (SCLC) stood front and center in the civil rights movement. King served as its president until his death. The civil suit *King v. Jowers* happened in 1999, the trial far more spectacle than an actual legal proceeding (chapter 18). Its outcome was never in doubt, the finding of an official conspiracy to kill King inevitable considering the slant of the evidence from both sides. No true adversarial court proceeding has ever seriously considered the King assassination. Twice Congress has investigated, but both efforts were tainted by politics. To this day, countless questions remain unanswered.

The operation known as Bishop's Pawn is all my creation. Except for the two mentioned earlier from chapter 27, the FBI memos (which start in chapter 23) are mine. But I utilized the style, and some of the wording, from actual memos. One phrase that is repeated a lot in those is *a confidential source who has furnished reliable information in the past* (chapter 27). We now know that those words meant the information came from an illegal wiretap, the nomenclature a covert way to shield that fact. In the context of this novel, it means Benjamin Foster. All of the information contained in the memos from chapter 27 and the conversations in chapters 58 and 61 accurately reflect King's own words and thoughts. What happened to Jimmie Lee Jackson, James Reeb, and Viola Liuzzo (as described in chapter 61) is fact. We tend to forget, these so many decades later, that people died during the civil rights movement.

J. Edgar Hoover hated Martin Luther King Jr. It was a deep, visceral, personal hate, which seems to have started in 1962 when King openly criticized the FBI for having no black agents and for showing partiality to southern law enforcement (chapter 21). King also challenged Hoover's belief that communists were involved in the civil rights movement, eventually calling on Hoover to resign. When Hoover tried to schedule a meeting with King and talk their differences over, his calls went unanswered. Not intentionally, but only because King was terrible at returning calls (chapter 46). No matter, the rebuff was perceived as deliberate and Hoover set out to destroy King.

In January 1964 the FBI secretly recorded a party at the Willard Hotel where they first learned of King's private dalliances (chapter 26). In December 1964 a package of tapes were sent anonymously to King's home, along with the note quoted in chapter 26. The tapes revealed King's extramarital affairs and his use of raunchy language in private. Coretta King listened to the recordings, but refused to give Hoover the satisfaction of winning, and did not end her marriage. The description of Hoover's home (chapter 51) is accurate, but the presence of Juan Lopez Valdez is my invention.

The city of St. Augustine, Florida, played a central role in the civil rights struggle. King did in fact call it *the most lawless community* he'd ever visited (chapter 34). A huge KKK rally happened in the city's central plaza, and violence directed against three local black activists eventually motivated King to come to the city. In the summer of 1964 St. Augustine became the epicenter of the racial struggle. The Monson Motor Lodge became famous for its owner pouring acid into a pool filled with protestors (chapter 31). King was arrested, as were many others, including three young people who spent six months in jail for ordering a Coke and a hamburger (chapter 34). But their efforts were not in vain, as the ongoing filibuster in the U.S. Senate was broken on June 10, 1964, allowing for the passage of the Civil Rights Act.

In 2011 a memorial was finally erected to that great struggle, which now stands in the Plaza de la Constitución. As related in the novel (chapter 34), it took a change to the St. Augustine city code for that to happen, as no memorials to events after 1826 were allowed. The Woolworths that was once there is gone. But its lunch counter remains on public display inside the building, now occupied by a bank.

As to the other St. Augustine locales in the novel: The Columbia restaurant is one of my and Elizabeth's favorites (chapter 36). St. George Street (chapter 35) reeks of history. The green tourist trollies that look like trains run all through the city. The so-called slave market stands in the main plaza. And the Café Alcazar occupies the deep end of what was once the largest indoor pool in America (chapter 37).

The Bay of Pigs invasion of Cuba is historical fact (chapter 33), as is Operation Northwoods, which was proposed (chapter 37) but ultimately rejected by President Kennedy. Of course, Valdez had nothing to do with either.

I've been wanting for many years to include Disney World in a novel. Finally, I have the chance.

The Pirates of the Caribbean, Disney's statue, the covered porch at the end of Main Street outside the train station, Main Street itself, and the Jungle Cruise are all real. Purists might notice differences between what stood twenty years ago and what I have described. I decided to stick with what's there now, unless I knew better. The bowels of the Pirates of the Caribbean attraction are my invention, though surely some variation on those exist. All of the other aspects of the attraction are accurate. The construction area in chapter 52 is my creation, though I recall a lot of changes constantly being made to that section of the Magic Kingdom. Today that area houses Fantasyland.

This novel focuses heavily on the last year of Martin Luther King Jr.'s life. On April 4, 1967, when King publicly came out against the Vietnam War, he began a steady downward spiral that included deep bouts of depression. A terrific account of that fall is contained in *Death of a King*, by Tavis Smiley. By April 4, 1968 (the date of his death) King's public status had changed significantly. Certainly, he remained one of the premier voices for equality in America, his words still important, but other more militant voices had begun to rise in volume. The movement itself became severely fractured over violence versus nonviolence. The hostile SCLC meeting of March 30, 1968, described at several points throughout the story, where King walked out in anger, happened and is illustrative of that conflict. Without question, King was not what he had been only two years before.

The "mountaintop speech" quoted in chapter 60 is an abridgement of King's actual words delivered the night of April 3. I eliminated only the aspects of it that did not address mortality. What remains in chapter 60 are King's words, not mine. He spoke without notes, from the heart. If you have never read or listened to the entire speech, I urge you to do so. Every word sounds like a man who knew he was about to die.

Consider this: Why would King stand out in the open, on the balcony of the Lorraine Motel, for several minutes? There'd been numerous death threats, and violence had already happened a few days earlier at the first march he led through Memphis. He'd been warned not to make himself a target, yet there he stood.

It's an interesting question.

To which we will never have the answer.

In the 1930s, the poet Langston Hughes wrote "Lenox Avenue Mural," where he asked, *What happens to a dream deferred?* Does it dry up? Or just explode?

Hard to say.

What will become of King's dream remains to be seen.

We are now fifty years beyond his death and his work still feels unfinished. By the time he died King had concluded that racism, poverty, and the Vietnam War were intricately linked. Together they were sapping the country of its core strength. His hope was that his Poor People's March, set for Washington, DC, in the summer of 1969, would raise awareness of all three. In the "mountaintop speech," delivered the night before he died, he framed his legacy. He told that final audience he was proud to have been a part of the fight. Then he ended his remarks with some prophetic words.

Like anybody, I would like to live a long life.

Longevity has its place.

But I'm not concerned about that now. I just want to do God's will. And He's allowed me to go up to the mountain.

And I've looked over.

I've seen the promised land.

I may not get there with you. But I want you to know tonight that we, as a people, will get to the promised land.

And so I'm happy tonight.

I'm not worried about anything.

I'm not fearing any man.

Mine eyes have seen the glory of the coming of the Lord.

Rana Faure

Steve Berry is the *New York Times* and #1 internationally best-selling author of fourteen Cotton Malone novels and four standalones. He has twenty-three million books in print, translated into forty languages. With his wife, Elizabeth, he is the founder of History Matters, which is dedicated to historic preservation. He is also a founding member of International Thriller Writers, formerly serving as its copresident, and is an emeritus member of the Smithsonian Libraries Advisory Board. Visit his website at www.steveberry.org.

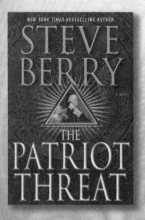
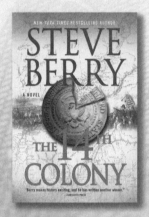
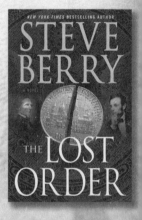
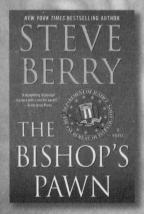
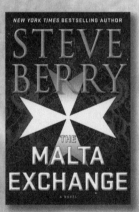
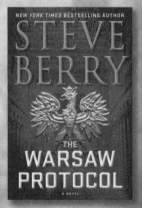